Triple Threat

Book 5 Rule of Three

Ann Grech

Blurb

She's picked her team. Now she just has to score.

When a summer storm sweeps in, Ava finds herself road tripping across the state with two sexy-as-sin strangers. A flat tyre delays their trip, and the only hotel in town with a vacancy has just one bed.

Even though the two men are complete opposites, both have her captivated. The only thing hotter than being with Bryce, the handsome footballer with a perpetual smile, and Cole, the dark and broody construction worker, is watching them together.

Their holiday fling soon turns into more, but the odds are stacked against them. Threats come in threes, and Bryce has to face one that will change the path of both his future and career.

But Ava's playing for keeps. Can this trio emerge as the victors?

Triple Threat is the feel-good, out-for-you MMF romance that concludes the Rule of Three series. Featuring a swoony cinnamon bun, a grump, and the woman who captures both their hearts, you'll fall in love with all three.

I lost my dad to a heart attack on 31 October 2022. I'm not ready to dedicate the ending of a series to him. Even though he's gone I'm not ready to say goodbye. I don't know if I ever will be. So, this story is dedicated to Mum, for her strength and resilience through this nightmare. I love you so very much, Mum. You are incredible.

ACKNOWLEDGEMENTS

I wrote this story as a novella and Ava, Bryce and Cole whispered to me when I wrote their original ending that they had a hell of a lot more to say. So, when I got the chance, I knew I had to revisit them. I had a blast doing it. Ava, Bryce and Cole were the perfect ending to this series-- my very own slice of sunshine, hissing alley cat and rock to ground them both.

I have a long list of people to thank for getting me to this point in this story. My family—my beautiful husband and kids, Mum, my cousin, aunts, my sister and brother and their families, and my best friend, Robyn (who I count as a sister)—all of you were the rocks that I needed so badly. Words will never be enough.

Korey Williams, thank you for all your answers to my ridiculous rugby questions!

Becky Johnson and the team at Hot Tree Editing, the manuscript I gave you was a mess. Thank you for weaving your magic and turning it into something I'm proud to release into the world.

Kariss Stone, your friendship and suggestions to get me out of the holes that Ava, Bryce and Cole had fallen into meant the world. Thank you for our late night chats that always end up going far too late.

i

My beautiful friends who make up the MM DreaMMers authors (Viva Gold, LJ Harris, JJ Harper, Angelique Jurd, Tracy McKay and Megs Pritchard), thank you for always being there. I'm grateful every day for you being in my life.

To Kristie and Amber, thank you for the work you've both done to keep me in line and organized. I appreciate it, always.

Clarise Tan from CT Cover Creations, thank you for your amazing work on both the photographic and illustrated covers for the series. Your talent is incredible.

Linda Russell from Foreword PR, my friend, you are amazing. I love working with you. Thank you for all the work you've done and always do behind the scenes for every one of my releases. It's truly appreciated.

To my A-Teamers, I love you guys and girls. You're my safe space to fall and you were there for me when I hit rock bottom.

Last and most certainly not least, thank you to you, the readers and bloggers, for your unending love and support. Sharing, reviews, general shout outs and, importantly, reading our words means the world to every author. I've said this a few times now, but I never imagined it would be possible to make a career out of my childhood dream, but you've made it a reality. I'll forever be grateful.

Ann xx

GLOSSARY

This story is set in Queensland, Australia. It uses Australian English. There are some terms that you might not have heard before, so I have set out a few for you. If you come across more, please let me know and I'll explain the terms. You might also want to take a peek at my website too – I'll add more there as they come up.

Bloke – a man.
Boardies – board shorts
Bottle-o – liquor store.
Boxing Day – the day after Christmas Day. It is a public holiday in Australia.
Brekkie – breakfast.
Brick shithouse – an outhouse made of bricks.
Building Code – short for the Building Code of Australia, a document that regulates the construction of buildings to minimum standards.
Bush – forest.
Car park – parking lot.
Centimetre – a metric unit of measurement. One inch is the equivalent of 2.54 centimetres.
Chippie – carpenter.
Dunny – toilet.
Esky – cooler bin
Flatmate – roommate.

Forward pass – a type of illegal pass in rugby.

Fridge – refrigerator.

Goldie – Gold Coast.

Hooker – in the context of this story, a rugby league position.

Ks – short for kilometres, a metric unit of measurement. One mile is the equivalent of 1.6 kilometres.

Kitchen bench – kitchen countertop.

League – rugby league, a full contact sport played be-tween two teams for two forty minute halves where the objective is to score more than the other team by carrying the ball over the 'try line' and, after making a try, kicking the ball between the posts to add an extra two points to the score (called a conversion).

Maccas – McDonalds.

Metre – a unit of measurement (approximately 3 feet).

Mobile or mobile phone – cell phone.

Nappies – diapers.

NRL – National Rugby League, the organization that manages professional rugby league in Australia.

Premiership – the Australian rugby league's (NRL) equivalent of the Superbowl.

PJs – pyjamas.

Portaloo – portable toilet.

Prop – in the context of this story, a rugby league position.

Queenslander – a style of architecture for houses built in Queensland to suit the varied climate in the state (sub-tropical to desert). Traditionally, the houses are constructed on stilts to allow for ventilation and flood waters to pass under the house, with wide verandas and windows all around the house. Painted in a light colour, the combination ensures cooling shade and cross ventilation.

Scrum – a method of restarting play in rugby league where players line up in a three-two-one tightly-packed formation, face off with the opposing team and attempt to get the ball from their opponents.

Scrum half – a rugby league position.

Shitter – toilet.

Shopping centre – mall.

Spewing – in the context of this story, being upset or disappointed.

State of Origin – rugby match between the mighty Queensland Maroons (the Cane Toads) and the meh at best New South Wales Blues (the Cockroaches). Usually the Blues have the blues because even though the stubborn bastards will never admit it, Queensland is by far the better team. Go Queenslander!

Sunnies – sunglasses.

Swimmers – swimwear.

Tap – faucet.

Tea – depending on the context, either a hot beverage or dinner.

Thongs – flip flops.

Try line – the line a rugby player must cross on the football field to score.

Uni – university.

Ute – a pick-up truck.

Utility – in the context of this story, a rugby league position

Winger – a rugby league position.

ONE

Ava

"Jingle Bell Rock" was playing, the happy tune being piped through the speakers at Sydney Airport. Ava hummed along with it as she wheeled her suitcase into the terminal, passing the giant koala in a pair of boardies, sunnies, and a straw hat, which marked the entrance to the check-in area. Surfboards, images of the Bondi lifeguards, and the world-famous break decorated the walls.

Ava loved it. Summer was her favourite season, but this year's vacation had taken far too long to arrive. She rubbed her eyes before yawning behind her hand. It was early—the sun hadn't risen yet—but that wasn't the cause of her sleepiness. She'd been working long hours, grinding away to make sure she left with everything squared up. When she returned, she would be taking over a new role—her promotion to development manager had been approved only a couple of weeks earlier. She couldn't wait to get started.

Tucking her hair behind her ear, Ava tried to keep the strands off her face. The heat would soon force her to pull it back. At least the terminal was air-conditioned; the predicted wind blowing straight from the red centre that day would make the space uncomfortably warm otherwise. Record temperatures were likely in the city, too—it always happened when the wind blew in from the desert.

But the weather at her destination was expected to be perfect. Her annual holiday to the Gold Coast was a reward for a year of hard work. Relaxing by the pool or on the beach would be heaven after the crazy few months she'd had. It was worth it, though. Her promotion had come far earlier than even she expected. The twelve townhouse development she was now responsible for wasn't the largest project on the company's books. But Ava was twenty-four. She'd only graduated university a few years earlier. Getting the promotion to take it on was a pretty remarkable achievement.

She shook her head. That responsibility—and challenge—would still be there ten days from now. And, boy, did she need a break from it. The grind, the pressure, and the pace were all so intense. It left her working impossibly long hours and perpetually stressed. So, today, she was determined not to think about anything except tropical beaches and cocktails.

Her sandals clicked on the tiled floor of the terminal as she joined the queue to check her luggage and collect a boarding pass. Ava's flight wasn't the only one leaving pre-dawn. People were milling around everywhere, but there were few smiles and a lot of grumbling. Apparently, not everyone was looking forward to their break as much as she was. She practically vibrated with anticipation.

Excitement ratcheted up as she watched the first rays of dawn break. The glass wall along one side of the terminal that overlooked the runways framed the scene spectacularly.

The sun rose, peeking over the horizon. The colours were magnificent. Pinks and oranges, so unusually vivid that she stopped and watched as the scene unfolded before her. The sky grew brighter, but oddly, it didn't morph into its usual shade of rich summer blue. Instead, the depth of the red haze increased until the entire sky looked like it was on fire. It was otherworldly. She could have been staring at a scene taken straight from a sci-fi movie.

It was eerie. Creepy, in fact.

Apocalyptic even. What in the world was going on?

Ava tore her eyes away from the windows and focussed on the morning talk shows playing on the wall-mounted televisions. Apparently, it wasn't just her eyesight gone mad. A dust storm was settling over the city. Ava swallowed hard, the buzzing anticipation turning to dread. A storm that lit the sky red didn't bode well for her flight. She hadn't bothered to check her departure time before she'd left home — she was on the first flight out. They weren't supposed to be delayed. Would the weather throw her carefully crafted plans into chaos? She was loath to check but had to know. Ava turned to the departure and arrival monitors, and her gut sank, disappointment stealing her breath.

Every flight on the boards was delayed. Every. Single. One.

"Shit," she muttered under her breath. How long was she going to be stuck there? She needed to find out. People were leaving the check-in queue in droves, but Ava did the opposite, beelining to the closest one to get some answers. At the very least, she'd be first to check her baggage when the gates were opened. There was no way a little delay was getting in the way of her holiday.

The line shrunk before her eyes, and Ava moved closer to the front, eventually coming to stand second after a man she couldn't help but ogle. Skin tanned to deep olive, with short, perfectly styled black hair and dark brown eyes the colour of melted chocolate, he was captivating. He had an air of mystery surrounding him that left Ava watching his every move to glean something about him. Mr Enigmatic Hottie acknowledged her with a nod, sending butterflies swooping in her belly. But there was no accompanying smile from him, only a bored fidget of the strap on his duffel.

Ava studied him from the corner of her eye. Forearms tattooed with dark ink disappeared under a T-shirt fitted over muscular shoulders. But those muscles weren't sculpted in a gym. His physique screamed wiry strength. She'd seen it often on the worksites she was inspecting. Tradies built their core strength from lifting and constantly balancing their own weight on ladders and beams, not through pumping iron in a gym. His rough hands suggested she was in the ballpark, but as to the type of trade, she was clueless.

A crackle sounded over the loudspeaker, and the cheery carols ceased. "Attention, ladies and gentlemen, due to inclement weather, all flights are now delayed. Please periodically check the monitors for updated status reports and cancellation advisory notices."

Ava ignored the disappointment dropping like an anvil, pulled back her shoulders, and lifted her chin. She would get on that plane, even if it happened through sheer force of will. She needed this break. Was almost desperate for it. If she stayed in Sydney, she'd work, and for the sake of her sanity, she needed to step away.

But reality came crashing down on her with the dawning fireball sky. It was a hard pill to swallow. Helplessness surged through her, and Ava groaned. It didn't matter how much she wanted this break—or how much she needed it. If the weather was too dangerous to fly in, there was no way any planes would be taking off.

Blinking back frustrated tears, she clenched her jaw and shook her head. Damn it, this wasn't supposed to happen. She was supposed to check in, embark, and be in paradise in an hour.

The man in front of her sighed and his face morphed from disinterest into a frustrated scowl, his brown eyes flashing. "Looks like we're gonna be here for a while."

She nodded, pursing her lips to bite back a curse. "Yeah. Great start to my holiday."

"Right? Not a single thing has gone smoothly today."

"Could be worse" came a voice from behind. Ava turned and looked at miles of golden skin and a muscular set of rounded pecs only partially hidden behind a loose tank top. Her gaze travelled way up over shoulders as broad as a doorway to a set of kissable lips split in a wide grin, and warm blue eyes, topped with a blond mop of messy hair. He was the complete opposite of the scowling man on the other side of her, but just as handsome. Baby-faced, his smile lit up the room, and Ava couldn't help but grin back at him.

"Oh yeah?" the other man asked, his tone challenging.

"We could be in the air in that." Blondie pointed outside. In the few minutes they'd been talking, the sky had darkened to an ominous russet colour. Clouds of what could only be dust from the country's red centre were rolling in. The sky was alive, the clouds tangling as they shifted on the wind currents. Like smoke haze at ground level, even the air inside the terminal building was gritty. But up in the sky, she could only imagine how blind pilots would be while flying.

"Yeah, okay, Mr Glass Half Full. Fair call." Ava laughed and shook her head at the cutie.

He shrugged and grinned wider, his gaze bouncing between the two of them. "Always gotta look on the bright side."

The man beside her reached into his back pocket and pulled out his phone, swiping his thumb across it, evidently to answer a call. "Hey," he said, as if greeting a friend.

Ava couldn't hear the conversation, but the crease between his eyebrows deepened, and his lips tilted downwards. She didn't think he was receiving the greatest of news. Her chest tightened, the slump in his shoulders making her want to reach out for him. Being stuck in public when he probably wanted somewhere private to talk was awful. Instead of reaching for him, she turned, giving him privacy and coming face to face with the blond cutie again.

This time her eyes were drawn down to a trim waist tapering down to narrow hips and thick legs. He wore silky rugby shorts that did nothing to hide the generous bulges of muscle and a well-proportioned package. He radiated strength, but his boyish good looks and the laughter in his voice made her instantly comfortable. "I'm Ava," she said, extending her hand.

His hand was the size of a bear's paw, and it engulfed hers as he shook it. His grip was firm, and the calluses on his palm tickled her own soft skin. "Bryce. Happy holidays."

"You too." She smiled again, her belly flip-flopping with his responding wink.

"Are you two together?" He motioned between Ava and the other man and grinned when she shook her head.

"Thank fuck," dark and stormy uttered.

Bryce studied the other man momentarily, his gaze roving over his face. "Everything okay?"

He huffed. "I've just been stood up. My ah... friend decided not to come." He shook his head and rolled his eyes.

"S-Sorry to hear that," she stuttered. It was a lame response, but Ava was shocked speechless. Who would do that? The insane urge to comfort him returned. He was already grumpy, and the call only intensified the waves of discontent rolling off him.

"Yeah, sucks," Bryce said before blinking out of his solemness and smiling. He held out his hand. "I'm Bryce and this is Ava. Good to meet you. Happy holidays."

"Cole." They shook and Cole regarded Bryce, narrowing his eyes at the other man and tilting his head to the side. Ava couldn't imagine what was going through that head of his, his expression locked in a fierce frown. Bryce met his gaze with a grin and a soft chuckle, and Cole turned, scowling deeper. Ava bit back a laugh at their differences—Bryce was like a big puppy dog, happy and excitable, all laughter and light, while Cole was a stray alley cat, hissing with his claws out.

Ava and Bryce fell into an easy conversation, talking about where they were travelling to—they happened to be staying quite close to each other, and what they did for a living. Bryce explained, "I'm a student—studying property."

"Really? I'm a development manager." It was rare that Ava had an instant connection with someone, but the way Bryce's features lit up when she spoke, Ava could have talked to him all day. Watching his excitement bubble over as he talked about his studies and questioned her on what her job entailed was breathtaking.

Cole stayed silent the entire time, watching them like a sentinel with those deep brown eyes until the frustrated groan and accompanying curse from a nearby passenger captured all their attention. "Bloody weather apps are useless."

He reached for his phone again and tapped away at it. Cole muttered, "Shit. We aren't going anywhere. Look at this." He turned his screen to them, and Ava's hope for the holiday she desperately needed crashed and burned in a fiery death. The map showed a bird's eye view of the state, with land depicted in brown and green and the ocean in pale blue. A line of dark red storms headed directly toward the entire Greater Sydney area, the tail extending out to cover half the state. There wouldn't be an hour or two's delay. No, they'd be lucky to get out at all in the next forty-eight hours.

No staff stood at the check-in desks. The conveyor belts were all roped off, and the lights turned out too. Heaviness settled over her, the spark of excitement over holidaying in the tropics flickering like a candle starved of oxygen ready to be snuffed out.

"It's okay. Just a bump in the road," Bryce soothed. "We'll be on our way in no ti—"

"Attention, ladies and gentlemen. We regret to inform you of the cancellation of all flights this morning due to strong winds and low visibility. Further significant delays are expected for flights this afternoon and evening. Please check with your individual carriers to rebook your flights." Ava looked between Bryce and Cole. Cole's jaw was tight, clenched so hard again she was surprised she couldn't hear his molars cracking. His brown eyes were flat; the spark of mystery lighting them up had turned them to flint. Bryce's smile slipped a notch too, but Ava could practically see the gears in his brain turning. Whether it was for an upside to this cluster or a way out of it, she had no idea. But Ava almost wished he'd pull a rabbit out of a hat. She sure as hell couldn't think of anything to get them in the air.

Then it hit her. She didn't need to be in the air. She just needed to be on her way. Ava grinned, buoyant once more as she extended the handle on her suitcase. "Nice talking to you, boys, but I'm going to find a rental."

Bryce's smile was dazzling. "What a great idea. If we leave now, we can be on the Gold Coast by tonight."

"What do you mean 'we'?" Cole asked.

"Bryce has a point," Ava conceded thoughtfully, surprising herself. The lessons drilled into her since childhood — don't talk to strangers, don't go anywhere with them — somehow didn't seem to apply to these two men. Maybe it was the lure of a holiday in paradise making her see them through rose-coloured glasses, but Ava instinctively trusted both Bryce and Cole, even if the latter seemed completely walled off. "We could get a car together and drive up."

Cole furrowed his brow and huffed before looking between them. His gaze was incredulous, but when he shrugged, Ava knew he was in. "Sure. Whatever."

She smiled, those butterflies in her belly flapping up a storm, and Bryce grinned, bouncing on his toes. She motioned to the car hire booths and added, "Seems like everyone has the same idea as us. We should get a move on." She led the charge, hustling over to the stands with the boys on her heels, and joined the line.

But within minutes, the car hire companies were issuing apologies. They'd run out of cars. "Well, there goes that idea," Ava grumbled, disappointment souring her tone.

Cole asked, "Do you not have a car?"

"No, I drive a company vehicle, and when I'm not at work, I catch public transport. I live right in the city, and I try to minimize my carbon footprint wherever I can."

"I'd offer my work truck, but it only carries two people, and it's filled with tools. It's also filthy," Cole said, and Ava stored the tiny piece of information Cole had shared like a precious gift. He was a tradie. Good with his hands and unafraid to get dirty. Damn, the visual of all that strength and competence was hotter than hell.

"We could take my truck?" Bryce suggested, those puppy dog eyes pleading. "It's old, but big and reliable. We'll fit comfortably, and my place is walking distance from Central Station. We could be there in twenty minutes tops."

They looked between each other, and Ava figured it was as good an idea as any. Road tripping was hardly the start to her holiday she'd imagined, but at least she could still get there on the same day. Without Bryce's offer, she'd be high-tailing it back into the city and trying to rebook a flight for the coming days or finding another rental.

"You guys aren't serial killers, are you?" Ava asked, half-joking, half concerned that she was actually considering this and completely fine with it.

Bryce laughed and shook his head, and Cole paled. "No," he uttered, his voice laced with horror.

Ava grinned and nudged him gently with her elbow. "Come on, a girl has to ask."

Cole looked away, colour staining his cheeks pink. It was the first time she'd seen a chink in his scowl that he wore like a wall of armour.

"Why the hell not, then? Let's do this."

Two

Cole

Cole had slept like shit, tossing and turning over whether to bail. Should he? Shouldn't he? The questions chased each other around in his head, going faster and faster until his mind was spinning. Lack of sleep and not enough caffeine left him testy. Kicking the bed and nearly breaking his toe was the icing on a fucked-up morning cake. The universe was definitely sending him a message. Maybe he should have stayed home. He grumbled unhappily, gritting his teeth and shaking his head, hoping the blocked nose he had was the worst of his allergies. Fucking dust storm.

The pressure was building, wisps of steam escaping — and not just from his sinuses. He was like a volcano about to erupt. Every little thing that had gone wrong in the last few months was one more crack in the surface. One more weakness in the paper-thin crust holding back a cataclysmic eruption.

He was on the edge.

Ready to detonate.

Cole wanted to roar until his voice was hoarse and every person on the planet had disappeared.

He needed on that plane yesterday. Cole closed his eyes and forced his thoughts into happier territory, one that didn't revolve around work and his relationship that was on the verge of falling apart. He just... didn't want to deal with people. The ideal trip crystallized, a picture forming in his mind of a week with no interruptions, no banal conversation, and no Mitch. Shit. His shoulders slumped.

His phone rang and Cole's gut clenched. He held his breath, not sure if he wanted the confirmation that would come with the telephone call if it was in fact Mitch.

He looked at his screen. Mitch. Fuck. Mitch. He groaned, checking his watch for the time. His boyfriend was late. Not that it mattered if their plane was delayed.

Maybe he won't come.

No, that's too much to ask.

He wasn't supposed to be hoping to avoid his boyfriend. Cole knew it wasn't a healthy position for their relationship to be in. But it had been rocky between them for a while—the bad times now outweighed the good. Being Mitch's dirty little secret was never Cole's preference, but he'd done it for his guy. Naïvely, he'd thought things would change when Mitch got settled in at work. Then there was the big deal he was trying to snag, then the promotion... Cole understood—he did—and he would never force Mitch to come out before he was ready. So Cole had agreed to keep their relationship a secret.

But then things had started changing. Mitch was breaking out some sort of bossy-arse persona. He thought it was sexy slapping Cole around and demanding his compliance. But he'd never once asked whether Cole was into it. Never checked that he was okay. Being forced to his knees when he walked into Mitch's apartment was one thing. Getting a cock shoved so far down his throat that he couldn't breathe and held there despite his protests made him want to lash out. It didn't turn him on. No, it pissed him off. He was lucky that Cole hadn't dented Mitch's pretty nose.

It didn't help that work had been shithouse too.

But the phone in his hand wasn't going to answer itself. "Hey," he said cautiously, forcing a calmness into his voice that was a total lie.

"So, um, yeah... I wanted to speak with you about our holiday."

"Okay," Cole responded, dragging out the word. If Mitch wanted to make this work, he'd try. But alarm bells sounded in his head, his gut telling him to proceed with caution even if he did.

"I wanted to talk about expectations. I want more from you." Cole froze, his mouth popping open and his breath rushing out of his lungs. Was he serious? Wasn't Cole giving him enough already? His dignity sure as hell thought so. "I want you to submit to me. This is your chance to please me."

"Yeah, nah," he responded, shaking his head. There was no way. They were already on an uneven keel. Mitch already dictated everything to do with their relationship, always worried about being seen. He wanted to hide what they had, entirely separating his personal and professional lives, but it wasn't that easy. Cole was Mitch's dirty little secret, and Cole couldn't bring himself to give up what little control he had over his own body. There was no empowerment for him when Mitch took over, because he'd never been asked to relinquish control. Mitch had simply tried to take it.

"You won't get another chance, Cole," Mitch warned, as if it was supposed to change Cole's mind. "I'm giving you a gift here."

"It's not a gift when I've told you before it's not something I want. I'm not into it, plain and simple."

"You should—"

"Look, I've been second-guessing this trip because I've been concerned about where we're at in this relationship. Spell it out for me precisely, Mitch. Is this an ultimatum?"

"Yes." Mitch's voice was matter of fact. Emotionless.

Cole blew out a breath, trying to calm down. Every time he thought about Mitch forcing him to his knees and treating him like a sex toy, righteous anger stole over him, outweighing the hurt and disappointment.

"I don't want it." He was being vague, but the alternative was spelling out exactly what he didn't want, and even though he generally hated peopling, he didn't want to be cruel. Telling Mitch he didn't want him, that he didn't like the person he'd become was too much. "I can't be that person for you."

"Very well. Looks like you'll be doing the trip solo then."

The weight he'd been carrying lifted off him, dissipating like fog in the morning sunshine. The blanket of unhappiness that had been shrouding him was pulled back, freeing him from its heavy confines. But he was oddly bereft too. Mitch had been a constant for him for two years. Ending things was right, but it didn't make the idea of change any easier. "All the best, Mitch."

"Yeah, you too. If you change your mind—"

"I won't." They said their goodbyes and he hung up, relieved that both the conversation and their relationship was over. "Thank fuck," he muttered, then winced at how cold it sounded.

He felt eyes on him and looked up, his gaze clashing with the big-guy hottie.

"Everything okay?" the other man asked.

Cole nodded, pursing his lips, and furrowing his brow. He didn't want to get into details, but it seemed important—both to them because of their expectant gazes and to something inside him—that he explain. "I've just been stood up. My ah... friend decided not to come."

* * * * *

Cole had noticed Ava's perfume first, its light floral scent heady as she stepped up behind him at the airport. He'd inhaled slowly, taking it in as he tried to conjure up a picture of her in his mind's eye. But his imagination hadn't come close to picturing her beauty. He was drawn to Ava, her frustration at the delayed flights and the take-no-shit attitude she possessed hot as hell.

But as much as he wanted to be pressed up against her, there was another person who was in the box seat. Bryce. Not all was lost though. In the crush of the train carriage, Cole was shoved up against him, their bodies aligning until the warmth emanating from Bryce soaked into him.

Bryce shifted, but lost his balance, stepping on someone's bag that had been carelessly thrown on the floor. Arms flailing, he reached for the railing. Cole didn't hesitate, wrapping an arm around Bryce's waist and hauling him against his chest. Bryce was bigger and probably stronger than him, but Cole could usually hold his own. His wiry strength had been built from hours of lifting beams and heavy tools and balancing on hard-to-reach places.

Cole halted his fall, but it presented another problem. His cock was tenting his cutoffs and there was no way Bryce could miss it. But he didn't push away angrily. He didn't shove Cole or call him something derogatory. It was almost as if Bryce had leaned into him. But that was just wishful thinking. The lurch of the train starting its journey pushed the already off-balance man against Cole.

Cross-eyed with lust, Cole breathed deeply, trying to will his cock under control. It was useless, though. Bryce's rich scent filled his nose, and as he drew a deeper breath, he imagined the microscopic scent cells filling his lungs, taking that small part of Bryce into him until it was impossible to separate them.

It was a hell of a turnaround for a man who'd been in a relationship only a few moments earlier. But had he? He and Mitch had never discussed being exclusive. Cole was, but he knew that Mitch took women out to keep up the façade of an eligible, straight bachelor. How else would he have pulled it off?

But as he took in the man before him—Bryce's broad back, his muscles rippling as he held onto the rail above his head, and his perfect bubble butt—it occurred to Cole that the affection and attraction he'd once had for Mitch had been waning. It was virtually non-existent nowadays, far longer than even he'd realized. It wasn't like he was going to jump into bed with Bryce, or even Ava, but the knowledge that he was ready to move on was somehow comforting. He might have been a cold-hearted bastard for not being in love with Mitch, except that Mitch didn't love him either.

From his peripheral, Cole watched as a man edged closer to Ava, eyeing her like a piece of meat. Cole gritted his teeth, shifting his position and trying to block the man's path, but Cole was hemmed in—suitcases on one side and Bryce on the other. But he need not have worried. Bryce shifted, using his big body to block the path of the man.

A wave of affection washed over him, dousing the protectiveness that had erupted in him. It was as if he'd poured water on a bonfire, the sizzle and hiss indicating the settling of the fire. Somehow he'd ended up tagging along with two people far too gorgeous for their own good, and he didn't hate it.

Swaying closer together, Bryce said something to her, his voice low and raspy and the glint in his eye wicked. Ava laughed, her smile lighting up her whole being. Sparks ignited when their gazes locked and she slowly inhaled, her chest rising and her nipples hardening under Cole's stare.

Cole looked his fill at them as Ava dipped her gaze eating up Bryce's sheer size like she'd done in the airport. Her tongue poked out between her lips, briefly licking them before she bit down on her bottom lip, catching the plump pink skin under straight white teeth. She was looking at Bryce like he was a lollipop she wanted to lick. Cole could relate. Where she was tall and moved like a cat, effortlessly graceful and sexy, he was huge. Built like a brick shithouse, and all golden tanned and smiley. He was the epitome of the all-Aussie bloke.

Cole was openly staring, but he didn't give a rat's arse. Neither did the others if Bryce's smile and Ava's coy look was anything to go by. Bryce grinned in his direction and followed the movement of Cole's hand as he reached down trying to discreetly adjust himself. Bryce bit back a laugh and Cole rolled his eyes, unsure whether to be annoyed or embarrassed.

Apparently, Bryce didn't care. Even Bryce's blue eyes were smiling, sparkling with some inner happiness he had going on. People like that annoyed Cole. All cheery and filled with positivity, they never looked at the hard reality of things. Bryce probably hadn't been around long enough to see the shitty side of life. But at the same time, he drew Cole in like the sun held the planets captive.

Energy buzzed around him, and Cole got swept up in Bryce's gravitational current.

They were both impossible to ignore.

"This is us." Bryce motioned to the upcoming station, and Ava turned so she could slip behind Bryce and follow in his wake rather than having to cut through the path of people herself. Flicking his gaze to her, Cole's breath caught in the same way it had when he'd first seen her. He nearly swallowed his tongue. Her body was gorgeous—curvy in all the right places and petite yet tall at the same time. The denim cutoffs she wore barely covered her arse and left no need for his imagination to summon up images of what her creamy thighs would look like. Of course, that left room for him to imagine them wrapped around his waist. Or his head.

Her flowy green singlet set off her emerald-green eyes, and her dark hair framed her pale skin like a halo. The sparkly sandals were cute on her feet and Cole found himself wanting to start right there, taking off every stitch of clothing as he kissed his way up her body.

She was breathtaking, and the instant desire that slammed into him had the strength of an ocean liner. He lingered, taking in every detail, and when their gazes had finally locked, Cole swallowed. He was instantly unmoored by the keen intelligence in her eyes and the way they darkened when she watched him eat her up.

His thoughts scrambled, and while he was drowning in her potency, Bryce nudged his shoulder and beelined for the exit of the crowded carriage.

THREE

Bryce

I n the space of ten minutes, his day had been turned on its head. But Bryce didn't care. He was on holidays and about to head up the coast to see his family.

Uni had been good. He'd managed half-decent marks for each of his subjects and had killed it on the field. He loved playing rugby league. Bryce was going to play professionally. There was no doubt in his mind, but he appreciated being forced to have a fallback. He'd chosen property because flipping houses or developing new ones seemed like something Bryce could do no matter where in his football career he was. He hadn't in his wildest dreams thought it would give him something in common with the beautiful woman walking next to him, though. How good was his luck?

It was even better now that they were getting started on their road trip. Bryce grinned, his cheeks hurting with how wide his smile stretched. He'd have the whole day to get to know both Cole and Ava, if the surly bloke actually decided to speak. It didn't matter, though. Bryce could admire him while he seethed quietly in the passenger seat.

Thankfully the train ride had been a quick one. Every carriage was full to brimming with people leaving the airport—there was no point sticking around when all flights were cancelled for the morning.

But it was pure torture too. The doors had opened at Central Station and Bryce launched himself out, pushing past people with their luggage until the three of them were standing on the crowded platform. He wasn't claustrophobic. But he was human. He was also a twenty-one-year-old dude whose dick stood at attention from a light breeze. With Ava pressed to his front, her subtle perfume winding its way into his senses, his brain had short-circuited. His hands had itched to grasp her waist, to see how big they looked on her slim but supple frame. The ghost of her body against his was electrifying.

Then there was Cole pressed to his back, with barely a sliver of space between them. Never mind short-circuiting. His brain had completely melted when Cole had hauled Bryce against him to stop him tripping. The press of his hard-as-nails dick between his arse cheeks had made his own throb, pre-cum leaking into his underwear. His body knew what it wanted, all but throwing out the welcome mats.

A split second into their ride and Bryce had worked out exactly what his ultimate fantasy was—a man behind him and a woman in front of him, connected as deep as they could go.

His balls drew up close to his body as he held onto the memory of being plastered between them only a few minutes earlier. It was sweet torture, and it had taken every ounce of self-control to avoid coming in his shorts like a randy teenager. Then the train started moving and all Bryce could do was hold on, squeeze his eyes closed, and pray to the rugby gods that he didn't humiliate himself. The rocking of the train was reminiscent of being on a boat, the pull and push of their bodies as the train slowed and sped up with each station, moving them as one.

Bryce inhaled deeply, taking in the stale city air filled with smog and exhaust fumes. It was a sure-fire way to pull him back from the edge. He'd come damn close to the point of no return on the train, and he could still clearly see the outline of his semi against his tight rugby shorts. His pressing issue was still there for everyone to see. Bryce untucked the front of his singlet, covering the unmistakeable bulge at his groin and hoped that no one else noticed.

Ava hadn't missed it. They came to a stop at the intersection near his apartment building and he watched as she blushed and flicked her gaze away. Ava was focussing on anything but him, but Bryce was patient. He wanted her eyes on him. It wasn't long before she gave in, letting herself look. She stared at his legs, her stare holding there. His thighs were one of his best assets, thick and powerful after he focussed so much time on building the muscle there. Bryce flexed, his imagination running wild as he pictured Ava's legs wrapped around him, or Cole's bracketing his.

"Where to?" Cole snapped, making Ava jerk in surprise. Colour rose in her cheeks, and she fanned her face before pushing her dark sunglasses up her nose. Bryce wanted to hate on the dude, but Cole was right. He just didn't need to get all shitty. He could definitely lose the haughty tone. He did a great job acting all growly. The perpetual scowl Cole wore was a nice touch too, but Bryce had a feeling that once Cole let go of the prickly attitude he wore like an armour, he'd be a different man. Bryce would love to see the tiger purr.

He'd be first in line to put his hand up to try to make it happen. Not that he really knew anything about looking after a bloke. While he wasn't a stranger to being attracted to men, he hadn't had much experience. Any if he was honest. Uni was supposed to be the place where people could finally try out new things, experiment to find themselves. But Bryce's experience was a little different. He had to stay quiet. He couldn't risk his secret becoming common knowledge.

His parents and brothers wanted him to be himself, but he couldn't risk it. Bryce wasn't stupid—his chances of getting signed to a professional team were better if he was thought of as straight. So he'd done what he had to do, and he'd keep doing it until his professional career was over. And all he had to do was ignore the pull he experienced around anyone but women. They were safe. No whispered rumours would accidentally get leaked to the media about a footballer being with a woman. No one would give him a second glance with a woman on his arm.

He felt like a fraud forcing himself to concentrate on only one of the genders he was attracted to, but it was the price he had to pay. He had ten, maybe fifteen years of professional football in him if he could make the cut. He just had to wait to experience what it was like until after he finished playing professionally.

Simple.

So far it had been… okay. Beauty was easy to find. It came in so many different forms. Strength, no matter what that looked like, was such a turn on and he thrived on finding the element of uniqueness in people. For him, attraction was all about the click. The moment where he felt the pull.

Funny that he'd experienced it within moments of meeting both Ava and Cole.

Bryce bounced on the balls of his feet and smiled his happy-go-lucky, eye-crinkling smile, his belly flip-flopping at the possibility of getting to spend more time with them. It had absolutely nothing to do with those perfect bowtie lips or her generous boobs he wanted to bury his face into. Or even her long legs he desperately wanted hooked over his shoulders. Or maybe Cole's shoulders while Bryce licked his way down the other man's body. Absolutely nothing at all.

Bryce bit his tongue, trying to rein in his wayward thoughts. This wasn't the time to be breaking promises to himself. Zero controversy. No hook-ups coming out of the woodwork. He wanted to be one of those dream rookies that teams fought over, not the one constantly looking over his shoulder.

Cole raised his eyebrow at Bryce's silence and his smile turned embarrassed. Bryce pointed the way across the road to the corner apartment. It was literally a stone's throw from the train station, but it was nothing to write home about. The six-storey red brick building was built in the 1970s and had seen better days. Its two tiny bedrooms meant that he could share the astronomical rent with a flat-mate, and the fact that it didn't smell and was close enough to everything made the expense worth it. Every cent he got from playing in the reserves went to rent, and his parents transferred an allowance to him to cover the balance and live on.

He'd wanted to get a job and pay his own way, but his mum had refused. She was his biggest cheerleader, con-vinced he'd turn pro. He loved her for it too. Leaving his old teammates and everything he knew back on the Coast had been hard; without them, loneliness had hit Bryce like a sucker punch to the gut. But meeting new people was his jam, and after a not-so-subtle reminder from his mum that he was being a stick-in-the-mud, he'd woken up and gotten on with it.

"We can get to the car park from the lift," Bryce ex-plained when they reached the building. He took them downstairs and unlocked his truck. It was as old as him, the colour a faded red between the patches of bog where he'd cut out the rust, but the CD player still worked, and the bench seat was comfortable. Shelby was reliable too, the old girl never missing a beat in the entire time his dad and older brothers had driven it.

Cole's poker face was once again fixed in place but his flinch when Bryce dropped the tailgate with a loud squeak was enough. Bryce couldn't help his laughter, a carefree chuckle breaking loose at the other man's reaction. Would he get in the car? Or would he walk away? Bryce shifted his weight from side to side, waiting on tenterhooks for Cole's verdict.

The frown that had only momentarily left Cole's face didn't budge as he looked between them. Bryce could tell Cole was analyzing him as much has his truck. He was probably trying to figure out whether Bryce had this much energy all the time. He knew he was a lot to take, but the fact that Cole hadn't walked away yet made Bryce even happier. Until he did, they were in with an even chance he'd say yes.

If toning down his enthusiasm would help their case, Bryce was all for it. He pressed his fingertips to his thumbs in succession, using the techniques he'd been taught as an overactive kid to focus his energy. Bryce held his breath too.

Would Cole take the leap?

Bryce wanted to push. He wanted Cole with them. After all, it wasn't a road trip without being able to play corners. But he hesitated. He also needed Cole to choose to be there.

Cole sighed and mumbled, "Let's go." His attitude screamed meh, but Bryce saw a glimpse of something simmering underneath. A wildfire about to burn. The man had an intensity that Bryce was drawn to like a moth to the flame. Where Ava was all about cool, calm competence like waves lapping at the shore, Cole was an inferno. Maybe he was… an analogy escaped him. Whatever, it didn't matter anyway. He could be the go between for them. No, bad Bryce.

He whooped, fist pumping the air, anticipation bubbling through his veins. Their trio was born, and this road trip was gonna be epic.

Cole rolled his eyes and Bryce wondered how old the man was. He didn't seem that much older, except for his attitude. The dude was like a grumpy eighty-year-old man stuck in a twenty-five-year-old's body. Bryce snorted out a laugh.

Ava's expression was easier to interpret. Her tight smile and slight pause when he'd pointed to the truck screamed scepticism. He could practically read the questions running through her mind as if she'd asked them out loud. *Will it start? Will it fall apart before we get there?*

The door creaked as Cole pulled it open, the rusty metallic squeak high-pitched in the quiet of the car park. He motioned for Ava to get in and Bryce blew out a breath. This was really happening. They were really doing it. A road trip with two strangers was impulsive and pretty crazy, but it was right up Bryce's alley. He jogged around to the driver's side and hopped in, slamming the door closed after him.

Bring. It. On.

FOUR

Ava

Cole pulled the door open and motioned for her to get in. Her lips tilted up in a shy smile, colour staining her cheeks when she caught Cole's bitten-back grin followed by an instant frown. She'd thought of him as a hissing alley cat only half an hour earlier, but she was intrigued. A crack had appeared in the façade, and she could see his squishy marshmallow centre.

There was a whole lot more to Cole than what he let the world see.

Ava's breath caught in her throat, a healthy dose of excitement and incredulity pulsing through her as she lifted her foot to the step. She couldn't believe that she was actually going ahead with this crazy plan. Not just with two strangers, but with two male strangers, no less. Despite that, her gut told her to trust them. It was crazy to think of either man as familiar when she'd literally only just met them, but it was instinctual. Cole's scowl and Bryce's cheeky grin were already growing on her.

Their gestures spoke louder than any words could too. They'd already put her safety and comfort above their own. Bryce had sheltered her on the train, angling her and using his own body to give her as much room as possible during the short, but overcrowded trip.

Even though Bryce had given her room, he'd also stuck close. That had been... enlightening. He'd tried his best to hide it, but there was no mistaking what he was packing. The way he'd used his size to eke out a pathway for her to follow and escape the chaos was sweet. His constant checking over his shoulder to make sure he knew where she and Cole were, left her in no doubt that he'd look after her.

Then there was Cole. With his hand on the small of her back, he'd steered her behind Bryce, flanking her and taking care of both their suitcases. She didn't think he'd wanted her to see, but he'd also gone back to assist an elderly man step off the train. The whole exchange was heart-warming, and she'd bitten back a laugh at the scowl he'd flashed at her when she waved to the man. Cole may be broody and may want the world to steer clear of him, but Ava saw through his façade.

They were both good men, and that was far more important to her than the length of time she'd known them.

It hit her when Ava reached for the grab rail. She was about to get into Bryce's truck. The sense of freedom that washed over her was overwhelming. Like she could take on the world and win. The weight of expectation and pressure hovering over her for as long as she'd remembered lifted, leaving her weightless. It was one of those stand-at-the-bow-of-the-Titanic-and-fly moments and she was sure her blinding smile and giddy laugh reflected that.

Cole bit down on his lip and gave her body a slow perusal, igniting a different kind of desire in her. The kind that wanted her to be a little wild too. When he lifted his eyes, their gazes clashed and held. Heat flared, dancing in his blown pupils. White-knuckling the door, Ava was drawn to his hands. Scarred and tanned, they were the hands of a craftsman. Flashes in her mind's eye of them sliding along her naked body lit her on fire.

Nothing revved Ava's engine more than sexy hands, and Cole's were gorgeous. Long, strong fingers with veins that ran like a spiderweb up to his wrist with a light dusting of dark hair. They were strong, and yet talented too; every tradesperson was.

The tip of his tattoo ended at his wrist. She'd noticed them before but couldn't study the ink without acting like a weirdo. Standing close now, though, she'd underestimated just how intricate their design was. The pieces told a story, every gorgeous millimetre etched into his skin with a level of care and talent that Ava was in awe of.

Without thinking, she reached out, running her fingertips over the precise lines of the sundial on his forearm. The shadows on the rope and centuries-old-style map further up his arm gave the imagery a three-dimensional look.

Cole sucked in a sharp breath, and Ava's gaze bounced to his. His pupils dilated and he exhaled a shaky breath.

Fuck me.

Cole was gorgeous. People's sexiest man alive level hotness. It took all Ava's strength not to strip him naked just for her viewing pleasure. Instead, she grasped his offered hand and hauled herself in. So what if she stuck her butt out a little more just to give him an eyeful of the evidence of the seventy-bajillion squats her PT made her do every week?

Bryce smiled shyly and straightened his leg, the muscles bunching as he pressed the clutch and reached between hers, shifting the gearstick into first. Ava groaned out loud. The man sported muscles on muscles and those hands.... Good lord, what was she getting herself into? Pressed between two warm bodies, both of whom were sexier than sin, Ava swallowed hard.

Nine hours of being in close quarters with them. Ava was doomed. Well, her panties were anyway. They'd be soaked through before they even managed to get out of the basement.

She fanned herself and didn't miss the teasing smirk Bryce sent her way before he looked to Cole, who was, once again, on his phone. He cleared his throat, his eyes never leaving the screen. "It's pretty much a straight run from here. Literally, three turns to get onto the highway." Cole pointed to the roller door. "Head for the Harbour Bridge, then take the signs to go north."

"No problem. Let's get a move on." Bryce fiddled with the air-conditioning, increasing the flow, and Ava's skin prickled, her nipples hardening at the blast of cold air caressing her skin. His gaze lingered on her breasts, and a shiver passed through her, want sizzling low in her belly. Bryce flicked his gaze to Cole, staring intently at the man for a moment. Bryce's smile was replaced with an intensity in his eyes that took Ava's breath away.

When he blinked, it was as if Bryce came back to himself, jolting to attention once more. Pulling out of the garage after the door had hissed and scraped open, Bryce revved the engine of the old truck, easing it onto the deserted street.

Visibility wasn't too bad until they climbed higher, ready to traverse the bridge. Then it became terrible. The steel girders were almost invisible, the clouds of fine red dust hanging heavy in the air like a fog. The outline of the abutment tower came up on them as they rose to cross the bridge, and Bryce changed gears, reading the growl of the engine.

Without lifting his baseball-mitt-sized hand from the gearstick, he flicked on the radio to a classic rock station. She usually skipped over it—listening to songs from the prior century wasn't really her thing... except on road trips. She grinned, her excitement ratcheting up again when Cole murmured, "Nice." It seemed that they all enjoyed it on this kind of trip.

Bryce hummed along with the song, his fingers tapping away in time with the drumbeat. "This is an awesome song. Do you know it?"

"I think I've heard it before, but I wouldn't say I know it," Ava answered, adding, "But I like it."

"'Time of Your Life' was our end of season song back in the day. I played on the same team as my brothers, and when I hit my teens, with the adults, so they all knew it."

"What sport?" Ava asked, looking up at him. She was probably staring, but she couldn't help it. He was so damn pretty. Happiness radiated from him even when he was concentrating on the unenviable task of driving through red mist.

"League," he replied like the answer was obvious before he shot her a cheeky grin. He was teasing her, but all Ava could think about were the muscles stacked on muscles that she spied from the side of his loose singlet, and those deft hands. A quiver skittered through her.

"What position?" She cleared her throat, her voice an octave higher than normal.

"I'm a prop." Her eyes widened, and he must have mistaken it for cluelessness because he laughed good-naturedly and added, "It's on the front row. I'm one of the battering rams that push the other team's defence back so we can get the ball to the try line. You do know what a try line is, don't you?"

Ava narrowed her gaze and elbowed him gently in the side. "I know what a try line is. I know what a prop does too, and most of the rules... of league, at least. Not so much union." Bryce flicked his eyes down at her, and the approval in his gaze warmed her insides. His grin never left his lips, but it had turned hungry.

"Would we know the team you play for?" Cole asked, startling her. It wasn't that Ava had forgotten he was there—how could she when their shoulders were brushing—but she hadn't expected him to speak. Cole ran the backs of his fingertips down her arm, soothing her fright and leaving tingles in his wake. Ava swallowed, her eyes slipping closed as she shivered.

"Easts." Bryce's voice was low and the rasp in it was sexy as hell.

It took a moment for the team to register. Easts Lightning were one of the oldest and biggest clubs in the league. They were her team, one she followed religiously. "You're a professional player? I thought you were a student?" Why hadn't she seen his name or photograph before? She thought she knew every player on the roster.

"I'm in the reserves for the moment. But I'll get there. What about you, Cole?" Bryce asked, redirecting their conversation.

"I work construction. I'm a chippie."

Ava slid her gaze sideways, watching the serious man curiously. He frowned, the line on his forehead deepening as his lips turned down. His jaw flexed like he was clenching it, and his fingers tapped out a staccato rhythm on his knee.

"I supervise a few crews who look after putting up house frames, but that's only new. I prefer being more hands-on; I'm better on the tools." He went quiet for a moment before sighing. "I've done plenty of other carpentry work—fix outs, some specialized joinery work—building decorative timber screens, fretwork and corbels, custom window framing, that sort of thing. But, yeah, I prefer being on the tools."

Ava clasped her hands together, resisting the urge to reach out to Cole. Something told her that this was an intensely personal moment he'd shared, and he needed to work through his emotions.

They passed through the inner city without seeing more than a handful of cars, their headlights casting an eerie glow in the haze, and headed north. The whole scene was unnerving. Red dust blanketed the city, permeating everything. It swirled around them like mist, the gusts of wind funnelled by the buildings buffeting the truck. Even with the air on recycle, the dust in the truck's cab was palpable. A fine layer had settled on them, the green of her singlet smudged with red marks where it came to rest in the folds.

When Bon Jovi's "Livin' on a Prayer" came on, Bryce belted out the lyrics with gusto and a sparkle in his eye while Ava relaxed back against the seat watching him. He was so at home in his own body, so sure of himself. He wasn't shy or self-conscious, and Ava admired that confidence. It certainly hadn't come easy to her. She'd much rather curl up on the couch and read a book than socialize. That and her competitiveness reflected her lack of friends. She just hadn't ever found her people. At least she hoped that was it. It didn't matter anyway; work kept her busy enough that it was only a couple of nights a week she missed having company.

She tucked a wayward lock of hair behind her ear, going back to staring at Cole out of the corner of her eye. God, he was beautiful. Even the line marring his forehead—the "what the fuck?" crease she saw on anyone who worked with a lot of people—was sexy.

The piece of hair fell straight back into place, blocking her view. Ava's hair wasn't perfectly straight, but not curly either, and the layers her hairdresser had cut in it were frustrating her. She lifted her butt up enough that she could slip her hand awkwardly into the back pocket to try and snag her tie.

Gentle fingers on her face stilled her movement, and she turned to Cole once more as he tucked the lock back behind her ear. She sucked in a breath at the raw heat in his eyes. His lips glistened from where his tongue darted out to lick them before his teeth slowly sank down. Ava's heart beat wildly, and she leaned into him, instinctively closing the gap between them.

Fingertips grazed the leg she had pressed against Bryce, and she startled, freezing in place. Eyes wide and breath sawing in and out of her lungs, Ava blinked, snapping herself out of the lusty spell Cole had weaved. She faced forward, clenched her jaw, and crossed her legs, fighting against their willingness to throw themselves open for either of these gorgeous men. Or both.

It was temporary insanity. She was overwhelmed by the pheromones in the truck. That's what it was. It had to be that.

Or maybe it was them. Maybe they made her brave enough to try something crazy. It wasn't just their attention either. It was the instant cocoon that wrapped around her in their presence, protecting her while at the same time lifting her up and letting her fly free. For the first time, Ava knew in her gut that she could do anything. She was proud of her achievements, but she'd had to work incredibly hard for every one of them. Right now, the sensation of floating fizzed in her veins, like she was riding high and flying free. The weightlessness and the excitement felt a lot like potential. It was as if doors were opening and she was seeing a new path before her, one she didn't even know existed, never mind wanted to follow.

* * * * *

The first few hours flew by, and Ava enjoyed the easy company. She and Bryce talked and laughed while Cole rolled his eyes and scowled. They listened to music and played a really bad game of I-spy.

But as they hit the fifth hour in the truck together, time crawled to a halt. They'd stopped for fuel once and Cole offered to drive, he and Bryce swapping seats. Ava was still pressed between them. She was still breathing in their spicy scents too, making her brain fuzzy and her body antsy.

At least when they filled up next, Ava could stretch her legs and snap out of her lust-soaked daze with some icy water. She needed to shake out the excess energy too, because if she didn't, Ava was going to combust.

The windows were wound down, having finally outrun the storm, but the breeze was stifling. Bush surrounded them on either side of the highway. Forests filled with towering gum trees and hardy bushes seemed to envelop them despite being a few metres away from the road. Long, dry grass edged both sides of the asphalt strip, cutting an almost straight line through the bushland. It made for boring scenery when repeated for hours on end, so it was a good thing that Cole and Bryce didn't seem to mind her staring at them.

The traffic was heavy too, travelling slower than the speed limit. Ava groaned and shifted, sliding down the seat a little more, and Cole shot her a look.

"Sit still, will you?" he groused.

Ava huffed and shuffled up the seat again. "I can't. I need to get out and walk around. I can't sit still for this long."

"Take this exit, Cole. I've had enough of this big sook," Bryce directed Cole and playfully poked Ava in the ribs, his fingertips lingering as he brushed them down her waist to her hip. "Let's stop for a bite to eat and go for a swim before we get back on the road."

Cole indicated, changed lanes, and took the exit, heading toward a village Ava had never heard of. But it didn't take long to see signs of life. The trees cleared, and a cattle farm appeared on one side of the road, while on the other, rows and rows of crops thrived. Fields of different coloured leaves, separated by a dirt track wide enough for a tractor stretched down into a valley and beyond.

They drove on, through lush undulating landscapes and up a rise. They crested it, and for a moment, Ava was speechless. The Pacific Ocean stretched before them, a rich blue twinkling in the early afternoon sun, the perfectly formed waves like corrugations on iron. To their left—north of them—lay the mouth of a river, a small delta forming between the sandbanks. Deeper channels snaked through in places, the colour of the water varying between the aqua of shallow waters on white sandy beaches and a deeper blue-green.

Ava could just imagine snorkelling there, seeing a wealth of fish swimming in the protected seaweed beds. On the southern side of the delta was a deep-water inlet with fishing boats and yachts gently rocking in the breeze where they were anchored, and a pier reaching out into the darkest part of the water. Directly before them, the road meandered down to a grand old bridge straddling the river's banks, high enough that all but the tall sailing ships could travel below its expanse.

"Oh, wow," Ava murmured, gobsmacked at the beauty that lay before her. It was picture-perfect.

"I had no idea this place even existed," Cole uttered as he shifted down a gear.

A bang sounded. Loud like a gunshot.

The truck shuddered, juddering along the road as the rear end fishtailed. Bryce reached for the grab bar with one hand while Ava clutched him and let out a yelp, instinctively gripping the arm he threw out to brace both her and Cole.

Bryce's touch was gentle. Protective. Comforting in the heart-thumping moment. Cole was rock steady, gripping the wheel and steering the truck to the side of the road while it decelerated. Ava was grateful for the waves of calm radiating from both of them. She breathed hard, her heart beating triple time as she slowly relaxed her trembling grip on Bryce's arm.

"Everyone okay?" Bryce asked with a wobble in his voice, his gaze bouncing between her and Cole.

"Yeah," Ava squeaked, nodding.

Cole blew out a breath and nodded before slowly un-curling his fingers from the wheel. It was the only indication that his feathers were even remotely ruffled. He cleared his throat and answered in a low voice, "I'm right, but I dunno about your truck, mate."

Bryce released Ava from his protective grip with a wan smile and patted her knee. "Sorry," he apologized, eyeing the spot where he'd had his hand on Cole's body. "Gimme a sec and I'll check the truck out." Bryce opened the door and slowly unfolded himself from the cab. His expression dropped and he cursed.

"What happened?" Cole asked as he eased out from be-hind the driver's side, and Ava slid out Bryce's side. They had a flat, the rim sitting on the folded rubber against the asphalt. When Cole joined them, he surveyed the damage with a frown. "We can change it."

"There's just one problem with that," Bryce mumbled, rubbing his forehead and sighing. "That was my spare. I had a flat a while back, and I meant to get it fixed, but I was broke. The spare was a full-sized one, so I didn't worry about it. Figured I'd just get it patched when I had the cash." His shoulders dropped and the perpetual smile he wore slid off his face. "Sorry, this is going to delay us for a bit until I can get them both fixed."

The prospect of a delay didn't worry Ava. She was away from work, and they were only a few hours from their destination. They had plenty of time and the scenery was fan-freaking-tastic, and not just the view outside the truck. Surely, there was a mechanic nearby who could help them, and while they waited the hour or two it would take, they could wander around the picturesque little town. Bryce frowned and cursed again under his breath and Ava's gut twisted. He wasn't supposed to get upset. Bryce was the one who radiated sunshine and happy vibes, brightening everything in his presence. She wanted to smooth the downturn in his lips back into a smile. When his happiness dimmed, it was as if the sun had disappeared behind storm clouds. Ava yearned to lift him up and bring back that charming grin.

Cole's expression hardened, but the flash of emotion as he focussed on Bryce was unmistakeable. It wasn't anger their travelling companion was giving off. It was something deeper, something he was trying to hide. He reached out, hesitating a moment before letting his hand fall away instead of squeezing Bryce's shoulder like he looked to be contemplating. His brows squeezed together and his lips flattened. Ava could practically hear the wheels grinding in his brain. He harrumphed and shook his head, like he was at war with himself. He paced away, his footfalls loud on the gravel as it crunched underfoot, his hands tangling in his hair and tugging on the ends.

Bryce curled in on himself, his expression crumpling. It was as if Cole had kicked him when he was down. Bryce's disappointment in himself ratcheted up, the agony she saw in his gaze flaying her open.

Ava wanted to slap Cole silly. Why was he making it harder on Bryce? He'd done them a favour. He'd rescued all their plans, and this is how Cole repaid him? With anger and frustration? Oh, hell no. Every protective instinct in her flared and she stepped closer, rubbing Bryce's arm while shooting daggers at Cole. "It's okay," she reassured Bryce quietly. "It's nothing we can't fix."

Cole spun around and stomped back over to them, coming to a stop in front of Bryce and blowing out a breath. Ava stood up straighter, ready to tear the man a new one, but his tone was gentle when he spoke to Bryce. "Let's see where we can fix a couple of flats, and I'll organize a tow truck to get us there." He shot his gaze toward Ava, and she nodded in encouragement. He seemed to be over his hissy fit. "While we wait, we can have that swim and lunch like you suggested."

This time he did reach out to Bryce, his hand lingering on the other man's shoulder as Cole squeezed it gently. He tilted Bryce's chin up with his other hand and held his stare until Bryce gave him a small nod. Cole shook his head and raised an eyebrow, communicating silently with Bryce. The other man seemed to melt, a flush rising up his throat to his cheeks and his lips turning up in a shy smile. Cole grinned, his smile indulgent.

Ava tried to breathe, but she couldn't get any air. Cole's smile was stunning. It transformed Cole's face, challenging both of them to resist him. Ava wanted to jump him right there and then. The tilt of his lips spoke of heat and whispered promises delivered with screaming orgasms. If she came across him in a dark forest, he was the kind of wolf she'd beg to devour her. Rapacious in an I-want-to-eat-you kind of way, Cole's smile was magnificent.

The contrast between the sensual promise in Cole's smirk and the boyish joy returning to Bryce's face was vast. It wouldn't be a hardship if the mechanic took longer than a couple of hours to fix the flats just so she could watch them together like this.

FIVE

Bryce

"Thank you for calling DS Mechanical. Our office hours are 8:00 a.m. to 5:00 p.m. Monday to Friday and 9:00 a.m. to 12:00 noon on Saturdays…." Cole walked away from him, and Bryce tuned out the rest of the message.

He turned his face to the rolling ocean and breathed in the clean air. The warm, salty breeze whispered of home to him. He was getting closer, and with every kilometre they travelled, he smiled harder.

He loved Sydney, but there was nothing like the Gold Coast. Glitz and glamour, nightclubs and tanned bodies with skimpy bikinis and muscles pouring out of tight-fitting board shorts, it was a study in contrasts. The city lay nestled between the perfect beaches along the Pacific Ocean to the east and a forest-covered hinterland to the west. The place called to him, begging him to come home. The Goldie was laid back and bustling, a unique mix of city and decidedly suburban, all neatly packaged within an hour's drive of the tropical paradise.

When he turned back to Cole and Ava, his companions were sitting on the tailgate, talking and showing each other their phone screens. Ava nodded as Bryce joined them asking, "How did you go getting a tow?"

"No one's open till Monday morning," Cole replied, his voice gruff. Bryce's gut sank and he struggled to find the silver lining in the cloud that settled over him.

"But it's okay," Ava added. "We can still have lunch and go for a swim at the beach and then dinner too. We get to have a little extra time here; I love it already."

"It is nice here," Cole mumbled, looking like it pained him to say the words.

"I found a room at the pub where we can stay for the night too," Ava stated brightly, nudging Cole with her elbow. He plastered on a wide smile that looked every bit the grimace.

Bryce snorted out a laugh. "You look thrilled, Cole."

"I just..." He groaned and scrubbed his hand over his face. He looked weary. "Urgh, peopling isn't my strength."

"You're doing okay." Ava shot him a smile and Cole's shoulders dropped, the frown that creased his forehead smoothing out. He looked away, but Bryce caught the way his lips tilted up in a reluctant smile, alighting those tingly flutters under his skin once more. He liked the grump.

* * * * *

The village was surreal. Surfing and fishing were a way of life around the town, but it was as if Santa had opened his sack and sprinkled Christmas dust everywhere too. In among the surfboards leaning against walls and bait and tackle signs, every window along the main street was decorated. Flags hung from the light poles, and carols played over speaker systems from the stores. Many of the houses they'd passed had lights strung on their roofs and inflatable reindeers, sleighs, and even a Santa on a surfboard in their yards. A towering pine, decorated with thick tinsel and baubles the size of basketballs, topped with a star at least a metre high, stood proudly at the beach-end of the main street.

It was hot, the humidity finally starting to kick in in earnest, but this little village was decked out in all its Northern Hemisphere Christmas-themed glory. And it wasn't even tongue in cheek. With Bryce and Cole flanking Ava, the three of them walked down the wide paths, making their way to the waterfront pub.

It was further than he realized, but it was worth the walk when they rounded the corner and saw the building. A modern double-storey structure sprawled before them, complete with a large, open eating area at ground level. A Sunday session was in full swing, a band playing somewhere in the back, while waitstaff dressed in jean shorts, white tees, and Santa hats welcomed patrons and served drinks.

Ava collected the room key from the lockbox and led the way up the outdoor stairs sheltered by palms reaching up to roof height. Their room was at the end of the building and Bryce could already see both the beach and the park adjacent to the mouth of the river. He was impressed; it was pretty damn good for a last-minute booking.

She turned the key and Bryce reached over her, pushing the door open. It was stuffy, the room hot after being locked up during the heat of the day, but it was fancy too. The polished timber floors gleamed, and a blue rug, the colour of the summer sky, covered the centre of the room. He hated the feel of carpet. Its fibres made him squirm and not in the good way. But Ava had already kicked off her sandals and was wiggling her toes in the thick rug. White furniture contrasted with a pale blue cover on the king-sized bed, and windows lined two of the walls, covered by white gauzy curtains. There was a small table, just big enough for two to eat at in the corner, and a spare chair sat against the wall.

Bryce looked around, counting the places to sleep. He guessed that the owners hadn't intended for three adults to sleep in the king, despite it being a decent size. The tiny sofa facing the water instead of the television hanging inconspicuously on the wall had to be for the third person.

He leaned back and watched, waiting for the others to clue on. Cole opened his mouth, the frown on his face deepening as he must have reached the same conclusion. When Bryce pressed his index finger to his lips in a "be quiet" motion, Cole snapped his mouth shut and propped his hip against the couch. Ava was busy opening the sliding windows, breathing out a sigh as the ocean breeze gusted in.

The door slammed, enclosing them in the cosy space.

She froze before turning slowly, the excited grin sliding off her face. Bryce tracked his gaze down her delectable body before he could stop himself and her reaction was palpable. She squeezed her legs together, fisting the hem of her shirt as her vision bounced between them. Bryce couldn't help the laughter bubbling up within him. She hadn't yet clued on. Or maybe she had and was braver than he'd thought.

He watched as Cole pinned her with his gaze and stalked closer, each step eating up the distance between them until they were chest to chest, only a whisper of space between them. Ava sucked in a breath and held it, her ribs expanding until her breasts brushed against Cole's chest.

"There's only one bed," he growled, the timbre of his voice a low rasp that shot straight to Bryce's balls.

She paled and snapped her mouth closed, her gaze darting to the bed. "Oh shit," she breathed. Bryce saw the moment her thoughts crashed into her, reminding her that she was about to spend the night with two relative strangers.

And there was only one bed.

She flushed, looking at the closed door. Bryce held out his hand, encouraging her to sit. Cole had an intensity about him, intimidating in its force, and the last thing he wanted was for her to be scared of them. Even if Cole's motives ended up being untoward, there was no way Bryce would let anything happen to her.

Ava's pupils dilated and a soft shudder passed through her as he took her hand. Her palms were clammy, and she was breathing fast, her chest rising and falling with each rapid inhale and exhale. She held on tight as he led her to the bed, patting it so she could sit.

Cole cleared his throat, the spell between them seemingly broken. "I'll, ah, take the couch," he murmured as Bryce explained, "I don't mind sleeping on the floor. You can have the bed. Solo."

Ava shook her head, fire in her eyes as she bit her lip. "Let's sort sleeping arrangements out later. I could eat a horse." She jumped up and raced over to the suitcase he'd wheeled in for her and placed in the corner, fished inside for a change of clothes, and plucked out something white with tiny patterns on it.

Before he could say another thing, the bathroom door slammed, and the lock engaged. Barely a moment later, the shower turned on.

"Way to scare her, dickhead," Bryce grumbled.

Cole snapped his head up and pinned Bryce with a glare. "I was teasing her." When Bryce's eyebrows hit his hairline and he choked out a shocked laugh, Cole huffed, "I fucking hate people."

"No, you don't. Not all the time. But you need to be... I dunno. Less intimidating?"

"I'm not intimidating," he protested indignantly.

Bryce stepped up to him so that they were chest to chest and stared him down, raising an eyebrow at Cole when he narrowed his eyes. Bryce growled, the noise a deep rumble in the back of his throat as he leaned in close and snapped his jaw closed. He really did want to bite the man. Take a big old chunk of his bubble butt and leave a nice round mark on it. Instead, he inhaled his spicy scent and held it in his lungs, getting drunk on him. But Bryce also needed to remind Cole of just what he'd done to Ava.

"No, you just growled at her," he muttered, his voice deeper and raspier than it normally was. Cole's eyelids fluttered closed, and his breath hitched. God, Bryce was so tempted to reach out and caress all that olive skin and taste those tattoos, but he'd forbidden himself. He couldn't go there. Not now, not when his career was only starting.

One taste, one kiss would be his undoing. There was no way he'd be able to give it up if he did. Bryce tapped Cole's nose, taking the only touch he'd allow himself. "Make sure she's not scared of you."

Even that touch was enough to get his heart racing and his dick twitching in his shorts. Bryce needed to get away from him, to put some distance between them.

He spun on his heel and headed to his bag before he did something stupid. Like give into desire. He didn't even know how Cole would react, but from the prickly pear reception he'd gotten most of the day, he could just as likely end up in a fist fight with the man as on his knees for him.

Bryce sank to one knee, clenching his jaw and refusing to look at Cole. Why did he have to find two people that ticked every one of his boxes for attraction to do an impromptu road trip with. Frustrated with himself, he pulled the first pieces of clothing out of his bag he touched—a white tee and pair of tan chinos. It was what he'd packed for Christmas lunch, but it didn't matter. He could wash them.

Unable to resist the temptation any further, he cast a glance over his shoulder, wanting a glimpse of the man. Cole hadn't moved, except to lower his head and clench and unclench his fists. His shoulders relaxed and Cole visibly blew out a breath before grasping the neck of his shirt and pulling it up.

Bryce was awestruck. Paralyzed with desire pulsing through him. He groaned quietly, the ripped body Cole revealed inch by inch as he lifted his shirt, a work of art. More of those dark tattoos curled around his stomach, dipping below the waistband of his low-slung faded cutoff jeans. The same jean shorts that cupped his perfect arse and those sexy-as-sin legs right down to his knees.

Bryce drew his eyes up, captivated by the dark images that contrasted against the paler skin of his abs. The ridges and valleys of a perfect six-pack had Bryce mesmerized. He couldn't tear his eyes away from them.

The door behind him opened and Bryce startled, tearing his gaze away from Cole. But by doing that, he came face to face with Ava. She was wearing a white mini dress that hugged every curve of her supple body. The straps were as thin as spaghetti, and they only made him want to tug on them until they snapped so he could peel her out of it. Bryce ground his teeth, his dick rock-hard and pulsing with the need for relief. If he didn't get some distance, he was going to embarrass himself. Pressing the clothes against his groin, he stood and dashed into the bathroom, slamming the door closed before he went off like a bottle rocket.

This wasn't the time to jack off, not with the two hotties immediately outside the door. They'd hear every stroke, every.... No, Bryce, shake out of it. He shoved his shorts down to his ankles and pinched the head of his dick hard enough that he whimpered. Like a deflating balloon, his cock retreated, trying to put as much distance between itself and his fingers as possible. He showered quickly, the water freezing cold, then dressed and swore at himself for not taking his toiletries in with him.

He wasn't sure what he'd find when he exited the room, but Cole's hands at Ava's waist wasn't it. His fingers lingered as he tied the bow at the small of her back, those shoestring straps crisscrossing over the smooth planes of her back. She shot a flirty look over her shoulder, her lips turned up in a cute-as-fuck smile aimed squarely at Cole. She blushed and Cole brushed a lock of hair off her shoulder before clearing his throat.

"Right, yeah," he mumbled, his gaze colliding with Bryce's.

Ava bent, giving them an eyeful of her sweetheart arse, and from the corner of his eye, he spied Cole adjusting himself. At least he wasn't the only one with a problem.

Bryce threw on his Vans as Cole ducked into the bathroom and emerged a few minutes later, showered and wearing white pants that showed just enough ankle to be sexy, one side of his dark shirt tucked in. Damn. They both knew how to wear a set of clothes.

"Boozy lunch?" Ava asked.

They headed downstairs, beelining for the tables set out on the grassy slope leading down to the beach. Shaded by the giant poincianas, their low-hanging branches created intimate spaces for each set of tables under their canopy. Bryce relaxed into his seat, sighing happily. Cocktails, an antipasto platter, and the crashing waves of the Pacific Ocean only a stone's throw away made for a perfect afternoon. This was the life.

Ava tipped her head back, the broad brim of her straw hat brushing her shoulders and exposing her throat. That desire to bite came back, except this time, it was accompanied with the visual of a whole lot of kissing and sucking.

The band played a mix of new and old-school rock, and Bryce grinned, pleased with the playlist. He hummed along, occasionally singing a few lines.

"You've got a good voice," Cole remarked, only to go still, tensing as he froze. Bryce smiled when he saw Cole's flush and the scowl return. He couldn't help but laugh. Cole was too easy. He wanted to wall himself off, to be feared so no one would mess with him or even talk to him. But Bryce wanted to get a deeper glimpse of what lay beyond the spikey exterior.

Ava agreed and Bryce's grin turned sheepish as he reached out, gently lifting Ava's strap back up to her shoulder. Her breath caught and she slow blinked. Bryce was tempted to tug it down again just so he could repeat the action. But Cole moved faster, resting his arm along the back of her chair. Bryce watched as he trailed his fingertips along her arm and her breath left her in a rush.

Goosebumps erupted over her body and her nipples hardened, the little nubs peaking under her dress. He wanted to push. In fact, he wanted to fall to his knees, push hers open and find out just how she tasted.

Instead, Bryce downed the remainder of his drink and motioned to the waiter, who nodded at his unspoken request for another round.

More cocktails were delivered to their table and Cole ordered a platter of hot food. Seafood, barbecued wings, and sliced beef was delivered and the three of them feasted as Ava grilled him on growing up on the Goldie, his family, and the crazy things he and his older brothers got up to. When he added in his cousin, Levi, and Connor, his best friend, there was a football team's worth of boys hanging around.

Now Levi, Connor and their girlfriend, Katy, truly were inseparable. The three of them had been together only a few months, but with the benefit of hindsight, Bryce could see that it had been a long time coming. Levi loved Katy with his whole heart, and he was completely besotted with Connor, finally being able to show the friend he'd grown up with exactly what he meant to them.

Bryce so desperately wanted that—a love for all the ages—but just like his cousin, there would be life-altering consequences if he reached out to grasp it.

It wasn't never; it was just not now.

Bryce recalled how, as kids, they'd decided to build a flying fox from his brother's window to the treehouse in their backyard. He laughed as he told the story. They hadn't counted on two things—first, that the tree was higher than the window so their attempt to bust his brother out of his grounding failed. Their other problem was tying the rope to the gutter, which definitely wasn't strong enough to hold their individual weight, never mind combined.

That first ride had been their last and the damage they'd caused spectacular. Ripping the gutter off an entire side of the house together with the downpipe wasn't even the worst. No, that was reserved for the smashed window when the metal sheeting twisted and pierced it, and the broken outdoor furniture when Bryce and his brothers had fallen, landing on it.

Ava listened, laughing along with him, and even Cole's scowl seemed smaller.

"You need to become a professional speaker," Ava advised after he'd finished explaining how his parents had done it tough raising the five of them. "I mean, as well as football, you should be a public speaker. You can tell stories like no one I've ever met."

Bryce shuddered, horror pulsing through him. Some people were scared of spiders or snakes. Not him. No, he was terrified of speaking in front of crowds. "Not a chance in hell. There's nothing worse than having to do a presentation or something like that."

"Pretend they're all naked," Cole instructed before tipping his head back and letting an oyster slide down his throat. Ava watched him, and Bryce watched her. There was no doubt she found Cole attractive. Hell, anyone would.

Bryce choked out a strangled laugh, trying to get his traitorous dick back under control. "Yeah, I'll get right on that."

The direction of the conversation changed again, the focus shifting to Cole. He was tight-lipped, divulging only that he had an older sister, but they hadn't spoken in years. Same with his parents. Bryce couldn't help but wonder what the cause of the rift between them was. But instead of prying, he asked what he hoped was an easier question on Cole, "You single, mate?"

Cole's lips curled, genuine relief lighting his eyes, Bryce guessing because of the redirect in conversation. "The phone call you saw me take at the airport was from the guy I'd been seeing. It started off okay, but he got a little too controlling for my liking. It was a mutual decision to break up, and he suggested that I go away alone."

Huh. Bryce swallowed, nodding in sympathy.

"Are you gay?" Ava asked.

Cole shook his head. "No, bi." He picked at a long thread on his shirt. "Is that an issue?"

"Not for me," Ava assured him, slipping her hand into his. When Cole flicked his gaze toward Bryce with a question in his eyes, Bryce wished he could open up. He wanted to share his secret and finally be himself. His parents knew and so did his brothers, but that was it. Not a single other person on the planet knew he was pansexual. But now wasn't the time, and being surrounded by people meant it certainly wasn't the place either.

"No problem for me either." He swallowed, his smile dimming. "Is that why you don't speak to your family?" Cole nodded and Bryce couldn't help reaching for him. With a squeeze of his forearm, the one draped over Ava's chair, he added, "It's their loss, but doesn't make it easier to deal with."

Cole bobbed his head, the cool detachment in his dark eyes flickering for a moment and revealing a depth of pain that Bryce instinctively wanted to shield him from. He was kind of jealous of Ava's ability to comfort him in public. Bryce wanted more than simply rolling around with the man. Getting one of those rare smiles would be spectacular.

Ava patted his knee and grinned at Cole before popping a quick kiss on his cheek. "Come on, boys. Let's get this show on the road." They didn't have anything planned and they couldn't exactly get on with their trip, so Bryce had no idea what she was talking about. But following her seemed like a good enough idea. He downed the two cocktails sitting on the table in front of him and swayed when he stood.

Cole insisted on paying and they wandered out of the pub when he'd returned. Bryce tugged Ava's straw hat off her head and popped it on Cole's, laughing as he tried to bat Bryce's hand away. "Suits you." Bryce poked his tongue out at Cole and cackled when Ava slapped his butt.

Six

Cole

His vision spun just a little, the cocktails having kicked in. But as Ava led them away from the pub and along the beach toward the park, the cool early evening air in his lungs was sobering. She tugged them toward the sound of people to a gathering on the grassy foreshore and Cole inwardly groaned. People. Urgh.

Laughter floated on the air and there were kids playing and squealing, running along the pathways leading to the market stalls. "Oh, let's head over there," Ava exclaimed excitedly before grasping their hands. Her grip was strong; he was coming to realize that there was no arguing with her once she'd set her mind to something. She was a pocket rocket that seemed to be used to corralling people where she needed them to go. If the projects she worked on were anything like the ones he did, it was no wonder she needed to be assertive.

Dry grass crunched underfoot, and Ava laughed as Bryce ran for the swing set. Cole rolled his eyes, not willing to let them see how much he was enjoying their light-hearted

banter. They let him sit quietly and observe rather than in-
sisting he join in every conversation, and yet, he never felt
left out. Most of the time he preferred people ignoring him
completely, but not these two.

"Get on!" Bryce ordered with a drunken laugh as he collapsed onto the seat. He was a big bloke, but despite his
size, he was a lightweight. Even Ava held her liquor better
than he did. She snagged the remaining seat, and Cole
stood back watching as they started to swing. "Push meee,"
Bryce whined, and Cole moved behind him purely so he
never had to hear him shout like that again.

Cole gripped the seat and pushed with all his strength
until they were flying high and squealing with delight. He
remembered the last time he'd been on a swing—he was
only a kid—but he'd never forget the swooping in his belly
and the rush of wind on his face as he saw nothing but sky.
Cole missed that freedom. The childlike giddiness that came
with a simple pleasure like being pushed on a swing. He kind
of wished that he could let go and enjoy himself like his travelling companions were, but it was better that he didn't.
Having fun and making friends was awfully domestic, and it
paved the way for heartbreak, something Cole wouldn't put
himself through again.

He missed his family, but Bryce was right—it was their
loss. He'd couch surfed for months after he'd tried to intro-
duce his first boyfriend to them and they'd kicked him out.
His friends were great, taking him in when he needed them,
but they'd gradually drifted apart as people often did when

they finished school. Then it was just Cole, and it was so much easier that way.

Lonely, but easier.

Even Mitch hadn't lessened the loneliness.

Bryce had the attention span of a toddler, throwing himself off the swing before it had even come to a complete stop and grasping his and Ava's hands. His paw closed around Cole's and its gentle strength and warmth surprised him. He was going insane. Since when did he even give a shit about holding someone's hand? That was relationship crap right there.

Cole stopped. He blinked. *Relationship crap.* He'd been in a relationship for two years and he'd hated being a secret, but he'd never once wanted to hold Mitch's hand. He'd thought he wanted them to become a normal couple doing coupley things together. But he'd been happy with seeing Mitch between his appointments and the nights he'd worked late. They hadn't been in a real relationship. It was a friends-with-benefits arrangement, and they weren't even that close. How had he been so blind?

Dragging them toward the markets, Bryce declared in a tipsy shout, "We need gingerbread."

"We could watch a Christmas movie." Ava smiled, and a pretty flush rose in her cheeks. She looked totally enamoured with the idea of a childlike Christmas. He hadn't celebrated the season since he'd left his family, and there was no way he was starting now.

"*Die Hard*," Cole mumbled before he could censor himself. Shut up, you idiot. He may not have celebrated it, but he also wanted to make Ava smile. Bryce too.

She gasped, horrified. "That's not a Christmas movie!"

"One hundred percent is." Bryce nodded in Cole's direction, still holding his hand, but Ava stopped walking, crossing her arms over her chest and narrowing her eyes.

"If we watch *Die Hard*, we're watching a movie I pick too." Her pout was cute. His dick took notice, and he had the urge to poke the spitfire just to see her rear up ready to attack.

"Yippee ki-yay, motherfucker," Cole responded with a raised eyebrow. The man walking next to them with kids in tow mumbled disgruntledly, and Ava nodded sympathetically to him. The look she shot him was murderous, her eyes flashing and her lips pursed in annoyance. One look at her and Bryce was in a fit of giggles.

Cole watched as Ava's expression softened, her lips tilting upward as she focussed on Bryce. The big oaf was like a puppy dog with boundless enthusiasm and energy, and a dose of sexy too. Bryce threw his arm around Cole's shoulder. He was a touchy-feely drunk and Cole didn't hate it. He didn't let himself get close enough to anyone to cuddle, but with Bryce, he couldn't seem to pull away.

The big man lunged for Ava again, but she dodged, shaking her head. She crossed her arms and stomped her foot, the whole tantrum losing any effect with the smile she was trying, and failing, to hide. "Oh, come on, boo," Bryce implored, holding out his free arm to her. "Come to Brycey."

"You're a bloody teddy bear." She poked Bryce in the ribs and wrapped her arms around him, adding, "And you… don't even get me started. Christmas movie, my arse."

Cole rolled his eyes, biting back a laugh.

"Dessert first, movies later." Bryce steered them in the direction of the markets. Cole hadn't imagined his night would turn out like this. Hell, his whole day had been like he was living in the twilight zone, but he was… happy. He was enjoying himself. Cole furrowed his brow, trying to think of the last time he'd been this light. He didn't usually get drunk. It took too much control away from him, and he needed to maintain an awareness of his surroundings. He didn't trust anyone enough to completely let go. But he wasn't drunk either. He had a bit of a buzz, but it was quickly fading. No, this wasn't the alcohol talking. It was being around them.

"Uh-oh, Cole's got his thinking face on," Bryce whisper-shouted to Ava. "Or he's constipated."

"I'm not fucking constipated," Cole mumbled, trailing off as the scent of fresh baked goods hit him. His mouth watered as he breathed in the sweet spices. Bryce had his hands on the biggest bag of gingerbread he could find within seconds—the big guy moved like lightning—and Ava held up a bag of cookies to Cole, silently asking him if he wanted some. A sliver of a smile quirked up his lips and Ava's corresponding beaming grin lifted them even further. Yeah, he liked these two. They didn't expect anything from him, not even a conversation, but when he did reach out, they rewarded him with pretty smiles and hugs. That usually would have been enough to make him run, but Cole wanted the cookies.

Ava opened the box as soon as they'd moved onto the next stall and offered it straight to him. He was itching to dive in and devour everything, but he resisted the temptation. Barely. But how did he choose? Chocolate chip and walnut were his faves, but double chocolate and white chocolate and macadamia looked gooey and delicious. He hesitated too long, and Ava reached in, picking a chocolate chip one for him.

The cookie melted in his mouth as they walked. It was almost better than sex. Almost. The moan that bubbled up his throat as he chewed, savouring every bite, was one of undisguised ecstasy.

They stopped in different stalls, Ava buying a photograph of the view from the rise they'd broken down on. Bryce went for the soaps and bath bombs, mulling over which to pick. Cole could tell he wanted more, but he held off getting them.

He stopped at the wood carvings, in awe of the craftsmanship it took to chip away at the raw lumber until it resembled the animals and abstract people the artist had created. He ran his fingers reverently over the smooth curves and snapped his gaze up when the man behind the table spoke to him.

"They're all made locally."

"Are you the artist?"

"I am." The man's chest swelled in pride and Cole touched the wedge-tailed eagle he had at the front of the table. Even with its wings outstretched, it wasn't large—not even half the size of an A4 piece of paper—but the detail was so intricate that it was breathtaking. Cole loved it, loved the freedom a bird in flight inspired. But that bird was a little too personal too. They mated for life, they built their nests and returned there year on year—they had a home.

Deep down, it was what he wanted, but he wouldn't go there. Families broke apart.

He bought the keychain of the coiled snake instead.

Then he saw the boiled lollies and handmade candy canes and Cole was like a pig in mud. It wasn't until they were browsing the roasted nut stand that he realized Ava hadn't bought any snacks. "You in the mood for anything?" Cole asked her.

Ava tilted her head in thought and nodded slowly. "I'd like to try eggnog. But not the store-bought crap. I wonder if anyone makes it."

"There's a stall up the other end of the market that sells vegan food. The eggnog is delicious," the lady behind the counter said as she handed Bryce some change. He screwed up his nose, but she continued unperturbed. "It's made from coconut cream, cashews, and local cane sugar. There's a bottle-o down the road, too, where you can get some whiskey for it."

Ava smiled and Cole's breath hitched. She was beautiful. "That's what I'm having then."

On their way, they paused at another handmade jewellery stall. Her fingers lingered over the turquoise opal mounted in chunky silver rings before moving on to look at the crystals. Blue, green, pink, and amethyst earrings, pendants, and hairpins were artfully displayed on pieces of driftwood and black velvet. She didn't buy anything, but Cole knew exactly what she wanted.

Ava rushed ahead to the stall to taste the eggnog and before he could blink, she'd bought a bottle. "Oh my god, that is delicious," she raved as she returned to them.

"Bottle shop's up there." Bryce pointed to the road they'd crossed as they walked to the pub. "But first, we need a Santa photo."

We? Oh, hell no.

Ava's question mirrored his thoughts. "Where are we going to get one of those on a Sunday night out here? There are literally no shopping centres in a twenty-k radius and none of them would stay open this late anyway."

"Right there." Bryce pointed to the rotunda at the end of the markets, a dozen stalls past where she'd bought the eggnog. Cole could see Santa sitting on a throne under harsh fluorescent lights wearing a red coat with no arms and a beanie. It wasn't until he stood to shake the hand of someone getting a photo that Cole saw the lime green boardies he'd paired the outfit with. No doubt he'd be wearing thongs too. Gum trees formed the background to the photo, and a surfboard leaning up against a post gave an unmistakeably Aussie feel to the whole scene. An Esky sat at his feet, and camping chairs with beach towels hanging over the armrests surrounded Santa's seat. Shit.

"You're kidding, right?" Cole asked warily.

"Oh, smile for once in your life, Mr Party Pooper," Ava chastised him. "Bryce wants to take a photo."

He didn't want to diss Bryce. It was cool if he wanted a photo. As long as the "we" he'd referred to didn't include him, it was fine. "I mean—"

"With both of you too." *Well, there goes that hope.* Bryce grinned like a kid at... Christmas and dashed off to stand in the line.

"I hate photos," Cole muttered, protesting, but he couldn't help following Ava as she joined Bryce in the line. The bloody puppy dog was getting to him, and Ava's enthusiasm to make him happy wasn't irritating like he'd expected it to be but endearing.

He paid for their photo to be printed, deciding on the spur of the moment to get it in triplicate, and lingered, waiting for Ava and Bryce to sit with Santa.

Apparently, Bryce wasn't having it. He was on his feet in a flash, coming at Cole like the battering ram he was. But instead of knocking him down, Cole was in the air, being picked up like a damn bride. He struggled, squirming so Bryce would let him go and groused, "Put me down, you dumb-arse."

"Hush," Bryce ordered, his muscles bulging as he carried him and sat down on the Esky.

Cole's protest caught in his throat as Bryce held him tight and Ava leaned over, laughing as she said, "You aren't getting out of it that easily." She ruffled his hair as Bryce poked his tongue out with a shit-eating grin. Cole couldn't help his snort of laughter.

The flash went off and the photographer called, "Say 'Merry Christmas!'"

Bugger it. If they were all taking what they wanted, he would too. Ava smiled and squeaked when he wrapped his arm around her nape, tugging her down to meet his lips. She froze and his hold relaxed, making sure she could pull away. Cole held his breath, her pheromones sending his into a tailspin. Bloody hell, she smelled so good—they both did. A mix of something fresh and sweet mixed with a citrus scent that Cole couldn't get enough of.

She relaxed into his hold and Cole kissed her properly, his tongue sliding against hers. Her lips were pillowy soft. His were demanding. She was confident and he was un-yielding. Ava slid her fingers into his hair and Bryce adjusted his hold, pulling him tighter. The dude was sporting one hell of a boner. Cole moaned, picturing just how gorgeous he'd be naked. Both of them would be. He thrust his tongue in deeper, tasting Ava's mouth. Her moan in response was quiet but it seemed to echo over their suddenly silent sur-rounds.

Cole blinked open his eyes, realizing exactly where they were and what he'd done. Fuck.

He leapt up and staggered away, rushing as far from them as he could go in the darkness that beckoned.

It wasn't long before trees blocked his path, the criss-cross roots of the mangroves that grew along the riverbank like an impenetrable fortress. Hands on his knees trying not to puke, Cole wished he hadn't been as impulsive. As reck-less.

What the hell was he thinking? He shouldn't have kissed her. He'd wanted to, but he should have stayed out of it. Ava and Bryce were better for each other. She smiled when Bryce did. She held his hand and blushed when he teased her. They laughed together and talked non-stop. He was like the dark shadow that dimmed their happy. The black hole that sucked the life out of them.

He felt Bryce's presence before he saw him. Cole waited on tenterhooks, unsure of how he would react.

A gentle hand on his shoulder wasn't what he expected. Cole straightened, meeting Bryce's gaze. "I'm sorry," he whispered, ashamed that he'd probably ruined the night.

"For what?" Bryce asked, his head tilted to the side, curious.

"For everything. I shouldn't have kissed Ava—"

Bryce barked out a laugh. "You need to apologize to her for that, but Ava seemed pretty into it to me."

"But you and her...."

"Are no different to you and her." Cole shook his head, and Bryce's grin turned wicked. His gaze fell, taking in every inch of Cole, slowly perusing him like he was eating him up. Heat flashed through him and his knees wobbled. Bryce was potent and the rasp in his voice had Cole's cock thickening.

A twig snapped behind him and Cole turned, seeing Ava with all their bags. "Shit," he muttered, racing over to her, and relieving her of half of them.

"Let me," Bryce implored, taking the rest. "You can carry the whiskey. I think we might need it."

* * * * *

The door clicked closed behind them as he toed out of his loafers while Ava went for her laptop. Bryce placed the bags he was carrying down by the sideboard. When Cole made his way there, depositing his own, he saw that Ava had made herself comfortable. Lounging in the middle of the bed, she was a sweet temptation.

He danced around Bryce awkwardly, every step tentative and filled with an awareness of what the other man had said. Electricity sparked in the air, anticipation sizzling through his veins at the tension ratcheting up. Three glasses landed on the counter in front of him and Cole realized he'd been leaning against it, knuckles holding him up for too long. He met Bryce's stare, heat sizzling in the other man's gaze. He wanted Ava as much as Cole did. Bryce poured three shots and brought one of the glasses to his lips, tipping back the amber liquid and letting it slide down his throat like a seasoned pro. Cole watched entranced as his Adam's apple moved, wishing he had a chance with Bryce too.

Cole filled the glasses with eggnog and let Bryce top his up with another shot of whiskey. He flashed Cole a confident smile, his eyes glittering wickedly in the lamps Ava had switched on. Want curled low in Cole's belly.

A gust of wind straight off the ocean cooled his skin, the gauzy, white curtains billowing with each gust. Cole loaded the glasses onto a tray, needing a moment to gather his wits and stop himself from jumping the gorgeous man before him.

"This was not the movie we agreed to," Bryce teased, his deep voice rumbling through Cole as he sat on the edge of the mattress, those chinos stretching tight over his thick thighs. When he saw Bryce's fingers dancing circles on Ava's petite ankles, Cole's mouth went as dry as the Sahara.

"I need to be far more intoxicated to watch that rubbish excuse for a Christmas movie than I am now." She held her hand out to Cole for the glass, the movement making the strap on her dress fall to the side. He wanted to pull it down. With his teeth. "Hit me up."

Cole swallowed hard and shook his head. "We're staying on this side of sober tonight," he instructed.

When Ava wet her lips and shivered, Cole reacted on instinct, setting down the tray with a frown. Reaching for the throw at the foot of the bed, he wrapped it around her shoulders. Why hadn't Ava said something if she was cold?

She smiled sweetly. "I'm okay, Cole. Just come and sit here with us." She patted the spot next to her and Bryce scooted closer too, pressing up against her opposite side. Cole copied him. He needed to get a grip. He had enough self-control to focus only on Ava. At least he thought he did.

Dear god, he wanted to be consumed by them. His heart thudded, and his breaths shallowed out.

No, he didn't want to be consumed by them. He wanted to do the devouring.

Ava closed her laptop and put it aside. He wasn't going to complain and by the bulge in Bryce's pants, neither was he. She motioned to Cole for the whiskey bottle, and he passed it to her, hoping she wasn't going to scull it. He'd made it clear what he expected. If Ava was going to get blackout drunk, he'd take the floor and Bryce could sleep on the couch. The deal was off if any one of them were drunk—none of them could afford hazy memories and un-answered questions.

She flipped around, facing them, and laid the bottle down before murmuring, "How about instead of watching a movie, we get to know each other better. Truth or dare, or—" She slowly spun the neck of the bottle using a finger. "—spin the bottle?"

Cole stilled, an inferno burning through him. "Be careful what you wish for," he cautioned, his voice a gravelly rasp.

Ava's chest rose and fell in quick succession, and Bryce flat-out laughed. "She's more than capable of making up her own mind."

She high-fived Bryce when Cole opened his mouth to voice his agreement, and Ava agreed, "I am capable of mak-ing a decision."

"Are you?" Bryce asked him, his own eyes widening at the question.

Cole see-sawed between want and a fear that he'd touch Bryce in a way that the other man wouldn't appreci-ate. He didn't feel like getting the shit beaten out of him or having to find the way to the Gold Coast from the tiny vil-lage by himself. But he could keep his hands to himself. Cole just needed to stay in complete control. He wouldn't be having anything more to drink, and keeping Ava between them the whole time would reduce the chance of him fucking up.

Cole exhaled slowly and nodded, a plan forming in his mind. Concentrating solely on Ava wouldn't be a hardship either—she was a wet dream, exactly the type of woman he had a hard-on for.

"Yeah," he rasped, his dick pulsing at the thought of touching the woman before him. But Cole's words seemed to have the opposite effect on Bryce.

He wrung his hands and bit down on that pillowy lip. He curled into himself, hanging his head and letting his shoulders droop. He ran his hands through his hair, tugging on the ends and groaned out a pained sigh. There was clearly something going on with the man. Cole flicked his gaze to Ava. She shook her head, clearly clueless as to the sudden flip in his mood.

"Dude, are you sure you're okay going through with this?" Cole asked. He didn't want to push, especially if having a threesome was something Bryce was nervous or uncertain about. Cole was just as happy to snack on their haul and watch shitty Christmas movies if that's what made Bryce and Ava happy.

Bryce looked up at him and slowly pulled his shoulders back, sitting up straighter. He gave Cole a small nod, a glimmer of a smile tilting his lips up, and nodded again with more certainty in Ava's direction.

"We can watch *Die Hard*," Ava offered.

Bryce chuckled, his grin lighting up his face, and added, "Nah, let's play."

Ava spun the bottle, but Cole couldn't take his eyes off the people before him. She touched his knee and he realized he hadn't even seen where it landed. The bottle hadn't made a full revolution, pointing squarely at him. He reached down, turning the neck until it faced Bryce. "It didn't make a full turn," he explained, wanting Bryce to make the first move if he really was okay with this threesome. "And it's important we follow the rules."

Bryce reached for Ava, and Cole's heart doubled its rate. He traced his thick fingertips over her cheek, before running his thumb over Ava's jaw and tilting her chin up. Bryce was infinitely gentle, his big hands dwarfing her petite frame. Leaning in, the man brushed his lips over hers in a sweet, chaste kiss. He licked her bottom lip, and Ava opened to him, their tongues touching gently as he explored her mouth. Ava shuffled closer and ran her hands up his chest and over those sculpted muscles that Cole wanted to lick.

When they finally broke apart, Cole was hard and desperately wanted another taste of her sweet lips. "Spin the bottle again, Ava," he directed.

SEVEN

Ava

S he blinked, coming back from an out-of-body experience. With Bryce's kiss on her tongue and Cole's
voice in her ear, it was as if she'd been floating in
outer space while galaxies of starbursts lit up behind her
closed eyelids.

Slowly, Cole's words registered, and she turned the base
of the bottle toward Bryce. "You know, if we're sticking with
the rules of the game, it should actually be Bryce's spin."

Bryce raised an eyebrow as if in question and tilted his
head toward Ava, a silent conversation passing between
them. Heat flared within and Ava bit back a whimper when
Cole inclined his head and Bryce's eyes sparked with mis-
chief. His lips turned up in a wicked grin full of promise as
he placed the bottle on the nightstand.

Ava couldn't help the snort of laughter that escaped
when Bryce bounced toward her, his big body reminiscent
of a goofy puppy. A moment ago, the sexual tension was
thick enough to have been cut with a knife. But Bryce's

uncanny ability to remind her to have fun had loosened the nerves around the tension, morphing it into anticipation.

Cole prowled forward on his knees, the glint in his eye and the way he wiped his lower lip with this thumb sending a thrill through her. She couldn't wait to taste him again. To touch him like she wanted to. He was intense, and being on the receiving end of that laser-like focus was reminiscent of being on a stage lit by a million spotlights.

Cole pressed his leg against hers, closing the distance between them. Shoulders brushing against Bryce's, they reached for her. Gooseflesh rose where their rough hands skated along her arms and her clit pulsed, her pussy throbbing. *Oh god, this was really happening.*

Cupping her face, Cole tilted her head just so. Desperation clawed at her as he stared down into her eyes, their mouths only a hair's breadth apart. His heated breath washed over her, and Ava's eyes fluttered closed, her lips parting as she sought him out.

She needed to touch them both to stop herself floating away from the high she was already experiencing and to reassure herself that this was real. Slipping her hands under each of their shirts, Ava moaned at the hot ridges of muscle rippling under her fingertips. Chest heaving, Cole pulled her closer and his mouth descended on hers, crashing their lips together. He kissed her like she was the oxygen he needed to breathe. It was passion and fire. All-consuming. His tongue demanded entrance and she immediately acquiesced, desperate to taste him again. His sweetness, now mixed with the warmth of the whiskey, and a flavour unmistakeably Cole, burst onto her tongue. Ava moaned, diving deeper into him.

He scraped his teeth over her bottom lip. Her moan turned into a whimper. She loved the possessive act, the control he exerted over her body as if it was his for the taking.

Bryce's warmth pressed in closer, and Ava wrapped her arm around his waist, tugging him toward her. She couldn't explain the need to have his hands on her too—having one of them should have been enough, but Ava was powerless to stop the overwhelming urge to claim them both.

Being the centre of their combined attention ratcheted up the sexual tension between them, the air thickening with anticipation. Her breath hitched and a ripple of nervous excitement fluttered through her. Ava's body flushed hot, her pulse thrumming through her veins as her nipples tightened.

Cole tangled his hand in her hair, tilting her face just so. His other hand teased a line up her inner leg, skating closer to her core. Bryce scraped his five o'clock shadow over her shoulder, brushing her hair back before nipping at the soft skin on her collarbone. Laying a trail of kisses up her neck, he nibbled her skin. Gooseflesh appeared all over, puckering her nipples. He fingered the thin strap of her dress and Ava tore her mouth away from Cole's to beg, "Do it."

Bryce slipped it down her arm and his mouth followed as he licked a path back along her collarbone to her breast, flicking his tongue over her pebbled nipple as Cole's kiss stole her breath. Bryce gently sucked the peak into his mouth, laving his tongue over her sensitive skin. Sparks lit up behind her eyes. Ava arched into him, steadying herself on her men's broad shoulders. Cole hummed and copied Bryce's moves, kissing his way down her throat and over her décolletage until he lashed his tongue over her nipple. Ava cried out, her pussy throbbing as need crashed into her like a star going supernova. She rubbed her legs together, needing friction against her core, and squirmed with the evidence of her desire slicking her upper thighs.

Tugging on their silky hair, Ava held them tight against her, her incomprehensible pleas echoing around the otherwise quiet night. Her breath caught as Cole resumed his tease up and down her leg, stopping just shy of her centre. Ava would have been embarrassed by her soaking panties, but his growled approval dashed any fear that he'd be turned off.

"So wet," he murmured, the prickle of his stubble against her sensitive skin awakening a delicious shiver within her.

A second hand was there only a moment later, this one bigger than Cole's. Bryce cupped her pussy, humming as she clenched and involuntarily thrust into his gentle hold.

It wasn't enough.

Ava's whine was plaintive, the frustration in her tone obvious as she became increasingly desperate to be stretched and rubbed in all the right ways.

Bryce's lips turned up in a grin and two hands landed on her arse, squeezing her cheeks and pulling her up onto her knees. Hard bodies collided with hers, their steely cocks grinding against her hips. Ava reached for them, cupping their lengths through their clothes. Fuck me. They were both long and thick, and so so hard. Fingers brushed her thigh, higher this time, and Ava undulated her hips. "Fuck," she breathed, shaking as the men licked and sucked her throat, taking it in turns to kiss her.

She wasn't sure who moaned, but the deep rasp was hot as hell and Ava's last thread of restraint snapped. Her clit pulsed, their teasing riling her up, but not satisfying her hunger. The craving was a sweet torment, one that Ava couldn't stand any longer. She pulled her grip free from their cocks and squeezed the hand between her legs, pressing both of them closer.

"We've got you," Cole whispered.

Bryce guided her down with a gentle touch until she was lying between them. Her dress was soon bunched up around her waist, her white lace G-string on display. Hungry eyes ate her up and her heart hammered, her pulse thundering through her veins until she was convinced her men could hear it. The need for relief grew, and Ava rubbed her thighs together once more, groaning with the ache exploding inside her.

One of those silent conversations passed between them again, their stare intense. Cole's lips parted on a sharp inhale and his tongue darted out, touching his top lip. Bryce wavered closer, and Ava watched enraptured, her body thrumming with desire.

Bryce caught himself before he lost balance and broke the connection between him and Cole. The other man's lids fluttered closed, and a vein pulsed at his forehead, his jaw clenching. But it wasn't anger. The bulge at his groin flexed, the linen of his white pants doing a poor job of constraining the hard rod pressing against it.

They turned back to her as one and Ava knew she'd just become their prey. But instead of her fight-or-flight instinct kicking in, she wanted to throw open the gates and invite them in to party. Ava rubbed her thighs together, their hands on her legs sending a ripple of need through her.

Cole licked his lips as he eyed her pussy and Ava shot into the stratosphere, wanting to ride the high for as long as she could. But if she didn't get the friction she needed, she was going to explode. Sliding her hand down, she pressed her fingers against her clit unable to tear her eyes away from the visual of Bryce stroking his cock through his chinos. It reached to his hip and was as thick as her fist. Her core clenched, eager to have him seated deep within.

Cole unbuttoned his shirt enough that he could tug it off and toss it aside, Bryce's shirt following only a moment later. A whiff of their aftershaves floated by as the shirts sailed over her head. Ava arched up, chasing more as she dipped her finger into her core before circling the nub of nerves at her clit again.

They were beautiful. Bryce was all golden skin and thick muscles. She couldn't get enough. Sitting up, she licked at his abs, the sweet taste of his skin as addictive as a drug. Ava moaned, desperate to take her fill as she traced a line up the middle of his body and nibbled on the flat disk of his nipple. She sucked, licking away the slight sting of her teeth when he gasped and she trailed her fingers down to his waistband.

"Fuck it," Bryce mumbled and palmed the back of his head, drawing Cole close. Their gazes clashed and she saw the moment the wildfire between them ignited. Cole's lids grew heavy as Bryce effortlessly tugged him closer. Cole gripped his shoulders, massaging the thick muscle there, the moment stretching out and speeding up at the same time.

Bryce crashed their lips together, his kiss ferocious. She hadn't realized it was even possible, but Bryce hauled Cole closer, his arm banding around Cole's waist. Their hips crashed together, and Cole tangled his fingers in Bryce's hair, taking what he wanted from Bryce as their tongues tangled.

The strength of the two men before her, their muscles rippling and stubble scraping as they devoured each other was the sexiest thing Ava had ever seen. The noises they made were an aphrodisiac, one she could listen to for hours. But they were beautiful together too, because for all that aggression and heat, there was a tenderness. It was in the way Cole pulled back and nuzzled their noses together, slowing their kiss, and the brush of Bryce's knuckles along Cole's jaw.

Panting, Bryce ducked his head and his cheeks flamed before panic crept in and she watched him swallow, his eyes wide as he flicked his gaze to hers. Cole cupped his face, tilting it back to him as he pressed a soft kiss to his cheek. "I'll never break your confidence, Bryce. It stays between us. Always."

"Thank you," he whispered, his lashes lowering. The flush on his cheeks deepened and Bryce's lips turned up in a shy smile before he sobered again. "I feel like I'm lying to myself most of the time. Denying it was always the plan—if I never acted on my attraction then I'd never get caught out. I was gonna wait until I retired. But then you two came along."

Bryce threaded his fingers into Ava's hair and her heart thudded against her ribs, her chest tight. She hated that he even had to worry about keeping a part of him secret, but Ava was no idiot. She saw how toxic masculinity infiltrated every aspect of the game. Sure, the league had policies on inclusivity, but it said more about the current state of play that there wasn't a single out professional player in the men's league. Her heart broke for him, knowing he would have to walk this journey without ever being open and honest with his teammates unless he wanted to be the one to walk the path first.

Bryce tilted her face up, his eyes wary and his expression guarded. "Are you okay with this?"

"One hundred percent. I'm very okay with it." She kissed him then, a soft lingering press of their lips that spoke more of comfort and affection than a wild night of sex. "Your secret's safe with me too." It was an easy promise to make. This man had already made an indelible mark on her heart. Bryce kissed her again, deepening it quickly.

Pressed against the two men, she shivered as Cole's hand skated down her belly before sliding between them and palming Bryce's cock. His lips landed on her throat, nibbling a path to the sensitive spot below her ear as his knuckles rubbed her clit while he stroked Bryce.

Bryce pulled back and groaned, his hips punching forward as Cole squeezed. "You're killing me," he moaned, shuddering. "Shit."

Ava turned her attention to Cole and unbuttoned his pants as he tried to push Bryce's down one-handed while cupping her breast with the other. He reached down, licking at her nipple but lurched forward, losing his balance.

Bryce snorted out a laugh as they went sprawling across the bed. "How much have you had to drink?"

Pressed between them, hard muscle flanking her, Ava moaned. Yes! This is what I want. Bryce curled his fingers around her hips and ground his dick against her. Ava cried out again. Before she could stop him, Cole lifted off, her body instantly missing the warmth and hot and heavy man pressed against her.

But Cole didn't go far.

He shucked his pants before positioning himself over her. Ava shifted, widening her legs so he could crawl between them as he blew softly on her skin, sending desire ricocheting through her before lapping at her breasts. He pressed his knee against her pussy and Ava shamelessly rubbed herself on that thick muscle.

Cole uttered, "Oh, I'm sober," in a deep growl against the dip between her breasts. He looked up, his gaze meeting hers before flicking to Bryce's. As if by unspoken agreement, they moved, tugging her on top of Bryce fully. Bryce pushed her dress down and Cole grasped it together with her panties, sliding them off until her legs were up in the air and the clothes were sailing toward the floor. Cole gripped her calves and spread her open, exposing every intimate detail of her body to him. Kneeling between her outstretched legs, Bryce's bracketing Cole's knees, she could picture exactly what they would look like as Cole and Bryce both sank into her.

Her juices leaked from her core and Cole hummed. "What did you just think of Ava?"

"Both of you inside me," she gushed breathlessly as Cole stroked up her leg, his fingertip circling the folds of her pussy.

"Mmm," Bryce moaned, thrusting up as he held her hips steady. With her ankles hooked over his shoulders, Cole reached between her and Bryce and tugged gracelessly on the waistband of the chinos, stopping her fantasy coming to life. Bryce took over and shucked them, Ava feeling the heat of his flesh slap against her butt.

"Oh yeah," Cole murmured, hooking her legs over Bryce's knees and pushing his legs further apart. Her pussy clenched again, needing both their touch. Cole's knuckles brushed her pussy as he took Bryce in hand, and she moaned. "Okay?" he asked, and Ava felt Bryce's quick exhale and nod.

With his other hand, Cole pressed a thumb against her clit, rubbing it slowly. Completely exposed to them, vulnerable and aching, Ava gave herself over to them as lust pulsed through her. She reached back, threading her fingers through Bryce's hair as he cupped her breasts, gently flicking her nipples with his thumbs. Cole laved his tongue over her heated skin, taking both her nipple and Bryce's thumb into his mouth. Sensation ricocheted through her, lightning zapping straight through her core to her clit. She moaned, and Bryce thrust his hips up, his hard cock tunnelling into Cole's fist at her openings.

His gaze never leaving hers, Cole moved down, running his tongue over her belly down to the crease at her hip. Ava squirmed, desire heating her blood. Bryce looked over her shoulder, his hot breath tickling her ear as he held her in place. "Fuck, that's sexy," he purred.

Cole ran his tongue down her slit, his eyes rolling back in his head. "Believe me, I'll be jacking off to this moment for a long time," he uttered before swiping his tongue over Bryce's cockhead and her pussy again. Over and over, he licked them until fireworks lit up below her skin, her nerve endings sizzling. Bryce's hisses and his low groans were like catnip, ratcheting up her own desire. But it was the sincerity shining in Cole's eyes that had Ava moaning. There was an attraction between the three of them, sure, but suddenly it felt like a whole lot more too.

Their moves were unhurried, their touch sensual as both men worshipped her and explored each other. Fingers and tongues, lips, and whispered words sent her to the edge. She hovered there, her pussy quivering and clit pulsing as the tide rose. One more thrust of Cole's fingers deep within her, a brush of teeth against her over-sensitized clit and the bite of pain from Bryce pinching her nipples and she was tossed over, her orgasm crashing over her like a tsunami.

Her inner walls contracted, clamping tight and holding Cole's fingers in place as Ava moaned incoherently. The ripple of ecstasy from their touch consumed her whole.

Cole didn't stop until she was wrung out and trembling. Then he kissed a line up her belly, smiling as she quivered at his touch. Wrapped in Bryce's arms, she was secure, but she needed both of them to ground her. To bring her back to earth gently.

Ava cupped his nape, tugging him closer. But as soon as he was close enough, Bryce lurched up in a half crunch and dragged Cole the rest of the way down until they were pressed together.

Her skin was dewy with sweat, and the warmth bracketing her blocking the cool wash of the ocean's evening breeze was like falling into heaven. Cole's spicy cologne and Bryce's citrus one, mixed with the heady scent of sex surrounded her, ratcheting up her need once more. Walls of muscle moved against her pliant body. Cole's briefs-covered cock nestled against her still-clenching pussy and Bryce's tree-trunk sized package prodded her as he thrust up, seeking friction in his needy state. Ava moaned, squirming between them. She'd just come, but she wanted more. She wanted it all.

She wanted the fantasy—the sex she didn't know she craved until she'd met these two men.

Bryce crashed his and Cole's lips together, and Cole ground down, dragging his hard length against her clit. Ava cried out, her body climbing again already. But she wanted a taste, just like Cole had stolen. She needed to be able to touch them and drive them wild with desire too.

Because if there was one thing Ava loved, it was being on her knees and bringing a man to his. Having two was like a damn Vegas buffet, and she was going to gorge herself.

"Let me taste you," she moaned, slipping her hands down to cup both men. Their moans were deep and throaty, punctuated with a snap of their hips as they both chased more of her touch.

Cole pressed his lips to hers, his mouth owning hers. She tasted herself and Bryce on his tongue and couldn't help but suck on it to get more of their combined essence.

When he pulled back, his eyes blazed with need. His lips glistened and parted as he choked out a cry when Bryce squeezed him. Cole looked down the length of her body, his gaze a caress. Her nipples puckered, her pussy clenching tightly as he ran a fingertip between her breasts to her navel, circling it gently, before pinching her clit. Ava cried out, shuddering with the force of the need exploding in her.

But this was about more than just her. Ava rolled sideways, clambering off Bryce so she could get Cole naked too. On her knees, she pushed Cole's underwear down and tugged him forward by his cock, bringing them together and wrapping her hands around their thick lengths.

They were opposites in many ways, even in their cocks, but there was an equal level of perfection in them. Cole's olive skin tone was concentrated in his cock, his shaft a few shades darker than the rest of his fine body, and the head a blush-pink. A thatch of dark, trimmed hair framed his long dick to perfection. Bryce's cock was a complete contrast. It was about the same length, but twice as thick, the veiny surface much paler than the rest of his golden skin.

Beads of pre-cum pooled at their slits and Ava spread her knees, hiking her butt up in the air so she could dive in for a taste.

She licked at their salty essence, the tangy liquid spurring her on to devour more. She lapped at them, sucking one of them deep before alternating to the other and using her hands to elicit moans.

They thrust against each other, frotting their cocks in her fisted hands. Stroking them, Ava couldn't wait to have both these men inside her. Their silky skin encasing an iron-hard core would hit her in every spot she needed.

Their hands tangled in her hair, holding it out of the way as Ava took her fill. Thick fingers speared her pussy, pumping in and out before slipping out and up, teasing her back passage. Ava moaned, pushing back against the thick digits. When a finger pressed against her rim, she cried out, begging for more.

One of the men worked his fingers into her hole. The stretch was unfamiliar, the feeling of fullness strange, but one she was desperate to experience in this moment. Another set of fingers speared into her pussy. Her body desperate for another orgasm, Ava moaned. The heady scent of sex hit her, and she wanted it all. She couldn't get enough. Opening wider, she did her best to fit both their cockheads between her lips while pushing back against their roaming hands, silently begging them to fill her.

Cole choked out a cry and shuddered, pulling back and gripping the base of his cock. A string of pre-cum still connected him to her mouth until Ava wrapped her hand around his tip and stroked down. "I'm too close," he gasped with a shudder as Bryce moaned, his cock pulsing in her mouth.

She pulled off and rocked back against their fingers, shamelessly taking what they were offering. "I need you both inside me."

Cole's nostrils flared and Bryce hissed before grasping his sac and pulling it roughly down, tugging his balls away from his body. "Bloody hell," he groaned as Cole added, "I want your arse."

"Thank fuck. I don't know if Bryce would fit."

Bryce groaned painfully, and he strangled his cock in a white-knuckled grip. "I'm gonna go off like a damn firework."

"How quickly can you get it up again?" Cole asked, his eyes onyx with desire.

"At this rate, I dunno if I'll even soften."

"Good." Cole batted Bryce's hand out of the way, leaned down to suck a mark onto his thigh, and jacked him hard and fast. Bryce shuddered and cried out before jerking his hips forward, pressing deeper into Cole's fist.

"Fuck," he gasped. "I'm there." Cole pumped him, his fingers gliding over the swollen head of his cock as Bryce thrust into the tight circle of his rough fingers. Thick muscles in Bryce's legs and arse tensed as he chased his orgasm. His abs rippled, and Ava bent, sucking one of his balls into her mouth. Bryce shouted and shuddered in their hold, coming undone at the seams and painting her hair and his belly with cum.

He breathed hard as he trembled, shooting Ava a glassy-eyed smile. He threw his forearm over his eyes and Ava turned her face, licking up his still-hard shaft to get another taste of him. Bryce groaned, still slowly pumping his finger inside her arse while Cole leaned forward and licked up his chiselled belly, cleaning every droplet of cum from Bryce.

Bryce never softened. Never even looked like he was going to, and when he began to thrust gently into her mouth in shallow pushes and pulls, Ava knew he was ready. "Do you have protection?" she asked, and Cole nodded, slipping his fingers free of her pussy and going to his bag. Her channel clenched, trying to keep the feel of him inside her. Ava had never experienced a reaction with anyone quite like this before. All she wanted was for them to be connected. To fill her and chase out the emptiness that had wormed its way inside her.

A bottle of lube and a single foil packet landed next to her, and disappointment crashed through her. One? That was it? She couldn't have both of them? Ava's shoulders fell and she bit back a sob.

Cole cleared his throat. "I'm smaller than you, Bryce. My rubbers won't fit you."

Ava blinked her eyes open as Bryce huffed out an embarrassed laugh. "Sorry, my brains are still scrambled. Front pocket of my bag." She couldn't help the sob that hitched in her throat this time, and Bryce chuckled. "We wouldn't have left you hanging, hon."

The laugh turned into a whimper when Cole gave them an unsurpassed view of his tight body—long legs and a high arse that Ava wanted to bite—when he bent. Legs spread, he put his hole on show for Bryce, whose cock flexed in her hand. He liked what he saw too—who wouldn't?

"Fuck," he groaned, and Ava smiled wickedly.

"Maybe you can get all up in there," she whispered, swiping a lick over his cockhead when pre-cum bloomed at his slit.

"I want all up in you first," he growled.

That was A-okay with her.

Cole passed her a magnum-sized foil, and she tore the wrapper open, rolling the thin latex over Bryce's shaft. Cole kneeled behind her and wet Bryce's cock with lube-slicked hands, then helped Ava balance as she shifted forward. She was soaked, but the lube helped ease him inside her. Ava had never been stretched so tight. She rocked slowly, working herself onto him until he was impaled deep within her. She shuddered, stuffed full of his meaty cock, and Bryce let out a strangled cry.

Her fingers flexed on his thick chest, and his muscles rippled as he closed his big hands around her hips, holding her steady. Holy fucking hell, he was big. He filled her to bursting, stretching her pussy tight.

"Shit," he hissed. "You're strangling my dick."

Ava gasped her response. "No, you're just super-sized." Even talking made her pussy clamp down and Bryce's response was immediate and without hesitation. The thrust of his hips and arch of his neck pressed him deeper into her. Ava cried out, riding the knife-edge of pain and pleasure.

"This is gonna be over quick," Bryce ground out between clenched teeth. "But I'll get you there." He slid his hand forward, pressing his thumb against her clit and she shuddered, spasming around his girth.

"Not yet," Cole soothed, running his fingertips down her sides to her arse. He kissed a soft line up her throat to her ear, his movements slow and sensual. He bit down on her lobe and whispered, "Relax, sexy. Lean forward and let me prep you properly."

She planted her hands on either side of Bryce's broad shoulders and held her weight on stretched arms, her pussy fluttering around the massive shaft impaling her. Cool lube-covered fingers slid down her arse to her hole and rubbed. Sparks of sensation ricocheted through her. Ava shivered and moaned when Cole pressed inside, pausing to let her adjust before quickly adding a second finger. The heat of his body pressed against hers and the slow slide of Bryce's cock in her pussy made her gasp for more. Cole obliged, sinking in deeper. The stretch increased, the feeling of fullness too, but there was no burn.

He did something then, rotated his finger and pressed against the thin wall between her arse and pussy, and Ava's back arched. Bryce cried out, his cock flexing inside her. The chuckle from behind was low and rough, and Cole kept going, stretching her, twisting his fingers, and adding a third until she was panting and desperate. Bryce wasn't faring any better either, his jaw clenched tight as his movements became jerky.

"I'm ready," she cried in frustration. "Hurry up and fuck me."

"I don't want to hurt you," Cole soothed, but then his fingers were gone and the emptiness in his wake left her bereft.

This was it.

She needed to be connected to them. Joined.

She wanted to share this moment with them—even if it was the only time they were together. She needed them both.

The tearing of the foil packet was like a siren's call to Ava. Her taut muscles relaxed, and Cole hummed as he pet her back soothingly.

"That's it, sexy. Nice and relaxed." Bryce sat up in a crunch and licked her nipple, distracting her as he spread his legs wider and planted his feet on the bed. "Stay right there, Bryce," Cole instructed. More lube, and then the press of Cole's cock against her entrance. Ava arched back, inviting him inside her, and moaned as he pushed forward. The stretch and burn were intense. She cried out, but not from pain. Cole stilled until she rocked her hips, trying to take more of him inside. He pushed forward slowly, and the burn returned. "I'm in," he breathed, his voice tight. "I'll go slow for the rest."

"That was just the tip?" Ava squeaked.

"Yeah, sexy, it was. You're doing so well. So fuckin' hot. I wish you could see how hot you look taking both of us. So tight too."

"Take a photo," she gasped, wanting to be able to see the evidence of them inside her as well as feeling it. Bryce shuddered and moaned, the jerk of his hips a telling sign of just how much he liked that idea.

Bryce reached up, grabbing his phone from the nightstand and handed it to Cole. She heard the artificial click of the camera and the thud as it landed on the bed next to her.

His hands landed on her hips once more and Cole thrust forward achingly slowly, her nerve endings firing. She was filled to bursting, but she needed them to move. To take her to heaven. She was being carried away, riding a high. She was up among the stars, her company comets and constellations that burned her up inside with ecstasy so great she never wanted the ride to end.

They moved in counterpoint. On Bryce's upstroke, Cole pulled out, and then they swapped. Their grunts and moans, the catch of breath, and whispered encouragement took her higher with every passing moment.

Ava reached back, wrapping her hand around Cole's sweaty nape as he buried his face in her neck. Her breasts bounced as they kept up the steady momentum, not too fast or rough but enough that with every stroke they lifted her, rocking her closer to the precipice. Bryce shifted his hands, one cupping her breast and teasing her nipple, the other sliding down to her clit.

Her channel spasmed, clenching tight as the orgasm crashed over her. Like waves curling and washing ashore, the ebb and flow of nirvana pulsed through her, turning her bones to noodles and her voice to a hoarse rasp. Ava cried out over and over again as they took what they needed, quickening their pace until there were twin shouts in the air.

Boneless, Ava collapsed forward, landing on firm, sweaty muscles on the broadest chest she'd ever known. Warmth surrounded her, the sound of Bryce's heartbeat steadying her as their lips on her shoulder, hair, and face and fingertips on her skin settled the desire burning within from the raging wildfire it had been only moments earlier to embers.

EIGHT

Bryce

He woke with an octopus wrapped around him, pinning him in place. Dressed, Ava was a vision. Naked, she was a goddess. One of the kinds the ancient Greeks and Romans would have carved marble statues of. But the heavy arm that lay across his belly wasn't hers. It was Cole's. Behind her, Cole's arm encircled them both, keeping them tucked to his side.

The man was an enigma, and one that was far too easy to lose his head over. Barely twenty-four hours ago, Bryce was standing at Sydney Airport waiting for his flight. Since then, he'd broken every rule. The ones his parents had taught him when he was a kid—don't talk to strangers and don't accept rides from strangers—to the ones he'd made for himself—don't have a taste because once you've had some, you'll want it all.

His instincts had been right.

One kiss from the man, one touch that was less than platonic, and everything in Bryce settled. He really was pansexual. He'd popped that cherry and now he was going to have to try to fit the genie back in the bottle. Or however the saying went.

"I can hear you thinking from here," Cole mumbled, shifting to his elbow. He ran his fingers over Ava's hair, and added, "Want to talk about it?"

"I dunno to be honest." He sighed. "But I think I need to."

"I'm not a bad listener." Bryce had no doubt. While Cole had been prickly to them at the beginning, the night before he'd shown a different side. Patient and passionate, he looked after them before himself, not taking anything until he'd given it all to his partners. That said more than enough about the man's character.

"I told myself I wouldn't go there with a man." Cole opened his mouth to interrupt, but Bryce shook his head, needing to finish speaking. "I don't have any regrets that I did. Only now, I'm terrified. How do I give it up? How do I turn my back knowing what it was like with you. With women, it's easy. It's safe. I don't need to look over my shoulder to see who's gonna throw shade at me."

"How bad does it get?"

"I dunno. There's never been anyone who's been brave—or stupid—enough to come out while they were playing. Every team has contingencies in place for it, but..." He shrugged, not knowing how to express what he wanted to say.

"It would put you under the spotlight for all the wrong reasons," Cole murmured, understanding his exact worries.

Ava ran her hand gently over his chest, nuzzling her face in his shoulder. "Morning," she mumbled before shifting closer to him, pressing every inch of their bodies together. Bryce kissed her hair, breathing in the faint smell of her shampoo and the heady aroma of sex still lingering on her skin. His morning wood saluted the sunshine, and his lovers' lingering touches were spurring it on.

"I remember the rugby player who got caught up making gay porn. The pics surfaced years after it happened," Cole murmured sympathetically. *Motherfucker. Yep, that would get rid of the boner.*

Bryce cleared his throat, squeezing his eyes closed and hating the clawing fear that got its bony hands around his throat. Picturing himself in that position freaked him out, and while normally he was happy and pumped about everything, this terrified him. "Yeah, he said it started off as modelling and turned into something completely different. Sucked for him." His gut twisted.

Before last night, being singled out and having every encounter in his past analyzed wouldn't have made a difference—his record was squeaky clean. But now? Everything had changed. Bryce trusted Cole and Ava; they weren't the issue. But what if someone had footage of them together at the park buried somewhere on their phone. It wouldn't surface now—he was a nobody. But after he'd won the State of Origin? After he was the most sought-after prop in the game? He'd be recognizable and someone looking through an old video or photos would see him.

The difference with the other player was that he was only under the pump for a few weeks. It had died down pretty quickly; no one thought anything more of it. But that guy had been straight. Young and desperate, he'd also been taken advantage of. He hadn't known that there was a dude on the other side of the glory hole. It was a far cry from Bryce being pan and hooking up with or having a relationship with a man.

"But it did settle down," Ava reassured him. "He's still playing."

"I don't want to be the first to come out, you know? Or be outed." He couldn't look at them. Throwing his hand over his eyes again, he blew out a shaky breath.

Thick fingers threaded through his and a soft kiss landed on his chest. Cole drew their joined hands down and Ava turned his face to hers, kissing him softly.

When she pulled back, Cole promised, "I'd never do that. Out you, I mean." There was fire in his voice, a passion and conviction Bryce hadn't heard before. "I brought my first boyfriend home because my high school principal found out about us kissing. He thought my sexuality and the fact that I wasn't burying it under a wall of shame was something that my parents should know about. He threatened to out me, so I tried to be proactive and control how they'd find out. I thought if they could meet my boyfriend, they'd see why I liked him. I lost everything because of that bastard teacher. I'd never do that to you. I know my word is meaningless, but I promise you that I'll never break your confidence, Bryce."

Bryce hadn't thought he'd needed to hear the words again until Cole said them. He trusted the man. It was why he'd let his guard down and acted on instinct, kissing him like he'd done to Ava. Bryce had wanted them from the moment he'd seen them. He was content to admire both from afar, but then fate intervened and he'd ended up here.

Cole's eyes shined with sincerity in the early morning sunlight filtering in through the gauzy curtains. His lips were pursed in a frown and the crease in his forehead from his drawn eyebrows was deep. This time Bryce wanted to give the reassurance. "I know, but thank you for telling me. Your word is the most important thing you could give me."

"You're safe with us," Ava reassured him, snuggling against his shoulder once more.

Bryce grinned, the weight lifting from his shoulders. There would always be the niggling fear of getting found out, but he knew neither Cole nor Ava would be the ones to start the rumours. He'd just need to make sure he didn't do this kind of thing again. The smile slipped from his face. Shit. Never again. Cutting himself off cold turkey was the only way he would be able to last years before he felt the scrape of another man's beard between his legs.

Even that thought sat heavily in his gut and turned his stomach. When he closed his eyes, he could no longer imagine some random guy's face between his legs. No, the one he pictured had dark hair and eyes that were almost as deep with a perpetual furrow in his brows and an intensity about him that sent Bryce's pulse skyrocketing. It was the same when he imagined a woman. There were no blondes or redheads. No, the woman he wanted had vivid emerald-green eyes, pale skin, and dark hair that offset her features beautifully.

He was in deep shit.

Choosing to ignore the battle he was waging against getting attached, Bryce rolled over and kissed Ava until she was breathless. He buried his fingers deep in her soaked pussy and worked her clit with his thumb until she was on the edge of coming. He loved the way she clenched around him, her silken channel gripping his fingers and trying to keep them where she needed them. Her nipples were hard, and Cole nibbling at the pebbled peaks was hot as hell. Fingers circled his dick and Bryce cried out, his cock weeping pre-cum as he thrust into the tight, rough fist.

God damn, these two were potent.

"Suit up, Bryce. Get inside our girl," Cole directed. His deep voice, raspy with desire, sent a bolt of awareness through Bryce, his cock swelling in Cole's grip. "I wanna watch you fuck her until she screams."

Bryce wanted that too. Hell, almost more than anything, but he needed something else too. "I don't want you to watch. I want to taste you."

Cole groaned. "Fuck yeah." He paused, his teeth biting down on those pouty lips Bryce loved kissing. He ran his hand down Bryce's flank, slipping his fingers between Bryce's cheeks to circle his hole. Bryce shivered, his star clenching with want. Bryce had played there before, slipping a finger in and shooting his load after a few measly rubs of his prostate. A cock up there? Hell yes. But he was terrified too.

Cole growled when Bryce pushed back, encouraging him. "One day I'll bury myself inside you so deep you won't know where you end and I begin. But not today." Cole shifted, his hard cock slapping against his belly as he slid off the bed and went to Bryce's bag again. When he came back, he nudged Bryce. "On your back. Scoot over here so your head's off the edge of the bed." Bryce got himself positioned and Cole kissed Ava, pressing the condom into her hand. "Work that pretty pussy down his cock and ride him."

Her deft fingers rolled the condom down his length and Bryce arched his back, his eyes crossing with the sensation overload. He cried out when the tight clench of her pussy enveloped his cockhead. With her fingers working her clit, Ava began a slow rock, a deep grind that curled his toes. Her breathy moans contrasted with his strangled cry as a ripple in her pussy sent a shiver of lust through him.

"Make sure you don't blow," Cole ordered as he pointed the head of his cock to Bryce's lips, painting them with pre-cum. He licked it away, the salty tang bursting on his tongue. It wasn't his favourite flavour—he wasn't likely to go out and buy a cock juice lip balm anytime soon—but the knowledge that it was Cole, that he was tasting a dick for the first time was heady. Or maybe it was the blood rushing to his head from hanging off the edge of the bed. Bryce licked at it again, savouring the silken feel of steel against his tongue.

"Open up." Cole pressed forward, nudging his cockhead into Bryce's mouth. He knew Cole was being gentle, letting Bryce take this at his own pace, but he was ready for more. Ava pinched his nipple and Bryce thrust up into her depths as he reached for Cole's butt and pulled him forward, slurping at his dick.

Cole hit his tonsils and Bryce gagged, prompting his man to pull back a fraction. Bryce couldn't believe it. His jaw was stretched wide, a cock in his mouth and his hands on Cole's ass while Cole rocked into him. "Hold my cheeks open," Cole rasped. The flick of a cap sounded, and Bryce did what he was told, humming in agreement. Cole bucked into Bryce's mouth, choking out a cry as a wash of pre-cum landed on his tongue.

"That's so sexy," Ava breathed. "Gets me all worked up watching you two." She ground her hips down again and Bryce punched his forward, rocking into her as her pussy tightened.

Knuckles slick with cold lube brushed his and Bryce moaned, sending another shiver through Cole. "Fuck. Oh God, I'm coming," Ava breathed on a cry as her pussy clamped down, the ripple of the contractions in her core vibrating through Bryce until he was on the edge. He squeezed Cole's butt tighter and pushed him deeper, wanting Cole to come before he did. Ava kept moving, rocking slowly as she rode the high of her orgasm. He could imagine what she would look like, her head thrown back and her dark hair cascading down her back, her tits bouncing as she undulated her hips. Bryce squeezed his eyes closed, begging his dick to hold off blowing until he'd made it just as good for Cole.

"Stop," his man begged in a strangled voice, pulling back until his cockhead teased Bryce's lips once more. A pearl of precum leaked from the tip and Bryce licked at it, earning another groan. "Fuck I'm too close."

"Come down my throat."

"No, I want you to fuck me now."

Bryce blinked. Had he heard that right? Cole wanted him to fuck him.

Cole and Ava were already moving, the beautiful woman falling to his side and their man ripping off the condom to replace it with a fresh one. Even through the thin latex barrier, he felt the cool lube Cole slicked him with. Bryce punched his hips forward, fucking Cole's fist as he shuffled down the bed so he could watch every moment of this experience.

When Cole had straddled him, Bryce gripped his dick, holding it up so Cole could sink onto him. "Don't thrust up. I'm not properly stretched and you're fucking huge. I need to take it slow."

"Let me help," Ava offered, scrambling up and reaching for the lube. Kneeling behind Cole, she nudged him forward until their mouths were a hair's breadth apart. Bryce couldn't resist the temptation of those lips, and he reached up, cradling Cole's face as he kissed him deeply. Their tongues tangled and Cole moaned, their cocks brushing against each other as Ava stretched him. Sticky tracks of pre-cum slicked Bryce's belly and he kissed Cole harder, wanting every part of him. Wishing it was his mouth Cole was leaking into.

Long moments later, Cole squirming on his lap, his breath catching with every pump of Ava's fingers in his hole, Bryce heard another of the clicks from a camera app. The photo Cole had taken the night before was downright illicit. Their cocks stuffed Ava full; her pussy and arse stretched around them both. He couldn't wait to see what this one looked like. If it was on his phone again, it'd be spank bank material for years.

"I'm ready," Cole gasped, fucking back onto Ava's fingers and grinding their cocks together. Bryce was already on the edge, the respite from Ava climbing off him long gone when Cole started frotting against him.

Cole shifted so he was squatting and slowly lowered himself onto Bryce's waiting dick. The tight clasp of his ring of muscle strangled him, instantly shooting him to the edge of an embarrassingly quick orgasm. "Fuuuck," he groaned, his feet scrambling for purchase and his hands gripping the sheets in a white-knuckled hold.

Cole paused, his muscles straining and his breathing shallow as he adjusted. If it felt half as tight a fit for Cole as it did Bryce, Cole would be struggling. He wanted to soothe him. Wanted to say something to help ease the discomfort, but Bryce was utterly incapable of stringing anything together other than incoherent grunts.

Ava did it though. She gripped his softening cock, rolling his balls in her other hand and dropped her mouth to him, sucking him deep if the sudden jerk of his hips forward was anything to go by.

The slick heat surrounding him lowered further onto his cock, moving slowly but surely until their hips were locked together. Bryce panted, his entire being focussed on the part where he was joined with Cole. Fucking hell. If the world ended in this moment, he'd die a happy man. "I can feel you at the back of my damn tonsils," Cole ground out, shifting his hips and sending a flare of sensation through Bryce's nerve endings, lighting them up.

"I'm not gonna last long," Bryce breathed, struggling to speak as his balls drew up tight.

Cole lifted himself up to the head of Bryce's cock and surged back down again. Once more and Bryce was lost. Gone. There was no hope of holding back. Bryce hit the point of no return and he shuddered, the orgasm rocketing through him.

"Fuck, fuck!" he swore, slamming his hips up and riding a tidal wave of ecstasy that had his balls unloading into the catch of the condom. He could just imagine what it would be like to be inside Cole and Ava bare and have that silken heat wrapped so tightly around him. He cried out, his cock throbbing every time a jet of cum surged through his cock. Jerky thrusts of his hips extended out his orgasm, but he knew Cole hadn't gotten there yet and there was no way Bryce was leaving him hanging.

He sat up, pushing Cole back until he was lying between Bryce's spread legs and shuffled back, his cock slipping from Cole's channel. It was the sexiest thing he'd ever seen, second to nothing except them both being buried inside Ava. Bryce tore off the full condom, knotted it and scrambled for his bag. "Ava, sit on his face. I'm not done with him yet and you need to be looked after."

"Please get hard again quick," Cole begged, his legs hanging open, his stretched hole on display. It hadn't closed fully yet, the usually tight ring of muscle still a touch slack from his intrusion. A surge of possession ran through Bryce. That was his hole. His and Ava's cock. His and Ava's man.

She straddled Cole's shoulders, bracing her arms on the white shelf that served as the bed head, grinding her hips as Cole stuck out his tongue and licked her. He could watch them together all day, but Bryce had a man to satisfy and a woman to give another orgasm to as well.

He pumped his cock, not needing much stimulation to get it to steely again when the moans Cole was eliciting from Ava were pornographic, and rolled the condom on fast, coating himself in a generous helping of slick. Crawling up the bed again, he gripped Cole's ankles, spread him as wide as he could, and guided his cock to Cole's waiting hole. Sliding in slowly, he bottomed out quickly and paused, waiting for him to adjust again. Tight, wet heat surrounded him, every instinct in his body screaming at him to move. He'd come once already, but it had barely taken the edge off.

"Move," Cole demanded, and the thread of control Bryce held snapped. He withdrew to his cockhead and slammed forward, rocking the bed with the sheer force of his thrust. A shiver racked Cole's body and he shouted, the noise muffled by Ava's pussy on his face. Bryce couldn't get enough. He pumped into him hard and fast, Cole's cock leaking with every thrust. Soon pre-cum had pooled in his navel and was about to overflow. Bryce scooped up the liquid with his thumb and sucked on it, loving that he managed to draw it from him. It was proof of Cole's steady climb to nirvana.

He dragged them down the bed, wanting Ava to bend over further so he could have a better view. With every withdrawal from Cole, the other man slid his tongue into Ava's pussy, fucking her with it, and with every one of Bryce's surges forward, Cole withdrew, moaning.

Bryce collapsed onto his elbows and craned his head so he could reach Ava's pussy too. His and Cole's tongues tangled, licking at her entrance and her clit, the three of them connected in a circle of never-ending ecstasy. Ava cried out and Bryce drove his hips forward, slapping hard against Cole's arse. His man's dick was pressed between them rubbing along the washboard of his abs. The soft grunts Cole let loose were hot, but Bryce wanted him to shout the walls down.

Ava's pussy rippled, the rhythmic clenching about to start. They worked her together and Bryce squeezed Cole's cock in his fist. Cole drove his hips up, fucking into Bryce's grip.

Yes, that's it, baby.

Hard and fast, Bryce concentrated all his effort on getting both Cole and Ava to the ledge and throwing them off, wanting them both to float in that mind-altering post-orgasmic daze he'd experienced the night before when he'd come.

Every muscle in Cole's body locked up tight, his arse clamping down on Bryce's dick. Cum shot from his cock, hitting Cole's throat with the force as he shouted, the noise echoing around their room. With his tongue buried in one lover, her pussy contracting and releasing as she cried out, and his cock wrapped in the tightest hole he'd ever been in, Bryce shot to the edge. His balls drew up again, ready to fire off a second time when Cole's arse relaxed its hold for a moment. It was enough for Bryce to withdraw and surge forward once more, tagging Cole's P-spot again. He shouted, his hole squeezing Bryce tight again, trapping him in place. It was one Bryce never wanted to leave.

With every shot of cum from Cole's cock and every breathless moan from Ava, Bryce edged closer. She collapsed to the side boneless, and Cole hugged her close before surging up, and latching their mouths together. The first press of Cole's tongue in Bryce's mouth was enough. He shuddered in Cole's arms and pumped his hips forward once more, emptying his balls into the condom.

Breathless, sweat dripping from the end of his nose and tips of his hair, Bryce rested his weight on the man still clutching him.

"Fuck me," Cole mumbled, breathless.

"Can't move," he responded, incapable of anything more coherent. But his cock was taking matters into its own hands, slipping free of Cole's channel and earning a hiss from the man underneath him. "You okay?"

"Mmhmm." Cole breathed out a laugh. "Don't think I've ever had as good a dicking before."

"Never want to stop." Bryce froze, the words still ringing in his ears. But the kernel of truth was undeniable. He didn't want to stop.

He propped himself up on his elbow, first looking at Cole and then at Ava. Both were staring at him. He knew they were waiting for him to expand on his thoughts. But his mouth had gone dry, the words lodged in his throat. Their time was coming to an end—the metaphorical cliff that their dream-come-true night would end at. Either they Thelma and Louise'd the crap out of it and jumped together, or they needed to wave to each other from a distance, each of them taking their own road and knowing it may never intersect again. If he let his dick do the talking, the answer was easy—jump together. But the implications for his future, his dream NRL career could be catastrophic.

Bryce swallowed, shifting off Cole and tied off the condom. With his back to them, he mumbled with a squeak in his voice, "So, yeah." He cleared his throat, hoping he could rescue himself from firmly wedging his foot in his mouth. "Should we, ah, go for a swim while we can? The air might be good for all of us."

There was a pause and Bryce's shoulders slumped.

"Yeah, we should," Ava replied, resting her forehead on his back, and wrapping her arms around his waist. Cole shifted forward, too, joining them. They sat there quietly for a moment, just breathing each other in and holding tight.

"We'll need to eat too. Breakfast after?"

"Yeah," Bryce agreed with a hitch in his voice. "Sounds great."

After their swim, they indulged in a long breakfast, picking up his truck hours after the tyre company called to say it was ready. They detoured, checking out the marina, and lingering until they agreed to stop for takeaway coffees before they left the little village.

* * * * *

Now that they were passing the Welcome to Queensland sign, marking the border between the two states, Bryce wished he'd been brave enough to say something, or perhaps smarter to have not said anything earlier. He wasn't ready to leave them, but time was fast running out.

In half an hour, he would have dropped both Ava and Cole off.

They'd all been lost in their thoughts during the latter part of their drive. Barely a word had been spoken since the turn off to Byron Bay. Bryce didn't know what to say. But he also realized he wasn't just thinking with his dick. He'd never dated anyone who he'd had such an instant connection with. Ava was perfect for him. Smart as hell and gorgeous; it was as if she'd stepped out of his dreams. And then there was Cole. The deep scowly frown was planted firmly on his face again, his lips pursed and knee jiggling as he gritted his teeth. Bryce loved peeling the layers of his personality back while dodging the spikes. He wanted more time with both of them. But how did he get it?

He was being selfish, though. It'd be better for everyone, and especially his career, if they ended things here. His head told him he should remember their time together as the moment he'd lived out his fantasy—the one and only time he got to be with a man before retirement. But his body? His heart? They were singing from a whole other song sheet. His gut sank, clenching at the prospect of letting them walk out of his life. Could he take a chance?

Bryce chewed on his lip, debating his options. Another hook-up? A holiday fling? Even more than that? Secrecy was the only way of making any of it work. Both Ava and Cole had already promised they wouldn't out him, except that only worked for something casual. The more Bryce thought about it, the more he could see himself with them. They'd clicked.

But he was being stupid. They'd had one night together, and Bryce was already prepared to bend the rules, making exceptions for them. He had to stay the course. He had to keep focussed on the dream. Being pan and a professional footballer weren't mutually exclusive—he was positive of that—but he did have to make sacrifices.

Being open about who he was just wasn't an option, and anything less than that wasn't fair to the person or people he was with.

This fling had happened at the worst possible time. He was playing in the reserves and hoping to get an invitation to train with the professional team. He'd gotten to where he was by following the rules—his rules as much as the rules of the game—and being the best at what he did. He tried to be the nice bloke. He'd always led the field, been the golden boy. He'd kept his nose clean and worked hard. When every other one of his mates were out doing stupid shit, he was singularly focussed on training and getting to the NRL.

He was an expert at anticipating players' movements and reactions. He knew when to charge forward, putting his shoulder down and mowing through the resistance, and when to pivot. Was this one of those times where he had to step back so he could gain ground rather than crashing head on into a tackle? Or was he destined to drop the ball? He didn't even know which analogy was worse—whether stepping back meant walking away or seeing their incredible day together from a different perspective. Had he scored the match winning try, or was he about to lose everything?

There was that tug again. A whisper that the storm that put them on this path was more than just serendipitous. It was as if the universe was telling him to sidestep. To take a chance. To reach out and grasp what was in front of him.

The decision was a whole lot harder than it had been a day earlier, and that meant something. He loved sex, but this was different. This was more than just fantastic orgasms. Walking away had never been an issue until now. The fact that he was having trouble letting go of the desire to see both Ava and Cole again told him just how unique their connection was.

But surely what he wanted was impossible. Wasn't it?

Threesomes weren't exactly the norm. They were a fantasy. A one-off or a kink. They weren't for real people, and absolutely not for people who would, by default, be in the public eye. Would he do it again, though? As long as it was with Cole and Ava, there was no question. His answer was a resounding yes.

So maybe that was his solution. Another night to get his fill. One more night together to satiate the quiet whisper of "more" in the back of his mind.

Bryce nearly missed the exit from the motorway for Cole's hotel. At least it would have been a good excuse to stay together. But he couldn't. Slowing down as he took the turn, he watched Cole tighten his arm around Ava's shoulders and press a lingering kiss to her temple. She squeezed Bryce's thigh and his chest responded in kind. He needed to say something. He just didn't know what.

Cole was staying at Currumbin beach. His beach. The very same one he'd grown up surfing at. He and his brothers rode there every day after school with their surfboards. The familiar waves grew closer as they crossed the bridge he'd jumped off once before, and he smiled wistfully at the estuary he'd spent entire summers at as a kid.

Ava was staying only a stone's throw away. It was as if they had a homing beacon, keeping them close to one another. Of all the hotels along the tourist strip, of all the towns they could have picked, they'd all chosen to stay within a ten-minute drive. It couldn't have been a coincidence. But Elephant Rock and Currumbin Hill, the park he'd had birthdays at and the beach that he'd missed with a soul-deep yearning did nothing to snap Bryce back into his happy-go-lucky mindset when they rounded the corner.

Bryce pulled up in the visitor car park and Cole opened the door, casting them one last look. Cole slid out and paused, patting the door like he wanted to say something. Instead, he closed his mouth, pressed his lips together in a frown, and moved to the tray.

No. Bryce couldn't do it. He couldn't just let either of them walk away without at least saying something. He was crazy for doing it—his head screamed at him to let them go—but every other instinct cheered him on.

Bryce slid out and jogged to the back of the truck, only to see Ava doing the same.

"Do—"

"I don't—"

"Are you—"

They laughed, his sounding awkward and nervous. "You first." He motioned to Ava, and Cole nodded encouragingly.

"Do you want to see each other again? I'm... I'd love to see you again. Both of you. Or either one of you. For a drink, or whatever..."

"I don't have your numbers. But I'd like them," Cole said. "I want to see both of you again too."

Bryce couldn't help the laugh bubbling up from the depths of his chest, excitement curling low in his belly and making him bounce on his toes. He grinned one of those sappy smiles at the knowledge he wasn't alone in his thoughts. Before he could catch himself, he asked, "Are you spending Christmas alone? I have a family thing, but it's super casual, and Mum wouldn't mind if I brought friends. We usually have loads of people tagging along. Half the neighbourhood."

Ava blinked. She opened her mouth and snapped it closed again. "I don't want to put your parents out—"

"Ah—" Cole started, stepping back as if to physically distance himself from Bryce's ridiculous suggestion. Of course they wouldn't want to have a family Christmas with him. What the hell was he thinking?

He blinked, turning away from them, about to dismiss the suggestion as rubbish when Cole started talking again. "I'd love to. What do you need me to bring?"

Bryce's gaze snapped to his. He wasn't expecting Cole to be smiling shyly, his cheeks flushing as he did. But there it was in all its glory. Cole's smile was like a ray of sunshine breaking through storm clouds. If Bryce did nothing else right, putting that smile on Cole's face was enough.

It took a moment for Cole's words to penetrate the fluttery sex-drunk excitement in his belly, and he lifted his eyes to meet the other man's gaze. They gravitated toward each other, Cole wrapping his arm around Bryce. It was a move that could be interpreted as a hug from a mate, but Bryce leaned in, enjoying the moment of intimacy.

"Sorry, Ava. I shouldn't have suggested it—"

"I want to come." She rushed her words out, falling over herself to cut him off. Her small hand closed over his forearm, and he shivered, wishing they were in private so he could show them exactly how much they meant. Ava added, "I want to see you again too. Both of you. I was trying to be polite and ask whether you needed to check with your parents first."

He pursed his lips, embarrassment making his cheeks flush and a smile crawl across his mouth. Bryce lifted one shoulder in a kind of shrug, trying to play what he'd done off as no big deal. It had happened when Cole was ordering coffees and Ava was in the bathroom. He hadn't intended to tell his parents about them at all, but there was no hiding from them. "I kind of already did."

Ava leaned in, going to her tiptoes and pressing a kiss to his cheek. "Then I'd love to."

Cole wrapped his free hand around her shoulders and pulled her against him until they were standing in a tight circle. Cole ran his thumb down Bryce's throat in a caress. It was the subtlest of movements, but he left a tingling in his trail. Bryce bit back a moan. Their gazes met and it took every ounce of strength he possessed not to lean in and kiss Cole, no matter the consequences.

Instead, he looked to Ava. She must have seen the desperation in him, the need to be close. Rising on tiptoes again, she pressed a lingering kiss to his lips. Tangling his free hand in her hair—the other one wrapped firmly around Cole's waist—he swiped his tongue along her lip, and she opened to him immediately, welcoming the move with her own tongue.

Cole moaned and his fingers tightened against Bryce's throat. His hoarse whisper went straight to Bryce's cock. "I wanna invite you both up so bad." Cole shifted, pressing his hard cock against Bryce's hip. The move sent a shudder through him. God, he really wanted to taste that meaty cock again, but as Bryce reached for him, Cole pulled back. "You need to get home to your family."

"Two days. Then we'll see each other again," Ava breathed against his lips.

It couldn't come soon enough.

NINE

Cole

He thought he wanted to be alone, but the moment his hotel room door closed behind him, the emptiness inside Cole reverberated like a gunshot echoing through a canyon. Wandering around and trailing his fingertips over the outdated but clean surfaces, he missed the space they'd shared with a fierceness that surprised him.

Cole couldn't fathom the change that had happened in less than forty-eight hours. He was a different person, but at the same time, it was as if he'd shed the disguise that he showed to the rest of the world.

The silence was deafening. Inexplicably, he needed to be around people. Cole opened the balcony doors and slipped outside, taking in the resort's pool and outdoor bar area. Voices floated up on the ocean breeze and Cole closed his eyes, trying to pretend that the children's giggles and deeper voices of their parents were Ava and Bryce.

Exhaustion enveloped him and Cole stretched out on the sun lounge as the afternoon sun dipped below the

towering cliffs directly behind the resort. His stomach rumbled. He had been looking forward to a week of being able
to relax and eat alone, but after the events of the last day,
he wished for some company. Not just any company,
though. He wanted Bryce and Ava there with him.

Cole startled hours later. All he could hear was the crash
of the ocean against the shore and the calls of the night
birds in the trees nearby. Stars as bright as diamonds glit-
tered in the inky sky, his eyes drawn to the moon sitting
high above the horizon. There was a slight chill in the air
from the ocean breeze, and his body ached from how well
used he had been that morning.

He sighed and scrubbed a hand over his forehead,
groaning at the immediate direction of his thoughts. His
dreams had been filled with husky laughs and the ghost of
gentle touches and passionate kisses. At this rate, the next
couple of days were going to stretch into eternity, Cole's
sleep just as utterly consumed by his two travelling companions as his waking moments.

* * * * *

Cole stared at the latest text from Bryce. It was only a
few words—his address and "see you soon"—but Cole was
reading a whole lot more into it. The prospect of spending
a day with the people who had been on his mind without
respite had excitement thrumming through him. A little of
that excitement was reserved for meeting Bryce's family

too. He'd heard Bryce's mum talking in the background when they'd spoken, and she seemed totally cool—nothing like the rigid trio his parents and sister had turned into when he'd last seen them. She'd yelled her invitation out to him, leaving Cole in no doubt that he was welcome there.

He looked up at the house, double-checking the number, but there was no need. Bryce's truck was parked on the drive and the ride share was already peeling away. He tightened his grip on the gift bags he was carrying and crossed the spongy lawn to the front door.

He knocked and the door swung open after only a moment, the man before him a welcome sight. He was bouncing on his toes and grinning at Cole like he was jumping out of his skin with excitement. The red shirt and Santa hat suited him—he was exactly like a kid at Christmas.

Bryce's excitement eased Cole's antsy nerves—he wasn't the only one who'd been looking forward to their meeting.

"Come in," Bryce mumbled, his voice a rough rasp. Bryce looked up and down the hall conspiratorially before taking Cole's hand and quickly dragging him in the opposite direction to the voices at the back of the house. Bryce tugged him through a doorway into a bedroom and slammed the door closed behind Cole, pushing him against it.

Connected from shoulder to knee, Bryce's big body trapped him in place. In a daze, Cole dropped the gift bags on the floor and reached for his man, threading his fingers into Bryce's silky locks and sinking into the kiss. It was a heady mix of frantic passion and rediscovering each other. Their tongues tangled and Cole moaned, his body arching into the hard one grinding on him.

Bryce moved his lips to Cole's throat, pulling his collar down to suck a mark in the dip above his collarbone. His big hand closed over his cock and Cole's breath hitched. This was... he shouldn't.... The protests died on his tongue when Bryce fell to his knees, tugged open his pants and freed his steely cock.

Cole bit down on his hand as Bryce licked his head and hummed before engulfing him to the root. Cole had no hope of resisting when the suction the other man applied had his toes curling in his loafers. There was no finesse, but Bryce's enthusiasm made up for it, and as shudders racked Cole's body, he threaded his fingers into Bryce's hair and tentatively rocked his hips.

Bryce's deep moan vibrated around his shaft, and the room spun, Cole's knees going weak as he crested, hovering in that split-second moment between the climb and the freefall into orgasm. He bit down on his lip, trying to stifle the shout that bubbled up his throat as Bryce rolled his balls and sucked him down again, drawing his orgasm from the depths of his body.

He saw stars, constellations bursting into life at the beginning of time as his cock pulsed and he erupted. He floated. The ripple of ecstasy thrummed through his body like an electric charge.

Shaking, his limbs like limp noodles, he slid to his arse. The sight before him stole his breath, and Cole moaned, another pulse of orgasmic bliss ricocheting through him as he watched Bryce jack off. It was the sexiest thing he'd ever seen—equalled only by Ava playing with herself while she'd watched them touch. But watching wasn't enough; he needed to touch.

"Come in my mouth, Bryce," he growled, needing another taste of the man before him.

Bryce didn't hesitate, standing and straddling Cole's hips, squatting until his cockhead touched Cole's lips. It only took one swipe of his tongue and another tug on his cock before Bryce shuddered out his orgasm, coating Cole's tongue in his essence. He moaned quietly, finally satisfied. That taste was what he'd needed. The reassurance that he hadn't imagined the desperate desire that he was filled with whenever he thought about the two people he'd missed with every ounce of his being in the time they'd been separated.

Bryce collapsed to his knees and his glassy eyes darkened, his nostrils flaring as he growled possessively. Tilting Cole's chin, Bryce licked up his throat to his lips, kissing him deeply until Cole was a quivering mess.

"Seeing my cum dripping from your mouth. Fuck," Bryce groaned. "So hot." He pressed their foreheads together and Cole relaxed, his breathing slowing. Bryce pulled back and his smile turned shy. "Hi."

"Hi." Cole laughed and cradled Bryce's face in his palms, pressing a lingering kiss to his lips. "That was quite a welcome."

"Is it weird if I say I missed that? Felt like I've been crawling out of my skin since I dropped you both off."

"No." Cole shook his head. "I... me too."

Tension that he hadn't even seen Bryce holding leeched out of the bigger man's shoulders and a relieved smile tilted his lips. "We better head out or someone'll come looking for me. You ready to meet everyone?"

"Might need a breath mint."

Bryce snorted out a laugh, rolling his eyes and standing effortlessly while holding out his hand to pull Cole up. Standing, they tucked themselves in and Bryce opened the door a crack before looking down at the bags.

"What's that?"

"Something small for you and Ava, and your parents."

Bryce's smile was cheeky. "Aw, boo, you didn't have to do that." He smacked a kiss to Cole's lips and motioned for him to go first.

Cole placed their gifts under the tree and took the extra bag he'd bought for Bryce's parents. He was waiting for the fear to claw at his throat, but the high from his orgasm lingered and Cole narrowed his eyes at Bryce, murmuring under his breath, "You did that intentionally, didn't you?"

"What?" Bryce furrowed his brows at Cole's question, his grin not dimming.

He leaned in close and replied, "Got me off so that I wouldn't be freaking out about meeting your parents."

Bryce barked out a laugh and wrapped his arm around Cole's shoulder in a bro-hug. "No, but call it a happy coincidence."

They rounded the corner into a large indoor-outdoor room with the furniture pushed to the side and two groups of joined tables surrounded by an assortment of chairs and stools. Kids played in the pool and the adults mingled, walking between groups of people, some sitting, some standing.

A slim man with salt-and-pepper hair, who only reached Cole's shoulder, made his way over to them. "You must be Cole," he said with a smile that was uncannily similar to Bryce's. He extended his hand and Cole gripped it, surprised at the strength there. "I'm his dad. Everyone calls me Mal."

Cole swallowed hard, the nervous butterflies erupting in his belly. So much for not being freaked out. "Nice to meet you, Mr Flaharty," he squeaked. "This is for you." He held out the gift bag with the bottle of wine he'd bought. The older man barked out a laugh, the same laugh as Bryce, and clapped him on the shoulder.

"Jenny's going to like you, but please don't call her Mrs Flaharty. Doc or Jen only or she'll rouse on you—she always says that Mrs Flaharty is my mother and they never got along." He leaned closer and whispered conspiratorially, "My mother thought she corrupted me." With that, he turned and yelled out, "Jen, we have another guest."

He looked to Bryce wide-eyed, and his lover chuckled, his arm never loosening his grip around Cole's shoulders. He steered him to the kitchen where a blonde-haired woman with a generous bosom and an apron around her waist that said "I'd rather be reading" was lifting a monstrous turkey out of the oven.

"Shit, Mum, let me help." Bryce stepped forward, reaching for the steaming tray, and was met with her back when she spun agilely.

"No," she snapped, her tone a clear warning. "It's hot. Bryce, when are you going to learn that you can't just grab things straight from the oven."

Cole stopped short, watching the exchange between them. He'd thought that there was a familial resemblance between Bryce and his dad, but he was the spitting image of his mum.

Bryce rolled his eyes and grinned mischievously. "At least one more time, Mum." He went back to Cole and nudged his shoulder with his own while his mum put the tray down on a thick timber board. "Mum, I'd like you to meet Cole."

Tossing the oven mitts she'd been wearing to the side, and wiping her hands on the apron, Bryce's mum sauntered over with a smile that lit up her features. Holding her hand out to shake, she exclaimed, "It's a pleasure to meet you, Cole. Thank you for celebrating with us."

"No, thank you, Dr Flaharty." He screwed up his nose, wincing at how Bryce's eyes widened. "Mr Flaharty told me to call you Doc. Sorry if I got it wrong."

She snorted out a laugh and closed her other hand around their combined ones. "Jen or Jenny is fine. Same with Mal. We aren't at all formal."

He nodded, still a little awkward and unsure of what to say. It was a good thing he'd brought an icebreaker. He held out the bottle of wine. "This is something small to say thank you for having me today."

She took it, gushing about how sweet he was. It was the least he could do given he didn't even know them.

His mum shooed them out of the kitchen and Bryce guided them around the outskirts of the conversations, introducing Cole to all the important people in his life—his brothers and their partners, his aunts and uncles, cousins and friends—and Cole marvelled at how friendly everyone was, and at how much they laughed together. Everyone was smiling like one of those TV special happy families. Truth be told, he'd never been more envious. He'd once had that himself. But it was stolen away, ripped from him before he could appreciate just how incredible it was.

"You're frowning again," Bryce whispered conspiratorially.

"Just thinking." He left off who he was thinking about. He didn't need to drag Bryce's mood down. Bryce's expression softened, his smile sad. He leaned in, pressing their shoulders together in a pseudo hug, one that Cole wanted to sink into.

The big guy might always be smiling, but he was perceptive too. Or maybe he'd opened up enough to Ava and Bryce that they could read him.

"Yo, Bryce, your other friend's here," his brother called out, motioning to the lounge room where a woman was depositing some presents under the tree.

TEN

Ava

Ava knocked on the door of the unassuming house in the suburbs. It was probably thirty years old. Single storey, the warm grey bricks and dark roof contrasted. Set in a tropical jungle-like garden, there was every kind of palm tree she could imagine, flowers in all colours of the rainbow and lush grass. She walked up the drive, hearing the party out back—laughter and loud talking, kids' happy squeals, and Christmas carols.

Ava blew out a breath. This was it.

Nerves fluttered around in her belly. It wasn't normal to meet the parents of the man she'd had a one-night stand with, much less a threesome. But here she was.

She pressed the doorbell and waited.

When the door swung open, Ava plastered on a polite smile. But it wasn't Bryce who appeared. His brother, perhaps, or another relative. The blond man who greeted her looked vaguely familiar, but she struggled to place him. "Hi." He was holding beer bottles and had a bottle of wine tucked under each arm. "I'm Levi. Guessing you're Bryce's friend. Sorry, I'd shake your hand but—"

"No, that's okay. I'm Ava." She shrugged, her own hands full with presents for her guys and the host. "I'd offer to help but..."

Levi grinned. "Come on in. Bryce is out back." He led her through the comfortable family home, down a wide light-filled hallway, its walls jam-packed with family photos. She spotted a few of Bryce—geeky school photos and one proudly wearing his black, blue, and white rugby uniform. She would have loved to linger and look at the rest, but Levi walked on ahead, explaining that Cole was already there, but she wasn't the last to arrive.

Double doors opened to the left into a large living room. A tree with its tip pressed against the ceiling was positioned in the centre of the window.

"Can I?" Ava motioned to it, and Levi nodded. "Wait, I've just placed you. You're Bryce's cousin, aren't you? You used to have that TV show. I've listened to your podcast too. I loved the interview you did with the ship captain and his boyfriend. That was a cool episode."

"Thank you, I appreciate it." He smiled back and rocked on his heels, hands still clutching the bottles. It was as if he wanted to say something more but was hesitating. When he licked his lips, Ava braced herself. "Bryce mentioned you, too—"

"You're here," Bryce exclaimed, brushing past Levi and wrapping her up in a hug.

Ava melted into him. His big body surrounding hers was like coming home. He smiled, and the sun beamed, warmth filling her chest and spreading throughout. She held on just as tight, burying her face in the collar of Bryce's red shirt and breathing him in. It had only been a few days, and they'd spoken every day since they'd parted, but damn, she'd missed him. When Bryce pulled back, Ava saw Cole leaning against the doorjamb.

"Cole!" Ava exclaimed and reached out, pulling him into their embrace without letting Bryce go.

"Hi, sexy," he breathed, his voice a whisper in her ear. Cole pressed a kiss on the sensitive skin below, and shivers erupted all over her.

A throat cleared behind them and Levi smirked, motioning with the slightest tilt of his head to an older man with salt-and-pepper hair walking up the hall. Levi took his leave as Bryce slipped his hand into hers, his big paw gently clasping her fingers.

"Dad, this is Ava, my other friend who's having lunch with us today."

The man, who was, physically, about as different to Bryce as Ava could imagine, held out his hand and smiled. There was no doubt they were related, though. Bryce had his dad's smile. It lit his entire face, the warmth he generated from it contagious.

"Nice to meet you, Ava. I'm Mal. Merry Christmas."

"You too, Mal. Thanks for letting me join you. I hope it's no bother that I'm here."

"You're welcome anytime. A friend of Bryce's is a friend of ours too. Like I said to young Cole here, it's not Christmas if you're on your own, so we're glad you could make it." He turned to Bryce and added, "Uncle Max wanted to try the cider. Could you please bring a bottle out for him."

"Sure."

He pottered along the hall, disappearing through a door that could only lead to the garage. Bryce ushered them into another room, still clutching Ava's hand. "Come in here."

They were in the laundry and Bryce closed the door after Cole had slipped in behind her. Pulling Ava into his arms, Cole hooked a finger under her chin before pressing a kiss to her lips and teasing her mouth open with his tongue. Ava held him tight, reaching for Bryce too. She wanted each of them as fiercely as the other. There was no choosing between them. It was all or nothing, and she wasn't settling until she had it all.

Stepping behind her, Bryce held her close and trailed a line of kisses up her throat. She gasped and threaded her fingers into his hair, holding him in place as Bryce grasped her breasts, flicking his thumb over her nipples while Cole kissed her breathless.

"Bryce—" The three of them froze, Bryce biting her lobe while Cole's tongue remained in her mouth. Ava blinked her eyes open and shivered as her lovers pulled back, their heat disappearing and leaving her bereft.

"Mum!" Bryce squeaked, stepping in front of Ava to block his mum's view. She fixed the straps of her gauzy singlet, straightening the rest of her clothes before touching

Bryce's waist. He shifted, and Ava came face to face with his mother.

Bryce had his dad's smile, but otherwise he was his mum. She was tall and broad-shouldered, big-breasted, and her smile turned radiant. "Be a dear, Bryce, and pass me the drink your uncle is waiting on before he comes in here looking for it himself." When Bryce went for the bottles stacked in ice in the sink, she turned her gaze to Ava and beamed wider. "You must be the lovely woman my son hasn't stopped speaking about since he arrived home. Welcome, Ava."

"Mum!"

"I'll stop harassing your dates, Bryce, if you get me the drinks."

He handed a few bottles to his mum and held open the door, as if begging her to exit.

"Thank you, dear." She winked and chuckled when Bryce groaned. "When you're ready, we'll see you for lunch."

"Fuck me," Bryce hissed. "Why did I think this was a good idea?"

"I think they're great," Cole answered.

"So do I," Ava added, brushing her thumb over Bryce's flushed cheek.

He huffed out a laugh, looked away, and bit down on his lip. She loved the shy side of him. It was such a contrast from the way he threw himself at life full of sunshiny gusto and the unyielding force she'd discovered him to be while playing rugby.

She'd watched every video of him she'd found online, but this vision of Bryce was her favourite. Ava loved these private moments she'd been able to steal with both Bryce and Cole, where this side of him stepped forth. Cole kissed his temple, lingering there a moment before they headed out into the fray.

* * * * *

Much later, after lunch had finished, they sat alone in the lounge room by the tree. Ava leaned into Cole's side, and Bryce sat on the floor between their legs, enjoying Cole's fingers in his hair. This peace, the warmth, and comfort was so much better than her fantasy.

Ava sighed happily, delighting in the weight of the iridescent blue jewelled earrings Cole and Bryce had bought for her from the markets.

"Can you pass up the presents in the green boxes, Bryce?" It was now or never. All or nothing time. When Bryce handed them over, she took one and passed it to Cole.

Cole slowly undid the bow she'd tied on the box before lifting the lid. Ava held her breath as he froze, his eyes snapping to hers. It was the carved eagle he'd admired. She hadn't bought it that night, but Bryce had snagged a business card and when he'd suggested calling them to have it delivered, she knew she hadn't imagined how long Cole had lingered, looking at it.

"I don't know what to say," he mumbled, the deep crease in his forehead betraying how much he was struggling to come up with words.

"Do you like it?" Ava asked, resting her hand on his knee.

Cole nodded, bobbing his head enthusiastically. "It's perfect," he replied, his voice catching. He cleared his throat and gave her a small smile that made Ava's heart clench and unshed tears burn her eyes. He ran his fingers through Bryce's hair and tilted his face up, giving him one of those sad smiles. It was obvious how much he wanted to show Bryce how grateful he was, but neither one of them had done more than place a hand on the other's shoulder or stand a little too close. Bryce was apparently out to his parents and brothers, but not to his wider family, and none of them would risk it.

He didn't hesitate with her, though, pressing a lingering kiss to her lips. It was warmth and affection, and Ava was desperate to give him the comfort he needed.

Pulling away, his smile was easier, his eyes less haunted by emotion. "Now you, Bryce," he urged.

Bryce had been easy to buy for. He'd only chosen a couple of the soaps and bath bombs he'd been eyeing, but had lingered, tossing up which ones to get. Ava had found similar handmade soaps, compressed coconut oil bars that melted into massage lotion and fizzing bath salts that he could relax with. Cole had loved the suggestion.

Bryce took her hand in his and lifted her knuckles to his lips. "Thank you. This is..." He trailed off and looked around the pile of small gifts that she and Cole had decided on together. "Incredible. No one ever buys me this stuff, but I love it. You're the first people who saw what I really wanted."

"I'm glad you like it," Cole murmured, doing the only thing he could to show Bryce a modicum of affection—playing with his hair.

"Do you wanna get out of here?" Bryce asked. "I, ah, kind of want some time alone with you both. It's selfish, I know, but…" He shrugged, trying to play it down, but his blush gave him away.

"So do I," Cole reassured him. "And you aren't being selfish. I understand. We both do."

"Here's the thing," Ava started, pausing to get her words straight in her mind. "I don't just want another one-night stand. I want more. I know we can't be open—Bryce doesn't have that choice, and a woman dating two men would be water cooler talk around my office for months, but I want it all. Dating, everything. With both of you."

Bryce shifted, spinning around so he was kneeling in front of her, and Cole tucked his foot under his knee, turning to face her.

"With Cole and I together too?" Bryce asked.

When Ava nodded, his lips tilted up in a radiant smile. Cole hooked his finger under her chin and pressed his lips to hers slowly and surely until she was kiss-drunk and ready to combust.

"Let's go," he whispered, squeezing Bryce's shoulder.

After they said hurried goodbyes, they left, each of the boys flanking Ava as they walked down the path to Bryce's truck. "Which of your hotel rooms has a bath big enough to fit us all in it?"

"Mine." Ava grinned, her insides fluttering with excitement as she thought about what the night would bring.

ELEVEN

Ava

THREE WEEKS LATER

Ava sighed and pressed her fingers against her temples. She had the beginnings of a killer headache. *The first week back at work is the hardest.* At least that's what Ava hoped. Her new job was always going to be a challenge, but Ava had been drowning from the moment she stepped into the office. Everything had gone wrong from the get-go.

She was under pressure to fix the on-site delays and cost blowouts plaguing the project. For one so early in its construction phase, she was surprised at the sheer mess it was in. The previous project manager had ignored most of it in favour of ploughing ahead and digging the project deeper into the red. But it didn't matter. It was literally her job to get it back on track.

Ava scanned the spreadsheet itemizing every cost outlay incurred so far, cross-referencing them with the staged budgeted amounts. She groaned. Numbers swam on the page, and it was barely 11:00 a.m.

The phone on her desk rang, startling her. "This is Ava," she answered.

"I have a delivery here for you, Ava. Shall I have it sent back to you?"

"Yes, please." Whatever it was would be a welcome distraction from the mess on her desk. A soft knock sounded a few moments later, and she answered, "Come in."

She saw the white gift box first with its ruby red bow and cascading ribbon holding it together. She didn't even take notice of the person carrying it, so when he shifted it, revealing his face, she squealed. Jumping out of the chair, Ava crash-tackled Bryce, jumping into his strong arms and peppering his laughing face with kisses. "You're here. I didn't think I'd see you," she exclaimed between kisses, her belly flip-flopping with excitement at seeing her guy. "I can't believe you're here." Ava breathed him in, inhaling his citrus scent and loving the way his face was lit with a radiant smile.

"Mmm, I'm between training and a meeting. Thought I'd dash over and see you." He captured her lips, kissing her with long, languid strokes of his tongue and one hand on her butt, holding her weight. His brute strength contrasted with the tender way he held her. Ava's toes curled in her steel-capped boots. Tangling her fingers into his hair, Ava rubbed herself on him like a cat. Fantasies of Bryce swiping everything off her desk and reminding her why she was addicted to him ran through her mind. She bit back a moan while sucking on his tongue.

"Do you have time for lunch?" she asked, snuggling into his arms.

"No." The disappointment in his voice gutted her. She'd probably stop to eat something with the girls in the office, but Ava's hopes had been unrealistically buoyed by seeing him.

"I have a meeting with the team's player liaison and the uni. They want me to get enrolled in my subjects early so I can make my schedule work. The team asked me to train with the professional group."

"Bryce, that's brilliant." Ava's voice was a high-pitched squeal, and she hugged him tighter.

"I think—"

"Ava—" her boss said, barging through the door, concern in his voice. She froze, her mouth agape and her eyes wide as she turned to him. He rested his forearm on the doorframe and laughed, shaking his head. "Sorry. I thought.... You screamed. I thought something was wrong. I'll leave you to it."

"No wait." Ava let her legs fall from around Bryce's hips, sliding to the floor. She adjusted her shirt where it had pulled loose and tucked it in again.

"Bryce, this is John, the head of residential development here. John, Bryce."

"Nice to meet you, John." Bryce held out his hand, shaking John's with a smile. "Thanks for looking out for her."

"Likewise. Sorry, I didn't realize Ava had a visitor. I'll leave you to it." John closed the door and Bryce gazed at her, adoration in his smile.

"He seems great."

"He is. Everyone is. I couldn't have asked for a better place to work." Bryce leaned in and kissed her with a smile on his lips, walking her back until her butt hit the desk. His tongue did wicked things, conjuring up the most delicious shivers through her. He played with her hair, running the backs of his fingers against her throat and down to her breasts. His thick thigh between her legs gave Ava the friction she needed, and she shamelessly rode him.

But it wasn't enough.

She reached behind her, trying to swipe everything off the desk.

"Uh-uh," he whispered, tugging on her wrist and returning her hands to his body. His sculpted pecs filled her palms, and she ran one hand down and around to his arse and the other up to his nape. Bryce kissed a trail down her throat, nibbling on the sensitive part that always got her going.

Ava moaned softly, tangling her fingers in his hair.

"Open your present, Ava," he directed, teasing her with words whispered in a rumbly growl against her throat and pulling back.

Pressing her legs together, she groaned at the throb and reached for the box. Instead, Bryce spun her around, pulling her against him until his hard cock was pressed between her butt cheeks. He snaked his hand down to cup her pussy and Ava moaned again, her hole clenching as she imagined him working his way inside while he fingered her clit. She'd never imagined wanting to get off in her office knowing there were people on the other side of the door and in offices across the road who had the perfect view, but now? She shivered, her pussy quivering.

"Mmm, I can feel you. Are your panties soaked, beautiful?"

Ava nodded, unable to form any coherent words. Bryce flicked the button on her khaki work trousers before sliding the zip down. Ava whimpered, desperate for his confident touch against her core.

He stilled as she reached out, holding him to her and chuckled. "Open your present, Ava, then you can have your orgasm."

She tugged on the ribbon, the bow slipping free and slithering to her desk. Bryce slid his hand into her underwear, one finger dipping into her pussy. They were just the right amount of rough to overload her senses. Ava bit her lip to stop the illicit moan bubbling up her throat.

"More," she begged.

"Lift the lid," he ordered.

She did, and he added another finger, his thumb flicking against her clit. Ava gasped, sensation rocketing through her as he stretched her pussy and lit up her nerve endings.

"You're drenched, beautiful. I can't wait to taste you. Then when I have, I'm gonna slide inside you and make you scream. Cole and I are gonna fuck you boneless tonight, baby."

Her pussy clenched, trying to hold his fingers in place, but Bryce was teasing her, only adding a third finger when she whimpered in frustration. He took pity on her, giving her what she so desperately needed. He pumped inside her, filling her pussy with his deft fingers and grinding his thick cock against her arse. She began the steady climb as he played her body like an instrument.

"Look up, beautiful. See those offices across the road? They want to be me right now, sinking into your tight pussy. They want you like we do. But you're ours, aren't you?" He popped the button on her shirt and slid his hand inside her bra, pinching her nipple. With his other hand, he flicked her clit and jammed his fingers inside her.

Ava arched against him, trembling as her orgasm swept through her, obliterating every thought. Her being narrowed down to the points on her body he was touching, his warmth adding fire to the heat burning through her. Ava bit her hand to stifle the scream she wanted to let loose as he upped the pressure against her clit. Her body responded, her orgasm reigniting and firing through her again.

Three orgasms later, Bryce finally withdrew his fingers from her still-twitching core. With a wicked glint in his eyes, he licked them clean, humming. Ava's pussy clenched again at the sight. On jelly legs, she would have collapsed to the floor—a good thing so she could get a taste of him—but Bryce stopped her. He lifted her onto the desk and adjusted himself, placing the open box in front of her with his now-clean hand.

"I'm saving this for later," he murmured against her lips, his hand gripping his cock until his bulge wasn't so prominent. He kissed her, lazy swipes of his tongue as he shared her arousal.

Lightheaded and trembling, Ava huffed out an exhausted laugh and resisted the temptation to lie down, spread her legs and demand that he slide into her now.

"Right now, you need to check out what I made for you."

She lifted the tissue paper. Her eyes widened, her mouth popping open. The detail was magnificent. A single red origami rose lay on another bed of white tissue paper. Its stem was decorated with a delicately folded leaf and another bud. Bryce must have spent hours—hell, days—getting it perfect. She touched her fingertips to the rose, making sure it was real and not a hallucination.

Bryce nuzzled her throat, his nose nudging her hair as he murmured, "Do you like it?"

"Bryce, it's beautiful. I love it." Her voice was barely a whisper. "Thank you."

"Sorry I couldn't get you anything expensive." He sighed, his voice an annoyed rumble. "I'm so sick of being broke."

"Hush." She nudged him. "This is… everything. I've never received anything this beautiful before."

Bryce's eyes brightened and a shy smile lit up his face.

Ava leaned into him, kissing him again. It was as if she was an overfull well, emotion spilling over and pouring out as she tried to show him just how much his handmade present meant. "Bryce, it's perfect."

He gently cupped her face and whispered against her lips, "Happy birthday, Ava." He pressed a lingering kiss to her mouth, and Ava smiled, her heart fluttering at how damn sweet he was. "I *really* need to go."

"I'll walk you out." It was easier said than done. Ava's legs were wobbly, and she walked like a newborn foal, happy hormones coursing through her bloodstream.

With Bryce's hand on the small of her back, she led him back through the narrow hallway and past the bullpen where most of the staff sat. Their eyes followed her, most of them with grins on their faces when Ava shot them a self-satisfied smirk. They may not know what she'd just gotten up to, but the ladies there could appreciate a beautiful man when they saw one, and Bryce was gorgeous.

Pushing through the door to reception, she waved and smiled like a lovesick fool as Bryce flashed an adoring grin and walked backward out of the front doors.

Ava was on cloud nine as she floated to John's office. She knocked, politely waiting for him to invite her in. "Did you want to see me?"

"I didn't, then I heard you shriek, and I freaked out. I thought something had happened." John motioned for her to close the door and sit down. "But I've just gotten off the phone with the directors. They want a few reports to be prepared this afternoon. I know you're working on one of them, but I also need an updated program for your project. I'm speaking with accounts about getting the updated cash flow too."

"Are they shutting it down?" she asked, her high from a moment earlier crashing. Ava slumped in the chair opposite his and furrowed her brow. What would it mean for her job if they shut down her only project?

He smiled reassuringly and the vice around Ava's chest loosened. "No, they're looking at every project we have on as well as retail's projects. I'd say it's just planning for this quarter and beyond. They do it every now and then."

"Okay, I should get onto it then." Ava motioned over her shoulder and John nodded.

"That'd be great. Thank you." Ava exited the office but just as she was about to close his door, he called out again. "Was that a birthday present Bryce was bringing you?"

"Yeah." She flushed, her love-struck love-heart-eyes smile firmly back in place.

"Well then, happy birthday. Make sure you take off early today. Get those reports done and get out of here."

Ava thanked him and walking on air again, she dashed to her office to get started.

Ava poured herself into her work, prioritizing the reports John had requested. One of the main things she'd learnt from him was that it was better to be a little generous with time, than to underestimate. Jason, the former project manager for her townhouse complex, had done the opposite. Every deadline had been missed, some by days, others by weeks. When she calculated the daily interest the company was paying on their loans for the site, her mind boggled.

The updated program finished, she emailed it off to John and rubbed her temples. The cash flow reports were being looked after, and she'd mostly finished reviewing the budget, adding in the cost overruns as well as the updated quotes. Materials prices had skyrocketed, and it was affecting every aspect of the build price. Most subcontractors had held their labour rates steady, despite paying their employees and contractors more, but the budget was months out of date.

Thankfully, property prices were up too, so they could still make back their outlays with the townhouses they were yet to sell. Hopefully, the softening in prices would hold off long enough to make a decent profit on the project. But it was looking dicey.

When her phone rang again, Ava yawned and rubbed her eyes. She'd just sent the updated budget to John and was exhausted.

"This is Ava."

"Ava, I have your 2:00 p.m. meeting in reception."

She frowned. "Ah, hold on." She didn't have any meetings scheduled. Frantically, she ran through her mental checklist of who she'd spoken to throughout the week. "Lisa, can you please discreetly get some more information for me. I don't know who I'm supposed to be meeting."

"Oh, sorry, did you not see my email?" she asked, her voice low enough that it wouldn't travel across the reception area. She hadn't. She'd been too focussed on updating figures, ignoring everything that had come in. "Mr Saxon rang when your earlier visitor was here. He asked me to confirm you'd blocked out your afternoon from 2:00 p.m. Apparently, you'd spoken with him and arranged it, but you didn't have anything in your diary. I added Mr Saxon in." Mr Saxon... Cole?

"Dark hair? Grumpy?"

"Yes," Lisa answered brightly.

Ava's belly swooped, excitement pulsing through her. "Give me a couple of minutes. I'll be right out."

Ava tidied up her office, closing down her laptop and tablet, picked up the roll of plans that she needed to look at over the weekend, and packed everything she could fit into her messenger bag. Taking her phone off charge, Ava touched the rose from Bryce and only stopped to confirm with John that it was okay to leave.

After getting his okay, she pushed through the door to reception, and bit back the groan trying to break free. Cole stood there, legs shoulder-width apart in chunky steel-capped boots with his hands shoved into the pockets of his khaki cargo shorts. His dusty high-vis shirt stretched across his shoulders and his dark eyes glimmered with promise as he watched her stride across the tiled floor to him. He held out his hand for her to shake and Ava couldn't help the ex-cited smile that stretched her lips.

All he was missing was the tool belt. Damn what a visual that would have made. She bit her lip painfully hard, men-tally cataloguing how sexy he'd be in just the boots and belt. Yummy.

Cole narrowed his eyes, watching her as she fought the overwhelming physical reaction to him. When he flicked his eyes down, seeing her hardened nipples through the thin fabric of her bra, he tilted one side of his mouth up in the ghost of a self-satisfied smirk. The twinkle in his eyes as he met her gaze once more spoke of wicked promises that she knew he'd deliver on.

Clasping his rough hand, Ava suppressed a shiver, failing miserably when he ran his thumb over her wrist.

"Mr Saxon, thank you for coming by." Her voice was breathy, anticipation fizzing through her veins like champagne.

"It was a priority," he answered with a rumble, a sensual tease in his promise. "It couldn't wait."

"You're in luck. I'm finished up for the afternoon. Should we head out?" Ava needed to be alone with Cole and now. She didn't want to hang around the office any longer than necessary, especially because her workmates would no doubt be gossiping about the two hotties that had come to visit her that afternoon.

"We're heading out, Lisa. I won't be back this arvo and I'm not contactable."

"Okay, no worries. Enjoy your weekend."

Ava waved, walking in front of Cole to the lift.

As soon as the doors closed behind them, Cole pressed her against the wall. She dropped her satchel, and it landed with a thud on the luxurious carpet. Cole threaded their fingers together, his thick between hers. Lifting her hands above her head, he pinned her there, his lean body holding her in place.

Cole kissed her senseless, and Ava hooked her leg over his hip. His tongue explored her mouth in a lazy dance, and his hips rocked against her core. Breathless, the room spun, and she was desperate to touch him, to climb him like a tree. "Cole," she breathed, begging him to do more.

"Tell me, sexy. Did you like Bryce's present?"

"God, yes," she moaned.

"Mmm, and what were you thinking about when you walked out and saw me waiting for you?" he challenged, a tease in his voice. Ava choked out an embarrassed laugh and Cole continued, his mouth panty-meltingly close to her ear, his breath tickling the sensitive spot on her throat, "You had your sex face on."

This time Ava did laugh. "My sex face?"

Cole growled against her skin, punching his hips forward and licking a line up her throat before sucking on her lobe. "Mmm, you get all shivery and your eyes go dark. You bite your lip too like you need something in your mouth. What did you want in your mouth, hmm?"

"Your cock." Ava gasped as he ground his rock-solid length against her core. "I was picturing you in your boots and belt, and that's it."

"You want me to nail you? Hammer you deep? Screw you in place?" he answered, his eyes dancing with mirth as he spoke.

She pinned him with her gaze, her pussy throbbing when he looked like he was having trouble tearing his vision away from her lips. "Hell yes." She paused, and Cole sucked in a breath, his cock thickening against her belly. "Then I want you to do it all to Bryce. Or let him do it to you. Either way suits me." She bit her lip and hummed, picturing her gorgeous men bending each other over, their thick cocks sliding in and out of the other's body.

Cole cleared his throat, loosening his grip on her hand and palming his dick. "Tonight. But first you need to eat. Keep your strength up." The lift dinged, the doors sliding open to a waiting audience. Cole picked up her bag and motioned for Ava to exit first, his hand on the small of her back as they walked out.

"How did you get the afternoon off work?" she asked as they meandered hand in hand along the busy street. "I thought you were super busy."

He shrugged. "Eh, busy enough, but that's why I worked back the last couple of days and started early this morning. I wanted to make sure I could pick you up. I was hoping to go home first and get changed but traffic was a shithouse, and I didn't want to be too late." He led her to one of her favourite hole-in-the-wall Korean takeaways and collected an order waiting for them. "Come on," he instructed, pointing out his white ute, the aluminium tray filled with oversized toolboxes, ladders, and rolled-up extension leads.

Cole seemed to know exactly where he was going as he drove through the city streets toward the Harbour. He'd clearly put a bit of thought into their plans, and when he backed up into a street, illegally parking in a no stopping zone, Ava smiled. She knew this spot. It wasn't the closest vantage point, but the prettiest. The view of the bridge,

Luna Park, and all the boats travelling along the busy waters was unparalleled on this side of the Harbour.

She stayed put as Cole walked around the ute, opening her door and taking their lunch from her hands. Sitting on the tailgate, overlooking the most spectacular view, he cracked open the lids and fed her kimchi and bulgogi. They sipped steaming samgyetang soup from takeaway cups, and Ava couldn't help her gushy smile and the way she leaned into his touch. Korean food was some of her favourite and the takeaway he'd chosen was famous for their chicken and ginseng soup as well as the meat and vegetable dishes he'd chosen.

"You and Bryce have spoilt me rotten today," she gushed as Cole chuckled and nudged her with his shoulder.

"It's our job."

"He made me a rose." Cole raised an eyebrow in question and her cheeks heated. "An origami rose. It's beautiful."

"He was practicing when I called him last night. Said he had one that was perfect but wanted to try one more in case he could make it better. He sent me a photo—he has a whole vase of them at his place."

"He's too sweet."

Cole nodded and lifted the nearest toolbox lid, plucking out a square brown cardboard box. "It's only just dry so I haven't had time to wrap it properly." Handing it to her, Ava furrowed her brow. Cole had made her something too? She peered inside and her breath caught. Rich, dark-toned timber gleamed at her. The impeccably smooth egg, its curves perfect, rested on a piece of folded newspaper.

"You made this?" Her voice was quiet, filled with awe.

"I did. Turned it on my lathe a few days ago and I've been sanding, painting, and staining it since. It opens too. Look inside."

Gingerly, she lifted it out, the ovoid filling her joined palms. She marvelled at the precise line between the base and its lid. Balancing it on one hand, Ava lifted the top half and gasped.

"Oh my god," she whispered. Staring back at her was a miniature ocean in the hollowed-out interior. Waves crashed on the beach; the timber stained a much lighter sand colour in that spot. Whitewash mingled with the azure waves and indigo blue depths; the whole painting shiny as if it was wet.

"You and Bryce inspired me to play around with my lathe again. I haven't used it since I was an apprentice, but then Bryce told me he was making you a gift and I saw this block of timber. I wanted to make something for you."

She touched the line of the waves and shook her head, dumbstruck at how beautifully it was finished.

"I made the waves out of resin."

"Cole... this is... I'm lost for words."

He lifted the egg from her hands, placing it gently back in its box before cupping her face. He kissed her long and slow, making love to her mouth and scrambling her brain just like Bryce had done earlier. They sat like that, slowly making out until the afternoon sun shifted, its rays burning Ava's skin.

"Let's get out of this sun," Cole suggested. "Want to show me your townhouse project?"

She grinned, happiness suffusing her veins. "Let's go."

* * * * *

Ava walked into the office on Monday morning, gingerly sitting on her chair. She was sore from the marathon sex she'd had over the weekend, but she wouldn't have changed it for the world. Bryce and Cole were insatiable, taking her higher than any lover had ever gone before. They'd tried every position and combined their mouths, fingers, and cocks with all her toys, giving her orgasm after orgasm.

Ava smiled, still riding the high from her secret weekend when the knock on her door came. John stood there, his complexion pallid. "Are you okay?" she asked, concern etched into her voice.

"Not really. All-staff meeting is starting in a couple of minutes. Make sure you're logged in."

Ava opened her mouth ready to ask another question, but he disappeared from her office. Poking her head out the door, she saw the stunned faces of her colleagues and the whispered conversations between them.

"What's going on?" Ava murmured to Andrea, her closest neighbour.

"No idea. But an all-staff meeting? Since when do they happen?"

"It can't be good." Ava's gut in knots, she shut the door, and took a calming breath. Surely it was nothing bad.

As long as she kept telling herself that, she had a chance of believing it. But before she did anything, she had a bill to pay that morning. Ava logged onto her tablet and opened her banking app. She stared at the balance. The balance that was a whole paycheque less than it should be. Surely there must have been a mistake.

Ava's thoughts were cut off when a voice cleared, signifying the beginning of their meeting. Maybe the meeting was because there was an error with their wages. She hoped so.

She cursed out her empty coffee cup as a stranger took the lead.

One hour and the trajectory of her career had been flipped on its arse. It was ironic how two life-changing events could happen less than a month apart and have polar-opposite outcomes. An overwhelming weight now rested on her shoulders, the path before her shrouded in darkness.

What would happen now?

When Ava had graduated, the administrative position she'd scored at the company was like gold. A foot in the door and every opportunity laid out before her. Her first promotion to assistant development manager cemented the path she wanted to take. She wanted to be in charge of her own developments. Ava hadn't thought it was possible to achieve her goal anywhere near as fast as she did, but she'd wanted this job more than anything. She'd worked hard for it. She deserved it.

And now it was gone.

Her dream career had been snatched from within her grasp. Defeat stolen from the hands of victory, dissipating like smoke on the water.

She'd had one week. That was it. It hadn't been easy. There was a steep learning curve, made more difficult by the former project manager's incompetence. But Ava would have persisted. She would have mastered it. She would have fixed every one of the problems with that project until she'd completely turned it around. There was no doubting that it would still have been over budget, and certainly over time. But she could have delivered something the company was proud of.

Something she was proud of.

If only she had the time. If only the company had the money.

Instead, she was out on her arse. The redundancy package she was owed was unlikely to ever be paid. Her outstanding entitlements—including her wages for the last week—were pretty much a write off too. The company owed millions, and the assets it had were nowhere near enough to pay them. Administrators had been appointed and the company was being liquidated. Ava and every one of her colleagues were now officially unemployed.

Her only job now was to pack up her office and leave.

Low murmurs and shocked whispers sounded outside her office. Her boss's secretary was crying. Ava was on the verge too, her eyes burning with unshed tears. She wanted to demand answers. Why them? What had gone so wrong? But deep down she knew. It was mismanagement multiplied over whole portfolios. She'd seen it in the person she'd taken over from. The company lacked control over the projects that were being carried out. There were too many layers of management, and there wasn't enough accountability. Add in volatile economic conditions, rising material costs, and longer lead times for the few tradies they could get to work for them, and they discovered the company's bedrock foundation was actually quicksand.

Ava wiped the stray tear tracking down her cheek and sucked in a shuddery breath. Twenty-twenty hindsight was a bitch. She opened her desk drawer—the same one she'd opened for the first time a week ago—and rifled through the bundles of post-it notes and highlighters to find the lone USB stick in there. After she transferred her private files off her company laptop, she had to hand it to the administrators. Then she packed the only other personal items in her office—Cole's and Bryce's gifts.

The knowledge that this was the last time she would be standing in this very spot, the last time she would work with these people hit her like a ten-tonne wrecking ball. She gasped, holding her chest as it sank in. Tears tracked down her cheeks, and her hands shook. Everything she'd worked for, all the long hours she'd put in and the cloud of stress

Ava lived under most of the time had been for nothing. She had to start all over again with another company.

Goodbyes were short. She needed to get out of there and get some air. Then she needed to start looking for another job. But before that, she had some news to break. Ava closed her eyes. Bryce and Cole, her parents too. She knew they'd be there to help her—her parents always were—but she hated needing them to. They'd already done so much. This was supposed to be her time to take over and do it on her own.

TWELVE

Cole

Cole groaned and flopped forward, landing face first on his bed. It was going to be the week from hell. Two apprentices had called in sick after a weekend partying, and custom-made oak doors were stolen during a break-in on site. Cole was responsible to fix all of it. Why was he doing this to himself? Oh, right, because he was an idiot for accepting the promotion and now he was stuck peopling.

He just wanted to have a few beers, relax on the couch with Bryce and Ava, and switch off from the world. He couldn't handle having to talk to anyone, but his phone was ringing non-stop.

Pulling it out of his back pocket, he pursed his lips at the dusty mess encasing it and swiped to answer. "Hey, you," he greeted Bryce. "Have a good day?"

"Hi." Bryce's voice was warm, and Cole could just picture the shy grin and pink tinge to his man's cheeks when he answered. Cole didn't expect him to sigh, and he furrowed his brow pulling the phone away from his ear as he looked at it, waiting for an epiphany. "It was good up until a few minutes ago. But I think you'd better get over here. Ava was waiting for me when I got home and is pretty upset, but she won't tell me what happened."

Adrenaline pumped through his veins in an instant, all the worst-case scenarios darting to the forefront of his mind. Before he could even finish asking whether she was okay physically, Cole had stripped off his dusty work clothes and was reaching for a pair of well-worn jeans and a T-shirt.

"She looks completely put together for work but has barely said a word to me. When I walked up the hallway, she grabbed onto me like a koala and hasn't done much except cry. I'm freakin' out, Cole. I dunno what to do."

"I'm coming. Give me twenty and I'll be at your place." Cole didn't even bother with shoes, instead dashing out the front door of his apartment and down to the basement for his ute. At this time of afternoon, there wasn't much traffic on the road—it was still too early for peak hour—and Cole made it in fifteen minutes.

Tearing up the first flight of stairs to Bryce's shoebox apartment, Cole's heart thudded in his chest. His palms were sweaty, a crazy mix of fear and nervousness fighting for dominance in his mind. Three students carrying heavy backpacks laughed and joked around in the stairwell, one shoving the other on the landing. They were too slow, and he needed to hurry the hell up.

"Move," he ordered, his voice a sharp bark as he shouldered his way past them and dashed up another flight. Cole didn't care. He didn't have time to deal with them getting their panties in a bunch. Their protests were silenced when Cole shoved through the door to Bryce's level, and it slammed behind him.

Bryce's door was propped open with a shoe and Cole pushed through, kicking it out of the way. Right there before him, Ava sat curled up on Bryce's lap, his guy threading his fingers through her hair as he held her tightly and rocked them gently.

Relief washed over his face, Bryce's lips turning up in a tight smile at Cole. He probably looked like he was wild with panic, his hair likely sticking up in every direction from tugging on the ends as he'd waited for a red light to change. It would be a small miracle if he didn't end up with speeding fines from the trip.

Ava wiped her cheeks with the back of her hand and reached for him.

Cole was there, his legs taking him to her before he even registered it. He wrapped his arms around them, wanting nothing more than to shelter them both in his embrace. He kissed her hair, breathing her in before flicking his gaze to Bryce. The subtle shake of his head told Cole that she hadn't opened up yet.

"Baby, what happened?" he whispered, pressing gentle kisses to her forehead and temples.

"I'm sorry. I didn't mean to worry either one of you, but I didn't know where else to go."

"You came to the right place. We're always here for you, no matter what," Bryce murmured. Cole loved that about him. He was the first person to crack a smile, the first person to tell a joke, but Bryce was also one of the kindest people Cole knew.

"I lost my job," she whispered, her voice wobbling as fat tears dripped from Ava's eyes. Her growl of anger would have been adorable had Cole not been thunderstruck by her news. She'd had a week, literally five days in the position. How could they have sacked her when they just gave her a promotion?

Cole ground his teeth together, his molars cracking as he tried to bite back a caustic comment about her boss being an arsehole.

"What? Why?" Bryce asked. "How can they do that?"

Ava sighed, the fight draining out of her once more. "Administrators were appointed to the company over the weekend. It's broke. It's being closed down."

Cole closed his eyes and held her tighter, pressing another kiss to her silky hair.

When she continued, Cole met Bryce's concerned stare. Cole wasn't good at this; he didn't know how to comfort people. He could fix things, could make things happen, but there was absolutely nothing he could do for the two people who were fast becoming the most important in the world to him.

"I'm owed last week's pay, and thousands in entitlements. So, now instead of working on the townhouse project, I've got to look for a new job, and I don't even know where to start."

"Shit," Bryce swore under his breath, shaking his head and running his fingers through Ava's long hair again. "So unfair."

"It sucks, you know?" Ava's quiet words were like a sucker punch, gutting him. "I worked so hard to even be noticed by management. Then my boss saw me. He took me under his wing and pushed me. He gave me a chance to prove myself. When I wanted the promotion, he championed for me. He talked the executive into giving me a chance. And for what? I've had one week's experience as a project manager. I barely even met the team I was supposed to be working with, never mind actually managed anything." Ava huffed out a laugh, but it held no humour, only disappointment and disillusionment. "Now I have to find someone who will give me a chance to get my foot in the door so that I can start all over again. It's like the last few years have been a complete waste."

"Don't think like that, baby. It's just a bump in the road," Bryce encouraged. He looked at Cole with wide eyes and waited for him to reassure Ava too. Expectation pressed down on Cole, and he nodded slowly, stalling until the words came to him.

"Yeah," he squeaked before clearing his throat. "What Bryce said." Cole could have kicked himself. What a dumb thing to say. Bryce choked out a cough and glared at him in horror while Ava pulled back and blinked at him. Heat washed over his cheeks, the flush rising from his throat. Cole tried to pull back, both furious and frustrated with himself, but Ava stopped him with a gentle hand to his cheek.

She ran her thumb over his stubble, and he turned to place a gentle kiss to her palm.

"You're really bad at this, Cole, but I love that you're trying. Both of you, thank you."

His shoulders sagged in relief that she wasn't pissed, his breath rushing out of him. Capturing her lips in a slow kiss, he moaned when her breath hitched as he slid his tongue in alongside hers. He slipped his hand under Bryce's shirt and with the other cupping Ava's face, Cole apologized with actions rather than words.

* * * * *

"Are you kidding me? No fucking way."

"What else am I supposed to do?" Ava screeched, throwing her phone down on the couch. It bounced, clattering to the tiled floor.

"You can't! I won't let you do that to yourself," Cole shouted. His blood was boiling, fury making him shake. What Ava was proposing—no, what those fuckwits had asked of her—was beyond the pale. The company she'd applied to had a reputation for using and abusing their staff. He hadn't wanted her to even send her CV in, but she'd insisted. This fucked-up plan they'd hatched was just another shitty way of getting free labour.

It was a bloody ruse.

Get people invested, make them think there's a job so they work hard, and the company gets free labour.

Demanding job applicants do unpaid work for them was low. But making them do it for three months to even get a look-in was abhorrent. They wouldn't give her a firm answer on how many positions were available, who she was competing with, or the number of applicants. It was insanity to even contemplate investing all that time and effort into a company who'd screwed their employees over many times before. They were sure to do it again too. But he couldn't make her see sense.

Ava got all up in his face and poked him hard in the chest. Her voice was venomous, her eyes flashing with cold fury when she shouted back at him, "In what universe do you think it's acceptable for you to act like my keeper? I didn't ask your permission. I don't even remember asking you for an opinion. How. Dare. You."

Bryce tried to step between them, gently brushing Ava's hair off her shoulder and trying to calm her. He was the peacekeeper of the group, the happy-go-lucky joyful one, while Cole was the snarling dog, and today she was a hissing cat.

Apparently, Ava was done with being calm.

She locked eyes with Bryce, silently challenging him to push her. She was spoiling for a fight, lashing out at anyone who would dare challenge her. But she wouldn't be throwing down with Bryce, not when he flinched every time one of them raised their voices. Cole would protect that little bit of Bryce's innocence with his whole heart.

With his hands on his man's waist, Cole eased him gently to the side and stepped in front of him, facing off with Ava once more. "Calm the fuck down. This is ridiculous."

"Fuck you very much."

"Think about what they're asking. Do you think for a minute that they're not gonna treat you like shit? They want you to work for them for free. For three months. Three months! And for what? A promise that you might get a look-in at a position they won't even guarantee they'll have available at the end? Are you mad?"

"What other choice do I have?" She threw her hands up in the air, the frustration bleeding through her loud voice. "I'm not even getting interviews. For anything."

"Ava," Bryce implored, reaching for her hands. She shook out of his grasp. A momentary flash of hurt stole across Bryce's face before he buried it behind a wall of stoicism. But it was enough to cut Cole deeper than he was prepared to admit. Bryce sighed and added calmly, "You did get an interview. Sure, there was someone else more qualified for the job that time. But they were impressed with you. Give it time, you'll find the right position."

Cole lifted one eyebrow in a see-I-told-you-so motion and Ava erupted, her face reddening as she clenched her fists hard. It was obvious to anyone looking at her that she wanted to beat the shit out of him. He would have felt bad about it, but if it got her to see sense, so be it.

"You're siding with him now?" she spat at Bryce. "Mr I-think-I-own-my-girlfriend?" She crossed her arms over her chest, her narrow-eyed glare never leaving his man's.

Bryce withered and he stepped back. Oh hell no.

"You think yelling at Bryce is acceptable? Not on my watch, sweetheart," Cole growled, his voice harsh from the need to protect them. Both of them. He could handle the vitriol. The tirade of cruel words. He'd been on the receiving end of it before. But he wouldn't stand for someone hurting the people he loved.

Oh, hell. No, it couldn't be true. Nope, no and hell no. There is no way. Not after only a few weeks. It's not worth falling for them anyway. Not when people just get hurt. I'm not going there. I can't. It's too soon. It's too much. There's no way I'm doing that to myself. The last people I loved threw me away. They tossed me out and I lost everything. I nearly ended up on the streets.

An awareness hit him. Like a light at the end of a tunnel followed by a freight train, it slammed into him with the tact of... well a freight train. Was it really too soon? Too much? Or was it exactly right? Were they exactly right? Maybe being happy was enough. And he was happy, even if he was in the middle of a yelling match with one-half of his heart.

"Or you'll do what, arsehole?" Ava rounded on him, her eyes flashing with anger and her lips in a thin line. Even furious—maybe especially because of that—she was gorgeous. Her face flushed a darkening red, but Cole was done with this conversation.

He would stand in front of her and battle demons she didn't even know existed if it meant keeping her safe and happy. He took a step forward, crowding her. Ava was in bare feet, while he still wore his chunky work boots. Cole towered over her. Outrage at the unfairness of what the company was demanding overflowed like lava bursting forth from the earth.

"This," Cole muttered before he cupped her nape and curled his hand over her butt, hauling her to him. He smashed his mouth down on hers and took out all his frustration at those arseholes in his kiss. He lifted her effortlessly and groaned in satisfaction when Ava curled into him. She wrapped her arms and legs tightly around his body even though her mouth was unyielding. He pulled back and narrowed his eyes at her, growling, "Kiss me."

"Fuck off," she uttered but didn't give him a chance to respond, capturing his lips with a ferocious kiss of her own. He let her take over, submitting to her. Yielding to let her know she and Bryce would always be his first priority.

She bit his lip and Cole's cock pulsed in his jeans. His hardness pressed against her heat; he couldn't wait to strip her naked and bury himself inside her.

Cole stomped over to the couch and dumped Ava unceremoniously on the leather cushions, following her down as he kicked off his work boots and dusty jeans. Ava reached for his work shirt, tugging it over his head and tossing it on the floor before digging her blunt nails into his back and pulling him close again.

She was still fighting him, but her anger had morphed into a primal lust. The needy moans she let loose spurred him on, desire overwhelming him until his movements were choppy and his hands shook.

"Bryce, get that sexy arse over here," Cole directed. Maybe he was a masochist, or maybe it was because he loved playing with fire, he added, "Our girl needs something to suck on to shut her up." He knew he was pushing her buttons, trying to provoke a reaction. But how hard would she bite back?

Cole's stare was unwavering, silently daring Ava to respond. Her only move was to snap her teeth closed and narrow her eyes.

"Play nice, Cole," Bryce chastised. He knelt and cupped Ava's face, brushing her hair away from her eyes and kissed her gently. The move was in complete contrast to Cole's rough touch.

He unzipped her skinny jeans and yanked them and her panties down her legs, exposing her bottom half to his hungry gaze. She was beautiful. Smooth alabaster skin and curves for miles. Cole held her in place, his fingers curling gently around her throat. With his free hand, he pushed up her frilly tank top and licked at her breast through the lace of her bra. She shivered, her nipple pebbling.

Temptation was a wicked beast. Cole was driven to show her just how nicely he could play. Closing his lips around the peak, he sucked, then bit down hard enough on her nipple to sting like a mother. He tugged hard and Ava arched into him, moaning into Bryce's kiss.

Bryce snaked his fingers down Ava's prone form to her core and slid them through her creamy folds. He unerringly found her clit and Ava moaned. The sound was illicit, and Cole's cock throbbed. At Bryce's matching moan, Cole curled his fingers around the base of his dick and squeezed hard, pulling him away from the edge.

He watched as Bryce shoved his hand down the silky shorts clinging to his bubble butt like a second skin. Cole leaned over, balancing on his knees as he helped Bryce out of them. It was an excuse to touch his man, to touch all that warm skin on Bryce's spectacular arse and down his thick legs. When his cock bounced up, slapping against Bryce's belly, Cole's mouth watered. He wanted both their tastes on his tongue.

"You want him to fuck you, don't you, sexy?" Bryce asked against Ava's lips. "You're so wet, so tight."

Cole moaned, need rushing forth like lava exploding from the earth's crust, the heat blinding him and making his head spin.

"He can fuck off," Ava growled. But her body spoke a different language.

She widened her legs, lifting her knees and making room for Cole to crawl closer. She pressed her heels into his butt, closing the last remaining bit of distance between them. Instinct took over. He needed the connection between them. He had to eliminate the distance and walls that they'd erected with their harsh words.

Cole lined his cock up to her core, her wet heat branding him. He thrust deep into her with one sharp movement, his balls slapping against her butt and his hips connecting with hers. With his fingers still wrapped around her throat, he saw stars. Galaxies exploding behind his closed eyelids like a fireworks display. It was like heaven and hell all rolled into one. He hadn't experienced anything like it before—her tight, wet channel gripping him with a vice-like strength.

She shifted her legs, cradling him as his cock pulsed, and Cole fought off the instinct to chase his orgasm, even as she screamed. Her pussy spasmed around his length, Bryce working her clit even as Cole impaled her. He fought the overwhelming urge to blow right there and then, and wrapped his fingers around his sac, tugging hard to halt being sling-shotted into ecstasy.

"Yes," she moaned. "Again."

Ava slid her hand down, using Bryce's cock as a lead to pull him up. He propped one knee by her head and painted her lips with the pre-cum leaking from his tip.

"That's it, gorgeous. Suck him until our man blows," Cole encouraged, shifting his hand until it was just below her jaw. He wanted to feel Bryce's length pushing past her tonsils.

When Bryce pulled his hips back, Cole did the same until only the head of his cock breached her core. He reversed and slammed home again as Bryce gingerly dragged his cock along Ava's tongue and back into her throat. Over and over again, Cole pumped into her, hard and deep. Unrestrained. He watched as Bryce took much more care with her, always gentle, always considerate. His deft fingers never left her clit and when Ava's walls tightened around him and her breathing shallowed out, Cole reached the point of no return.

It was that moment of hovering before the freefall that always got him. Cole's orgasm rushed at him like a skydiver free-falling to the ground. She was too tight, too hot, too beautiful laid out before him to resist. Cole wanted to worship at the altar of her body for the rest of his life. He wanted to make her see stars and never for a moment regret the fireworks that sometimes went with them.

The tingling at the base of his spine grew, spreading outward in waves until his balls unloaded, shooting his seed deep into her. Once, twice, then three times his cock pulsed, and Cole shouted out. He didn't think he had anything left, but when Ava's pussy tightened on him, rhythmically clenching and releasing, she milked the last remaining drops. His shallow thrusts must have been enough to hit her G-spot over and over and her orgasm renewed.

His head spun and his limbs like jelly, Cole collapsed, resting his head on her breast and slipping free of her depths. He reached down ready to slip off the condom when he touched his own skin. Fuck! No wonder it had been so much better than anything he'd ever experienced before. He'd never once gone bare.

"Shit. Shit, shit, fuck." Panic clawed at him. They hadn't spoken about this. Ava hadn't given him the okay. He'd been so crazy out of his mind that he'd lost all sense of reason and responsibility.

"What's wrong?" Ava mumbled, her arm thrown across her face.

"I didn't use a condom. I'm so fuckin' sorry, Ava. I'm clear. I got tested just before I met you guys, but... fuck." Wide-eyed and his heart thumping hard against his ribs, which had nothing to do with his exertion only a moment earlier, he babbled, his words tripping over themselves to be heard as panic clawed through his veins.

She lifted her face and peered up at him before cupping his face. "Hey, it's okay. I got tested too and I've got an IUD in. There's virtually no chance I can fall pregnant."

He shook his head, his eyes burning. "I'm not worried about that. You didn't say I could. I broke your trust. I could have hurt you if I hadn't been tested. I didn't even think."

"Come here." She hooked her finger under his chin and Cole went willingly. The touch of her lips against his was soft. Gentle. She kissed him, made love to his mouth until every worry he had dissipated on the breeze of the air-conditioning blowing over their sweat-soaked skin. "I know you'd never hurt me."

Bryce kissed his temple and Cole reached for him, pressing their lips together and making out lazily. Bryce moaned, the sound needy, and Cole pulled back, blinking. His man's erection was steely hard, pre-cum dripping down his length. Veins stood out in sharp relief to his pale skin. "Please," Bryce begged, his voice pained.

Cole shifted, opening his mouth so Bryce could take what he needed but his man shook his head. "I need to see." He gripped the base of his cock, squeezing hard. "I need to see your cum in Ava's pussy.

"I want yours in there too, Bryce," Ava breathed, her fingers sliding down, dipping into her soaked folds. She lifted them to his mouth, and he whimpered, sucking ravenously on her digits. Cole made to shuffle back, but Bryce was one step ahead, lifting Ava off the couch and carrying her straight toward the bedroom.

Cole took a moment. He breathed deeply and let his head stop spinning. He wanted to give Bryce and Ava a moment without him. Ava hadn't been angry at him, but that didn't matter. He was disappointed in himself.

"Cole, get your butt in here," Ava called out, leaving no room to argue.

For the second time that afternoon, relief swam through his veins, turning his legs to jelly. He padded over and leaned against the doorjamb, watching as Bryce eased Ava's bra strap off her shoulder and kissed a path down her arm. He worshipped her, gently caressing and kissing her until she whispered something to him, and both their gazes connected with Cole's. With a wicked smile, Bryce lined himself up and slid slowly into Ava, her eyes slipping closed and neck arching back. Bryce's moan was deep and gravelly, the sound going straight to Cole's cock. His hole clenched with the memory of Bryce inside him. Their man was thick and so very long and the way he moved—almost like a dance—sent Cole into orbit every time.

Swiping his thumb over his bottom lip, Cole stared at the two people making love before him. The two people he loved. There really was no denying it anymore. Even wrapped up in each other, it was as if he was a part of them, their gentle touches and slow movements a beautiful extension of the warmth in his heart.

"You feel so good," Bryce breathed, his lips falling to Ava's collarbone for a lingering kiss. He snapped his hips forward at the same time as he turned and focussed back on Cole, holding out his hand.

Cole couldn't say no. He slid onto the bed next to Ava and kissed her shoulder, resting his hand low on her belly. He could feel Bryce moving within her, his deep thrusts shifting her body up the bed. He slid lower, finding her clit, and rolling the nub between his fingers.

Ava lifted her hips, meeting Bryce thrust for thrust. They lost themselves in each other, moving in perfect synchronicity. Bryce's thrusts became choppy as they neared the edge together. Ava fell first, her body locking as tightly as a strung bow. She cried out and Cole kissed her, swallowing her moans while Bryce grunted and pressed his hips tight against hers, riding out his own orgasm.

Breathless, his two lovers lay there, and Cole held Bryce's hand while he cuddled into Ava, unwilling to let either of them go for the moment.

"Thank you for fighting with me," Ava murmured.

Bryce's reaction was comical, his head snapping up and mouth popping open. "Are you kidding me? You wanted that?" He huffed out a disbelieving laugh and shook his head, wide-eyed with surprise.

"Not so much wanted as needed." Ava brushed a piece of Bryce's hair off his sweaty forehead and smiled softly at him. "I've been so frustrated. Everything was building up and I had no outlet to vent. But Cole gave me one."

"You didn't like us fighting." Cole didn't ask; he didn't need to. It had been obvious from the way Bryce tried to be the voice of reason, talking to Ava like she was a spooked animal and recoiling when he was on the receiving end of their shouts.

Bryce took that moment to shift from between Ava's legs, but he didn't go far and he didn't let go of Cole, mirroring his position on her other side. Eventually, he shook his head and Ava pressed a kiss to his forehead. "I'm sorry for yelling at you. Next time I'll only scream at Cole." She shot him a cheeky grin and Cole snorted out a laugh, biting her playfully on the shoulder.

Bryce smirked and rested his head on Ava's chest. "Or you could, you know, talk it out like adults?"

They laughed at Bryce's comment, but he was right. Talking things out should be their first approach. It wasn't fair to any of them that their arguments ended in yelling, even with the make-up sex afterward.

Cole spoke quietly, but he needed to be clear to Ava. He didn't want any misunderstandings. "For the record, I know I don't own you. But I hate the idea that you're going to work for them for nothing. You deserve so much better."

Ava sighed, the smile falling from her face. "I don't really have another option. I know it's only been three weeks. It's nothing in the grand scheme of things." She ran her fingers absently through Bryce's hair, pausing for a moment. "But if I get some more experience under my belt with a different company, it'll only help my chances. I'll keep applying for positions at the same time. If something else comes up that's more certain, great. If not, then at least I have three more months experience."

Cole nodded. Her argument made sense, but it killed him knowing she was going to be taken advantage of.

"I can't keep sitting around day after day and asking my parents to pay my bills for me. It's not fair to them."

"Can I help?" Bryce asked at the same time as Cole said, "Move in with me." He couldn't decide if his suggestion was madness or genius, but the silence that greeted him told him enough. He shook his head. "Never mind, I shouldn't have suggested it. You probably don't want to live with me."

"Well, I mean—"

"Why wouldn't you?" Bryce asked, then turned to Ava. "It's not the worst idea he's ever had. I mean, an hour ago he thought he owned you." Bryce's cheeky smile lit up his face, his eyes dancing with mirth as he teased Cole.

He rolled his eyes, biting back his laughter.

"I don't want to take advantage of you," Ava replied simply.

Cole looked up. She hadn't said no, but Bryce hadn't said yes either. Hope blossomed and he laugh-smiled, his chest lighter than it had been all week. "You won't be. I don't have all that much furniture. We could store the extra stuff in the spare room and then neither of you have to worry about paying rent—"

"What?" Bryce asked.

Cole shrugged. "I pay rent and utilities for here now as well as buy food, so you'd be doing me a favour really." Ava hiked up her brow and Cole swallowed. He hadn't exactly prepared a speech; he hadn't intended on asking them for a while yet. But moving the timeline forward made sense. They spent half the week at one another's apartments and the rest of the week facetiming. "Bryce, you could pay for food—overall it'd be cheaper than what you're paying now—and then when Ava starts working again, we can just work out what everyone's comfortable with."

Bryce opened his mouth then closed it again, looking to Ava. When she shook her head, Bryce's lips turned down in a frown and Cole's heart clenched. Bryce wanted it too, but he didn't want to influence Ava's decision.

"You shouldn't feel obligated to help me. That's not the right reason to move in together."

Bugger that. Cole needed to bring in the big guns. If he could get Bryce to say he wanted it out loud, Ava would cave. Neither of them could resist giving Bryce anything that made him happy. The smiles he rewarded them with were always worth it, and Bryce was so selfless anyway that often the way to please him was by making either Ava or Cole happy.

He lifted their clasped hands to his lips and pressed a kiss to Bryce's knuckles. "It's only a matter of time before you get the call up. I knew you were good, but watching you train last week was insane. You're better and fitter than half the pros on the team. It got me thinking that if we all lived together, then at least we've got an excuse to spend the night together. It's gonna look real strange when your mate keeps staying over at your's or your girlfriend's place. That's how rumours start and it's the last thing I want for you."

Bryce's gaze bounced between them, finally settling on Cole. "Why is Ava my girlfriend and not yours?" he asked, his brow furrowed but with a small, shy smile on his lips. He clearly liked what he'd heard.

Cole huffed out a laugh, trying to hide behind humour. It didn't work for him. He was always too serious to pull off joking about something. Ava had accused him of wanting to own her—it was far too accurate a sentiment. It wasn't because Cole thought of her or Bryce as possessions, but he did want them to be his, and his alone. He would freely admit to being a possessive arsehole, to want to mark them as his, if it wouldn't set Ava off again.

"Because I may not be able to claim you in public, but I'll be damned if I let anyone else think they have a chance," he growled. "No, you two are together and I'm your friend. That part's non-negotiable."

Ava's smile turned sappy as she playfully knocked her head against his. "Aw, I think Cole's getting all protective. He's been thinking about this for a while."

"Mmhmm, sounds like it," Bryce replied with a smirk that was equal parts wicked and teasing. "Also sounds as if he might like us."

"Sounds like you want an arse kicking." He narrowed his gaze at Bryce and the big guy barked out a laugh.

"I'd like to see you try. All I'd have to do is sit on you and you'd be begging for mercy."

Cole moaned, fantasies of Bryce sinking down onto his cock suddenly taking centre stage in his mind's eye. Fuck yeah, he'd be begging for mercy within mere moments if Bryce ever let him anywhere near his perfect hole.

"Hmm, then again, maybe you begging for it isn't such a bad thing."

THIRTEEN

Bryce

I t had been a week since their argument that ended in epic make-up sex. He'd hated the fight but loved the apology. Now he was back to hating—seeing Ava struggle so much was awful. She'd accepted the offer to do work experience at the development company she and Cole had fought over, and she was starting that day. Ava couldn't sit still, but it wasn't excitement. They'd stayed up late the night before, neither Cole nor Ava able to sleep. In their whispered conversations curled around each other in bed, she'd confided that it was fear more than happiness keeping her up. It was as if she could feel an expiry date on her career looming above her head and she couldn't do anything about it.

Then there was Cole. He was just downright miserable at work. He dragged his feet every morning, was losing weight, barely sleeping and his smiles were harder to pull out of him. It couldn't continue, but now that he was a supervisor, he felt trapped. He couldn't go backward; his only way now was to step up the ladder he was regretting ever getting on.

Bryce was powerless to help them, and it killed him. He wanted to wrap them up and hold them close, protect both his boyfriend and girlfriend from their stresses. The last thing he needed was to add thoughts about his career, but it was inevitable. His agent had texted him a few days earlier summoning him to a meeting. He was due at the Lightning's offices in an hour.

He still had a year left on his reserves contract with the Thunder, but his agent preferred setting up the conversations and expectations early. He'd been training well, doing everything asked of him and more. Bryce's form on the field was good—training with the professional team had improved his game immeasurably. If he kept going the way he was, Bryce was confident he could get another year. Their meeting would set up exactly what the team's expectations were, and his agent was talking long-term goals with the coach. It was pivotal to Bryce's chances to play professionally.

"You ready?" Ava asked, sticking her head in his bedroom and coming to stand between his legs. He dropped his phone and slid his hands onto her hips, cupping her pert butt. Those sharp emerald eyes he could stare into for hours assessed him, the affection in her gaze warming him. Ava's smile was a thing of beauty, one she gifted him with now.

She smoothed her hands down the lapels of his suit jacket and wiped a spot of shaving cream off his lobe and onto her jeans. "You look incredible, Bryce."

"Yeah?" He hooked a finger under the collar of his shirt, pulling it away from his throat, crossing his eyes and sticking out his tongue. "How do people wear these every day?"

Ava rolled her eyes, laughter dancing in them as she straightened his tie. Bending over, she kissed him, her tongue snaking out and teasing his as he pulled her close. Ava straddled him and Bryce wrapped her up in his arms, sinking into her gentle touch. He inhaled her sweet scent and kissed her deeper, then moaned when she threaded her fingers into his hair and ground her core against his semi.

Need was at war with responsibility. He wanted to say fuck the meeting and fuck her work experience commitments. Getting naked and burying himself inside his woman was a much better idea, but he couldn't. They both needed to be adults and do adulty things.

"We need to go or I'm going to be late," Ava murmured, sneaking another kiss. "Not a good look on my first day."

"Let's come back to this later," Bryce proposed, brushing his lips under the collar of her shirt as he squeezed her butt and slipped his fingers lower to tease her.

"Let's." Ava groaned a pained laugh before slipping off his lap and sashaying away from him. Curling her finger in a come-hither motion, she added, "We need to go, Mr Flaherty. We have a date with both our destinies."

She was quiet on the trip over. Tension gathered around her eyes and her deep frown concerned him. He knew she was worried, but she was a superstar. He had absolute faith that she was going to make a good impression and get her dream job. And if it wasn't with this company, so be it.

As soon as Ava's landlord gave the okay and his flatmate found a replacement for Bryce, they'd all be living together. They could help her out and she could take her time finding the right job for her. Ava was worried about... everything. She was so used to analyzing information before making a decision. The uncertainty she was now faced with was overwhelming.

Ava squeezed his leg as Bryce followed the slow line of traffic up the street. Her posture was rigid, but she was breathing long and slow, trying to calm herself. He slid his fingers through hers, trying to comfort her. If he could take away some of the uncertainty she was facing, he would.

It was exactly what Cole was trying to do when he'd asked them to move in with him. Bryce knew Cole was quietly freaking out about his suggestion too, but at the same time he knew Cole really did want them to live together. Both of them had given Cole the chance to rescind his offer. He'd shown a flash of vulnerability when they had, asking whether they didn't want to move in with him. Cole tried his hardest to keep the stony façade in place, but Bryce saw straight through him. Cole was a big marshmallow inside who just wanted to love and protect those around him. He wouldn't admit it, but his parents kicking him out and his sister's indifference to what had gone down scarred Cole deeply. It took a lot for him to trust, so asking them to live with him was a big deal. Bryce adored him for the growth he'd witnessed in his man. His prickly cactus had dropped some of his spines, only wielding them when he was talking to everyone else.

Bryce could see the training ground and team's offices up ahead at the end of the busy street. A rumble of nervous anticipation coursed through him. His heart thudded in his chest, his insides vibrating like he was plugged into an electrical socket. Bryce needed to work off some steam, get his blood pumping and mind on something other than what was going to happen in the meeting. If it went well, then it would be another check in the column of "fuck yeah."

He bit back the smile that was fighting to break free. He was excited, but Ava was having a professional crisis. He wanted to be there for her, and that meant tamping down his own enthusiasm so he could focus on her.

When he pulled into a car park at the club's headquarters, Ava turned to him, taking his other hand in hers. A thrill fluttered through him, buzzing in his veins and skittering across his skin at her touch. He held his breath, luxuriating in the quiet moment together.

"I'm so proud of you, Bryce. You're so close to making it. Another year on your contract and I know you can get there." Her eyes and smile were bright, determination that he would achieve his dreams burning fierce inside her. It was obvious even with the tension lines at her temples.

He hadn't realized how much he'd needed Ava to say the words until she had. The weight of guilt that something good might be happening to him and something shitty to her lifted. She was cheering him on. His confidence buoyed and his heart skipped a beat. Bryce couldn't help the delighted laughter that bubbled up his throat.

"I'm gonna do it. I'm gonna get that extra year on my contract." He nodded and this time let his giddy grin split his lips.

"You go get 'em, baby." Ava smiled, the spark in her eyes lighting up her face. She squeezed his hands tightly and he brought her knuckles to his lips, brushing a kiss to them.

"You're gonna kill it today." He tugged her forward until she laughed and nearly landed in his lap. He pressed a smiley kiss to her lips and pulled back reluctantly. Patting the dash, he added, "Take care of my baby."

She rolled her eyes and laughed as he jumped out of the truck. "I will. Break a leg," she called as she slid across the seat. Bryce backed away, waving at her while she reversed out of the spot.

Bryce pushed through the double glass doors to the office and admired the backlit images on the walls. Team photos for the whole of the club's history lined one section flanked by blown-up shots of premiership wins. Another area was their wall of fame—photos of the greats on the field proudly displayed in both black-and-white and colour. As he got closer to the reception desk, television screens played a slideshow of the current team members and replays of memorable moments in the last few seasons. One day, he wanted his plays to be on that reel. He wanted his photo with the rest of the team. He wanted that jersey.

He'd get there. He knew he would.

The receptionist blushed when he introduced himself and flashed her a boyish smile. She led the way, knocking on the door to a meeting room, not waiting for an answer before she opened it and motioned for Bryce to go through.

"Thanks." He grinned again, his heartbeat kicking up another notch when he saw who was seated at the table.

His agent was already there, as was his coach and another man he'd never met before.

"Bryce, good to see you, mate," Travis, his agent greeted, shaking his hand and gesturing to the spare chair. "You know Coach Latimer, obviously, but I don't think you've met Maxwell Denyer before. Maxwell is an independent board member who helps with player contracts."

"G'day, Coach. Good to see you." Bryce shook his hand and then greeted the other man in the room. He was... intimidating. Grey-blond hair and an expensive pin-striped suit and a thick gold watch at his wrist screamed money. He barely cracked a smile and had that look-down-his-nose-at-Bryce haughty feel about him that made Bryce feel like he was being scolded at school. But Bryce did the mature thing and held out his hand to shake. "Pleased to meet you, sir."

"Let's sit," Coach Latimer said, a warmth in his voice that the people close to him were familiar with. He was a man of few words. He came across as gruff, but he had the respect of every player and official in the game. When he spoke, people listened. Bryce unbuttoned his suit jacket and followed the others, sitting down on the last remaining chair.

"So, we've called his meeting today because the team's management wanted to talk to you about your future," Maxwell said.

Bryce blinked, his words taking a moment to sink in. He'd had no idea that the team called the meeting. He'd assumed his agent had requested it. Looking across to Travis, his agent smirked and shrugged his shoulder, unapologetic for not passing on that piece of information. Bryce didn't have time to dissect his feelings, though, because all eyes were on him.

"Okay," he squeaked before clearing his throat.

Coach took over, using the opening to get to the point. "I've been watching you carefully since you started training with the professional team, Bryce. You get along with all the players and your form has been exemplary."

Bryce couldn't help the proud smile that stole across his face. Coach had noticed. That was brilliant news for his chances at getting another extension. But if it wasn't his agent who'd requested the meeting, was that even what they were talking about? Butterflies danced in his belly as hope lit him up brightly.

"Thank you."

"So, the team has put together an offer for you to join the Eastern Lightning." Denyer kept talking but his words were white noise, a buzz in his ears.

Bryce swallowed and shook his head clearing the cobwebs and blinked a few times. "I'm sorry, did you just say you want me to join the professional team? As in, the NRL team? The Eastern Lightning?" His gaze bounced between

Travis's and Coach Latimer's and they both nodded, smiling proudly. He opened his mouth but there were no words. He was speechless. "Ah..." Bryce huffed out a laugh. "Not the Eastern Thunder?"

Coach Latimer laughed, a hearty chuckle filling the room. "No, son, not the reserves. We want you to join the professional team."

"No freaking way," he uttered, wide-eyed. His lips tilted up in a shocked smile, his body tingling. This was it, his dream come true. Never mind butterflies flapping in his belly. It was a rollercoaster zooming up and down and around loop-de-loops. He flushed hot and a rushing sounded in his ears. His hands shook and a laugh bubbled up his throat. "No way! I'm in. Where do I sign?"

His first instinct, the one that told him to shout out in glee, had him reaching for his phone. He wanted to get Cole and Ava in on this. His fingers closed around the device he'd slipped into the inside pocket of his jacket, and he paused. He couldn't let them know. Not yet. Not like this. He wanted to see their reactions face to face. He wanted to kiss and touch them and celebrate properly. He wanted to show them how falling in love with them had changed his life.

Bryce choked out a laugh. Holy shit. He loved them. He really did. Bryce dropped his phone back in his pocket. He couldn't wait to get home and tell them.

His agent opened his mouth to speak but the Denver dude beat him to it. "Read the paperwork and get advice on the terms. You must be aware of what you're agreeing to.

The conditions are important and one of them is non-negotiable."

"What are they?" Bryce asked, his excitement dimming.

Coach interjected, his hand clasping Bryce's shoulder warmly. "First, finish university. We want you to get your degree. I know you've got a year left, but if you need to stretch that out, it's fine."

Bryce nodded. He would have finished uni anyway. Even though he'd always wanted it as a backup, he still wanted to finish.

Seemingly satisfied with Bryce's response, Coach continued, "Aside from that, there's the behaviour clause. That's the mandatory one in every player's contract —"

"You're obligated not to engage in behaviour unbecoming of the team or the league." Denyer clasped his hands on the table in front of him and waited for Bryce to speak.

Bryce's mind worked a million miles a minute. All his hopes and dreams cascaded in waterfalls around him, filling him up and lifting him on a rising tide. This was really happening. He was going to get to play professionally. Sweet!

"Bryce?" his agent asked, an eyebrow raised in question. What were they talking about? Oh yeah, behaviour clause. No problem.

Bryce's grin stretched even further, his cheeks hurting with the movement. He nodded and responded, "Good behaviour. Got it. No problem."

Coach Latimer wasn't satisfied though. "As a rookie, you'll be in the spotlight, Bryce. The season is about to start and once you're announced, eyes will be on you everywhere. Photos and recordings of you getting up to anything you shouldn't will find their way to social media. Things will be taken out of context too. You're a good kid, so keep it that way. If your behaviour is exemplary, life will be easier."

"I trust that you'll take care of ensuring his social media profiles are either locked down or managed properly," Denyer directed to Travis.

"Yes, our firm has access to everything. We'll vet his existing posts and remove anything inappropriate."

"Right, let's talk signing bonus then."

FOURTEEN

Cole

They'd agreed to meet at his place that night and his knockoff time couldn't come quick enough. It was like Groundhog Day all over again. Mondays sucked, and not in the fun way.

"Cole, you want to check whether you're happy with how we've set out the stairwell and pantry?" his apprentice asked. It was an awkward design with the stairs cutting into the pantry space in the kitchen. The walls needed to be in precisely the right spot, or they'd have to rip them out and start again.

He stepped off the ladder and pulled out his measuring tape, following Sam to where he and the other apprentice had been working. "Where are the plans?"

"Over by the back door."

Cole rolled his eyes. The back door was far enough away that the boys wouldn't have been double-checking measurements as they went. Cole collected the page he needed, shaking his head when he looked up at the markings. Cole spread it out on the makeshift sawhorse that the apprentices had been using and sighed.

They winced, their wary gazes bouncing between each other and the plans.

"Have you double-checked all your measurements against the plan?"

Sam shook his head, and Cole grumbled, massaging his temples. He had to remember that they were fresh meat. Trainees. But this was basic shit that they shouldn't still be screwing up. And they had screwed it up. Cole spotted their mistake the moment he'd walked into the kitchen.

Ken patted his pockets down looking for a measuring tape, and Cole pursed his lips, biting back a snarky comment and handed over his. How could they do their jobs without one? He motioned to the space and waited while they measured the doorway and the four walls within the pantry.

"Looks good," Sam said with a satisfied smirk, letting his measuring tape snap closed. Cole raised an eyebrow and Sam withered under his stare. "Maybe?"

"What's the width of the stairwell?" It was a leading question, one that if they'd followed the plans properly, would be bigger than it currently was. This was the shit that frustrated him. But he should be grateful. At least they'd asked him to check rather than going ahead and fixing the frame down, cutting it to fit the wrong space.

"Seven fifty." Sam furrowed his brow and hummed.

Ah, now he sees the problem.

"And the length of this wall?" Cole asked flatly. Sam measured it and the pieces seemed to click into place.

"It's too long."

"How do you fix it?"

Ken shrugged and Cole tossed the plans at him.

"You start with the plans and a measuring tape. Day one on the job, guys. Measure twice, cut once."

Sam was the younger of the two and the one more eager to learn. Ken was a pain in the arse, thinking he was already an expert—he'd been around Jono, the other bloke on site, for too long. Cole focussed on him and let him think it through.

"If we shift all the markings by three hundred that way, the pantry will be the same size, but we'll have enough space to put in the stairs in."

Cole nodded. "Exactly."

"What's the minimum width we can have for the stairs?" Sam asked, and Cole explained the requirements of the Building Code, his apprentice making notes in his phone. He could and did get frustrated with all the boys on site, but at least Sam was open to learning. Jono's bad habits were rubbing off on Ken, and Jono himself slacked off more than any of them.

Speaking of Jono, where was he? He looked around for the man but couldn't see him. He needed to give Jono a briefing on when the flooring joists and the second load of framing timber were arriving. They were behind schedule on this build for no good reason. The clients were going to start making a fuss if they didn't get a boogie on to get it back on track, and that meant Cole copping it from the site supervisor.

Cole still had to get over to his other site and help push through the delays there too. "Where's Jono?"

"In the shitter." Ken pointed in the direction of the portaloo.

Cole sighed. He couldn't exactly stop his guys from using the facilities, but Jono spent forever in there. Cole couldn't imagine anything worse. The portable toilets stunk, and they weren't exactly clean. There was an endless number of blokes using it, and the longer it sat there, the worse it got. The dunnies were delivered sparkling, but they were never cleaned while they were on site. As far as Cole was concerned, almost anywhere was better to sit and scroll social media than a shared shitter that hadn't been disinfected for weeks.

Twenty minutes later and Jono emerged. Cole was beyond frustrated, angry that he was taking advantage of his seniority. Jono was working the apprentices while he slacked off. Cole needed to reallocate him to another site where there was a team that would push him. Except the very reason why Jono was working alone with the apprentices was that most of their other crews wouldn't have him on their site.

Cole cracked his neck, squeezing his shoulder muscles to loosen the knots there. But it was no use. This was why he should never have accepted the supervisor's job. He hated all the peopling.

Cole rushed through his update, ordering the boys not to knock off without having finished erecting the last remaining walls downstairs. "Call me once you're done. I need to report back that these walls are up. When the trusses get here tomorrow, we need to start getting them up. I'll be here first thing so make sure you're on site by 6:30 a.m. This frame was supposed to have been done two weeks ago."

"The deadlines are ridiculous," Jono answered with a sneer.

Cole's temper exploded and he opened his mouth before he could stop himself. "The deadlines are fine. If you didn't spend so much time sitting on your arse jacking off in the shitter you wouldn't have a problem."

"I'm stuck here with two apprentices who don't know shit," Jono shouted back.

"Show me a single wall that you've put up," he growled. "Oh, wait, there was one." Cole pointed to the back of the house to the area overlooking the massive entertaining patio. The wall—if you could call it that—was one big open space that a set of stacked sliding doors would fit into. The doors ran almost the full length of the opening so the wall itself was less than twenty lengths of timber with fewer than five cuts involved. He raised his index finger. "This whole house and you've put one wall up. The problem isn't them. It's you. Yeah, they fuck up, but they're apprentices. They're still learning. You just fuck around all day. Clean your shit up, Jono. It won't fly with me."

Cole stormed away, slamming the door to his ute closed and shutting him in the stifling heat of the cab. He groaned and leaned his head back against the rest. Fuck, he hated this job. He still had hours left of his day too. The other site was only fifteen k's away, but it would take him over an hour to get there with the car-park-like traffic on the freeway. Then when he got there, he had to figure out a way to slash how long it would take to finish the build.

The theft of the doors had put them weeks behind their already blown-out schedule. The company was paying the owners' rent as a penalty and shit had been hitting the fan for weeks. As lead chippie for the site, it was on Cole's back to fix.

His phone rang just as he stepped through the safety fencing erected around the massive site, Ava's name lighting up the screen. "Hey, gorgeous. How's your day been?"

"Interesting? I don't know how to describe it to be honest."

He could hear the disappointment and frustration in her voice, and Cole hated that he might have been right. He wanted nothing more than for her to find her dream job with this company, but it was only the first day. She'd likely sat in induction meetings for most of it and was bored shitless, so there was still hope.

"But that's actually not why I was calling. Have you heard from Bryce?"

"I got a text earlier after I'd left a message to say that his meeting had turned into a few more than he'd expected. Said he'd see us tonight." Cole didn't like not knowing but there was nothing he could do except wait.

"I'm a bit worried to be honest."

Cole refused to believe that Bryce hadn't managed to secure the extension on his contract. He shone every time he stepped on the field. Cole was in awe when he'd watched Bryce play in a practice match with the team. "He'll be right," Cole reassured her. "Bryce is bloody good. The team are blind if they can't see that."

"You're right. I just can't stop thinking about how he's going." There was noise in the background, talking and shuffling, and Ava spoke again, adding, "Sorry, hon. I have to go. See you at your place after work?"

"Can't wait." Cole hung up and trudged up the unmade driveway to check over the team's progress for the day and meet with the owners and site supervisor. He could handle working with the apprentices when they had their brains switched on. Picking up basic things like forgetting to measure where a wall should be placed was annoying, but he could deal. It was the other guys—the Jonos of their crew who didn't care about deadlines, or even much about the quality of their work, and the site supervisors who promised the world to owners—that drove him insane.

Cole rubbed his forehead before pressing his thumb and forefinger to the bridge of his nose. He already had a headache, and the worst of his meetings were yet to come.

Three hours later and Cole was finally pushing through his front door. A shower, cold drink, and pizza were calling his name, but first he needed to know how Bryce and Ava had gone. Neither had left his head for more than a few moments throughout the whole day. He'd spaced out time and again when he should have been concentrating on work and talking down the irate owners. They'd had no concept of the lead times involved with manufacturing products. They'd waited months for the original doors to be crafted and were demanding replacements by the end of the week. He'd had a go at them, snapping that it wasn't possible when they wouldn't listen to reason. He'd deserved the earful the site supervisor gave him, but instead of pushing him to do better, it only served to demotivate him.

He called Bryce, but it went straight to message bank. Ava was next, but the same thing happened. He sighed unhappily and stripped. He took a swig of his ice-cold beer and stepped into the shower.

The warm water sluicing over his tired muscles was exactly what he'd needed. Cole rested his free hand on the cold tiles and hung his head low, letting the shampoo wash from his hair before he scrubbed himself down. The high-pitched ring from the building's front door sounded just as he turned off the water. With only his towel around his waist and water dripping off him, he dashed across the apartment and buzzed in Bryce, his heart doing a fast thump-thump at the knowledge he'd see at least one of the two people who could always brighten his day.

"Come on up, the door's open," he said into the intercom before unlocking the front door. He hadn't even managed it halfway back to the bathroom to dry himself off when the ring sounded again. This time it was Ava, and the smile that split his lips was absurd. Cole huffed out a laugh at his ridiculousness. He was a sappy fool, excited beyond measure at seeing them.

While he was waiting for them to come up, he dried the floor with his towel, dumped it in the hamper, and grabbed a fresh one to dry off with. He swirled mouthwash around, spat it out, and threw on some deodorant. "In here," he called when he heard the front door shut.

A moment later, Bryce's strong arms wrapped around his waist. Cole melted into his touch, letting his eyes drift closed as Bryce nuzzled his nose against the wet hair at Cole's temple. It sent a shiver through him, and he felt Bryce's lips tilt up against his skin in a smile. When his man licked a drop of water sliding down his cheek, Cole moaned, his cock thickening.

"Hey, you," Bryce rumbled, the noise sending another shiver of desire straight to Cole's cock.

He opened his eyes, staring at their reflection. Cole looked wanton, his lips parted and his pupils blown. Bryce's golden skin and hair against Cole's darker complexion stood out in stark relief, but it was Bryce's smile that caught his attention and kept it.

Pure joy radiated from his man and Cole's heart swooped like a flock of birds in full flight.

He turned in Bryce's embrace, wrapping his arms around his man's shoulders and asked, "You got it?" His voice was high with excitement, and Bryce's ecstatic grin ratcheted up even further in response. Cole's heartbeat quickened in his veins.

"No, but I do have news. I want to tell you and Ava together." He stepped back, eyeing the bulge underneath Cole's towel while Cole drooled over him. He'd rolled the sleeves of his white dress shirt up, showing off thick forearms with a dusting of blond hair and veins that snaked their way up his arms. His top two buttons were undone, revealing the hint of just how perfectly rounded his pecs were. The grey tie hanging untied around his neck was perfect to grab him with and haul him close, and his navy blue slim-line pants moulded to his muscular thighs and calves.

Cole couldn't wait to wrap his legs around those wide hips.

Bryce's voice was a husky rasp when he added, "Don't get dressed. Better yet, lose this altogether." The front door closed again, and Bryce hooked a finger onto Cole's towel, backing out the door and taking it with him. "Oops." He shrugged and Cole snorted out a laugh.

He followed him out a moment later, watching as Ava buried her face in Bryce's chest, sighing when his arms closed around her. He couldn't hear what Bryce was whispering but Ava's headshake and the tension she was carrying in her shoulders were like an anvil to his gut.

Cole's buoyant mood from a moment ago slipped and he joined his guy in holding their girl tight.

Ava finally pulled back and plastered on a smile that didn't come close to reaching her eyes. "It'll be okay. How did you go? I've been waiting on tenterhooks all day."

"Let's sit down." Bryce motioned to the couch, and Ava took Cole's hand. It was cool and curled around his, gripping him tightly as if she needed his strength. He closed his other hand over hers too, and squeezed back, reassuring her without words that he was there.

"You a nudist now?" she asked with a tilt of her head and a ghost of a smile lifting her lips. She looked exhausted, as if she was carrying the weight of the world on her shoulders. Dark marks under her eyes marred her smooth complexion, and her face was paler than normal too. "Or are you looking to make my night a whole lot better than my day was?"

"Bryce stole my towel, but yeah, let's go with option two." Cole winked and led her to the couch, propping himself up on the armrest and patting the spot in front of him while Bryce sat sideways on the sofa.

Ava curled into Cole, resting her head on his chest so they could both see Bryce. Cole played with her hair, scratching her scalp and massaging her shoulders to release the knots of tightly wound tension there. No wonder she looked terrible—she must have been sporting one hell of a headache if the tightness was anything to go by.

"Spill," Ava ordered, and Bryce chuckled, picking up a thick white envelope off the coffee table.

Bryce didn't hesitate, slipping out a black, white and electric blue folder with the team's logo taking up most of the space on the front. "So, the team didn't want to talk about extending my reserve contract for another year—"

"What? How could they reject you?" Cole asked, disbelief and instant outrage warring for supremacy.

Bryce held up his hand and Cole snapped his mouth shut, biting back a tirade. What the hell? Bryce deserved that contract more than anyone. He couldn't believe they'd knocked him back. He must be crushed. Why was he smiling? He'd worked his butt off for this. What did it mean going forward? Could he swap reserve teams? Each of the professional teams in Sydney had one, so there were plenty to choose from, but if the Thunder had rejected him, did that mean he'd find it difficult to get into another? But if that were so, why was Bryce smiling?

"In fact, that wasn't even discussed."

Huh? How could he know that they'd rejected him if they didn't even talk about it? Cole tilted his head, his brows furrowed, and lips turned down as he tried to work out what Bryce was talking about.

Bryce gave them a small smile and opened the folder. "They offered me a spot with the Lightning. I'll be playing professionally this season."

Ava gasped and launched herself at Bryce, squealing as she peppered his face in kisses. Cole stared at him open-mouthed. He blinked and stood, his legs unsteadily holding him up as he stumbled over to the coffee table in front of Bryce before his legs gave out.

Taking Bryce's hand in his, Cole realized he was shaking. He laughed, the sound unsteady. "You're serious."

Bryce nodded, colour flaring in his cheeks. "I'm going pro, baby," he shouted, lifting his fists in the air.

Cole crash-tackled him, squashing Ava and taking his man's lips in a fierce kiss. Spearing his tongue into Bryce's mouth, he swallowed Bryce's moan and kissed him deeper. It was only when the room spun and his lungs were screaming for air that he pulled back and sucked in a breath, nipping and licking a line down Bryce's throat as Ava claimed his lips.

Cole's heart beat hard, jubilation rushing through him. It was heady. Pride and excitement and a fierce need to show Bryce, and Ava, just how much he lov— Woah. No, he wasn't doing that. He pushed down the fear, breathed through it. He loved them, and they cared about him too.

Cole straddled Bryce's leg, one hand cupping his nape and the other on Ava's back.

"There's more," Bryce said with a moan as Ava moved to the other side of his throat. Their hands met at the junction of Bryce's thick thighs, cupping the hardening length there. He lifted his hips chasing their touch as Cole pulled back and Ava shifted so she was no longer straddling him either. He opened the folder that had fallen to their side and flipped over a few pages before showing them a number. A very large number with a dollar sign in front of it and plenty of zeroes behind.

Shock held Cole immobile. He blinked, taking in the number again. Holy hell, that was a nice salary for Bryce to be getting.

"Bryce, oh my god, this is fantastic. Congratulations," Ava breathed.

"Your salary is… fucking hell." Cole shook his head, still gobsmacked at the number.

Bryce huffed out a laugh. "That's not my salary. That's my signing bonus. This is my salary." He flipped over the page and Cole's eyes nearly fell out of his head. On top of the signing fee, Bryce was going to be earning over a hundred grand a year, and there was a whole list of other bonuses that would increase his base pay well beyond that.

"Holy shit."

"Yeah, that's what I said." Bryce shook his head slowly and closed his eyes, chuckling again. "I'm still spinning. I can't believe it's happening, and those numbers... I had no idea what to do with that kind of money. But then I did."

"What are you gonna do?" Ava asked, bouncing in anticipation.

"I'm using it to fund our business."

Cole's head snapped up and Ava stilled, her smile slipping.

"Our business?" Cole asked dubiously, at the same time as Ava questioned, "What business?"

"Okay, so um... hear me out, yeah?" He rubbed his hand over the blond five o'clock shadow growing on his chin.

Cole reached for him, stilling his movements and Bryce flushed, colour rising in his cheeks as he shot Cole a shy grin. He just about melted into a puddle, his heart slamming against his ribs at the sight of Bryce's smile.

"Tell us," Cole encouraged, his voice cracking.

Bryce fanned his face and started unbuttoning his shirt, shrugging it off when it was undone, the pretty pink flush extending down to his chest. "I was doing my degree hoping it'd be my backup career if I didn't get a professional contract. If I did get one, I was planning on flipping houses after I retired. But then I realized I don't need to wait."

Bryce licked his lips and Cole's gut twisted. How could he be jealous of Bryce's tongue getting to touch those pouty lips? He flicked his gaze to Ava and knew he wasn't being ridiculous. Want flared in her eyes, her breath quickening as she watched him bite down. Cole wanted both of them with a fierceness that was terrifying.

"I'll get the bonus as soon as I sign on the dotted line. That gives me enough for a deposit and renovations on what would probably be a half-decent first home."

Ava nodded and gave him an encouraging smile.

Bryce pressed his lips in a flat line before continuing slowly, "It wasn't until I met the two of you that I realized I'll never be able to do it, though. I can't do the actual work. I'm not a tradie. I can't build things, and I'm not a project manager either. I can't line everything up so I can flip it quickly. I'm good at design elements. Fabric and colours, textures that sort of thing."

"I can help you with project managing it, Bryce."

"And I can do whatever work you wanted to get it looking how you want it," Cole offered.

"Good, because I can't flip houses by myself. It won't work. I need people I can trust who I want to build a business and a life with for the long term." He went quiet, his gaze bouncing between Cole and Ava. Bryce worried his thumbnail with his teeth and waited, but Cole didn't know what to think. He was stuck. Completely lost for words. The professional contract had flawed him. Bryce's signing bonus exploding his mind.

This? This was life changing.

"Say something," Bryce begged in a whisper.

"You want to buy a house and renovate it? With us?" Ava asked slowly, her brows furrowed as if she was confused.

Bryce nodded and Cole opened his mouth to clarify but wasn't actually sure what Bryce meant. He was speaking as if it was more than just his house.

"Yeah, but I don't want to hire you."

Cole responded with a nod and a smile. He wouldn't expect anything different. There was no way he would let Bryce pay him to do work on his house.

Bryce continued, adding, "I don't want to be your boss. I want to work as equal partners."

Wait, what?

"I'll supply the initial cash investment. You supply the knowhow." He lifted Ava's hand to his lips, pressed a lingering kiss there, and turned to Cole. "And you supply the manpower. We'll be a triple threat."

"Bryce, I…" Ava hesitated, then looked to Cole, worrying her lip and giving him a minute shrug and shake of her head.

Cole asked, "What are you suggesting, Bryce? Spell it out for us."

He looked between them, his eyes widening, clueing in on their confusion. "A business between the three of us. Equal partners. We decide unanimously on what projects we do. I'll tell you what look we should go for and you two tell me if it's possible. Then, Ava, you project manage it. Cole, you could work on site back on the tools, creating the looks we decide on. No supervision of idiots, no stressing about owners who don't understand the process. Equal split of the profits."

Cole swallowed. It sounded too good to be true. He wished every day that he could turn back time and undo his decision to take the promotion. He wanted the days of creating things without all the angst and frustration of supervising people that he didn't even enjoy working with. Going into business with Ava and Bryce could be amazing. It could also backfire spectacularly. They hadn't been together long, barely any time at all. What if they got sick of him?

A cold dread settled in his stomach, and he couldn't help voice the fears as they piled on top of him. "What if you want out? What if we don't work? If we break up? You'll want to leave sooner or later. I don't want to tie you down."

Bryce's face fell. "I won't, Cole. I've never been more certain of anything than I am of you and Ava. Not even playing." He took Cole's trembling hand in his and brushed his thumbs over Cole's rough knuckles. "Hey," Bryce murmured, and Cole lifted his chin.

He waited for Cole to meet his stare, but it took him far longer than he was proud of to work up the courage to meet Bryce's gaze. The sincerity Bryce was staring at him with undid him. He gripped Bryce's hand harder, needing every bit of his strength he was prepared to impart.

With his free hand, Bryce cupped his face, drawing him closer until their lips hovered a hair's breadth apart. Cole forced his eyes to stay open, not wanting to miss a moment between them. "I love you, Cole. I'm not walking away, and I'm absolutely not gonna push you away." Bryce's smile was small but earnest.

Cole opened his mouth to respond, but once again he was speechless. It was as if he'd been caught up in a tornado, lifting him and spinning him around and around until he didn't know which way was up. But right there in the centre of it all, in the eye of the storm waiting for him to come down were Bryce and Ava.

Bryce turned away, but his hand tightened on Cole's, keeping him close. Bryce left him with no doubt that he was still right there, still in this conversation as much as Cole was.

When Bryce turned his attention to Ava, his smile was warm and filled with adoration. "I love you too, Ava." Bryce laughed, his face lighting up with joy. "I'm in love with both of you and I want it all. Everything. I wanna live, work, and play together."

She leaned in and pressed her lips to Bryce's, lingering there in a sweet, chaste kiss. "I love you too. Both of you."

Cole shook his head, his chest tight and his lungs seizing. He stood and turned away, giving them his back. He stumbled over to the window, needing air.

Crossing his arms across his chest, he hid from them. He was exposed in more ways than one. Hearing their words rubbed him raw, like rough sandpaper over soft timber.

He sucked in a breath, but no air entered his lungs. His vision spotted, his knees nearly buckling under him.

Reaching out, he grasped the windowsill, trying to halt his slide to the floor.

Cole stared unseeingly out the window. What was happening? Why now? Why this?

He needed…. He didn't know what.

Cole choked out a sob, when a warm hand landed on the small of his back, rubbing gentle circles. Bryce had startled him. His man leaned in close and blanketed Cole with his strength. A soft kiss was pressed to his shoulder and Ava's long hair brushed against his arm as she leaned her head against him.

"I don't expect you to say anything," Bryce reassured him. "I get it if you don't feel the same."

Cole's chest clenched and the burning behind his eyes increased. He blinked, but it did nothing. His throat was closed, a boulder sitting there, stopping him from swallowing.

Ava whispered, "Do you know why I want to flip houses, Cole? I want to mend something that was broken. We can give it a new life and fill it with love. I want it to give it a family. I want it to shine, because even though it might not know how beautiful it is, it really is." She gripped his forearm.

Cole's heart slammed against his ribs, the breath squeezing out of his lungs. He gasped in a shuddery breath and another sob broke free. Their arms wound around his waist and shoulders, and he buried his face in Bryce's neck. Tears tracked down his cheeks, soaking Bryce's skin, but his man never let go. Neither did Ava. She pressed herself against his back and held tightly, kissing his shoulder.

"We want you, Cole. We always will. You're an incredible man. You're so worthy of love," Ava whispered. He couldn't help the tears that fell when he cried harder. But Ava and Bryce still didn't let go. If anything, they held tighter.

"I'll do whatever it takes to make you happy," Bryce promised. "Both of you."

"What if you change your minds?" Cole asked, his voice small. "I can't lose you."

Bryce tightened his hold around Cole's shoulder and threaded his fingers into Cole's hair, kissing his forehead. "You won't be alone again, Cole. I promise you. I'm all in."

"Me too."

Cole sucked in a slow breath and wound his arm around Bryce's waist. His warmth gave him the strength to reach for Ava. He held them close. Cole was scared stupid. But in their arms, he found his courage.

Bryce and Ava wanted him. He'd walked away from them when they told him they loved him. Instead of getting angry or hurt, they were comforting him. But that was what you did when you loved someone. You made sure they were okay. You didn't toss them aside. You didn't impose conditions on your love. You kept your promises, and you were all in. Just like he'd asked them to move in with him, they wanted to work together too.

Light dawned on him. The crushing weight in his chest loosened and warmth surrounded him. They wanted it all, and he... he wanted it too. Logically, he knew that there was always the possibility that things might go south. Nothing was guaranteed. But his life hadn't been the same since Ava and Bryce crashed into his world. They'd turned everything upside down, lighting him up with their warmth.

They were sunshine and fire. They were love.

Just like going with them the first time was the right move, Cole knew in his gut that this was the right move too.

He pressed a kiss to Ava's temple and slipped his hand under Bryce's shirt, needing to feel his smooth skin under his palm. Ava and Cole had held him close and shown him day after day that he mattered to them. They hadn't been together for long—barely even two months, but he knew. In his gut and in his heart, he knew. They were the ones for him.

They were his home.

He pulled back and looked at them, both their eyes red and glassy with emotion. Bryce's beautiful face, one that was usually filled with smiles and happiness, was drawn tight, and Ava's was filled with devastation.

Cole wrapped his hand around their napes and drew their foreheads together. He closed his eyes and breathed them in, steadying his racing heart and shaking hands. In their arms, Cole finally found the courage to let them in. To smash those walls down and give himself permission to love again. He took a deep breath and soaked in their strength and support. "Me three," he whispered.

The fear that had held him in its grasp didn't magically disappear after saying he was in. He thought he'd exorcized the ghosts of his past. His parents weren't supposed to hold any sway over him anymore, but they apparently did. Ava and Bryce's reactions at least went a long way in helping to shake loose his insecurities. It was as if the admission and permission he'd given himself to fall for them had taken the weight off his soul. It was as if he'd reclaimed his heart from the rubble.

Bryce laughed, the sound so full of joy that he couldn't help his own smile, and Ava squeezed him, pulling his face down to hers. Her lips pressed against his and her tongue demanded entry. He didn't hesitate, diving into her and devouring her moans until she was breathless and he was hard.

FIFTEEN

Bryce

A FEW MONTHS LATER

Bryce pulled his truck up at their worksite. He loved that—their site. It was obviously theirs too. Ava had invested in canvas signs that hung on the safety fences surrounding the block announcing that it was "Another build by Triple Threat Enterprises." He grinned, getting a kick out of it. He'd never imagined that his pitch would be the basis for their name.

He'd wanted to show them that they made the perfect team. He had no idea how his brain had conjured up those words at that very moment, but it had stuck. The name was the easiest part of their business to set up—it was their very first unanimous decision.

He slipped through the fence and secured the padlock in place. Bryce was tired and achy from practice, but he was pumped too. It was Cole's birthday, and he and Ava had spent the day together while Bryce was at training, and Bryce knew that not much work had been done. It was his time to spoil his beau now, and he had every intention of making his man come apart again.

"Cole," he called, closing the front door behind him. There was a fresh coat of paint on the walls that completely changed the mishmash of colours it had been when they'd first seen this house. This flip was a simple one—on the inside Cole had demolished a couple of walls to open up the living spaces, they'd updated the bathrooms and laundry, changed the kitchen bench, repainted, and replaced the window coverings. The outside was a matter of updating the gardens, adding a few more plants in to replace the dead ones, and trimming back a few overgrown trees.

"In here," he responded, and Bryce paused to light the candle on the cupcake he'd bought before following the sound of his voice.

He took a moment to admire his man. Dressed in khaki work shorts, tan steel-capped boots, and a high-vis polo shirt, Cole was hotness personified. Bryce wanted to drool. But it was the tool belt that did it for him. Ava had confided how she'd imagined what Cole would look like in just his belt and boots. Ever since their conversation, he'd been like one of Pavlov's dogs. Cole pulled out the belt and Bryce drooled. Watching him in action up a step ladder adjusting the hinge on a cupboard door was a fantasy he didn't even realize he had.

"Happy birthday to you," Bryce sang when Cole turned and spied him staring. His grin turned sappy as Bryce kept singing. He probably looked absurd in a party hat, wrapped in streamers and carrying the cupcake, but getting a smile like that out of Cole was worth it every time.

"You're ridiculous, you know that?" Cole said, sauntering over to him and blowing out the candle. He didn't wait for Bryce to put it down, instead wrapping his arms around Bryce's shoulders. His belly flip-flopped. The smile that Cole gifted him with was radiant. It shone from within, something that he'd seen more and more of in the last few months. "But you brought me cake, so you can keep being as ridiculous as you like."

"Happy birthday, babe," Bryce murmured against his lips before stealing a kiss. His soft stubble brushed Bryce's lips as Cole kissed a line down his throat, and Bryce shivered, imagining it between his legs. But it wasn't about him today.

"Nrgh," Cole half mumbled, half whimpered as Bryce slid his free hand up under his shirt and flicked his nipple.

"This tool belt gets me every time," Bryce murmured, fingering the clip and moving back to Cole's mouth. He tossed the cupcake on the kitchen bench, uncaring whether it landed the right way up, and threaded his fingers into Cole's hair, holding him in place while he devoured him.

Cole rocked into him, grinding his hard length against the leg Bryce had pressed between his, kicking Bryce into action. He danced Cole's shirt up his body and tossed it aside. Falling to his knees, he licked and nipped at every inch of Cole's chest and abs on his way down. And damn those abs. Tight and dusted with a dark treasure trail and decorated with tattoos, Bryce couldn't help follow the directions to the pot of gold—or whatever the metaphor was. He couldn't think straight. His brains were scrambled by his hot-as-hell lover's hands in his hair, tugging at the overgrown length, while he rubbed his cock against Bryce's face all but begging for friction.

Bryce was happy to oblige.

He flicked open the button on Cole's cargo pants and lowered the zip, slowly revealing a pair of tight black boxer briefs trapping Cole's thick length. He mouthed the head, being rewarded with a taste of pre-cum, and breathed his man in.

"Please," Cole begged, and Bryce drew down his shorts and underwear in one go, baring his man to him.

He'd never get sick of the sight before him—Cole wanton and desperate. His dark cock was throbbing, the veins along its length standing out in stark relief to the smooth shaft. The blush-pink head was decorated with a drop of pre-cum as another slid down his length. His man was desperate and needy, even after having come multiple times that day already.

Bryce loved it.

He buried his nose in the thatch of dark, trimmed hair at the base of his cock and breathed his subtle spicey musk in, nudging Cole's balls with his nose before licking them.

Cole cried out and Bryce licked up his shaft, capturing his crown between his lips. Sucking deeply on the downstroke, Bryce tongued his cock, slowly releasing the suction as he pulled off. Over and over he did it until Cole was riding the edge of an orgasm, leaking onto Bryce's tongue. He loved his taste, couldn't get enough of it, but that wasn't how Cole was coming this afternoon. No, Bryce had plans on just how he wanted to make his man scream.

He spun Cole around, guiding his hands to the kitchen bench. "Lean over and hold tight," he instructed, his voice a low rasp. Bryce's cock was steely and seeing that perfect arse framed by the tool belt hanging down his legs, Bryce thanked his lucky stars for tradies.

Smoothing his hands up Cole's lean legs, the dark hairs tickled his palms and then his lips as he trailed them along the same path, circling ever closer to his tight hole. Bryce licked and nipped at Cole's skin, tasting the faint musk of sex on his tongue. Bryce sucked a mark onto Cole's skin right at the crease where his cheek met thigh and he moaned.

Cole gasped pushing his butt closer to Bryce's wondering fingers. He brushed over the pucker he desperately needed to be inside of, and Cole clenched, a shiver passing through him.

Bryce's dark chuckle was strained, his fingers shaking as he reached for the travel lube he'd stuffed in his wallet. He coated his fingers and pressed in achingly slowly, drawing out Cole's moan as he did. Tight heat surrounded his fingers and Cole's cry bounced around the room at the same time as Bryce gasped. God damn, he was on the edge already and he hadn't even managed to get a second finger in yet.

Cole canted his arse, begging for more and Bryce dipped a second finger in, breaching his tight ring and stretching him for his cock. Every time he brushed the spongey pad of Cole's prostate, his man shuddered, crying out. Pre-cum leaked from his cock like a dripping tap and his balls were drawn up tight. His pleas and moans were incoherent, but his body spoke loud and clear. He was riding the edge on the brink of an orgasm that would turn into an out-of-body experience for his man.

When he begged Bryce to get a move on, he knew he was almost at the point of no return. Cole wasn't the only one. Bryce hadn't touched his cock, but watching Cole's reactions, seeing how he responded to every one of Bryce's touches had him towing the line too.

Slipping his fingers free, he nearly swallowed his tongue as Cole's hole stayed partially open. Fuck me. It was the hottest thing he'd ever seen. Bryce was on his feet in a split second and clumsily pushing his track pants over his hips as he slicked himself up with another sachet of lube.

He needed to be close to his man. To be connected with him from top to toe.

Blanketing Cole's body with his own, Bryce pressed a line of kisses along his shoulders as he lined himself up and slowly pushed inside. The resistance gave way and with just the head of his cock in nirvana, Bryce paused, letting Cole get used to the intrusion. He wasn't small, and although he'd prepared Cole thoroughly, he didn't want there to even be the slightest bite of pain for his man.

Cole wound his fingers back in Bryce's too long hair and arched into his touch, crying out as he shifted, inching forward into his channel. Bryce couldn't pull him close enough. He couldn't get enough of him.

Hands and lips trailing along every centimetre of skin he could reach, Bryce held one of the loves of his life close and made love to him. With slow, deep thrusts, he swallowed Cole's cries with every kiss. With every swivel of his hips, they neared the precipice. With every caress of their tongues, he climbed higher.

Cole trembled in his arms, but his sweat-soaked skin flushed hot. Bryce nuzzled the spot below his ear, the one that always made Cole shiver, and he sucked on his lobe. Cole moaned long and low, his hips shifting forward before driving back again, meeting Bryce thrust for thrust as he instinctively searched for friction on his dick.

Bryce was close, the tingling at the base of his spine radiating outward in waves. His balls drew tight and his cock hardened even more. He needed Cole right there with him. He wanted his man to come from his dick buried deep in him. Could he do it? Could he make Cole come without touching his cock? He knew Cole was almost there too, but with every tunnel forward into his tight heat, the chances Bryce could hold out lessened.

Desperation overtaking him, Bryce closed his fist over Cole's throbbing length and stroked him. Up and down once, then twice, and Cole shouted out, his body locking tight as he erupted, shooting pulse after pulse of his seed against the kitchen cabinets. His channel clenched and released in time with each spurt and any hope that Bryce could hold out shattered. He buried himself deep, pressing his hips against Cole's and hurtled off the edge, floating in bliss as he emptied his load into Cole's channel.

Choirs could have been singing and fireworks going off in the same room, but all Bryce could concentrate on was Cole. The musky scent of their sex in the air, the feel of his warm skin pressed up against Bryce. The weight of his body as he went boneless in his arms and the noises he made when he was still flying high from his drawn-out orgasm. Bryce had edged him over and over and Cole was revelling in the payoff.

Breathing hard, he held Cole to him, staying wrapped in each other's arms with their sweaty skin cooling in the late afternoon autumn chill. Bryce never wanted to leave this spot. Still buried deep but sated, he could happily stay in this very position until he could get it up again and go for round two.

When Cole came back to himself, he nuzzled Bryce's cheek, snuggling into him.

"Let's get you cleaned up," Bryce murmured as his cock slipped free of Cole's depths.

"Wait." He gripped Bryce's forearm, holding him firm. Bryce tightened his grip on his man and Cole relaxed into him once more, melting against his chest. He loved it when he could wrap Cole and Ava up in his arms and seemingly protect them from the world. "I…" Cole blew out a breath and pressed a soft kiss to Bryce's lips. "I love you."

Shock held him momentarily immobile. He knew Cole loved him. He showed him in everything he did, from the simple things like a kiss or a touch, all the way to making his and Ava's visions for their project come to life. He cooked their favourite foods and worshipped their bodies like he was a devout disciple at the altar. But he'd never said it back to them.

Neither Bryce nor Ava had pushed him. Just because they'd been ready to say it, it didn't mean Cole was. But to hear Cole tell him he loved him was, short of Ava telling him she loved him, the single greatest thing he'd ever heard.

When his brain kicked in, Bryce spun Cole in his arms and wrapped him up tight. Jubilation filled him, and Bryce wanted to shout from the rooftops that he was the luckiest bloke on the planet. He lifted Cole off his feet, twirling them around as he whooped. Laughter bounced off the walls of the empty house, the sound hearty and joyful. "I love you too." Smiling, Bryce kissed him, their lips melding and their tongues caressing as he worshipped Cole all over again.

Cole laughed as he pulled away, the sound a melody to Bryce's ears as he kissed a line down his man's throat. "How the fuck did I get so lucky?" he asked.

"I ask myself the same question every day," Bryce responded, running his lips over Cole's stubble. He pressed their foreheads together, letting his eyes flutter closed as he basked in the words his lover had spoken.

"Let's go home," Cole suggested. "I want to tell our girl I love her too."

"Yeah?" Bryce's smile made his cheeks hurt. He couldn't wait to see Ava's reaction.

Colour rose up Cole's throat, his smile turning shy. He nodded. "Yeah. I told her this morning, but I wanna tell her again."

SIXTEEN

Ava

They'd been lucky with their first couple of flips. Six months into their business and they were killing it. Their third house had just been listed with an agent and the photographer was swinging by the next day once Bryce had touched up their staging. He was flying in with the team later that night after their afternoon match on the Gold Coast wrapped up.

Ava wished she could have been there, but he'd insisted she stay and sort out the listing with the real estate agent. The market was turning and all three of them were nervous. Offloading this house was critical.

"A little to the right," Ava suggested. Cole tossed a smirk over his shoulder and lined up the level he was using to make sure the paintings were hung straight. The bubble lined up perfectly and Ava stuck out her tongue. "Fine, Mr Know-it-all. Don't change it."

Cole placed the level on the buffet and playfully narrowed his eyes. Ava squealed and threw the white cushion at his head before taking off and putting the kitchen island bench between them. Cole laughed and tossed the cushion carelessly on the couch before chasing her. She laugh-squealed again and dashed around the table, holding onto the chairback as if it were a shield. She'd use it against him too. Although truth be told, she'd never fight to stay away from either Cole or Bryce. They were her whole heart and these last few months working together had been a dream come true. She worked hard—longer hours than she'd ever worked before, but that was because she took ownership of every project. They were her babies. She wanted the best properties to create homes in and so far, they'd been spot on. Triple Threat was thriving. Three properties down and two more already on the books. One was awaiting approval for the extension they planned on adding and the other had already been demoed, ready for the new kitchens and bathrooms.

Cole faked a move left and chased right. Ava fell for his bluff, moving to the right. He laughed and lunged at her as she swore, wrapping her in a bear hug as she playfully fought to break free. Cole just dipped her back and Ava squeaked, gripping onto him to stop herself falling. He shook his head and sucked on her bottom lip until she moaned and hooked her leg over his calf, trying to bring them closer.

"I'll never let you fall," Cole murmured before kissing her again.

"Too late," she teased before licking his ear and scrambling out of his hold as soon as he reached up to wipe it off.

"You little shit." He laughed, the light in his eyes making her heart sing. He was still grumpy, and his resting face always had a frown, but nowadays, it was one of concentration rather than annoyance. He loved being back on the tools. He loved creating and learning new things and finding ways to build Bryce's visions. It was a privilege to be able to give that to him.

But the biggest change in Cole had occurred a few months earlier. When he'd finally allowed himself to tell them he loved them, it was as if he'd become a different person. Lighter, happier, and more open with his affections. It sucked that they were stuck showing that affection behind closed doors. It killed her not being able to demonstrate to him the same love in public she could give to Bryce, but he hadn't budged on his insistence that she was Bryce's girlfriend and he was their flatmate.

Ava darted around the couch. She thought she'd dodged him, but Cole didn't even slow down, vaulting over it like he was a kangaroo. Open-mouthed, Ava hesitated for a fraction of a second, but it was all he needed. He grabbed her in a headlock and ruffled her hair. Ava fought dirty, grabbing a handful of that luscious butt with one hand and the other sliding her hand along the front of his cargo pants. It did the trick, halting Cole's movements as he rolled his hips into her hand.

"You win," he grunted, sliding his arms down so they were around her waist. "But that's cheating."

She rubbed him, squeezing his cock and watching raptly as his gaze glassed over and he tilted his head back. "All's fair in love and war." She leaned in, nuzzling his throat before pressing a soft kiss there. "You noogied me. That wasn't very nice."

He stilled her hand with a squeeze and Ava pressed the heel of her palm harder against his length. He gasped and shuddered, thrusting into her touch. "I'll make it up to you."

"Good." Ava pulled back, wiggling out of his arms and winked.

"Jesus, woman, you're a tease today," he said with a pout.

"But you love me." She grinned and batted her eyelids innocently before Cole reached out, pulling her into his arms again.

He held her tight and tilted her chin up to meet his gaze. "I do." Their kiss was slow and deep, a complete contrast to the taunting she'd tortured him with a moment earlier. Their lips melded together. Tongues tangling, Ava pressed into him, loving being wrapped up in Cole's arms.

The knock at the door startled her. She pulled away reluctantly, not wanting to leave his arms to answer it.

A man in a suit that looked like it cost more than the deposit on this house was waiting for her. He shamelessly peered over her shoulder as she opened the door before ducking his head and peering at the gleaming crystal chandelier. It was a rescue from before the renovations had begun, and she'd painstakingly polished it to perfection.

"Afternoon," Ava greeted with a polite smile.

"Hello." He nodded, the complete lack of smile in response unnerving. "Maxwell Denyer." Ava held out her hand to shake and he flicked his eyes down before continuing, "Attorney for the Lightning. Bryce Flaharty is involved with your company, yes?" he asked, motioning to their signage still decorating the front of the house.

Ava dropped her hand and forced another smile. She was pleased that the team's solicitor had recognized their company name and was supportive of their guy, but this man was… intimidating as hell. "Yes, Bryce, Cole, and I are partners. This is our third renovation together." She swallowed back the desire to cut their conversation short and get back to Cole, but knew she had to play nice. "So how can I help you?"

"I'm in the market for a property." His words stopped her short. There was a potential sale here and she needed to step up the charm.

"Would you like to come in and see what we've done with the place?"

He gave her a curt nod after looking at his gold watch momentarily and Ava put on her most professional persona.

"Please, do come in."

She showed him around, pointing out the changes they'd made to the layout to open it up while keeping the original styling in the renovations. The aim had been to restore the home to its former glory, not to remove the period pieces. The furniture wasn't quite placed right yet — Bryce would primp and preen it until it was perfect—but the restoration work Cole had crafted was second to none.

White wainscoting on the walls and turned features marking informal dividers between rooms in the now open area created a timeless charm in the turn-of-the-century cottage. Dove-grey walls contrasted beautifully against the rich almost black timber floors that Cole had painstakingly sanded down and the painters had refinished. White gauzy curtains and modern furniture mixed with a few period pieces showed exactly how a family could make this space into their home and the splashes of colour in the rug and throw blanket lifted the room.

"It's close to the river too, isn't it?" Mr Denyer asked.

"It's only a five-minute walk. The parks there are beautiful—perfect for a growing family. It's the ideal location."

"Restaurants?" he asked, tapping his chin with his forefinger as he paused in the kitchen and tested the drawers. They'd installed soft closing runners and hinges on every one, so even though the kitchen looked traditional, it suited modern use.

Ava led him through to the dining area and the courtyard backyard. The original owners of the house had built a lovely garden that only required a good clean, a relatively small amount of TLC compared to the rest of the house. "The Village is near the river. It's set up on the weekend as farmers' markets and surrounding the forecourt are a few cafés and two restaurants. At night there are often performers and during summer they do art classes and yoga in the square, that sort of thing."

"The neighbours are friendly too," Cole added as she closed the door. Cole had a particular fondness for Mr

Moss, the elderly man two doors down. He'd tried to take his wheelie bin out, struggling to tilt it on the soft grass as he steadied himself with his cane. Cole had spent the day with him doing yard work, and a few days later, he and Bryce laid a concrete pad for his bins so that he didn't have to struggle. Cole had stopped by for a Friday arvo beer every week since, and Ava added a few things to their grocery list so she could make him scones and other sweets. He was like the grandfather she'd lost too young, and he was becoming a fast friend for Cole.

"Mr Denyer, this is Cole, our other partner. Cole, Mr Denyer is the Lightning's solicitor. He recognized our name on the sign as Bryce's company."

"Good to meet you, mate," Cole responded, holding out his hand.

"Hmm." Cole flicked his gaze to Ava and quirked an eyebrow as Mr Denyer continued to walk around, once again ignoring his outstretched hand. "I'm in the market for another investment property. This could work."

"It would definitely be suited as a high-end rental," Ava agreed.

"The design and location make it good for short-term rentals," he added thoughtfully.

"Like Airbnb?" Ava asked. She swallowed. It was always a possibility that buyers would put the property to that use. But with three other houses in the street already available for short-term rent, and a severe shortage of long-term rentals in the area, she wanted to hold firm to their promise. And call her sentimental, but the stately old home deserved to be loved as much as the former owners had. The neighbourhood had character and it was a close-knit community. She wanted to do her bit to keep it that way. The easiest way to do that would be for it to be used as a home not a revolving door for visitors.

"Exactly like Airbnb. I have a portfolio of holiday rentals and was looking to add to it." He fished out a card from his wallet and handed it to her. "Have your agent contact me. I'd be interested in putting in an offer."

"Ah, sure." She mustered a smile and pocketed his card. If Ava had her way, she wouldn't be selling the property to him. "Let me walk you out."

* * * * *

"Urgh, we should think about it as a business, shouldn't we. I didn't gel with him but that shouldn't matter. He's offering list price. It's a shorter settlement timeframe and he has his finance sorted. It's pretty much money in the bank for us," Ava mused, picking at her chicken salad.

Cole sipped his wine. Ava was already onto her second glass. It was crisp and delicious and from her favourite part of New Zealand's south island. "But?" he asked, already knowing where her concerns laid.

"Mr Moss, Mrs Elba, and Dr Chen all said the same thing to us—the holiday rentals weren't good for the area." She wasn't responsible and couldn't control what the eventual owner did with the property once they sold. But one of the things they'd written into their vision was that with every property they flipped, they would contribute positively to the community. They wanted to renovate houses and apartments into homes. They were about helping people in this rental and affordability crisis to get a foot into the market, not making it worse. Wasn't that exactly what they'd be doing if they sold the property, knowing it was going to lay vacant for much of the year? And on their third house? If they caved now, would their mission hold any value? What about going forward? It sounded awfully hypocritical if they only stuck with their guns when it suited them.

"How much are we in the hole for?" Bryce asked.

"Over a mil. But we won't have a problem covering that from the sale. We haven't over capitalized," Cole explained.

"I know that. I'm just trying to figure out how to calculate what it costs us per day to hold the property if we turn down the sale and have to wait a month or two for another offer."

Ava waved her hand and went to her laptop sitting on the desk, crammed in the corner of their living room. She had a spreadsheet to answer precisely those kinds of questions. "That's easy." She typed a few figures in and flipped the report page around to show them. "This is how much it costs us per day to hold onto the property. Based on a conservative estimate of the sale price—what Mr Denyer is offering—we'll turn this much profit." She pointed to the cell with the second lowest figure in it. "If we sell to the other people, we'll actually get less in hand even though it's a higher offer—the settlement date is a few weeks longer, so the extra mortgage costs offset the higher price." She motioned to the amounts at the higher end. "If we can achieve something more like this, we'll be better off, but the longer we wait, the lower those figures get. We have sixty days to sign a contract and another sixty days to settle before we start losing money at the lower end of the price range."

"So we have time," Bryce mused.

"Yes, but the market is turning. It's taking longer to sell property, even with how cheap it is for the area," Ava countered.

"This price range is cheap?" Bryce shook his head. "I'll never get used to Sydney prices. Over a million bucks for a small two-bedroom house on a tiny allotment is insane. No wonder people can't afford to buy."

Ava nodded. It really was ridiculous, but that was the property market they were dealing with.

Cole stretched out, propping his feet up on the free chair at the table. "How legit is this other offer the agent is promising?"

"No idea. If the buyers have got their finance in order, we're sweet, but we won't really know that until we get the okay from them."

"So we have time and a potential other buyer. There's always the possibility we'll get more if we wait, but as long as it's not an offer at the lower end after the full one-twenty days, we'll make money. I don't see what the issue is," Bryce countered with a shrug. "The agent said these people are looking to move into the property. I say we take the risk and sell to them."

"Cole?" Ava asked.

"I'm with both of you on this. Let's do the open home tomorrow, and if we don't get anything else, we'll sell to that couple." He twirled the wine glass, the stem delicate between his thick fingers, and Ava nodded. It was the right decision to make, but there was still something bothering her.

"Why are you worried?" Bryce asked, topping up his glass of water. "Mr Denyer will understand if he doesn't get it. He's a businessperson."

Ava shook her head and lifted a shoulder in a half shrug. "I don't know. I feel like we should give him priority because he's associated with the team, but at the same time I don't think it's the right decision for us to do that. I don't even know what I'm trying to say, but I've got this niggling feeling, you know? Maybe he just threw me."

"I didn't like him," Cole agreed. "Who doesn't shake hands with people? Although, I suppose it's not surprising given the last few years."

"He shook my hand," Bryce added, his brow furrowing while he pursed his plump lips. "I think. Maybe."

Cole finished off his wine and Ava watched as his Adam's apple bobbed while he swallowed. How was that so sexy?

"Another?" He held up his glass and took Ava's when she nodded.

She sighed happily as Cole leaned down and kissed her hair and squeezed her shoulder. "Okay, I'll send the agent the instructions to go ahead with the open house. We'll see what comes of it."

"There is something else I wanted to talk to you about," Cole added. "I'm thinking we should incorporate a charitable arm into the business." Ava's interest was immediately piqued. Cole wouldn't have suggested it unless he'd been thinking about this for a while, and he usually had a plan of attack before ever mentioning an idea.

"I love it," she encouraged. "Sell me on how to make it happen. What are you thinking?"

"Well, we join most of the Facebook groups for the suburbs we're renovating in to get a feel for the community. I've seen posts recently from support workers and teachers in the area, and a couple of single parents who were struggling, asking for help. The basics—nappies, food, schoolbooks, that sort of thing. People are doing it tough."

Bryce nodded and reached for his hand as Cole fiddled with his glass. He was nervous, and she loved that Bryce picked up on it and tried to soothe him. Ava scooted her chair around and rested her head on his shoulder, cuddling into his arm and tried to do the same.

"We're so lucky, and Bryce, I know it's because of you and all your hard work not luck, but we're sitting here talking about how much we can make on the sale of our third house. I know the market is changing and you're worried, Ava." He leaned into her, bending down to kiss her hair.

She smiled. Knowing he understood her concerns was one thing, but still wanting to help others took her already high respect for him up to a whole other level.

"But we've pulled this business together in only a few months and I know we can do more. People are having to choose between paying their rent and utilities or buying food. Others, like Mr Moss, have houses that they can't afford to or aren't able to maintain for other reasons. I just think maybe I could volunteer a couple of hours a week to help people do little things around the house, do a shop for them, that sort of thing—"

"On one condition," Ava said, pulling away from him to look Cole in the eye. "That I can do it too."

His eyes lit up, and his grin was like the sunrise after a dark night. "Yeah? I don't know how to organize it." Cole pursed his lips, but Bryce was there, turning his face.

"I do. The team has resources for us to help get involved in doing charitable work. They were totally into it when I told them I wanted to talk about cyber bullying. I know they'll love to get involved in setting up something of our own too."

SEVENTEEN

Bryce

DECEMBER

They were staying in a fancy hotel for the night. It was a dual celebration. Their tenth house had settled the day before, the money landing in their joint bank account, and the charity ball that he'd hosted the night before had gone off without a hitch—except for how awkward it had been with Mr Denyer.

He'd tried to talk Ava into selling their latest property to him for cost. He'd wanted it, but hadn't moved quickly enough, their agent lining up the purchase before the property even hit the market. Ava had refused politely. He wasn't happy, but he'd conceded graciously. It only got awkward when Bryce repeatedly felt eyes on him and he'd search out who it was, only to meet Mr Denyer's gaze over and over. Each time, he'd flash Bryce a smile, lift his glass in a toast or give him a polite nod and each time, it got more awkward.

He couldn't wait to get out of there by the end of the night.

The lift upstairs to their hotel room was the start of a change of tide though. By the time they pushed through the door, Bryce was so wound up that he'd taken great delight in stripping Cole out of his penguin suit and Ava out of her red silk floor-length gown. Bryce's own suit was strewn all the way through the hotel room to the foot of the bed. Both his lovers were sexy as hell dressed up and even better out of it, and he'd shown them both just how much he appreciated every inch of their delectable bodies.

Bryce propped himself up on his elbow and peered down through squinted eyes at his partners sleeping peacefully next to him. Cole was in the middle—in Ava's usual spot—the big spoon to Ava's little one. He pressed a kiss to Cole's shoulder and slid out from under the sheet. It was going to be another warm day, the sun already pumping out heat even though it was relatively early.

He did his business in the bathroom before ducking under the warm shower spray and quickly scrubbing himself clean. His stomach rumbled loudly, curling in on itself. The meal at the fancy fundraiser had been amazing, but most definitely on the tiny side. They'd been too preoccupied to do a late-night Maccas run, and he was regretting not eating now.

He and Ava traded places when he opened the door, his girl only stopping to plant a smacking kiss on his lips before she shut the door. "Morning," Cole mumbled, lying face down on the bed, the pillow he'd shared with Ava on his head.

Bryce leaned down and pressed a line of kisses along his shoulder, speaking quietly when he said, "I'll get you some water and painkillers."

"I'm okay, just feelin' a little seedy. Too much bourbon and not enough food." Bryce couldn't agree more, but he'd stayed mostly sober, only having a drink or two to loosen himself up for the speech. He had another motivation too—he got handsy when he was drunk and announcing his sexuality and his relationship with Cole in front of a room full of people wasn't in the plan.

Bryce fetched him a bottle of water, cracking the lid open before he tossed his wet towel at the end of the bed and slowly lowered himself next to Cole. He handed him the bottle and rubbed his back. "Once you're up, have a shower and we'll get some food."

He looked up nearby coffee shops and read the reviews—Grounds had the best rating and it was only a couple of blocks away.

It didn't take long for them to hit the street and only a few minutes later, the welcoming aroma of excellent coffee and breakfast food beckoned to them. He pushed through the door to the café and did a double take.

"Mate!" Liam, his football bud from back home, a player for the Gold Coast team strode over and gave Bryce a back-slapping hug. It was great to see him, but his enthusiastic reaction had gotten peoples' attention and he'd been hoping to fly under the radar.

He wasn't ready to go back to treating Cole as a friend just yet.

Liam touched the woman he was with on the elbow, and Bryce took her in. She was tiny, both short and petite. A good head shorter than Ava. But she also had presence. She may be the size of a mouse, but she didn't hold herself like one. Her hot-pink hair stood out, announcing her arrival, and her smile drew him to her. His initial impression said she would be smart too. Behind the smile were keen eyes that seemed to take in everything. He couldn't explain it, but Bryce just knew she would be able to tell a lot about someone just by their body language.

"Addy, this is Bryce. He plays for Easts. I was a senior in the training camps when Bryce was coming into them. He was my little buddy," Liam babbled, and Bryce snorted out a laugh. It was true, but only as far as their ages were concerned. Bryce was a few years younger than Liam but even before he'd hit his teenage growth spurt, he was both taller and broader than Liam. It suited both of them, though. Liam played on the wing. He had to be fast and duck and weave between the defensive line to score and to be able to keep up with the other side when they were on the attack. Bryce was on the front row too, but he was the brick wall that no one wanted to run into.

"Addy's a good friend of mine," Liam explained, but the tiny twist in his lips had Bryce blinking, replaying the moment in his head, trying to put his finger on whatever it was that Liam had inadvertently let slip.

"Great to meet you," Bryce responded automatically while his brain caught up.

He couldn't help the googly-eyed smile that no doubt lit up his face when he thought about who he was with. They lit up his world. "This is my girlfriend, Ava, and our roommate, Cole." The words were bitter on his tongue, a harsh contrast to the loved-up warmth of having his man in his arms all night. Usually he got the privilege of cuddling Ava, but Cole had needed them both the night before. He tried not to show it, but he'd been miserable being introduced as their flatmate over and over again. That was why their clothes had landed in piles on the floor as both he and Ava reminded Cole of just how important he was to them.

Cole touched the small of his back, a subtle move that no one else would have noticed and stepped away. Bryce kept the smile in place even with the frown appearing again on Cole's face. "How long are you here for?" he asked, knowing he couldn't do anything to soothe Cole.

"Just until tomorrow night. Addy's boyfriend and I fly back so I can train on Monday, but Addy has another week here after that."

Training for the Lightning had already begun too, and he was loving being back in the swing of it. Summer was surfing and swimming, but winter was rugby, and any chance he got to play was awesome. He couldn't deny that the couple of months off after the season had wrapped in September was good, though. Bryce had finished up his exams, leaving only a few more subjects from his degree to complete, which he could do remotely, and he'd helped finish the two builds they had on the go. It was a glimpse of Bryce's future after his playing career was over, and it was a hella good motivation to wrap up his degree the next year. He loved playing, and playing professionally was literally a dream come true, but he knew he had a future to look forward to working with Ava and Cole.

The problem—one Bryce was only realizing now that they were in front of friends—was that their relationship had become insular. Bryce hated hiding Cole, so it was easier to decline invitations to go out with mates or other couples than to explain why he'd tagged along. Both Ava and Cole were homebodies, so it didn't bother them, but Bryce had no idea how much he'd missed his friends until that very second.

On the spur of the moment, he asked, "If you feel like catching up for dinner tonight, give me a yell. I don't think we have anything planned, do we?" Bryce looked to Ava and Cole, hoping they didn't mind, but Ava's enthusiastic headshake and grin relaxed him.

Cole kept his serious face on, but the tiny tilt of his lips upward was enough to reassure Bryce that he was up for it. "No," Cole responded. "Nothing on."

"We're staying in the building across the road," Addy explained. "We could order takeout and stay there if you'd prefer that to going out. Save you being plastered all over social media."

"Sounds good," Liam confirmed, wrapping an arm around her. She snuggled into his embrace. They were comfortable together, their bodies pressed close. Bryce's smile was half shock, half blind hope that his mate was in some sort of three-way relationship with Addy and her boyfriend. Could they have stepped into the twilight zone and found someone who might actually understand his, Ava, and Cole's non-traditional relationship?

He beamed, shifting from foot to foot as excitement coursed through him. He wanted to catch up even more now.

"Will all of you come?" Liam asked.

"Yes," Bryce answered at the same time as Cole shook his head and said, "No."

Liam snorted out a laugh at their contradiction, but Bryce looked to his man, silently begging him to agree. They could be discreet, and they would be, but Bryce needed this and he couldn't bear leaving Cole home by himself. Cole inclined his head, just a tiny dip, and Bryce's smile turned triumphant. He resisted the urge to throw his arms up in the air and do a victory dance, but the laughter that bubbled up his throat said it all. "We'll all be there."

"Good. I'll message you to sort out the time."

* * * * *

Liam met them in the lobby of their apartment building. Bryce was riding a high, excited to not only catch up with an old friend, but to be able to spend the night talking and laughing with all of them together.

Cole wore a frown now, one Bryce hadn't seen in a long time, and it killed him seeing it. They'd been together almost a year and Cole smiled more often than not—his frowns reserved for when he was concentrating or when something went wrong on a build. He was nervous, closing those walls in on himself as a protective measure and wearing his scowl like a shield.

Bryce nudged his shoulder with his own and brushed his fingers over Cole's. His man's gaze snapped to his and Bryce stared back, wishing he could lean in and kiss him. Instead, he threaded their fingers together and squeezed, hiding their joined hands behind his body. Ava and Cole were his world, and Bryce may have selfishly wanted a night with friends, but he needed his man to know that they wouldn't stay if he was uncomfortable.

While Ava made herself at home helping Addy pour the wine and open a few beers, Bryce passed a plate to Cole and watched as Liam rested his chin on King's shoulder, snagging a spring roll off his plate. King, Addy's boyfriend and clearly Liam's friend, laughed and swatted his hand away. Liam looked giddy. His grin lit up his face and he shifted closer. Bryce turned to Cole, not wanting to intrude on what seemed like a private moment between Liam and King and met his man's gaze. The private smile Cole shot to Bryce, the tiny tilt of his lips upward and the heat in his eyes had Bryce putting his plate down and reaching for Cole, wanting that connection with him again, even if it was as simple as holding his hand.

"Excuse us for a moment," King said, tugging Liam out of the room.

Bryce paid them no notice. He was too busy concentrating on Cole. When the other two were gone and they were shielded from the ladies by the kitchen bench, Bryce reached out for Cole, joining their hands and squeezing. He mouthed, "I love you," to his man and Cole's shy smile in response lifted his spirits.

"Let's dish up," Cole murmured, grabbing two plates and heaping out a serving of the ginger chicken on each. Bryce did the same, adding rice and the garlic and pepper beef to theirs as well as the sweet and sour pork while Cole went for the rice. They were practiced moves. This was how they plated dinner every night, Ava looking after the drinks while they cooked or dished up the takeaway.

"Tuck in," Addy instructed them when they sat. "King and Lee won't be long." Just as she finished speaking, the two men in question walked through the door, Liam's smile dropping when they all turned to them. "What?"

"Is it just the two of you who're together, or all three of you?" Bryce asked, biting his lip against the hope bubbling up in his chest. The hints were small, but they were unmissable. He figured putting it out there and seeing where the chips fell.

Liam visibly swallowed and King stepped back, putting some distance between them. Oh no. "What makes you ask that?" Liam hedged, a line of sweat dotting his brow.

"The love-heart eyes you three have been making at one another all night has been a dead giveaway," Cole said blandly. "But the pash rash on your face makes it a no-brainer."

Liam brought his hands to his cheeks, the pink glow blooming on them a welcome change from the colour leeching from his skin only a moment earlier.

Bryce laughed, grateful that he hadn't completely screwed their night up. He got up from his spot on the couch.

"Is that like the love-heart eyes you two were flashing each other in the coffee shop?" Addy asked, hand on her hip and her eyebrow raised.

He knew she'd be a force to be reckoned with, not standing for any shit.

"They were?" Liam snapped his gaze to his girl and then back to where Bryce squeezed Cole's shoulder before moving to lean against the back of the couch. "You were?"

"Probably, but hiding sucks and I can't lie to save myself, so...." Bryce shrugged, like it was no big deal while his insides flip-flopped like a fish out of water in a nervous dance. Standing, simply because he couldn't sit still anymore, he clapped Liam on the shoulder and added, "You look good, man. Regardless of who you're with, we're happy for you."

"Hiding what?" Liam asked, focussing on what Bryce hadn't said.

Bryce laughed again, relieved at being called out and finally being able to be honest with someone other than his and Ava's families. "The three of us are together." He slung an arm around Liam's shoulders and nodded in the direction of Cole and Ava. "So, it's all good. If you and King are together, you won't get any judgement from us. We're stuck hiding too. We call Cole our flatmate, but he's not. I love him just as much as Ava."

Cole beamed and Ava's smiled softly, looking between them. Bryce's heart filled to bursting, and it took everything in him not to bounce on over to his people and crash-tackle them to the floor to kiss every inch of them.

"It's not just me and King," Liam rushed out, the tension lines on his face that Bryce hadn't even realized were there relaxing. "Addy, King, and I are together. We're only new, but we're together."

Bryce went back to Ava and Cole and picked up his plate where he'd left it, adding, "Just be careful who you're open with. You always have to be careful. We can't risk it getting out to the press, especially not in my rookie year. Can you imagine the media shitstorm?"

"How long?" Liam asked, sliding into the chair beside the armchair where Bryce had sat before.

"A year in a few days' time." Bryce pressed a kiss to Cole's temple, and Cole leaned in, wrapping his arm around Bryce's forearm while he reached for Ava's hand. It was a simple moment, one filled with intimacy, and Bryce's heart overflowed. This was what Cole needed.

Bryce nudged him and both Cole and Ava scooted over, making room for him on the tiny two-seater couch. He leaned into his man, loving that he could show him affection in front of someone other than Ava.

"But you've made it work. You're happy," Liam said, capturing Bryce's attention again. It was almost as if he was looking for reassurance.

Bryce grinned. The tables had turned—it was the first time he'd been able to advise Liam. It was a nice change, one that he was happy to do if it meant giving him comfort.

"We've made it work. There have been a few rocky parts, but we've never doubted each other," Ava confirmed.

It was true, they were rock-solid.

EIGHTEEN

Bryce

The January heat was brutal. The first Friday of the year and it had set a record for temps. Even in the air-conditioning in the shopping centre they were hanging around in, it was stifling. It had been like that for three days, and each day they'd gone for a swim after practice, then hotfooted it over to the shops. At least decent movies had been playing, so window shopping, then watching the latest flick was a good way of wiling away a few hours in the middle of the day when it was hottest. Then it was another swim in the afternoon when they could get a spot on the beach, or a few hours at the local pub having a couple of drinks and dinner before they'd rinse and repeat.

Their next renovation would have air-conditioning, and Bryce was determined that they were moving into it.

The chime on his phone alerted him to an email as they were leaving the cinema. He ignored it, too busy dodging the hoard of people that surrounded them. They were moving en masse, bustling from the theatre and spilling onto the main concourse of the mall.

It rang less than five minutes later—while they were lining up for ice cream—and although he didn't recognize the number, he picked it up. "Y'ello," he answered. It was probably some telemarketer or spam caller, but on the off chance it was important, he answered.

"Good afternoon, Mr Flaharty—I presume it is Mr Flaharty?" a woman asked him in a no-nonsense tone.

He hesitated. He didn't want to give out any information in case it was one of those scammers. "How can I help you?"

"My name is Rita Savage from News and Views." He recognized the name of the online site. They were notorious for trolling their targets, breaking stories that weren't often supported by truth. But they aimed for viral content and more often than not, got it.

"Right. I'm not interested, thank you."

He was about to hang up, but her harsh laugh stopped him. He met Ava's curious gaze and shook his head, dismissing her concerns. "I've sent you an email, Mr Flaharty. You should read it and respond. You have until noon on Sunday."

The line went dead, and Bryce laughed, rolling his eyes. Way to be dramatic. He was right—a spam caller. The whole conversation was an attempt to get something out of him, something he wasn't prepared to do.

"Who was that?" Ava asked.

"Someone saying they're a journalist and I needed to read one of their emails and respond by Sunday lunchtime." He put on a voice that the person—what was her name? Rita something?—had sounded like.

"You aren't gonna check?" Cole asked with a frown.

"Anything important would have come through my agent. This is that gossip site who makes their shit up and calls it news."

"Fair enough." Cole shrugged, but his frown didn't lift, even while checking out the menu and asking Ava, "What do you feel like?"

"Mango sorbet."

"Ooh, yum. I'll get that too," Bryce chipped in, his grin in place at the thought of the taste of summer.

He stretched out on the armchair, his leg hooked over one of the armrests as he played on his phone. It was too hot to do anything even though the sun had set hours earlier. He shook his head, noticing the reporter's name in his inbox. He rolled his eyes and clicked on the email. *What ridiculous thing have they come up with?*

He got to the second line and knew he was in trouble. The words blurred in front of him, his chest seizing with an equal measure of dread and panic. The rushing in his ears was so loud that he was woozy within seconds.

They'd found out.

They didn't have all the details—they thought Ava was his beard—but they knew enough to hit him like a sledge-hammer. They knew about his relationship with Cole. Or at least they said they did.

The reporter was presenting him with an ultimatum— she'd break the story on Sunday at noon. It was right in time for some momentum to build with their ravenous readers and make it onto the evening news. If they saw it, the article would be added to their programming. There was no doubt that it would be the topic of conversation on the Monday morning talk shows as well as the sport news on Sunday and Monday nights wrapping up the weekend's games.

He remembered when the NFL player came out and the Aussie soccer player too—both were international news stories in less than twenty-four hours. *Oh shit.*

The alternative she presented was doing an exclusive interview with them.

Anger coursed through his veins. Indignation too. How dare they. Why? What had he ever done to anybody? How would it impact Ava and Cole? They didn't need his shitstorm raining down on their shoulders. It'd be a nightmare.

But maybe... maybe it was all speculation. Maybe their evidence was nothing more than a photo of them doing something innocent together, something that flatmates would do. Could he stick with their story of Cole being his roomie? Maybe the whole thing was a weak attempt to have Bryce give weight to a ridiculous misinterpretation. But was it ridiculous if it was true?

He held his breath as he clicked on the attachments. Fuck. There was no way this could be played off as just roomies. His breath see-sawed out of his lungs and his heart thudded in his chest. His hands shook and sweat trickled down his back as he squeaked out, "Cole."

His boyfriend looked up from the couch next to him, a frown immediately appearing. Worry flickered in his eyes, and he sat up straighter, taking his feet off the coffee table.

Bryce's breath caught, and he tried to swallow past the lump in his throat as he passed his phone over to Cole.

"What the fuck?" he asked, his head snapping to Bryce when he looked at the image. He handed the phone to Ava and turned to Bryce. Fury twisted his face into a grimace and Bryce's gut sank. Cole was angry with him. He'd been careless, and now it was coming to bite him in the arse.

"Who took these?" Ava asked, her voice short and sharp like a whipcrack. She was a study in contrasts that night. Wearing a tiny cotton camisole and boxer brief PJ pants and her hair in pigtails, she looked like she belonged at a sleepover. The cocktail in her hand and the anger sharpening her features were almost out of place.

Bryce shook his head, his eyes burning with unshed tears. They were both pissed off, and he hated that he was the one who'd caused it, because even if they all should have been more careful, he was the one who strangers cared about what he did.

"Are they trying to blackmail you?"

"Read the email," he whispered, his voice a harsh rasp. Broken and devastated.

Cole vibrated with anger, his scowl deepening and his face turning a dark shade of red. His eyes flashed and Bryce could hear him grinding his teeth. Cole jumped up from the couch, roughly shoving their coffee table out of the way with his foot before pacing their small lounge room. He stomped, his heavy footfalls and harsh breathing the only noise as Ava read the email. Bryce buried his face in his hands, flinching when glass shattered and Cole shouted, "Fuck."

Bryce was on his feet in a split second, looking between his partners. Glass was shattered all over the floor, Ava's cocktail splashed on the tiles. "What happened?" he gasped, jumping into action to make sure she didn't have to clean up the mess.

Tears pooled in Ava's eyes, spilling down her cheeks. "This is so unfair," she whispered.

"Are you okay?"

"Yeah." She nodded, waving away his concern. "Just dropped it." She swallowed and sniffed, smiling gratefully at Cole when he picked up the pieces of broken glass and wiped the floor down.

With a sigh, Cole asked, "What are we gonna do?"

Bryce slumped into the armchair again, the wind going completely out of his sails. "I... I have no idea." His shoulders fell. Resting his elbows on his knees, he stared at the floor before covering his eyes. Maybe if he stuck his head in the sand, he could forget this was happening.

He'd made it into the league and had a decent rookie year—the team didn't make the finals, but they'd been close, really close. Now that he was in, he was supposed to be shoring up his career, stepping things up and getting as much on-field time as possible. He wanted a spot on the origin team. He wanted to play for Queensland, don the maroon jersey and run onto the field with the best of the best players in the league.

He knew it wouldn't happen immediately, but if he kept his nose clean, played an excellent game, and backed it up year on year, he'd get there. It was his five-year plan.

The thing was, he wanted to do it all with Ava and Cole by his side. Would they stick around if they had to face the media every time they stepped outside? What about the fans? The toxic ones who thought rugby was a game for men, and "real" men couldn't love other men.

This was going to be a nightmare for them. He'd deal with whatever was thrown his way. He wouldn't enjoy it, but it was the path he'd started down the first time he'd donned his footy boots. Bryce's dream was as interwoven with the negative side, the prejudice, as much as it was with the positives. But at least if the team knew about it, they wouldn't be blindsided.

"I better start with the team and Trav."

"Call Trav first," Ava advised, patting the seat next to her.

He shifted over to her. He needed them, their support and their love more than anything right now. If everything went to shit, at least he'd still have them. He hoped.

Bryce put the phone on speaker and dialled. Trav picked up after a couple of rings. "G'day, Bryce. What's up, my man?" There was noise in the background, talking and music like he was in a restaurant or bar.

"Ah, hey... I think we've got a problem, Trav. Can you get somewhere private?"

"Yeah, give me five and I'll call you back." He hung up and a few minutes later was returning his call. "Okay, hit me," he said.

Bryce explained how the email had come in a few hours earlier, but he'd ignored it, thinking it was fishing for information on something, then the cryptic call, and his realization that they had enough on him to expose a secret he'd been keeping.

"And you never thought to mention that you're gay?" Trav asked. "Dude, I could have at least had something ready to go so we weren't writing it on the fly."

"With all due respect, Travis," Cole interrupted from his spot on the coffee table, his legs bracketing Bryce's, "focus on Bryce. He didn't want to inconvenience you and add to your workload, but that's what you get paid for."

Bryce squeezed his hand, not knowing whether it was in thanks or begging him to stop talking.

Travis sputtered with indignation and Bryce took the opportunity to explain, "I'm not gay, Trav. I'm pansexual. Ava, Cole, and I are together, not just Cole and I."

"No one knows what pansexual is, Bryce. They don't understand ménage relationships either. They'll see pictures of you and Ava and say you cheated on her, or you used her. To them, you'll be the gay player hiding behind a woman you hurt. No matter how you spin it, you'll be the bad guy."

Ava wrapped her arm around his waist and leaned into him. Cole threaded their fingers together and he held on tight. His heart was shattering in his chest. He wasn't that guy. He wouldn't hurt them. He wouldn't cheat.

"Look, Bryce, I'm going to give it to you straight. Unless you craft your own story and head this off at the pass, it's going to ruin your reputation. Come out as gay on Insta — we can draft up a post for you — say that Ava is your closest friend. We can get you doing some charity work for LGBT community organizations, that sort of thing. If they see you as a guy who's coming out because it's time, who has the support of his best friend and boyfriend, then it'll at least work in your favour. You've finished your rookie year, so it makes sense that you'd choose now — before the new season starts — to come out. That way, by the time you start playing the bruhaha is going to have died down and you can get back to being you."

"That'd be fine, except I'm not gay. I don't want to cat-fish anyone."

"How is it different to what you've been doing?"

"That's not fair," Ava interrupted, leaping to his defence. "You know exactly why he hid his sexuality."

"I do. But trust me on this, Bryce. Do it my way and it'll be okay. Let me get on the phone with the club and I'll call you back."

"I'll speak to them," Bryce said, wanting to make sure they got the true story, not what the tabloid press wanted them to know or his agent's hairbrained scheme. "I can deal with it." He could and he would, but he was shit scared too.

"Let's conference call it then. I don't want you on the phone without representation."

Within an hour, Travis called him back. The team's PR rep and Mr Denyer were already on the line when he picked up. Apparently, they'd received a similar email and had been working behind the scenes on a strategy. Concern that they hadn't bothered to call him about it pricked his skin, wariness winding its way around him.

"Mr Flaharty," Ellie, the team's PR rep said without an ounce of emotion in her voice. "You've put the team in a very difficult position. Your relationship is about to become international news. The photos are explicit. This is not ideal."

"Someone took photos of me on private property with my boyfriend. It's an invasion of my privacy. Why are we not talking about that? Why are we focussing on the fact that I have a boyfriend? This isn't fair," Bryce retorted, frustration bleeding into his tone.

"Bryce," Travis cautioned. "We've gone over this."

"And I never agreed to do it your way," he snapped.

"Gentlemen, our concern as a team is the fallout from this news. It's not a good look for our star rookie to be stirring up controversy before his second season even starts," Ellie stated matter-of-factly.

"Once again, I did nothing wrong."

"I agree," Mr Denyer explained, his voice full of sympathy. Despite the awkwardness between them a few weeks earlier at the fundraiser, he seemed to be on their side. That had to be good news. "However, in this case, perception is everything. There will be calls made that you've engaged in behaviour unbecoming of the team and the league—"

"How is being with my boyfriend in private unbecoming of the team?" Bryce exploded, throwing his hands up in the air. His frustration billowed into anger. It took everything in him not to pick up the phone and throw it across the room. He couldn't believe what he was hearing.

Bryce tugged on the ends of his hair, trying to distract himself from the violation of being photographed without his consent in a private moment. It was Cole and Ava's touch that calmed him. The hand on his knee and another at the small of his back. He leaned into them, the fight leeching out of him.

"Bryce, perhaps these negotiations would be better off delayed," Travis suggested. "If we all calm down and come back to it in the next day or two, we can look at it with clearer heads."

"I don't have time for that, Travis," Bryce snapped. "Some fucking idiot trespassed onto my property, they took photos of my boyfriend and I in a private moment, and now they're threatening to expose us to the world."

"You're right," he conceded, then added, "So let me help. I'll draft up the post, you can do some charity work, and all this will go away soon. Then you can get back to playing."

"We're acting as if I've done something wrong. I'm being punished for having a boyfriend."

"It's not because you have a boyfriend. It's because you put it out there that you have a girlfriend. The perception will be that you lied," Denyer patiently explained, his voice even and calming.

His tone did nothing to ease Bryce, devastation taking the place of his earlier burst of anger. "I didn't lie. I do have a girlfriend. I've never cheated on them. Ava, Cole, and I are together."

"How do you propose explaining that to our heartland supporters, Bryce?" Ellie asked, her tone all business. She was a hard-arse. He'd had mad respect for her efficiency and professionalism when he'd been recruited. She'd reminded him of Ava, but now he saw how wrong he was. "Opinion polls taken during last year's elections from the electorates where 90 percent of our supporters live made it clear that traditional family values are a priority."

"You can't be serious," Ava snapped back. "Those traditional family values you speak of were transphobic rhetoric plagued with fear mongering. The candidate you're talking about who relied on labelling the trans community as paedophiles lost by a landslide."

"Be that as it may, the team is reluctant to have players on its roster who attract negative publicity. We're of the view that it's behaviour unbecoming of the team."

Her words smashed into Bryce like a Mack truck ploughing into him square in the chest. He shattered into a million tiny pieces. His shredded dreams fell apart, skittering into every crevice and niche. He'd never be able to put them back together.

"No," Cole ground out. His eyes flashed and his face was pulled tight with anger. He vibrated with a pent-up rage that would have been terrifying if Bryce hadn't known just how fiercely Cole would defend him. "Players beating their wives up and snorting coke in toilets is negative press. Bryce is in a steady relationship with us. We're committed and exclusive. We haven't done anything wrong. You and the team are discriminating against him because of his sexuality."

"Let's not be hasty," Mr Denyer cautioned. "No one wants to say anything they'll regret later."

When Ellie spoke again, her tone was placating. "I'm trying to protect everyone here. There are real consequences when a team's brand takes a hit like this. It will affect more than just Bryce, and it's my job to think of the team."

"While I sympathize with that, this is my client's life and his relationships we're talking about." Finally! Bryce breathed a sigh of relief that Travis was finally stepping up his game and actually representing him. "I think we're all in agreement that Bryce is either going to have to come out or be outed. Whether he comes out as gay or in a relationship with two people is fairly moot at this point. You're jumping to the conclusion that people will react negatively. The team should be spinning this to demonstrate how supportive of the LGBTQIA community the club is. Young players and fans who see themselves in their idols could become lifelong supporters if this is handled well."

"And in the meantime, existing members refund their memberships, ticket sales will plummet, and merchandise sales are affected. I understand the long game you're trying to play, Travis, but it's my job to look at how the team will be affected in the short term too. Do you really want that on your shoulders, Bryce?"

Bryce swallowed, not having a clue how to answer that question.

"Bryce, don't say a word," Travis snarled, as if reading his mind. "Your allegations that my client has engaged in conduct unbecoming of the team are flimsy at best. We'll be taking this to the players tribunal if there is even a hint of a sanction against him."

Mr Denyer interjected, "Bryce, I understand what you're going through. I'm sympathetic. I saw my son go through something similar to you. It was devastating for him. He was in a same-sex relationship and certain people didn't react well to it. They forced him out of his job and his apartment. His partner suffered greatly too. Let's get on the front foot with this. Release a statement and some photos to social media. Take the wind out of this tabloid's sails."

"Okay," Bryce murmured, his gut telling him that there was more to come, that the axe hadn't fallen just yet.

He continued talking as if Bryce hadn't said a word. "Look, it may not feel like it at the moment, but I have your welfare at heart too. It pains me to suggest this, but I'm worried about how the pressure will affect you, your playing game, your university marks, and your relationship with Cole and Ava. If you come out and your season doesn't result in a premiership win, there's someone out there who'll put it down to you folding under pressure. If it's the media who reaches that conclusion, your whole career could be tarnished."

There was a hum of agreement from Ellie. Bryce looked at Ava then Cole. He couldn't read either of their expressions other than the worry painted over their faces —lips drawn in straight lines, pinched brows, and tense shoulders.

"That kind of negativity can get in your head. You're incredibly talented, and we want to nurture that talent," he continued.

"What are you suggesting?" Travis asked.

"I think the best way of protecting Bryce is for him to play in the reserves this season." There it was: the axe falling. His lungs deflated and his shoulders slumped. He wanted to cry, but he was overwhelmed. In shock.

"Bryce, I know it's hard, but you won't be in the public eye every week. People won't be constantly reminded of what's happened, so you won't have to live with reporters camped out in front of your apartment. It's not a permanent situation by any means, but at least it will get you out from the public eye while things die down and you adjust to the change."

The call continued, Travis, Ellie, and Mr Denyer in a back and forth between them. Bryce barely listened. It was as if he was drowning. Underwater. He was gasping for breath and drifting deeper, away from the light. He could hear noise, but not make out what was being said. He couldn't yell for help. He couldn't fight the tide dragging him under.

Ava gently took the phone from him, pocketing it. It was as if he was watching the scene from outside of his body, his consciousness hovering somewhere above him. She ran the backs of her fingers against his cheek, her warm touch stitching him back together. Heat seeped back into his body from that simple gesture, thawing the block of ice inside him like the spring sunshine dawning in the arctic. Numbness had crept in and exhaustion plagued him. His limbs were heavy. His vision swam, dizziness making him nause-ous. Or maybe that was the feeling of his dreams slipping out of reach.

No. He couldn't think like that. He'd done it once. He could do it again. He would do it again.

Getting bumped back to the reserves wasn't his fault. It wasn't because he wasn't good enough, or he hadn't kept up his end of the bargain. He'd done everything expected of him. He was being punished for the narrow-minded views of the team's PR rep, and someone seeking a hefty pay day.

He'd be back, and he'd show them all. The haters would be left in awe. The PR rep would be spewing that she'd pulled him from the team. The lawyer... well, he'd actually been pretty cool. Bryce didn't have any hard feelings for him.

Bryce would be better than all of them. The selectors would be jumping over themselves to recruit him into Queensland's Origin team. He wasn't moving the timeline either. Five years and he'd be there. Seven and he'd be cap-tain.

Holy hell. Is this what Levi went through when he'd been outed? Levi had lost his career. It had come crashing down around him. No one wanted a kids' TV presenter who was sleeping with both a man and a woman, one who refused to deny them.

Bryce puffed up his chest, pride for his cousin hitting him square on. Now he understood why Levi had chosen to give up his career instead of the alternative. There was no way he would walk away either, not when Ava and Cole were the most important people in his world.

NINETEEN

Cole

Cole was shaking. It was something way beyond fury. He didn't even know how to label it. All he knew was that he needed to do something—anything—to... gah! Bryce. He needed to focus on Bryce. He had to pull his head out and focus on his boyfriend. His dreams had just been snatched away from him. Bryce had done nothing wrong, but he was the one copping the penalty. Shitty kind of justice.

Cole reached out, grasping Bryce's hands. They were cold, but he held onto Cole like a life preserver. He leaned into Ava's touch too, her brush of knuckles against his face a comfort for him.

"Bryce," Cole choked out, his voice hitching. He didn't know what to say; he had no idea what he needed.

His man looked at him, forlorn and lost, but as Cole looked closer, he spotted that steely determination underneath that drove Bryce. A fierce competitiveness that he thrived under. Cole's muscles unclenched. Bryce would be okay. He'd make sure of it.

Bryce opened his mouth as if to speak, but no words came. He would be okay, but it would take a bit of healing to get there. Cole's heart broke. Bryce was a big puppy dog and usually full of energy. Cole was used to seeing him bound around with a smile from ear to ear, but he was far more subdued. Cole hated seeing him like that.

He squeezed Bryce's hands, and his man lowered his gaze, focussing on where they were joined.

"How about a warm bath?" Ava suggested. "Or maybe a cup of tea?" She looked to Cole, her eyes wide and lips twisted, begging him to give her the answer, but he was just as clueless on what to do.

Bryce gave them a small smile, one that didn't reach his eyes as he stood, before walking to the window. Ava's gaze followed him, her lips turned down in a worried frown.

Cole squeezed her shoulder and went to Bryce, slipping his arms around his waist and kissing his nape. His man melted into his touch, leaning back against him and sighing softly. "Talk to us when you're ready. We want to help."

Bryce nodded but didn't say anything for a long while. The whole time Cole kept up his soft touches. He caressed the sensitive spot near Bryce's hip with his thumb, the beginning of that delicious V, and pressed lingering kisses to his throat, cheek, and temple.

He slid his hand up Bryce's bare chest and clasped his throat with just enough pressure to make Bryce moan. Turning his chin toward him, Cole pressed their lips together and kissed him.

Their touch went from zero to one hundred in a matter of moments, both unleashing their frustration and passion on each other. Their tongues tangled and Cole swallowed Bryce's moan as Ava stepped in front of him and ran her hands and lips over his chest. He hadn't intended to distract Bryce with sex, but any reaction was better than seeing his sunshine, the man who was always so full of life and bubbly energy, so untethered and lost. So quiet.

Breathless, Bryce pulled back, his chest heaving as he sucked in oxygen. Cole shifted his hand, palming Bryce's erection through his loose gym shorts. They were the summer equivalent of grey track pants and Cole loved the way they framed Bryce's package so perfectly.

"Let me look after you, Bryce," Cole pleaded. He loved bottoming for his man, had never expected to want to top him, but everything in Cole screamed at him to make love to Bryce. To take care of him and show him just how adored he was.

Everything Bryce had worked toward for most of his life had just been snatched away and Cole desperately needed to show him that there was still good left. He couldn't lose hope or the fiery determination he'd seen in his gaze buried under the bitter pain. Cole needed to show him exactly what it was like when Bryce made love to him.

"Please," Bryce whispered on a raspy moan.

"Come with us," Ava encouraged, taking Bryce's hand and leading him to their bedroom. Their king bed took up most of the space, but they wouldn't need anywhere near that amount of room tonight.

"Strip," Cole directed Ava. "Lie diagonally on the bed."

Bryce hummed and closed his fist over his shaft, squeezing it through the soft material of his shorts. There was already a wet spot of pre-cum dotting the light cotton.

"She's beautiful, isn't she?" Cole asked rhetorically, gripping Bryce's hips and grinding against his muscular bubble butt. "I know you want to spread her legs and taste how much she wants you, don't you? But tonight, it's all about you. Ava's pretty mouth is gonna be wrapped around your cock and I'm gonna get another taste of your perfect hole. When I finally sink into you, you're gonna be begging for it. Then you'll know."

Bryce gasped, pushing back against Cole's cock as it slid between his firm cheeks. "Know what?" he asked.

"That even though you've hit a snag because of me, I can make you feel good." Cole squeezed his eyes closed against the burning and swallowed past the lump in his throat. He'd thought they were being careful, but somebody had seen them. Somebody had been able to take those pictures. And it was his fault.

He remembered that day. He'd been teasing Bryce with brushes of his hand and talking dirty to him. He'd finally snapped and pinned Cole's chest against the wall, shoved his shorts down, and as soon as he'd felt the lube Cole had preprepared himself with, thrust home in one deep slide.

Cole thought they'd been hidden, even with the blinds being open—they were in a darkened corner at the back of the house. How was he supposed to know that someone would break in? He never imagined it, but he should have.

Bryce stilled at his words, snapped his gaze to Ava's, before he reared back and pinned Cole with his stare. His eyes were wide with surprise or shock, Cole wasn't sure which. "No, this isn't your fault." He shook his head, his eyes blazing with that same determination. His fists were clenched, his nostrils flared, and his body vibrated with ferocity. He pointed between himself and Cole, adding passionately, "This isn't either of our faults. This is Ellie's fault for not understanding. This is that damn website's fault for threatening to publish those pictures. This is the photographer's fault for breaching our privacy, for coming onto our property and taking pictures of us in a private moment without our consent." His chest heaved and his face was red from his outburst, but Bryce wasn't finished. "This is a violation, and because of closed-minded arseholes, I need to prove myself again. And I will, dammit. When I get back on that field as a professional player, no matter how long it takes me to get there, I'll be the best. I'll prove every one of those bastards wrong. I'll show them that it takes a real man to take a cock."

Cole didn't know what to say; words were a jumble in his head. He didn't even realize he was frowning until Bryce gripped his chin in one hand and smoothed his forehead with his thumb. "I..."

"I love you too. And Ava, I love you. As long as I have the two of you, I can get through anything." Bryce smirked, his wicked humour lighting up his eyes. "Now get that mouth on me and show me what I've been missing because I've been to chicken to let you get all up inside me."

A burst of laughter tore from Cole's chest, the weight of the guilt he was carrying lifting from his shoulders.

Cole fell to his knees and palmed Bryce's ample butt in his hands, nuzzling his flagging erection. Hooking his fingers under the elastic of the waistband, Cole slid Bryce's shorts down to expose his cheeks, mouthing his hardening shaft while he did.

"You'd better get on the bed then," he murmured against Bryce's cock so he could feel the vibrations from his voice. He tugged his shorts all the way down, letting them fall in a pile at his feet. Cole watched as Bryce's thick cock sprang back and slapped his belly. Cole's hole clenched, the memory of Bryce being inside him still fresh from his late-night railing the night before, after Bryce had taken Ava in much the same way. The two of them had been left satiated limp noodles, star-fished on the bed, sweat and cum soaked as Bryce jacked off over them taking his third orgasm for the night and painting them with his completion.

But this time they were doing things differently.

Cole closed his fist around Bryce's shaft and licked at his slit, tasting his pre-cum. He closed his lips around the wide mushroom head and sucked, moaning as he did. Bryce's body locked up tight and Cole snorted out a laugh. He pulled off with a pop and slapped his man on the butt before questioning, "What are you waiting for?"

Bryce bounded onto the bed with a laugh, hooking Ava's legs over his knees and bending down to kiss her.

Cole admired the view, his woman's and man's holes on display for him to taste and torment until they were shouting their orgasms into their private oasis. They kept the blinds drawn in their bedroom—a set of curtains pinned to the edge of the frame. It was so the light didn't blind them in the mornings, but it had another added benefit too.

No one would ever see in without their okay.

Cole crawled up behind Bryce and bit into the thick muscle of that gorgeous pale butt before licking his way down his leg and tasting all that skin on display for him. He nudged Bryce's sac with his nose and pulled his cock down to lick a stripe up his shaft. Bryce cried out, his balls drawing up tight to his body.

Trailing his tongue over his sac and up his taint, Cole watched as Bryce's hole clenched tight, his body finally ready to let Cole in.

But he wanted to look after their lady too. He dipped his head and licked at Ava, her breathy moans encouraging him to slide his fingers into her soaked pussy and nibble on her clit. Bryce trailed his fingers down, slipping them between Cole's tongue and Ava's core. Cole hummed, grateful that Bryce would look after Ava as well. With both their hands on her, Cole kissed his way back up Bryce's leg to the juncture of his thighs. He licked a circle around Bryce's hole and hummed as it clenched tight again.

Bryce's musky flavour filled his tongue and his cries of "Yes! Fuck, yes!" drove Cole to shoot him into the stratosphere.

He licked and nibbled, slowly relaxing the tight ring of muscle around his opening until Cole could spear the tip of his tongue inside Bryce. They'd done this before, but never had Bryce become an incoherent mess so quickly. He was ready for this next step, and for that Cole would always be grateful. Bryce was giving him something that no one had ever been privileged enough to have before.

Ava's pussy clenched around his fingers, her core contracting rhythmically as she rode out her orgasm and Bryce swallowed her moans. Breathless she begged, "Need to taste you, Bryce. Get your cock up here."

Bryce clambered up her body, his knees bracketing her shoulders and his arms bracing himself against their padded headboard. His hips were tilted up perfectly, giving Cole a view that would be burned into his memory.

Ava took as much of his cock as she could into her mouth and slid her fingers up, circling his pucker and pressing gently against it. She went in to her first knuckle before pulling out and doing it again. Bryce's legs shook, his gravelly moan spurring Cole on. He lunged for the lube sitting on their bedside table, straddled Ava's hips, and drizzled a line down Bryce's crease, watching as Ava gathered the slick on her finger and pressed in again, shallowly fucking him with her digit.

It was one hell of a sight, and Cole drove his hips forward, grinding against Ava's legs, the tip of his cock connecting with her mound. A muffled cry from Ava encouraged Cole to do it again, and he set a steady pace as his mouth joined her fingers in preparing Bryce.

Their man rocked his hips, alternating between pushing his arse into them and his cock into Ava's mouth. Cole pressed a finger in alongside Ava's, and they stretched and twisted inside of him, tagging his prostate relentlessly.

Cole and Ava each added a second finger, giving Bryce a chance to orient himself to the stretch. His breathing was ragged, each of their moans echoing in the room as Ava crested once more and Cole squeezed the base of his own cock to stop himself from coming at the sight of his woman's essence painting the insides of her thighs and his man stuffed full with their fingers. Cole reached for his phone, snapping a picture for Bryce and Ava to admire later.

"Fuck, I'm gonna come," Bryce uttered with a grunt as his hips snapped forward, making Ava gag. "Get inside me," he begged. "Need you inside me when I blow."

Cole slowly withdrew his fingers and Ava followed suit. Bryce's hole stayed open, and Cole couldn't resist taking another photo before diving in to taste the stretched skin. He tugged on his hips, shuffling Bryce down Ava's body until she could lift her knees and spread her legs. Cole looked over Bryce's shoulder, admiring Ava spread out like a buffet before them. Her nipples were drawn tight, the pebbled peaks making him want to nibble and lick them. Her dark hair was splayed out in a halo around her head and her long legs were open, inviting Bryce into her body. "She's so fuckin' pretty, isn't she?" Cole murmured to his man, before sucking a mark into the sensitive spot on his throat. Bryce's hand worked his cock and Cole's nudged at his hole. "Get your cock into our woman and make her scream, and I'll do the same to you."

Bryce didn't hesitate, hooking Ava's legs over his knees once again and sliding into her in one slow stroke. When Bryce's hips were flush with hers, Cole slathered himself in lube and drizzled more along Bryce's crack before he inched up the bed and notched the head of his cock against his man's hole.

"Do it," Bryce demanded impatiently.

Cole bit his lip, sensation already overwhelming him as he watched the head of his cock stretch Bryce open. Bryce hissed and he paused, before Bryce pushed against him once more. A hand to his hip steadied Bryce and Cole inched forward again, the ring of Bryce's muscle strangling his cock when he'd eased his mushroom head through the resistance.

"Oh, fuck," Bryce breathed, burying his face in the crook of Ava's neck.

She petted him, soothing the burn as Cole reached down to fondle his nuts. Bryce cried out and drove his hips back, impaling himself on Cole's cock in one go.

Cole grunted, squeezing Bryce's hips and holding him steady as his cock throbbed and his balls drew up tight. At this rate it would be the quickest fuck in history, Bryce's tight channel already sending Cole almost to the point of no return.

He breathed through clenched teeth and bent forward, blanketing Bryce's body with his own. Their thrusts were erratic for a few moments until they learned each other's rhythms and then, perfect synchronicity.

Cole rested his forehead on Bryce's bunched shoulder blades and pressed a gentle kiss to his back. "Fuck, you have no idea how much I love you both," he whispered.

Bryce reached back, threading his fingers through Cole's hair, and Cole kept up his long, slow thrusts, plunging into Bryce's body and driving him forward into Ava's. Sweat-slicked skin slid together and breathless moans filled the air. Cole hugged Bryce and Ava to him tightly, never wanting to let go of either one of them. He kept up his litany of praise, telling Bryce and Ava how sexy and beautiful they were, and how loved they were.

The tingling began at the base of his spine and Cole's movements stuttered. He didn't want this moment to end. Bryce's hot, slicked-up channel surrounded him, and the spongy pad of his prostate gave the full length of his cock an extra lick of sensation every time he thrust forward.

The smell of sex lingered heavily in the air and the writhing bodies below him pushed him ever closer to the edge. Ecstasy awaited, but Cole wouldn't be the first one to get there if it was the last thing he did.

Bryce clenched his tight ring of muscle and Cole saw stars. It was the beginning of a chain reaction, Ava catapulting over first as Bryce drove his hips into her. For a second time, Bryce's channel tightened around him, Bryce going rigid and grunting as he emptied his seed into Ava.

With his dick being strangled in the best possible way and the cacophony of moans below him, Cole ground his hips forward and unleashed, his orgasm ripping through him like a lightning strike electrifying every one of his nerve endings, the sizzle a painless nirvana. With each throb of his balls, Cole emptied himself, painting the inside of Bryce's channel with his cum. His shout of completion rent the air and his heavy breaths ghosted across Bryce's skin, raising a trail of gooseflesh in their wake.

He didn't want to leave the sanctuary of the bubble they had created in their bed, but his softening cock wouldn't allow him to stay. He pulled out and collapsed to the side, wishing he had a view of his cum dribbling out of Bryce.

Ava nudged their man, and he slid off her boneless. Her parted legs were slick with their combined essence and Cole wanted more than a visual. He eased himself down the bed, lapping at her folds until she rocked her hips and gripped his hair with both hands as she ground against him, claiming another orgasm from him. Both he and Bryce were hard again by the time he'd finished, and the way Bryce manhandled him so that they were sixty-nineing was so hot that Cole damn near came on the spot.

He resisted, barely, distracting himself by licking up the evidence of his arousal from between Bryce's cheeks before swallowing his man's cock. Bryce drove up into his throat and the first connection with his tonsils sent Cole over the edge once more. He shouted out around Bryce's shaft and swallowed as Bryce came down his throat.

* * * * *

Saturday morning dawned and Cole blinked open his eyes, his head pillowed on Bryce's leg where he'd passed out the night before. Ava was curled around Bryce, her fingers sliding into Cole's hair as she smiled softly at him.

He winced and adjusted his position. "Morning, beautiful," he rasped, his throat still saw from Bryce's cock lodged down it.

"Morning, grumpy cat." She huffed out a laugh when Cole stuck out his tongue. Bryce cracked open an eye and lifted his head up to peer at him.

"How are you doing today, babe?" Cole asked.

Bryce wiggled his hips as if he was testing out the movement and groaned. "I'm achy but not hurting. Might need a few days before we try that again."

Cole flipped around, using Bryce's thick arm as a pillow. "You don't have to do it again at all."

"Yes, I really do." Bryce's smile was lazy and supremely satisfied too, and Cole grinned happily, his heart fluttering at the thought that he'd made things good for Bryce. Almost as soon as he had the thought, Bryce's smile slipped, and he sighed.

"Hey, we'll work it out."

"I know. I meant what I said yesterday too. I'll get back there." Bryce's stomach rumbled at the same time as a buzzing began on the floor. "Urgh, they can bugger off," Bryce mumbled, but Ava was already on her feet, bending down and scooping up his phone. When she handed it to Bryce, Cole saw Travis's name on the screen. "Hey, mate," Bryce answered warily. "Do I want to know?"

"You absolutely do." The words loud and clear, even from where Cole lay.

Bryce perked up, pulling himself up to sitting. Leaning against the headboard, he put his phone on speaker.

"Hit me," he responded, bracing himself.

"I've spent all night on the phone. I reached out to every team who would take my call and after chatting with eight clubs, I narrowed it down to three and floated the idea of you transferring to them. Melbourne's roster is full and they're at the salary cap so can't take anyone else on."

Bryce nodded and made a non-committal noise. Cole's chest squeezed. The idea of Bryce moving to Melbourne sucked, but a long-distance relationship was a small price to pay if it meant he could play professionally.

"Of the two others, the Gold Coast was the most receptive. In the strictest of confidence, I explained what's going down with the Lightning and this bullshit article. They're supportive of however you want to handle it."

A rustling sounded on the phone and a yawn ripped out of Travis. "Sorry, I'm too damn old to be doing an all-nighter, especially when there's no sex or alcohol involved."

Bryce snorted out a laugh, Cole bit his lip and Ava rolled her eyes, her expression alight with humour.

"Their player recruitment manager got the team's PR rep on the phone while we were speaking. He suggested that they do an immediate announcement of your transfer, pending approval from your old club. They want to frame it as if they're poaching you to replace their retiring prop. Given you're still contracted to the Lightning, you'll need to be let out of the contract, but after Ellie's reaction, I can't imagine that the team will have too much of an issue letting you go." Travis took his first breath after the dump of information and launched straight back into talking. "They're a solid club, up and coming and have a great coach. They're putting together an offer for you as we speak. Bryce, I recommend accepting it, no matter what the terms are. Getting back into professional football is going to be harder than transferring sideways."

"Wow, okay," Bryce started. "Um... can I think about it?"

Cole watched as Ava threaded their fingers together. He rested his head on Bryce's shoulder, curling his hand around his man's forearm. He would support Bryce with whatever he needed and would back up whatever decision he made, but bloody hell, this sounded like a dream opportunity.

"Of course, but as I said, Bryce, this might be your best chance. In the meantime, I've had our marketing people draft up an Instagram post. I've emailed it to you already together with the Gold Coast's draft press release. Check them both, send me some photos that show you and Cole together, and I'll look after posting it on Instagram for you."

Cole's heart sank. He'd hated being the one who was hidden, even though it had been at his insistence. He'd do it again all day every day for the rest of their lives if it meant Bryce could have kept playing with the Lightning. But it wasn't fair to Ava to deny her. He didn't want to put her on the outer. It wasn't fair.

"Trav, we spoke about this. I'm not lying anymore. If I can't come out as poly, I won't say a single word to the media at all. Let them make up whatever they want about me if they aren't prepared to hear the truth."

A lump lodged in Cole's throat. Bryce's attitude was admirable, but what damage would it cause? How much worse would it be if he said nothing?

Travis sighed, frustration leaking into the sound. "I'm not recommending that approach, Bryce. But ultimately, it's your life and career on the line. I can't protect you if you don't want to be protected."

Ava slid her hand onto Bryce's leg, squeezing the thick muscle there and Bryce knocked his head back against the headboard. "Urgh, yeah. I know. We've still got a day. I'll have a decision to you in an hour."

"Okay. Now if you agree to the Gold Coast offer, they'll want a press conference with you at their headquarters first thing tomorrow. I'm booking you a flight early evening tonight." Cole's eyes flicked up to meet Ava's and at his unspoken question she gave him the barest of nods.

"Book three seats," Cole said. "Ava and I are coming."

* * * * *

"Why don't you call Liam?" Ava suggested when Bryce was no closer to an answer. He'd spent the better part of the hour he'd stalled for pacing. He was antsy and anxious, and Cole hated seeing him like that. It didn't help that they hadn't received the written offer from the Gold Coast team yet. Their coach had reached out telling him that Rogers left big shoes to fill, but he was sure if Bryce accepted the offer, he would fit in well with the team.

"He plays for the Gold Coast, doesn't he? He's good people too. He'll understand," Cole encouraged.

Bryce nodded. "He does, yeah. I don't know why I didn't think of that."

"You've had a lot on your mind. It's easy to forget you've got people who'll support you."

"This happened to my cousin. You remember Levi? Same thing, and it destroyed his career. I should call him too," Bryce mused.

Cole breathed a sigh of relief. Bryce was finally opening up and ready to talk. He hadn't said anything to his parents or brothers yet—another call they'd have to make—but Cole couldn't very well jump the gun and do it for him. Bryce was the centre of his story and Cole would support him in every aspect.

"Call them." Ava handed him his phone, smiling indulgently as he rolled his eyes and pressed a kiss to her forehead. They sat down, Bryce perching on the edge of the couch, Ava sitting on the coffee table. Cole sank to the floor on their plush rug as Bryce called, putting his phone on speaker.

"Bryce, mate, how are you?" Liam greeted warmly after he picked up. Before Bryce could get a word in, he added, "Would you believe I'm at a get-together with your cousin Levi?"

Bryce chuckled and Cole blinked.

"Small world. Cool." Bryce paused and Cole could see him struggling with what to say, how to even approach the conversation.

"You okay, mate?" Liam asked, concern lacing his voice. Noise in the background had Cole on edge. Was Liam somewhere private enough that his secret wouldn't be shared even earlier than it was going to be?

Bryce responded, his voice filled with pain. "No. Um, I... I've been bumped down to the reserves again. Easts don't want me playing professionally this season. I'm a liability."

Cole hated that they were prepared to dispose of him so readily when he'd had a killer first season.

"What do you mean a liability?" Liam asked, sounding a mixture of confused and irritated.

"I don't get it. You had the best rookie season I've seen in ages. You kicked arse."

"Apparently the team doesn't want bad publicity." Bryce sighed, the sound resigned. "We're about to be outed. I had the editor of an online newspaper email me photos. I either confirm our relationship and give them an exclusive piece, or they'll put up an exposé."

Clear as day, Cole heard Adelaide call out for Levi, saying, "We need you in here. We've got an emergency." A moment later, she came on the phone again. "Bryce, repeat what you've just told us. We've got a room full of friends who want to help."

Ava squeezed Bryce's hand as he spoke, relaying the email and their conversation with the team and Travis regarding his playing future. That Travis had been able to pull off that much was great news—a testament to Bryce's talent—but Bryce still sounded miserable, and Cole's heart clenched painfully when he thought about what it would mean for them.

"What's concerning you most?" King asked.

"Coming out. Being outed. I have no idea what it's going to mean for me, or for us. I knew that I'd be in the public eye, but now I'm dragging Ava and Cole into it too, and this isn't going to be pretty." Bryce paused, swallowing hard. He sounded defeated when he spoke again. "My agent wants me to deny we're a trio. He's suggested I come out as gay, tell everyone that Ava and I aren't really together and she's my closest friend. They want me to be the poster boy for gay athletes, and that'd be fine... except I'm not gay. I don't want to catfish anyone."

Cole could hear murmurs in the background, an understanding rippling through the group of people on the other end.

Bryce continued, "Then there's my playing career. I either move to the Gold Coast or I'm out of the NRL. I don't know whether to chuck it in and join Ava and Cole, or to move."

Ava shared a look with Cole. They faced a decision too. Bryce might feel like he needed to make an impossible choice—move to the Gold Coast or give up his dream—but they had a stake in matters too. If Bryce left, they'd be without him, but Triple Threat tied them to Sydney, at least temporarily. Until they could sell all their houses, they couldn't just up and leave.

Cole recognized Levi's voice when he spoke. "Okay, mate. Easts want to push you back to reserves. They seem to have made up their mind, so let's forget about them for the moment. Does the Gold Coast team know what's going on? What are they saying?"

Bryce's response sounded a little more hopeful, but he was still down. "The Gold Coast team have already done up a welcome announcement. They've worded the press release as if they poached me. It talks about my stats and says how I'm an asset that they're grateful to have. They have a one liner in there at the end which says they're ecstatic I get to be my authentic self and the entire team are 100 percent behind me in every way. They haven't mentioned my sexuality at all, but the conversation I had with the coach was good."

"Coach is good people," Liam stated. "He'll support you. The players are good guys too. They'll probably be put out because of the media circus that's coming, but I don't think anyone will be overly shitty."

A man, Nick, introduced himself as the cousin of one of Levi's partners. "What do you want to do? It's a big decision to move teams, especially with this hanging over your head.

"You're not quitting," Ava mumbled. "We'll make it work well before you need to give up your dream."

Bryce shot a sideways glance at their girl, and Cole grinned, pleased she'd nipped that in the bud before Bryce actually thought it was an option.

Bryce groaned. "I have no idea, but I need to have a game plan figured out so that I know how to respond. I'm floundering here."

"Let's put aside the contract and your agent for a moment and deal with the media," Nick advised. "You've got a few options on how to tackle them."

Levi added, "Agreed. If you'd like my help, I'm here for you."

"Yeah." Bryce cleared his throat, blinking back the emotion Cole could see building in his eyes.

"You're loved, Bryce. We're all here to help," Cole encouraged, dropping a kiss on his leg.

"I'm not really ready to come out, but I'm also not going to lie about Cole and Ava to anyone either." Bryce's eyes lit up and he sat up straighter. "You run a podcast, don't you?"

Cole's mouth popped open, his brain going a million miles a minute to catch up with Bryce's train of thought.

"I do," Levi answered proudly. That was it! "We can use it to take control of the narrative if that's what you're thinking,"

"Yeah, that's exactly what I'm thinking. How quickly can we set up a session?"

"I could be ready in twenty minutes, but I'm sure you'd need to speak with your agent and the Gold Coast team first."

Bryce nodded. "Yeah, I will. Assuming I get their okay, could we do it later tonight? My agent has us on an early evening flight to the Goldie tonight."

"Perfect. Where are you staying?"

"Mum and Dad's. I'm going to talk to them when we get there. Let them know what's happening."

"Let's pencil it in for tonight at like 10:00 p.m. It'll only take an hour." Before Bryce had a chance to answer, Levi asked, "Con, can you pick Bryce up and bring him to our place?"

"Absolutely," another man said.

"Assuming the terms of the offer are okay, I'll have a press conference tomorrow at noon in the club's media room. I guess the Lightning need to sign off on any deal, but my agent doesn't think it'll be a problem."

TWENTY

Bryce

Bryce undid the button on his suit jacket, tugged on the lapels to resituate it on his shoulders and re-buttoned it. He was borrowing the suit from Rogers, the prop he was replacing. The jacket wasn't a perfect fit—Rogers had thicker muscle than him, the pants were two sizes too big—but it was the best the team could do on a few hours' notice. Each suit was tailormade for a player, and his hadn't even been ordered yet. But the team's PR rep didn't want to advertise how last minute his acquisition actually was.

By announcing it early in an attempt to distract the media, they were doing him a huge favour. He was not going to complain.

Nerves churned in his belly, but he couldn't wipe the smile from his face. In fact, nothing could dim his happy. Except maybe one thing. Looking at what their lives would be like in a few months when they didn't see each other often was like an anvil sitting in his gut, but Ava and Cole had promised him they'd make it work. They weren't giving up on him, and that was all that mattered. So, he put aside the worries and basked in the knowledge that this team wanted him.

All the dreams he thought were dead in the water had been given a new lease on life. He'd walked into the team's offices at 9:00 a.m. sharp, as per Hayden, the PR rep's request. After his briefing, they joined the rest of the team. DJ, the player liaison, had given the team the full run-down and went through what to expect. By the time he'd walked in there, the team was firmly on his side, welcoming Bryce with back-slapping handshakes.

Liam had taken him under his wing, sticking close and introducing Bryce to everyone. The conversation flowed, the trays of food were demolished, and tea, coffee, and juices were drunk, and Bryce was jumping with excitement. There was a healthy dose of nerves too.

Cole and Ava, together with King and Adelaide, were waiting in the audience. The team was going to line up along the back wall, standing behind the table he and Coach would sit at. Hayden would be at the lectern, directing questions to each of them.

Every single player and all the staff he'd met had expressed their support, even though quite a few had no idea what the right terminology was. It was a weight lifted off his shoulders. He'd never been so open before—Bryce had always expected his sexuality to be a secret—but he'd had no idea how much it had weighed on him. This was the first time he'd walked into a room and everyone knew the piece of himself that he had kept under wraps. The best thing was that everyone had accepted him for it too. It only made Bryce smile wider, his cheeks hurting from the grin he didn't want to lose.

"You good, mate?" Liam asked as Bryce reached inside his pocket and blew out a breath at the text from Levi: **Podcast just hit the first thousand downloads. It's blowing up. You're definitely gonna get questions from the media.** Levi had been right. Both his agent and the team wanted to approve the podcast before it went live. Recording it the night before had come in handy—he'd forwarded a link to the raw recording and by morning, both had sent their requirements to Levi, who was only too happy to edit it as necessary.

Bryce showed Liam the message. "Shiiit. You aren't alone, okay? We're all here to back you up."

"Yeah." His smile came even easier now, from deeper inside. It wasn't just excitement, but contentment too. "As long as I have them, I'm good. But thank you for being here. This team…." He looked around the room, at the easy laughter and playfulness. The Lightning had the same sort of vibe, and he'd loved it there too. Knowing he wouldn't be back there was a bitter pill to swallow, but having a place on the Gold Coast team was worth it. "I know I'll be happy here."

Cole and Ava would be happy too. They had the business and each other. He could come and go, visiting them whenever his time allowed it. He could handle living alone—he would have to—because as Bryce stood there, basking in the acceptance of a team who he'd only just met but immediately knew he fit into, he desperately wanted to make it work. All of it.

"Time's up, gents. Let's get into position," Hayden announced. "Bryce, if you'd like to wait with me while everyone gets into place." Liam slapped him on the back, grinned and nodded, then filed out of the room with the others. "Do you have any other last-minute questions?"

"No, but just got a message from my cousin. He said that the podcast has already had a thousand downloads."

Hayden nodded. "The press release is already on the website. We're expecting it and are prepared. Only answer the questions you feel comfortable addressing. If you want me to field any of them, just look my way and nod."

"Will do."

Bryce walked through the door and swallowed, his smile dipping a little as his mouth went dry and his heart thudded in his chest. His forehead prickled with sweat as nerves hit him. The room was packed. A horde of media was seated at the ready, some taking photos and a few doing quick video clips in anticipation of the cross.

Three chairs were pushed in against a long table, a microphone in front of each seat. Coach pulled out the chair next to him and Bryce slipped into it, leaning in close when Coach rested a hand on his shoulder and murmured, "We've got your back. Literally."

Bryce nodded, a mixture of relief and excitement breaking through in his grin as he cast a glance over his shoulder at the team lined up against the wall. Liam gave him a thumbs-up and a couple of the other blokes gave him a chin-up nod.

Bryce guessed that the spare seat next to him was so Hayden could join them after he'd done the official opening at the lectern, but until then, he used it as an armrest, faking a relaxed pose. His eyes were drawn to the back of the room where Cole and Ava sat next to King and Addy. All four of them wore team jerseys, and Bryce laughed as Ava blew him a kiss and Cole pretended to snatch it out of the air and pocket it against his chest.

"Thanks for joining us, everyone," Hayden began, the room immediately silencing. "We have some exciting news to share with our fans. As you're aware, the team has been searching for the perfect prop to fill Rogers's sizeable shoes since his retirement. That search has taken us longer than expected, but we're very happy to announce Bryce Flaharty's appointment to the team. Bryce was an asset to the Lightning in his first year playing, and we're excited to have been fortunate enough to secure his agreement to return home to the Gold Coast. The Lightning agreed this morning to release Bryce from his contract. Please welcome the Gold Coast's newest team member."

The team cheered and clapped, a few of the players reaching forward to pat his shoulder. Bryce couldn't help the colour rising in his cheeks. He flicked his gaze to Ava and Cole. They were clapping and cheering the loudest, their smiles aimed solely at him.

He grinned happily and laughed when Coach nudged him with his elbow and pointed to the team. They were doing the wave, stepping forward, raising their arms and stepping back again back and forth.

Questions were fired at all three of them, Hayden and Coach fielding some of them and Bryce fumbling through answers as his nerves exploded. Cole mimed taking off his shirt and Bryce took a breath, collecting himself and looked around the room, remembering Cole's advice. Pretend everyone's naked. Amazingly enough, it helped.

But then it happened. "Bryce, did you leave the Lightning because they weren't supportive of your sexuality?"

The room silenced, a collective pause while Bryce absorbed the journalist's words. He flicked his gaze to Cole and Ava. They were holding hands, leaning forward as if hanging off his every word. A hand landed on his shoulder, squeezing tight in the way that Liam often did.

"I'd prefer not to talk about the Lightning's willingness to release me from their contract. The Gold Coast has welcomed me with open arms. That's what I'm going to focus on." There. He'd done it. Given the canned answer Hayden had coached him on. He didn't want to risk bad-mouthing the Lightning, but he wouldn't lie for them either.

"So you're confirming you're gay?"

This was what the Lightning were worried about—his sexuality overshadowing his playing achievements, distracting the team and getting their highly religious players offside. But the squeeze to his shoulder gave him strength, as did Coach leaning forward, prepared to answer for him.

"No, I'm not gay. I'm pansexual." Bryce smiled, closed his eyes, and basked in the feeling of being able to shout it from the rooftops. He was out. Officially and undeniably out. The momentary lull didn't last long though, the ruckus from shouted questions deafening. Liam slipped into the chair next to him, not taking his hand from Bryce's shoulder.

"Ladies and gentlemen, let's keep this press conference civil, please. One at a time," Hayden directed, pointing to a reporter sitting only a few seats away from Ava.

"Are you cheating on your girlfriend, Bryce?"

"No." He shook his head and flicked his gaze to Ava, giving her a small smile. "No, I'd never cheat on her."

"How do you explain the photos released by News and Views?"

Bryce blinked and Cole's face drained of colour. He'd naïvely thought that by coming out and announcing his transfer that News and Views would have their story trumped and the images would be buried. But apparently not.

"Those pictures were taken without Mr Flaharty or his partner's consent from private property. An investigation is being conducted to determine who the trespasser was, and appropriate action will be taken against them," Hayden answered in a no-nonsense tone. "In the meantime, we ask that you respect Mr Flaharty's privacy."

Question after question was fired at him, far too many about whether he could still play the game if he was gay. It was frustrating and unfortunately, everything Bryce expected. He wanted to rail and shout, to protest that he was the same person the media had complimented at the end of last season as the year's best-performing rookie. He wanted to tell them he'd done that with both Cole and Ava at his side. He was no different from what he'd been the entire season. It was just their perception that had changed. It was their understanding of who he was that had been altered.

Hayden refused to allow answers to some of the less respectful questions, even asking a journalist to leave if he couldn't be polite. Coach interrupted one of Hayden's answers, telling the reporter flat out that the question she'd asked was disrespectful of a professional team and its players. Bryce wanted to crawl into a hole and never come out when she'd asked Coach if they'd signed Bryce because his sexuality would get people talking more about the team.

"Let's focus on Bryce's playing ability, not his sexuality," Liam said matter-of-factly from beside him. "That's what we should be talking about."

"Why are you sticking up for Bryce? Are the two of you in a relationship? Are you the person he was cheating on his girlfriend with?" a dumb-arse journalist asked.

Liam laughed and Bryce couldn't help the twitch of his lips when he flicked his gaze toward Cole. The man looked murderous. His lips were set in a harsh line, the crease between his brows deep as he willed death on the reporter. Cole flushed red, his fists clutching the chair in front of him in a white-knuckled grip.

"No, he is my mate, though." Liam paused and Bryce tore his gaze away from Cole, looking to his friend. He blew out a breath and steeled his spine. "You're all assuming that Bryce is the only player in the men's competition who is LGBTQIA. Statistically speaking, it's highly unlikely. It's also homophobic. The level of toxic masculinity in this game is pretty horrifying sometimes, and from a group of educated people, it's disappointing that these are the questions that are being asked."

"Thanks," Bryce murmured, but Liam wasn't done talking.

"You've never questioned my playing ability. Why is that?" Liam raised an eyebrow and looked out over the sea of faces.

Bryce's mouth popped open, his eyes widening in panic. What was Liam doing? People would start talking. They would start rumours about him. He'd be put under the microscope.

"Is it because you assumed I'm straight? Is that why I'm a good enough player to be professional? Because of who I love?"

Murmurs went around the room, and Bryce looked out toward Adelaide and King, waiting for them to put a stop to this madness. Bryce gripped Liam's forearm, squeezing it and shaking his head.

"No," he murmured. "Liam, don't do this."

Liam patted his hand, and he watched as Liam met Adelaide and King's smiles with one of his own. They were proud of him. King's chest puffed up, a smile breaking over his handsome face, and Addy held a hand over her heart, smiling softly at him.

"Well, your assumption was wrong—"

"Liam, please," Bryce whispered, panic for his friend clawing at his throat. He didn't want him to be under the same kind of scrutiny as he was. He didn't want it to tip the team over and have them both on their butts without playing contracts. He didn't want the other players to turn on them. What if they wouldn't share a locker room with them any more? What if it destroyed the team dynamics? Liam didn't seem to be thinking about any of it.

Liam smiled, wrapped an arm around Bryce's shoulder and pulled him closer, murmuring under his breath, "I told you that you aren't in this alone."

"But—"

Liam leaned closer to the mic, cutting off Bryce mid-sentence. Bryce's belly swooped, and his chest clenched tight when his friend spoke.

"I'm pansexual too. I'm in a relationship with both a man and a woman."

The room erupted, questions being hurled at them, fingers typing on phones to tweet the news first. It was utter chaos. But Bryce was slowly sinking underwater, that same detachment he'd experienced before filling him again. He opened his mouth to suck in a breath, but it was like the noise had taken corporeal form. His lungs seemed to fill with water rather than air. He snapped his mouth closed again, concentrating on Liam's arm tightening around his shoulders. But just as suddenly as the overwhelming sensations crowded him, the air cleared, and his lungs emptied.

This was his chance to set the record straight. Another chance to control his story. To say the words out loud himself rather than letting strangers tell it for him.

He took a deep breath and leaned forward. The room hushed, anticipation rippling through them. "For clarity, Liam and I aren't together. But as he said, both of us are pansexual, and we both have a girlfriend and boyfriend. Like his, my girlfriend and boyfriend are together, too, and we love one another deeply." He shrugged, not knowing how to simplify this relationship any more than he already had. "There are three of us in our relationship. None of us are cheating on the other because we're all together."

Bryce knocked on the table, taking his time to choose his words and shove down the anger and desire to scrub his body clean from the feeling of being violated. He rested his elbows on the table and opened up to the people in front of him, saying, "Those photos that were taken of my boyfriend and I aren't me cheating. We're three adults in a committed, exclusive relationship. Regardless of what you think of it, surely we deserve the right to... I dunno... be together in our own house behind closed doors. The person who took them may have gotten a scoop, but they also committed a crime."

Liam squeezed his shoulder as Bryce's voice wobbled, and he sucked in a breath, blinking back the burning behind his eyes. Reporters were asking questions, challenging some of his comments and others expressing support. He appreciated that support. He'd at least made some of them think about what had happened. When he'd turned pro, Bryce knew he would be in the public eye. But he'd never imagined that the photogs would be so relentless to take images of him having sex.

The whole experience was appalling. He couldn't believe it was happening. Whose life had he fallen into? He wasn't a Kardashian. He wasn't worthy of a sex tape. Cole and Ava certainly didn't deserve it.

Bryce liked to see smiles on the people he was with. He wanted laughter and happiness surrounding him. He wanted love, and he'd go to the ends of the earth to defend those people who made him happy and loved him like Cole and Ava did.

He wanted to say a lot more than he had. He wanted to tell people to butt out of his relationship, that they would answer to him if they hurt the two people who meant the world to him. But he held his tongue.

"No, we're not together," Liam agreed. "I'm asking that readers and viewers don't share the images and boycott any publication who does. My friends deserve that respect."

"Thank you," Bryce murmured under his breath, forever grateful for the friendship that Liam had shown him. Liam, his cousin, and their friends hadn't hesitated to stop in the middle of a party—a celebration of another throuple's commitment to each other—to help. He hadn't met many of them yet, but they were there for them, giving them advice and lending an understanding ear.

Then there were his new teammates. They'd gone out of their way to welcome him. Even some of his old teammates had reached out, expressing how sorry they were for the way he, Cole, and Ava had been treated.

"Thank you for coming," Hayden announced. He tilted his head, motioning for the three of them to leave. They filed out to claps on shoulders and a few ruffles of Liam's hair. "On behalf of the team, I'm reiterating our press release and extending it to Mr Masters—we are all 100 percent supportive of both Bryce and Liam and their partners. They're brilliant players, but more importantly, they're part of our football family and they matter to us. We don't believe in paying lip service to equality. We believe in living it. Please stay tuned for an announcement in relation to LGBTQIA initiatives the team is undertaking to demonstrate our ongoing commitment."

Bryce followed Liam through the door in a daze, beyond relieved that the press conference was over, but also riding a high that he'd been able to express himself so genuinely. Voices surrounded them—the team filing into the room. The volume reached a crescendo, until he heard "Excuse me," in a sweet voice. It was Adelaide, pushing through the swell of men surrounding them. "I'm so damn proud of you, Lee," she said, wrapping him up in a hug. King was there, too, taking both his partners into his arms and kissing Liam's forehead.

"I knew it!" someone shouted at Liam and King, as Cole nudged his shoulder, brushing the backs of their hands together and Ava curled hers around his forearm, squeezing his arm before letting him go. Bryce knew they were respecting his boundaries, unsure whether they could engage in any form of PDA now they were out.

But Bryce had done enough worrying about it to last a lifetime. He needed them, needed their grounding touch and their love. If he was going to be out to the media—and no doubt the subject of many more photos—he was going to be himself in front of his new teammates too.

Bryce wrapped his arms around both Cole's and Ava's shoulders and pulled them tightly against him, breathing in their familiar scents and taking comfort from their touch. Standing there in a three-way embrace, their arms curled around one another's backs, Cole nuzzled his face into the crook of Bryce's neck, exhaling slowly.

"You're so brave," he breathed. "I could never do that. I'm in awe of you."

Warmth flared through his chest, and he held onto both of them a little tighter. He couldn't believe Cole was saying he was proud of him when what he'd been through paled in comparison to Cole's coming out. All he'd done was do a damn interview.

"I love you both. I'm sorry the journos were dicks."

"We're having an impromptu barbecue at our place if you want to join us," King offered, siding up next to them. "Liam thought it might be good to spend some time together with the team."

Bryce looked to his partners, grinning when they nodded. "Yeah, we can come for a few hours. Cole and Ava's flight home isn't until later tonight."

"You staying with your parents until you can get a place here?"

"Yeah." Bryce nodded, pursing his lips. "Not sure what I'll do yet though."

"I've got the perfect place for you. Little furnished granny flat above our friends' garage. Sweet spot near the beach, and garage parking too. I'll hook you up with them."

TWENTY-ONE

Ava

I t was the first night they'd spent apart in months. Ava hated it. She was comfortable lying in Cole's arms, but she missed Bryce's big body behind her. She missed his playful bouncing on the bed when they hopped in, and the laughter that seemed to light them up when he was near.

He was their sunshine, the bright spark in their day.

They'd facetimed Bryce, talking through their options for the future. Now that his playing contract was sorted, they had the breathing space to figure out where Ava and Cole would be long-term. Cole had asked the ninety-nine-dollar question: "Do we need to stay in Sydney?"

Ava hadn't hesitated, knowing in her gut that she wanted them to be together. They just needed to find a way to do it without losing too much money.

Bryce had started to drift, eventually falling asleep. The day had finally taken its toll on him, and it was as if the sun had set when his breathing had finally evened out. "He's exhausted, the poor bugger," Cole murmured.

"I don't blame him. Today was crazy, and we were just spectators."

"Yup."

Ava snuggled into Cole and sighed. "Are you okay after everything that's gone down? We've all been focussing on Bryce, but you were in those pictures too."

Cole grumbled under his breath, and Ava couldn't help but smile. These last few days had seen the return of Cole as a hissing cat, but even with it, he was still so different. A year had changed him. He still wasn't a fan of people in general, but the only ones who got his hackles up had hurt or upset Ava or Bryce. "I'm fine."

Ava propped herself up on her elbow, looking down at her lover. His dark eyes pierced into her with their intensity, but there was a melancholy there, a hurt that Ava wanted to scoop up in her arms and protect him from. She brushed her thumb over his bare chest and took solace in the steady beat of his heart under her palm. "Hey, it's okay to be upset, to feel angry or even violated. Someone was spying on you," Ava whispered.

He curled his hand around hers and nodded, slowly blowing out a breath. "I feel dirty. Not because of what Bryce and I did." He looked at her with wide eyes, pleading with her to understand.

She did. Nodding and smiling gently at him, Ava pressed a kiss to his chest, encouraging him to continue.

"I'd been teasing him. I wanted it so bad. I was completely on edge, and he knew." Cole smiled wistfully, the sadness in his eyes never leaving. "He made me feel so good. He looked after me, gave me everything I needed and more. Every time he sank into me, he did that thing with his hips." Cole shivered and Ava didn't miss the way his breathing hitched.

"But it was more than that. He didn't just fuck and run. As corny as it sounds, he made love to me. He showed me how much I mean to him, and through the whole thing, he told me how much both of you loved me. It was special, and they took that away from me."

"Oh, Cole." Ava hugged him close. "They didn't take it away. You still have that memory. You still have the knowledge that we will always love you as much as we did that day."

He shrugged, but Ava could see that he was trying to downplay his feelings, that the whole episode had cut him deep. "It's stupid, but the way they described me—as some random who Bryce was screwing—hurt, you know? I was worthless. I was just a hole for Bryce to get his dick wet in."

She didn't know what to say to that. She had no idea how to fix what they'd broken, but she had to try. "You mean everything to Bryce and me. You're so strong and brave. You'd literally stand in front of a bus to protect us. You're our counterbalance. You think things through way more than Bryce and I ever do—"

"You mean overthink."

"Eh, to-mah-toe, to-may-toe." Ava grinned at him, her smile cheeky as she pinched his nipple. "You make sure you've considered all the angles before you jump in, but when you do, you're all in. I love that you're a grumpy cat and all moody and broody with everyone except us."

Cole rolled his eyes. "I don't like people."

"They're arseholes most of the time," Ava agreed. "But you're safe with us, Cole. You're so loved, so special to us. Bryce may be our sunshine, but you're our strength. You're the one who holds us together." Ava huffed out a laugh. "Sometimes I wonder if the two of you should be together without me."

"You're our spitfire. Our go-getter. We wouldn't be half of what we are without you."

"See? Even when I'm trying to make you feel better, you'll take over and care for us. It's who you are, Cole, and we love you for it. You're so much more than what they saw. But that's good, because you're protected from them. That's how Bryce and I wanted it to be."

"I love you," he whispered, tugging her down so her head was on his chest. His sigh was loud in her ear, and Ava's heart broke for the stoic man in her arms. He had a heart of gold that had been battered and bruised before he'd met them, and Ava would do anything to protect him from more of that. "I miss him already."

"Me too." Ava ran her fingers through the hair on his chest and bit her lip, unsure of how to broach the question.

"So how do we wrap things up here?" he asked. "I mean, do we just power through the houses we've already started? We can drop any renovations that aren't essential and sell off the other ones with just a quick clean up."

"I think that's perfect." Ava popped her head up, her smile stretching wide across her lips. "Are we really going to do this? Move to be with Bryce?"

"To see that smile on your face?" He cupped her cheek, his callused palm rough against her skin. Ava leaned into his touch, loving the warm flutters that awoke in her belly when he looked at her with such adoration in his gaze. "I'd do anything. Absolutely. And I'm being selfish too—I want to be with him just as much as you do."

"Let's take a closer look at what we have." Ava pulled back, anticipation pulsing in her veins. She loved Triple Threat, loved the work they did and the way they were rescuing old houses. She loved working with Cole and Bryce, creating something from the ground up. But they could easily do the same work on the Gold Coast, and the city had one thing that Sydney no longer had—Bryce.

Cole sat up too, kicking off the sheet as he eased himself off the bed. His movements were graceful, and Ava enjoyed the view of his naked body as she followed him to their shared desk, excitement building as he collected the folders for each of their properties and she grabbed the laptop. With everything back in their bed, they worked at cutting back their projects to the barest minimum, repricing them and rechecking what sort of sales prices they could get. If they could break even on the three houses, all at different stages of renovation, they'd have a decent nest egg to start investing on the Gold Coast when they got there.

"We can always speak to the Lightning's lawyer. See if he wants to pick up any of them?" Cole suggested. Ava had already sent him an email and she smiled, turning the laptop to show him. Cole laughed, rolling his eyes at her blush, and leaned in to press a kiss to her forehead as she cuddled into his shoulder.

* * * * *

Ava grinned happily as Cole's peel of laughter and Bryce's soft chuckle filled the small space. Liam hadn't been kidding when he said that he had the perfect spot for Bryce to rent. It was a one-bedroom apartment on top of a garage, but its location was second to none. Two streets back from the beach in a quiet little enclave of old Queenslanders, nestled among the strip of high-rises that lined the main road.

"Come on, that's them." Bryce bounced excitedly on his toes as the creak of the garage door signalled it closing below them. He was out the door in a flash, Ava hot on his heels.

"Hi, Bryce," the woman with flowing blonde hair greeted him.

He relieved her of the grocery bags she was holding, and Ava got a good look at her. Bryce had mentioned her before—Cassie, his landlord. She was beautiful, glamorous in a classic kind of understated way, but dressed super casually in a pair of denim shorts, white bikini top, and flowing white linen shirt.

"Ava, Cole—" He looked around and Ava followed his gaze, spying Cole at the top of the steps. "Babe, come down here." Cole did, giving them a tight smile as he reached them.

Ava held out her hand for Cassie and they shook. "It's nice to meet you. Bryce has said so many good things about you."

"You too. I feel like I know you already." Cassie shook Cole's hand too and motioned over her shoulder to the men she was with. One looked like he'd wandered straight off the beach with his blond man-bun, board shorts, and lack of tan lines. The other was the complete opposite—dark features and buttoned up in a way that reminded Ava of a man who was used to suits but had dressed down once or twice and was completely out of his element. Even his polo shirt had the top button done up. "These are my husbands, Jake and Phoenix."

Ava flicked her gaze to Bryce, and he nodded, his grin like a kid at Christmas. He hadn't told her that he'd met another trio apart from his cousin and Liam, but he was clearly excited.

"This is my girlfriend, Ava, and boyfriend, Cole."

"Bryce said you'd be home tonight, so we organized an impromptu party to welcome you all here. Bring your swimmers. It'll still be warm enough," Cassie said, her smile open and welcoming.

Ava was blown away. Cassie was far more than Bryce's landlord. She reminded her of a mother hen, making sure everyone was welcome and looked after. "Can we help set up, or bring anything?"

"Nah, you're the guests," Jake answered.

Phoenix added, "We've got beer and wine, but if you'd like something different to drink, just bring that."

A few hours later with introductions done, Ava was riding cloud nine. Bryce, Liam and King, Connor and Levi, and Mike and Ezio were bonding over fitness stuff, while Mike watched his kids splashing with Nick and Emma's young daughter in the pool, calling out to them when it got too rough.

Jake peppered her and Cole with questions about their business and what they would do when they moved up. Jake and Cassie were apparently real estate agents, but while she looked after corporate spaces, he focussed on residential properties.

Jake grinned, his passion for his business and clients shining through. "I've got quite a few listings that I've been marketing as renovator's delights, but people can't see past the dated façades and bad kitchens. Great areas, solid houses, but people just don't want the hassle of renovating."

"That's our ideal property," Ava replied, thanking Phoenix for topping up her soda water and lime.

Jake tugged on his husband's belt loop and asked him to relax, Phoenix popped a kiss on his lips and replied, "Almost done with refills. I'll be with you in a second." He sauntered off, checking for empty glasses and opening and giving out a few new bottles of beer.

Ava watched Jake as his smile turned soft when Cassie caught Ava's attention. Her gaze followed her man, and the love in Phoenix's eyes when he caught Cassie watching him was enough to make Ava swoon.

"It is," Cole added, dragging her back into the conversation. He ran his hand down her back, stopping at the small of her waist. "We should look at them. If we find one, we might be able to get the keys around the time we're finishing up in Sydney. It'd be good to be able to jump right in."

Ava turned to Jake. "Apart from seeing Bryce, we came up to get an idea of what the property market here was like. Get a layout in our heads of the Coast and where the hot spots are. We holidayed up here Christmas before last and Bryce grew up on the Goldie, so we've got a bit of background, but not enough to start investing. If you could give us a recommendation or two, that'd be amazing."

"Yeah, no worries. I'll pick out a couple of the best listings for flipping and point you in the direction of the suburbs being gentrified."

Phoenix joined them again, wrapping his arms around Jake's waist. "We should get the food started."

"Mmm, we should." Jake excused himself to get the barbecue going, and Ava smiled at the way he and Phoenix gravitated to each other. Like all the men in the group, they were openly affectionate.

"You should go sit with Bryce," she encouraged Cole. "There aren't any arseholes here."

His lips tilted up, giving her the soft, shy smile he reserved for them and nodded. "Yeah, I think I'd like that."

Bryce held out his hand as she and Cole wandered over to them, pulling Cole into his arms the moment he got close enough. Ava waved them off when Cole did the same. She wanted to catch up with the ladies.

Ava wandered over to where Adelaide, Katy, Cassie, and two women she'd met that night—Robyn and Emma—were sitting. "This is great, Cassie. Thanks for making us feel so welcome."

"It was our pleasure. We thought it'd be nice to get to know a few people who you could be yourselves with after what you've been through, and then having to be separated because the Lightning wouldn't renew Bryce's contract."

"The Lightning cancelled his contract," Ava explained. "Bryce still had another two years to go, but they were going to bounce him to the reserves to get him out of the public eye. His agent worked his magic and got him in with the Gold Coast instead. The Lightning couldn't wait to wash their hands of him."

"Rogers retired at an awkward time," Adelaide explained. She was a massive football fan, even bigger than Ava was. "But it was such good timing. The Goldie missed out on the main trade timeframe at the end of the season, but because of that, they were looking at exactly the time Bryce became available. I still can't believe the Lightning were stupid and prejudiced enough to let go of the best rookie prop around."

"Prejudiced?" Robyn asked. "Sorry, I've had my head in the sand—been working on a big case."

"Yeah," Ava answered honestly, explaining their conversation with the team's PR rep.

"Shit," she swore. "That's disgusting."

"It's not unheard of though," Katy sympathized. "It crushed Levi when he lost his job."

Cassie squeezed Katy's arm and smiled warmly at Ava. "Like I said, we all wanted to let you know that you've got friends here."

They talked about nothing and everything, the conversation meandering from heavy to light when Jake called, "Come and get it." Ava's stomach rumbled, the delicious scent of grilled meat floating on the sea breeze over to them.

Within a few minutes, they were seated around a collection of tables lined up along the back deck paired with mismatched chairs. Cole slid into the seat next to her. Bryce was on his other side and immediately pulled his chair closer to Cole's. The private smile they shared and soft kiss Bryce planted on their man warmed Ava's heart.

"Sorry about the pics, man. You got screwed by that website," Phoenix grumbled as he sat opposite them. "Addy told me what happened at work, and it was kinda hard to miss the news a few weeks ago."

"You and Adelaide work together?" Ava asked. She knew her friend was a sex counsellor, or however she'd described it when they were talking earlier, but she had no idea what that had to do with Phoenix working at a bar.

"Yeah, I'm a bartender at the swingers club Addy consults at. Cass and Jake met her through Levi, Con, and Katy at Robyn, Mike, and Ez's housewarming. But none of us knew until recently that she, King, and Liam were together."

"How did you, Cassie, and Jake meet?" Cole asked.

Phoenix laughed, but the sound was tinged with sadness. "I was working as a barista while I was at uni in Sydney. Jake was showing an office nearby and he stopped in for coffee. He ordered what the dude in front of him did. It was the most disgusting mismatched blend of tastes that I'd ever made. He really only wanted an espresso—it's all he drinks—but he got tongue-tied around me and couldn't think straight." He knocked his shoulder into his husband's and laughed when Jake wrapped an arm around his shoulders and planted a kiss to his temple.

"Completely lost my head. Couldn't even string a sentence together."

"Anyway, Cassie came in to chat me up the next day because Jake spoke to her about me. We got together but then lost contact. I moved up here a few years later and started working at the club. Addy met Jake and Cass at the housewarming next door and gave them a card for the club. We ran into each other that first night and the rest is history."

Jake turned Phoenix's face, his hand cupping his lover's cheek. Phoenix's eyes slipped closed as Jake pressed their lips together ever so gently. When he pulled back, he whispered something against Phoenix's lips that prompted the other man to nod and kiss him again. It was chaste, nothing more than a slow press of lips together, but the love between them was captivating, and like ripples in a pond, radiated outward until they were all smiling goofily at the pair.

"How did you three meet?" Robyn asked as she tugged a balled-up piece of bread from Jax, her stepson's hand. He was glaring at his sister, about to throw it at her. "Is that the right thing to do?" she asked, getting a headshake in return, the little boy's shoulders dropping. She kissed his temple and gave him a new piece of bread. "Eat this one. No throwing, sweetheart."

Bryce grinned, regaling the group with the story of how they'd decided to do a road trip when their flights were cancelled, and Cole's gaze went wistful. Ava leaned in close, squeezing Cole's hand, and asked, "Are you okay?"

He nodded, his smile soft. "Yeah, just can't believe I'm sitting here with both of you among people who understand and accept us. I've never had that before, you know?"

"We're all lucky," Phoenix explained, clearly having overheard their murmured conversation and getting the attention of the others around the table. "I found my way back to Cass and Jake at my lowest point, and they and Addy all promised me I had friends I hadn't met yet who cared about me. Con was at his lowest too when he came home to Levi and Katy, and King and Addy were there for Liam when his world was falling apart. So were Mike, Ezio, and Robyn—they came together when the three of them were struggling for different reasons. I know it's been tough for all of you, but we understand. You're safe here."

"It took me—took us—years to come out." Jake motioned between himself and Phoenix. "Our one-night stand wasn't by choice. My dad was a bastard. He destroyed mine and Cassie's careers, then did the same to Phoenix after he found out about us. He scared Phoenix into cutting off all contact with us. We understand how hard it is. How shi—crappy the world can be."

"How did the site get the picture?" Connor asked.

"We don't know," Bryce replied with a shrug and a shake of his head. "But it was taken from the back of the house. Whoever it was, didn't just stumble past and see an opportunity to make a buck. We were careful."

"Who ratted you out?" Cole asked Levi.

Levi tilted his head in Katy's direction. "Her d-head brother. He got his five seconds of fame and lost half his family because of it."

"I wish we knew," Bryce mused with a frown. "I hate that it could have been someone we knew. Someone we trusted."

"I might know someone who can help," King volunteered hesitantly. "I was thinking about it the other night and found her number. She was one of my students a few years ago, a computer and maths prodigy. She might be able to look into it."

"How?" Bryce asked, his brows furrowed.

"I have no idea, but I know she's done this kind of thing before," King replied.

"Is that the person you referred me to?" Levi asked. When King nodded, he added, "She shut down a hack of the

LGBTQIA shelter's website within five minutes. Some right-wing group of nut-jobs were redirecting people to their site, then spamming them with hate messages. She's good at what she does."

"Let's speak with her," Ava agreed, nodding. "Can you give me her number?" Her guys deserved to know. Bryce was walking on eggshells, scared that someone they knew had sold them out—and given how small that list was, it was no surprise he was wary—and Cole needed the closure. He needed to feel empowered again after having his privacy ripped away from him so publicly.

"I'll pass on yours and ask her to call you if she thinks she can help."

* * * * *

They'd stayed up late the night before, talking into the early hours. Mike's, and Nick and Emma's kids had crashed out on the couches in the lounge room somewhere around the 9:00 p.m. mark after their movie wrapped up, and the adults had just stayed in the backyard talking.

Ava rolled over trying to shield her eyes from the blinding sunshine coming through the gap in the curtains, but she was awake. It was probably a good thing given the rattling around of her phone on the bedside table next to Bryce. He groaned and Ava clambered over him, reaching for it before it went to her message bank. It was a private number and Ava never normally answered those, but King had warned her that his friend would be calling from one.

"Hello, hold on for one sec," she croaked, clearing her throat from the sleep still clinging to her. Ava slipped on Bryce's shirt that he'd dropped to the floor the night before and padded out into the cosy lounge room, closing the bedroom door behind her. "Sorry, this is Ava."

"Hi Ava, I know King. He gave me a brief of what's happened to you and asked if I could help you find out where an image came from."

"Yes, oh my god, thank you for calling so quickly." She filled her in, giving her the whole sordid story, and the woman hummed thoughtfully between asking questions for more detail.

"Okay, I'll do some digging and let you know if I come up with anything. Give me a couple of days and I'll be able to tell you whether there's something there. Don't call me. I'll call you."

She couldn't call her anyway—the number was private.

"Sure, okay," Ava said slowly, pausing when she realized she had no idea what her name was. "Sorry, I'm usually more awake when I'm speaking with people. I didn't catch your name."

"I didn't give it to you." *Okay then. Who is this woman?*

"What are your rates? How do I pay you?"

"Call it a favour for a friend of a friend."

"No, I wouldn't feel right doing that," Ava insisted. "Look, it's important to do this the right way. I need to pay you."

The woman sighed as if she was running out of patience, and Ava winced. She didn't want to piss her off, especially not when she'd agreed to help them, but Ava drew the line at getting things for free.

"My fee depends on what I find. I've taken a quick look at the photos. They're professional, so it's likely a pap. I'll find out whether they were following Bryce, or if they were tipped off. If someone sold you out, and they're a piece of shit, I'll take my fee from their assets. I decide whether they're a piece of shit and how much I charge. You get no say in it at all. If that's not satisfactory to you, then we leave it and we both walk away right now."

Ava swallowed. Take her fee from their assets? Ava didn't know what exactly that would entail, and she wasn't sure she wanted to either. There was no way it could be legal. "What about if they're... not a piece of shit?"

The woman huffed out a dark laugh. Her voice was smoky and seductive, and Ava was a mixture of scared, a little excited, and a whole lot intimidated by her, whoever she was. "They rarely are. Tell me, would you consider a person who sneaks into someone's backyard, takes photos of them being intimate then sells them, decent?"

"No, but—"

"Neither do I, but I keep an open mind. In my line of work, I find information that people are trying to hide. Trust me, it's rare that I'm not paid. It actually makes a nice change when I don't."

"Are you sure? I mean—"

"Yes." This time her voice was sharp, and Ava snapped her mouth closed. There was a clicking on the other end of the line like the press of a computer keyboard. "If it makes you sleep better, donate some money to Bryce's e-safety charity, or the one you run."

Ava swallowed. Clearly this woman had done her research on them. Her voice came out as a squeak, timid when she was usually confident. "Okay. Yeah, we can do that."

The line went dead, and Ava pulled her phone away, blinking. The whole conversation had been surreal. Who was this woman? How did King know her? Ava jumped when Bryce's strong arms slid around her waist, laughing when he playfully kissed everywhere he could reach.

"Why are you up so early?" he whined, fake crying.

"I just got off the phone..."

TWENTY-TWO

Cole

Ava's hand shook as she flipped her phone over, looking at the caller ID as it rung. He had to give it to her. The woman Ava had spoken to was precise. Two days to the hour from her original call and she was on the phone again.

An anvil sat perched precariously in Cole's gut. He was ready for it to fall and take his already average mood with it. Fear sat heavily in him. He was terrified of finding out that one of the very limited group of people—Ava and Bryce's families and a group of friends he could count on one hand—had betrayed them. He desperately wanted it to have been just bad luck.

Was it possible that they were in the wrong place at the wrong time and seen by someone who took more than a passing interest? He wasn't sure what was worse—being stalked or betrayed.

Cole sucked in a breath and held it, counting each heartbeat as his pulse thudded through his veins. Lightheaded, he threaded his fingers through Ava's and gripped her hand, holding onto her for dear life as he slowly exhaled. She was his calm in the storm, his safe place, and he needed her in that moment more than anything.

The only thing missing was Bryce's presence, his exuberant happiness like a ray of sunshine over them.

Ava answered the call, putting it on speaker. Cole was surprised that the woman actually spoke to people. From the way Ava had talked about her, she was more than a little weird. Surely some sort of incognito message popping up after their computer screen blanked out and a lone curser appeared would be more appropriate. Who didn't tell people their name? Then again, giving out a name meant that she could potentially be found—social media, at her job. Then she'd have to be available to talk to people. Cole could relate to wanting to avoid that. Peopling at all was seriously overrated.

"Hello," Ava squeaked. She cleared her throat and shot a freaked-out look—wide-eyed and bunched eyebrows as she bit down on her lip—toward Cole before she continued, "Ava here. You're on speaker phone with my boyfriend Cole."

"Ava, Cole, I have news. Are you somewhere private?" The woman's voice was smoky. It immediately made him think of whiskey and cigars, dark corners in bars, and a red slinky dress on a beautiful woman. Except there was no seduction or sensuality in her voice. She was all business.

No wonder Ava was intimidated. He was a little of that himself.

"Yes, we're in one of our houses. We're the only people here," Ava responded as Cole pulled away from her and closed the last of the blinds to the room. Anyone outside could probably hear them—there was a gaping hole in the kitchen floor that they were standing right next to, but at least they couldn't see them. They were rarely inside now with blinds open anymore. It was depressing and made for constantly feeling like they were closed in, but at least there wouldn't be any more photos.

"Good. The photograph was taken by David Collingwood. He's a professional photographer but doesn't usually dabble in paparazzi images."

Ava looked to Cole, and he shrugged, not having any idea who the man was. He didn't know whether to be relieved or sweat on it that he didn't know the name. It didn't make a difference to his heart pounding in his chest or his gut clenching painfully.

"Collingwood is a contact of one of the principal agents at City Space, a man named Charles Frazer. Frazer briefed Collingwood, but there was a third person involved—the brains and bank behind the operation."

"Who?" Ava asked, reaching for Cole again.

He pulled her tight against him, sure she could feel his pulse fluttering under his skin and his heart beating a mile a minute.

"Collingwood reported to Frazer, but he was just a puppet. Their puppeteer is a powerful person. I'm surprised I haven't come across his name before," she mused thoughtfully.

Cole buried his face in Ava's hair and breathed in her floral scent, wishing that his nerves would settle. Bloody hell, did she have to drag things out? Couldn't she just put them out of their misery and give them a name?

"Maxwell Denyer," she added as if it was an afterthought.

It was as if Cole had punched through a frozen lake, the shock instantly seizing his lungs and every nerve ending in his body simultaneously sizzling and numbing. Screaming pain tore through him, the betrayal deep. Someone who was supposed to keep quiet—weren't lawyers like priests and had to take stuff like this to the grave?—had ratted them out.

The urge to lash out and destroy something, anything, like Denyer had done to them was overwhelming. "Fuck," he muttered. Tearing himself away from Ava, he spun away and shouted, "Fuuuck."

Cole kicked the cupboard door that always sat open. Now that the foundations were finally succumbing to the water leak that the previous owners had patched, but not bothered to fix, the whole section of the house had begun to sink. His mood had been headed in the same direction. Finding out that it was someone who'd been friendly to Bryce, who'd tried to influence his decision on his future, was the icing on a fucked-up shit sandwich.

The door hit the cabinets, banging loudly. He flinched. That pissed him off even more. It bounced open, swinging in the opposite direction. The timber splintered from the force of his steel-toed boot, the bottom half falling through the hole where the flooring had once been and into the sludgy ground below the house. The top half bent at an awkward angle, the hinge barely holding on. He wanted to destroy it. He wanted to destroy the whole fucking kitchen. The whole house. He wanted to burn it to the ground, to raze it from the earth.

No. That wasn't right.

He wanted to raze Denyer from the earth. He wanted to make him pay. Slowly and painfully. He wanted revenge. No one stole Bryce's dreams. No one humiliated Ava. No one tried to rip them apart. No one hurt the loves of his life.

He clenched his fists, his body taut like a rubber band about to snap. Ava's soft touch against his back brought him back from the edge. Cole gritted his teeth, focussing on the calm she gifted him with rather than the murderous thoughts coursing through his veins.

"As in the Lightning's lawyer?" Ava asked, her voice quiet. He spun only to see the colour draining from her face. "No, that…. No." Her legs gave out and she slid down the kitchen cupboard until her butt was on the floor and her phone hung loosely in her hand.

The anger fled. The desire to reap bloody revenge instantly dissipated. Ava needed him. She was hurting, and he needed to fix it. He'd already failed to protect her once. He wouldn't do it again by focussing on the wrong thing.

Cole fell to his knees, cupping her cheeks. "Breathe, baby," he whispered, stroking her face with his thumbs.

Her eyes filled with tears that spilled over her long lashes with every blink. Ava's voice sounded winded, the pain in her tone excruciating. Cole's chest tightened and he rubbed the spot where his heart was breaking.

"It's over a fucking house? Bryce got kicked off the team and we've had every journalist in the country digging up information on us because that bastard was pissed we wouldn't sell him a fucking house?" Ava's voice pitched higher with every word she spoke. She shook, her eyes hardening, that fiery strength burning within, even as her tears spilled freely down her cheeks.

"It appears that way," the woman on the line agreed sympathetically. "All he had to do was come up by a few thousand dollars and he would have been the highest bidder."

"We still wouldn't have sold it to him," Cole spat. God, if he could get his hands on him... He couldn't believe the piece of shit had walked into one of their builds, talking to them and playing nice only to throw his toys out the cot the moment he didn't get what he wanted.

Except his form of tantrum hurt Bryce and Ava, and Cole wouldn't stand for that.

"Why not?" she asked, curious.

Ava wiped away her tears. She blew out a breath, tucking her hair behind her ear. Pulling herself together like that when everything was crumbling at their feet, being their pillar of strength, was a feat that floored Cole every time Ava did it. She'd never wavered, the tears he'd witnessed a moment earlier her only show of weakness since Bryce had shown them that godforsaken email.

"Because he wanted to use it for holiday letting." Her voice wobbled, but she swallowed it down and continued, "The neighbours were worried about how many were popping up in the suburb. They were losing the community feel there because of it—people in and out all the time, partying at all hours, strangers walking around instead of friends, and empty houses the rest of the time."

Cole slid his hand into hers and thought back to the build Denyer had walked through. The neighbours had come to visit them early on, everyone except Mr Moss, the others calling him too grumpy to bother conversing with them. But Cole had seen something different in him. It had been too long since he'd seen the old man—weeks had gone by. He missed his blunt honesty, and now that they were leaving Sydney, Cole wanted to see him one more time.

Ava squeezed his fingers, and Cole spun around, sitting next to her so he could tuck her into his side. He explained, "Our company's objective is to restore houses for people to live in—"

"Not to perpetuate the housing crisis by locking more away for short-term use," Ava cried, passion infusing her voice. That addition to their mission statement was her condition. It was something she'd insisted on after seeing how profit-focussed the development industry was. Maybe it was the bad taste left after her first employer had gone under because they didn't care enough. Maybe it was the shitty conditions and high expectations at the company she'd worked for free at until their own was set up. Either way, Ava had wanted to do things differently with Triple

Threat, and Bryce had wholeheartedly agreed. So far their approach was working.

With the exception of Maxwell fucking Denyer.

All this mess was because they were trying to be good people and had turned him down. They were striving to make a difference and do some good in the community, rather than being solely focussed on the bottom line.

Cole pressed his fingers to the bridge of his nose and growled. All they'd wanted was to be together, and Denyer had ruined it.

The woman they were speaking to was silent, but after a few drawn-out moments, she replied, "I like you. Both of you. You have principles." Her sigh was resigned and a lot disappointed. "Look, this Denyer isn't who he seems. On the surface, he's a lawyer at a prestigious firm. He has some of the top clients in the country. But in reality, he has his fingers in dodgy dealings from east to west coast. I'm not done digging dirt up on him yet, but I've got enough to put him away for a long fucking time with what I have."

Red tinted his vision. It wasn't just them he'd screwed over. The man was supposed to be honourable or some shit, not break the law. He wanted Denyer in jail. He wanted him to rot in there and to see him destroyed.

"Find it all. I want him buried. I want him to burn," Cole gritted. Ava gasped, turning to him wide-eyed. He couldn't begin to process the shock etched in her features, but he swallowed, sucked in a breath and tried to calm down before he said something to her, he'd regret.

Clarity eventually won out over vengeance, and he calmed fractionally. Ava had explained how this lady would get paid—she'd take his assets. Cole wasn't an idiot—someone who'd been able to dig up this sort of dirt on someone in such a short timeframe wasn't doing it through proper channels either. But he had to ask. Putting him in jail wasn't worth bankrupting himself or their business. "How much do we owe you?"

The woman on the other end laughed, a husky sound that made his blood heat up and run cold at the same time. "Oh, sweetheart, you don't owe me anything. I'm going to clean this bastard out. Every single cent of it."

Ava swallowed. "How did you find out all this information? What if it wasn't really him?" She shook her head. "I don't believe I'm sticking up for him."

"The thing with people like Denyer is that they leave behind a trail of their dealings. It's like a stain. To the naked eye, it might appear to fade. But look closely enough in the right spot and you can see the shadow of it. And I know where to look. I know how to look." Shuffling like she was adjusting her phone sounded, and he could hear her clicking away on a keyboard. "He's guilty of far worse things than outing your boyfriend."

Ava added, "Bryce told us that Denyer spoke to him about his son. Did you find out anything about him?"

"Jacob Denyer. He doesn't appear to have anything to do with his son. They haven't spoken or emailed for the last few years. His son changed his name too. I'd say he knows exactly what kind of person his dad is and got out. He doesn't have any other children."

"Okay. Yeah, do it then. But I want to go to the police. Can you send what you have to them?" Ava asked.

"I'm not finished yet. I want to do a full workup on him. But when I'm done, I'll send it to my contact in the police. Leave it with me; I'll look after everything from here on out."

Relief washed over him like a summer breeze straight off the ocean. The same breeze he'd enjoyed that first night he, Ava, and Bryce were together. He was already lighter knowing that Denyer would get his comeuppance. "Thank you, um... it's so weird not knowing your name." He huffed out an uncomfortable laugh.

"My online alias is Queen."

"Like Queen Elizabeth?" Ava asked, pulling a face that Cole had to bite back a laugh at.

Queen chuckled. "No, like the chess piece. I can go anywhere. Boundaries other people set up don't stop me."

Ava's eyes widened and she nodded. "Right. Well, thank you, Queen. We appreciate everything you've done to help us."

"No worries. You won't hear from me again."

The line went dead, and Cole blinked, his eyebrows hiking up his forehead. She was... interesting. A little scary too. Fucking brilliant and slightly unhinged. Definitely a queen of old—that "boundaries... what are they?" attitude wouldn't fly for most people these days, but on her it was kind of hot.

"We should call Bryce," Ava murmured. Cole shook himself out of his thoughts and cocked an eyebrow at Ava when she laughed. "I had exactly the same reaction when I spoke to her too. She's kinda scary and maybe a little crazy too but hot at the same time."

"Mmm." He tugged her between his legs and licked her throat. With a growl, he added, "This might be a new fantasy for me."

Her reaction was immediate, a small shiver and an arch of her back, pressing her butt against his groin. His shaft thickened as she rocked against him.

"What might?" Bryce answered. Cole hadn't even realized she'd pressed call. "Actually, I don't care. I'm in."

Cole huffed out a laugh, his skin flushing hot with desire. "Ava and another woman."

"Deal. When and where? I'll be there." There was talking in the background, laughter too.

"Bryce," Ava interrupted, her tone serious. "We have news. Do you want to go somewhere more private?"

"I'm with Jake and Mike and all the partners and kids. Do I...?"

"If you're asking if it was them, the answer's no," Cole answered quickly. He wasn't going to drag this out any more than he had to. "It was Denyer."

"Denyer?" he shouted. "What the fuck?"

Cole expected a commotion in the background, but instead there was absolute silence.

"Denyer?" a man asked, his voice shaking. He sounded a lot like Jake, but Cole couldn't be certain. "Denyer, who?"

He heard the moment Bryce put them on speaker, the noise ratcheting up a level. But Bryce's response was quiet. He sounded robotic, so matter of fact and utterly devoid of emotion. He was fuming, and Cole hated fuckface Denyer even more for separating them. They should be there for Bryce. No, this shit should never have happened in the first place. "Maxwell Denyer, the Lightning's lawyer. He was the one who tipped off the media."

"I know that name," a woman answered.

There was a pregnant pause when another man asked, "How, Rob?" His deep voice was a dead giveaway—Mike.

"I haven't dealt with him before, but I remember seeing it written down…. Shit, how do I know that name?" the same woman answered, Robyn he assumed.

"I…," Bryce started.

Cole tried to tune out the background noise, but it was hard with the commotion.

"He's okay, Ez. It's an anxiety attack. Let Jake look after him. They need a moment together," Cassie said. "Hell, I need a moment." She paused, but when she spoke again, her voice was wobbly like she was fighting back tears. "We know him too. He's… We haven't heard that name in a long time, but it'll never be long enough. Maxwell is Jake's father. Jake changed his surname to Phillips—my surname—after we moved here."

"He…." Bryce trailed off again.

"That's it," Robyn uttered triumphantly, but her tone was tinged with disgust. "He's a partner at one of the big firms. I remember Western Mineral getting advice from him on who to donate campaign funds to. It was weird because he was in Sydney and we were in Perth, but he'd tell the board which of the candidates up for election were mining friendly and which were environmentalists. Whenever we had issues, the board would say 'who you gonna call?' and then I'd get instructions to leave the problem alone. A few days later, it was fixed."

"That sounds like him," Cassie agreed.

"He was the one who Aurelius Branigan, the CEO, called when I thought I'd been successful in burying the exploration permit for the caves. Then all of a sudden, the minister allows it."

Cole was curious. He wanted to know more about both Cassie's history with Denyer and Robyn's, but now wasn't the time. "He's a piece of shit," Cole agreed, but he had more pressing concerns. His boyfriend's silence was scaring him, and the distance between them wasn't helping. "Bryce, talk to us."

"He said his son had been hurt because of his relationship. Was it a lie or did Denyer hurt Jake?" Bryce asked, horror filling his voice. Cole hated the betrayal in his tone, but he understood far too well. Cole might have been angry, but Bryce had placed his trust in both the Lightning and Denyer. They'd let him down spectacularly.

"Denyer is the reason we don't live in Sydney. He's also why Phoenix no longer practices law." Cassie paused and he heard her sniffle. "He decided that no son of his could be a homo. Jake worked for Denyer's best mate—"

"The agent from City Scape," Ava interrupted.

"That's him. Charles. He fired Jake because Denyer told him to. Somehow, we still don't know how, his lease got terminated too."

"Bloody hell," Ava uttered.

"That's not all. I lost my job when he called up some of my clients and had them move their real estate work to another agency—probably City Scape. We were broke, couldn't get work because of our non-compete clauses, and were paying astronomical rent to live in the city. The cheapest option was to move here to my family's holiday home."

There were murmurings, and Cassie continued, "We had it easy. Denyer ruined Phoenix's career, his relationship with us, and his mental health."

"It's why he moved here," Robyn said, understanding dawning in her voice. "I've tried to persuade him to work for Nick and me, but he doesn't want to go back to law."

"I doubt he ever will either."

"Where do you want to take this?" Robyn asked. "I don't have any experience doing ethics work, but I'm sure Nick or one of his partners will. Do we have evidence that it was him? Can we take this further?"

"I don't know," Bryce whispered.

The fire in Cole's belly burned bright. He would protect his man. He'd get justice for him. He'd also get vengeance for Cassie, Jake, Phoenix, and even Robyn.

"We're going to fix this," Cole promised. "We've got someone on it. We're gonna stop him from hurting anyone else."

Ava squeezed his hand and added with absolute confidence, "She'll take him down."

TWENTY-THREE

Ava

Ava was still tired after being in the car for the all-day drive from Sydney, but she wouldn't be anywhere else. Bright lights shone in her eyes, the pitch-black sky above, clear. A crisp breeze blew outside, although they were somewhat sheltered in the stadium.

It was a home game and a Queensland derby—Bryce and Liam on the field together against the team's closest rivals, the Broncos.

She sat on the edge of her seat, her heart in her throat when the boundary ref called a forward pass to the other team. They'd been awarded a penalty, and although that was supposed to be good, the resulting scrum was the one thing in football that sent Ava into panic-mode quicker than Bryce getting tackled.

Play stopped and the men lined up, Bryce taking up his spot on the front row. His job was to propel his team forward into the line of the other team, controlling the play. What it really meant was that Bryce, with his arm around the player closest to him, would throw himself against the other team, locking his opponents in a wrestling grip and use the combined force of the men behind him to surge forward.

Scrums were better nowadays—less rough play and more finesse—but injuries still occurred, and Bryce was always black and blue for days after the hard hits.

Her guy was on the end of the scrum closest to them, his teammates backing him up in a three-two-one formation. He planted his feet, using his thick legs as propulsion.

Bryce's jersey moulded to his every muscle as he bent at the waist and waited for the play to begin. A split second later, they slammed forward, the sound of bodies crashing together audible even over the screaming fans.

Ava bit her thumbnail, watching in silence as the ball was rolled between the two teams who raked their feet back, trying to steal the ball. Ava held her breath, waiting as their hooker caught it on his heel, shoving it back through their scrum and into the waiting arms of the team's scrum half. Her breath whooshed out of her lungs as the scrum half moved like the wind, passing it back and away from the Broncos' defensive line, and the teams pulled apart.

One pass, then a second straight to Liam on the wing. He was one of the smaller men on the field, lightning fast and nimble on his feet. He hurdled one player who'd dove too early, trying to take out his legs, and sidestepped a second. But there were three more converging on him. He was trapped by the touchline to his left, the try line only a few metres away.

There was no way he'd make it.

Ava focussed on Bryce as he sprinted toward the melee. Nerves assailed her, excitement and fear vying for attention. It was the same with every game Bryce played. She was sure she aged a decade with every week during the season. Bryce put his body on the line every time he went near the play, and Ava locked her muscles tight, bracing for impact even though it was over the barriers on the field.

He'd come so far in only a few short months. His personal struggles had been motivation for him to step up his game again, and his training and skill level had taken another leap forward.

Adelaide choked out a cry as Liam waited until the last possible split second to pass. Her brother and Cole were shouting while King looked away, their eyes meeting and holding, fear and hope mingling in her friend's eyes.

Time seemed to slow as Liam flung the ball sideways, on a perfect backward arc to Bryce. It was a sublime pass, straight into Bryce's outstretched hands. Liam sidestepped, going down as he and the opposing wing crashed into each other.

But Ava was focussed on her man.

Bryce was a battering ram, charging forward with the ball tucked under his arm. He mowed down his opposition, not giving them the opportunity to tackle him. Two, then three men, hurled themselves on him. He looked around, searching for a clear line to pass. But there was none.

Ava gasped as Bryce seemed to make up his mind, surging forward again. Another half-step forward. The try line was only an outstretched arm away. Could he make it?

He stumbled. The weight of the footballers who'd tackled him dragged him down.

He pushed forward again, another few centimetres gained. Between the opposition's bodies he reached out, his huge paw gripping the ball tight. Forward momentum carried him, despite the press of players against him.

Ava covered her mouth with both hands, screaming in frustration. She was on her feet, her eyes locked on where her man went down, hitting the ground hard. Her breath whooshed out of her lungs and her chest seized, stopping her from sucking in a breath.

The ball was on the field still in Bryce's outstretched hand. Whistles blew. The line ref motioned for a try, referring the final decision to the video referee.

Ava was lightheaded, still unable to breathe. Was Bryce okay? He was still down. He hadn't moved. The big screens blanked out, the focus now on whether Bryce had scored. The try scoring sponsor's logo and decision pending flashed up. Cole wrapped his arm around her shoulders, equally as tense.

The players lying on Bryce gingerly lifted themselves up, freeing him from beneath them. He stayed still, unmoving.

The screens blacked out again before a flag unfurled with try written on it in bright green lettering lit up the screen. Bryce jumped up, punching the air and shouting. Ava's legs almost gave out from underneath her as tears sprang to her eyes and she choked out a sob. Bryce's teammates threw their arms around him, slapping his back and high-fiving him as the crowd roared. They were ecstatic. The try had nearly equalled the score, giving them a fighting chance. If their kicker managed a conversion, they'd be in the lead.

But all Ava could concentrate on was that Bryce was upright. Cole pulled her close. "Shh, it's okay, baby. He's okay."

"I fucking hate this game," she sobbed. "Every time I watch him, I want to go out and kill the other players for hurting him. Three on one, Cole. They could have broken something."

He chuckled but held her tighter. "He's strong. He knows how to fall so he isn't hurt. But yeah, I love and hate him being out there too." He pressed a kiss to her hair. "The kicker's lining up."

Ava turned her attention back to the field, but she didn't leave the safety of Cole's arms. Burying her head in his chest seemed like a good idea. As the kicker set the ball on the tee and stepped back, readying to land the conversion, Ava sought out Bryce. He was lined up with his teammates, Liam resting his arm on Bryce's shoulder. They were almost the same height, but they were so different in build, Liam looking downright scrawny next to Bryce's solid frame.

The kicker's boot connected with the ball, a loud thwomp amplified by the high grandstands in the stadium. The ball soared in a high arc, but it was too far to the right.

"Come on, come on! Get in there!" Adelaide shouted. The ball sailed ever closer to the post, but instead of flying over the crossbar, it bounced off the post.

"Damn it." Eli, Adelaide's brother yelled, clapping loudly, "Come on, boys, you can do it. One more." That's all they had time for too. The countdown clock was down to a handful of minutes.

The opposition took possession of the ball while Bryce's team lined up, ready to receive the kick in their defensive zone. The ball sailed high, dropping into their forty-metre zone. A catch, and they were moving forward, a row of men in red-and-orange uniforms running hard as they passed the ball, attempting to gain as much ground as possible before the first tackle.

The Gold Coast's utility caught it, immediately passing it to their number nine—the hooker. The Broncos were gaining on them, but they were already over the halfway line. The first tackle was on the way to the forty-metre line just as their kicker was positioning himself to punt a field goal. As soon as the ball was in play, their kicker was surrounded, the other team strangling any chance of a kick getting them the win.

It was slow going, the team barely making a couple of metres before they were taken to the ground again in the second tackle. King hissed as Liam was put down hard. He was slow to his feet, the hit looking like it had winded him.

The third and fourth tackles saw them take it over the twenty-metre line, with Bryce catching and passing it as the team slogged forward. Ava managed a squeak of a cheer when he caught it, but with her heart in her throat, it was hard to get anything out, and she was too on edge. The other team were on them like a rash, and it would only take a split-second hesitation in a pass to be dropped.

Ava dared another glimpse at the countdown clock. Two minutes. Two points behind. If they could score another try, they'd win. If not, Brisbane would walk away the victors.

The ball went back and forth between Bryce's teammates as they played keep away while inching closer to the try line.

"Come on, Bryce," Cole muttered as their boyfriend charged forward through a gap with the ball. He hurdled his counterpart, before rolling over another back-to-back. He dodged left. Faked a right. Lunged forward.

But the other team's two back rowers were waiting. They smashed into him like wrecking balls demolishing a building.

Ava held her breath.

The ball sailed backward, still in play. "Oh, god," she uttered, her palms sweating and her nails making half-moons in her hands.

It was as if time slowed, Ava's focus zeroing in on Bryce as he relaxed into the crush of bodies. It wasn't hard to miss the play for what it was—a ruse to attack the wrong player. Their captain was right behind Bryce, scooping up the ball mid-flight, charging forward.

That scary-as-fuck move was intentional? Ava's chest unclenched but her belly flipped, and not in a good way. She sucked in a breath, trying not to be sick at the thought of Bryce using his body as a roadblock.

The captain sidestepped, dodging out of reach of the players scrambling up from the ground. Bryce was up on his feet too, staying close to their captain's shadow, readying to catch the ball if a pass was necessary. The nausea stilled, like waters suddenly becoming calm, and Ava held onto her belly, wishing for a quicker end to the game than the remaining few second countdown.

Arms outstretched, ball gripped firmly in the captain's hands, he threw himself forward. Diving for the turf, he sailed over the try line. Slamming the ball down, his momentum carried him in a slide along the ground.

The ref's whistle sounded. She looked up at the countdown clock sitting on zero. Her eyes widened. Her mouth popped open. Holy. Shit. He'd scored. He'd done it. Even seeing it happen right before her eyes, Ava didn't believe it was real.

But it was.

They'd won. They'd actually won.

The captain was on his feet. Arms raised in the air with the ball held high. He pointed to Bryce. Raised his arm high and pointed to the scoreboard, lit up in green with try pulsing on it. He wrapped an arm around Bryce's beefy shoulders and pulled him into a hug.

Bryce's teammates surrounded them, adding to the group hug. The vision was beamed on the big screen, and Ava watched joyfully as every member joined in the back-slapping and hair ruffling. Bryce laughed, his grin radiant as he formed a fist, tapped his heart and held up two fingers.

It was an "I love both of you" from him to them. The acceptance from the team was real, not just lip service — the play and the congratulations made that as clear as day.

Their kicker broke away, lining up for the conversion. He'd missed the last one and worn a scowl on his face ever since. This was his chance at redemption.

The team settled down, spreading out to show their support as he placed the ball on the tee. He lined himself up, stepping backward so he could take a run up. Ava watched as he centred himself, finding his zone and rocking back and forth on the balls of his feet until he was ready. Three strides and he kicked, the thwomp echoing around the stadium.

Ava could see how different this kick was than the last one. It shot from the ground like a bullet, harder and faster than his earlier attempt at a conversion. It soared in an arc that took it dead centre to the posts.

The crowd erupted. Cheering, whistles, and feet stomped on the concrete floor. Music began pumping from the speakers. Ava recognized the team's song, but still didn't know the words. Cheerleaders danced along the sidelines as the players lined up and shook hands. Ava cheered and clapped while Cole whistled, and the rest of their group hollered the words to the team song.

It was easy to get carried away when the vision of the team's smiles were shown on the grounds. Sports reporters clambered onto the field, racing over to the players.

"Darren, congratulations on the win," the woman said to their team captain, the interview playing on the big screen.

"Thank you. It was definitely hard fought. We were the underdogs tonight, but we've come a long way as a team these last few years, and tonight we played the way we've aspired to."

"That last try was incredible. Tell me about it."

"Bryce and I have really clicked playing together. Something told me I needed to be there at that precise moment, so I got there. The play went off seamlessly."

"Has the media attention around Flaharty's and Masters' sexuality affected the team?"

"Does it look like it has?" He raised his eyebrow and added, "Thanks very much."

He walked away without another word, and Ava cheered harder, telling their captain just how appreciated the move was. Addy did the same, throwing up her hands and bumping hips with Ava until they were both dancing in the crowd.

Elation filled her, lifting her spirits like the incoming tide. Ava laughed, watching as Liam jumped on Bryce, wrapping his arms and legs around her man like a koala clinging to a tree.

It was hours before they heard the barrel of the lock turn, announcing Bryce's homecoming. They were staying at Bryce's little flat above Cassie, Jake, and Phoenix's garage, but it wouldn't be for long. Their furniture was being delivered in two days, in just enough time to fill the house they were renting only a few doors up from their current location.

They were diving straight into work too, starting with three small projects for the charitable arm of their business. One thing that the Lightning had done right by Bryce was throw resources at him when he explained to them what the mission of their charity was. Grass roots community helping community had always been the basis, and Ava could already see the urgent need for something like that on the Gold Coast.

But for now, Bryce was here, and they were finally seeing him after a very long few weeks apart.

TWENTY-FOUR

Bryce

"In the bedroom," Cole called out as Bryce pushed open the door.

He snorted out a tired laugh. The flat was literally three rooms—a combined lounge, dining, and kitchenette, a bedroom, and a bathroom. There were very few places they could hide, but if Cole and Ava were as antsy to see him as he was them, there'd be no hiding.

He walked in to a gorgeous sight.

Ava was on her back, splayed out for his viewing pleasure, the glow from the lamp next to the bed casting shadows over every dip and valley of her naked body. Cole was on his knees by her head, stroking his semi to full hardness, his six-pack and tattoos flexing as his muscles jumped from the stimulation.

Bryce licked his lips and eased his bag off his shoulder before dropping it unceremoniously to the floor. His suit jacket and tie went next as he toed out of his dress shoes, busy unbuttoning his shirt. Damn penguin suits. But the heat in Cole's gaze, and the way Ava traced her fingers down to her pussy and rubbed, her eyes never leaving his body, made the extra layers worth it.

He was stiff and sore, his bruises already darkening, but he'd live. If only for the chance to be with Ava and Cole again tonight.

He'd been dreaming about it all day, knowing they were making their way north from Sydney. They'd been right there in the crowd watching him. It certainly wasn't the first time, but now that they were all Gold Coast residents, it was extra motivation to make this one special. And it had been better than he could have imagined.

His cock was already throbbing, tenting his pants before he managed to undo the zip and kick them off. Bryce was moving slower than he usually would—there wouldn't be any jumping on the bed tonight—but his cock was up for the challenge. He just didn't know where to start. All that smooth skin, dark and light next to each other. Their taste, their reactions… he was torn between devouring both of them. How could he do it at the same time?

"I love walking into this," he uttered, his hoarse voice from shouting during the game, taking on a rasp as arousal flooded his veins. He closed his fist around his shaft, giving himself a stroke that sent his neurons firing and pleasure crashing through him. His balls were already drawn up tight, just waiting to get the party started. "But I don't know where to start." He huffed out a laugh. "Who do I get to taste first?"

"Ava," Cole replied. "You two are going to swap spots and she's gonna sit on your face while I suck you off."

Bryce moaned, loving how Cole took control so that he could just feel.

"Then I'm gonna prep one of you. Who wants me in their arse? Hmm?"

This time it was Bryce who volunteered his girlfriend. "Ava. I want you against me as we're buried inside her."

Ava whimpered and slid her fingers deeper, pressing them into her core.

"Get your hand off *my* cock, Bryce. On your back." Bryce hissed as he let go of his cock, the loss of sensation putting the brakes on his already steady climb to his orgasm.

"Easy," Ava cooed as he groaned when he sat, his sore body protesting. He would need the ice bath tomorrow, especially after the few hard hits he'd had. That final tackle was brutal—like being hit by two steamrollers—but it was worth it. The win was enough to get them in the top eight, and if they could keep building on that, they were headed for the finals.

When she finished plumping the pillow for him, Bryce laid back, his breath gushing out of his lungs as he relaxed into their nest.

"Jesus, you're black and blue," Cole grumbled as he ghosted his fingers over Bryce's shoulders and his ribs where a rogue knee had got him on a tackle. "If you're not up for it—"

"I'm up for it." He chuckled, fisting his cock and spreading his legs wide enough to fit Cole's shoulders. As Cole ran his fingertips down the insides of his thighs, Bryce's hips instinctively lifted off the bed, chasing the teasing touch. But the move made his ribs pinch and he gasped, tucking his elbow in to protect the tender area. "Just be gentle."

Ava kissed him, her lips soft against his as she teased his mouth open and slipped her tongue inside. They made out, long and slow, their hands and lips rediscovering each other again after being apart for so long. It was his flat, and even though Ava was the one who'd just arrived, her kiss was like he was coming home.

She shifted, pulling back to kiss a line down his throat, and Cole was there, his five o'clock shadow dark on his skin and scratchy against Bryce's face. But his lips were pillowy and his tongue playful as they kissed. With his hands buried in their hair, their bodies tangled together, Bryce let out the breath he'd seemingly been holding since he'd last seen his lovers.

They were together. Exactly where they were meant to be.

"Relax into it," Cole murmured, as he shuffled down between his legs and bent to take Bryce's cock between his lips.

Bryce moaned, the wet heat and suction of Cole's mouth shooting him straight to heaven. His cock ached, his balls already fit to burst, but he needed more. He threaded his fingers into Cole's hair, not to push him down, but rather for the extra connection. God, he'd missed this. He'd missed them.

"Come up here, babe," Bryce encouraged Ava, and she gingerly lifted her leg, kneeling over him. She was treating him like glass, and while it wasn't quite necessary, he appreciated it.

He cupped her butt with his free hand and looked up her body as she braced her arms on the headboard. She was stunning like this—the long, shapely lines of her body right there for his viewing pleasure. And her scent. It was intoxicating. Bryce touched his tongue to her core, her musky flavour bursting onto his tongue.

Cole pulled back, his mouth slipping off Bryce's hypersensitive shaft with a pop. Bryce moaned and Ava cried out, grinding down on his face. He gripped her butt tighter, massaging the supple muscle as he devoured her, licking her pussy and flicking his tongue over her clit.

Cool gel dripped onto his free hand and Bryce moaned his enthusiasm. Oh hell yeah. He couldn't wait to get all up inside their girl and feel Cole next to him. He slid his fingers between her cheeks and played with her hole, softening it as he gently nibbled her clit and lashed her with his tongue. His cock flexed as Ava arched into his touch, pushing back on the finger he had buried inside her tight heat. Bryce cried out, frustrated that Cole was neglecting his dick.

But then he was there, taking him to the back of his throat and swallowing around his cockhead. Suction, tight and hot, overwhelmed him and Bryce's breaths stuttered. His vision went hazy, and electricity zinged through him, a rushing beginning at the base of his spine. If Cole didn't let up soon, this party would be over far too quickly. Bryce needed a distraction and Ava was the perfect one.

He added another finger, stretching her for Cole as he doubled down on her clit.

Her pussy tightened around his tongue and her moan echoed through the room. The rhythmic clenching only made him remember what it was like with his cock buried inside her instead of his tongue. His dick hardened to the point of painful and his balls tingled, getting ready to paint Cole's throat with his seed.

He shouted as Cole kept up the suction but slowly pulled off his cock, every muscle in his body locking tight as Bryce's orgasm raced toward him like a freight train barrelling through a tunnel. The grip at the base of his cock was too tight to be comfortable, but it pulled him back from the edge. It was exactly what he needed.

Cole trailed his mouth lower, sucking one of Bryce's nuts into his mouth and laving him with his tongue. Bryce panted, trying to think of anything that would take the pressure off—what was gross enough to pull him back from the edge of a monster orgasm when he had his fingers buried in his woman, his mouth on her, and Cole's mouth on him?

He breached Ava with another finger, and she moaned, pressing her arse into his fingers, driving him deeper.

"Fuck, I'm ready. Now, guys, I don't want to come again without you inside me," she begged.

Cole breathed out on a hum as he let Bryce's testicle slip from his mouth, and Bryce cried out, his feet scrambling. He wasn't sure if he was pulling away or pushing back to get back in the wet heat of Cole's mouth.

Ava was moving too, pulling off him and shimmying back.

Bryce couldn't talk. He couldn't even think straight. His mind was completely blown, his body at his lovers' mercy. Panting, completely out of breath, he hissed as Ava brushed his sore ribs. He grasped her hips, stilling her movement before she sank down on him. He needed a moment—maybe a minute—to pull himself back together again or he'd lose it the second he was inside her.

Cole was next to him, kissing him again, lapping up Ava's essence from Bryce's chin and lips. Ava joined them in a messy three-way kiss that was all lips and tongues. He could do this all night—make out with his people—but his cock had other ideas.

Bryce flexed his hands on Ava's hips, and she pulled back.

"Finally," she breathed as she sank down onto him until his hips were pressed against her butt, his cock impaling deep into her. Her moan was illicit, her flood of arousal on his dick ratcheting his desire up to a whole other level.

Bryce sucked in a breath at the vice-like grip she held him in, her inner walls still clenched tight from her last orgasm as she rocked forward. He shivered, sweat breaking out on his brow as he fought his body's instinct to drive into her.

Cole moved, pulling away from him as he shifted behind Ava. As he straddled Bryce's legs, the flick of the cap was loud in the otherwise quiet room. Bryce reached up, gently pinching Ava's nipples. Her channel tightened around him. He grasped her nape and tugged her down against him until he could suck on the pebbled peaks of her breasts. She arched into him, pressing her chest against his mouth and lifting her arse to Cole.

The first press of Cole's cock against her hole had Bryce seeing stars. He fucking loved frotting. There was nothing hotter than rubbing off against his guy, unless they were doing it with Ava's thin barrier between them while they were buried inside her.

She choked out a cry when Cole's cockhead popped past her resistance and Bryce clenched his jaw, begging his body to calm the fuck down. He didn't want this to end, but especially after they'd only just gotten started.

Ava's breathy moans combined with Cole's deeper grunt and Bryce's gasps as Cole took control and pressed forward. His movements were slow, deep, as he made love to them.

Pinned down under them, Bryce couldn't move other than the tiniest thrust of his hips, but it was enough. Ava surrounded him, and Cole dragged his cock up and down Bryce's until he saw stars.

"Oh fuck," Ava breathed. "I'm gonna come again."

Bryce was there too, his body screaming at him to let go. It was as if he was standing on the edge of an abyss, waiting to jump.

"Do it," Cole rasped, his voice a deep growl as sweat dripped off his brow and his muscles shook with restraint.

Bryce slipped his hand down Ava's belly, pinching her clit as she rocked her hips. She cried out, her pussy clamping down as the wave of her orgasm peaked and she rode the crest. The clench and release and the stutter in Cole's thrusts was all Bryce needed. His own orgasm crashed into him, his back arching and his throat closing on a silent scream as his cock painted their girl in his seed. Every pulse started from deep in his balls, the sensation overwhelming as he marked her.

His orgasm was renewed when Cole choked out a cry as pulse after pulse of his cum shot into Ava, his cock throbbing with every one.

Breathless, Bryce's muscles turned into limp noodles. He huffed out a laugh and used every ounce of strength he possessed to reach out and touch Ava's cheek and Cole's forearm. Ava slumped down beside him, groaning as he and Cole slipped free of her.

Cole hit the other side of the mattress and pressed a kiss to Bryce's shoulders. "We've missed you."

"So much," Ava agreed on a mumble.

"Me too. Don't want to be apart again."

"Never."

* * * * *

The noise woke him far earlier than he wanted to be awake. Ava was still tucked into his side, barely having moved after Cole cleaned them up. Cole was facing away from him, using Bryce's arm as a pillow, but he was holding it to his chest in a vice grip. Bryce couldn't get up even if he wanted to. He blinked his eyes open as Ava nuzzled into him and he gasped. Fuck, that hurt.

She was instantly awake, shifting back in a panic. "You okay? What happened?"

He looked down at his torso and winced. His side was a mottled purple. Bryce opened his mouth to speak when the banging sounded again. That was what had woken him. "What time is it?" he rasped.

"Too early," Cole mumbled.

"Bryce, open up. You need to see this," Jake called.

Ava slid out of bed, pulled on Bryce's shirt, and padded out the door, closing it behind her. Cole sighed.

"If we hide in here, do you think they'll go away?"

"Doubtful," Bryce mumbled, rolling onto his side with a choked cry as he stretched his bruised side and cuddled into Cole.

"Bryce, Cole, seriously get up," Ava announced, her voice a higher pitch than normal. It wasn't panic; it was something else. But hearing her tone was enough to jolt them into action.

Bryce moved like an old man, his ribs tender. Bending down to reach for the pair of track pants he kept in the bottom of the wardrobe was a mission, but they were easy to get on. When he was finally decent, he admired Cole's butt in his training shorts. He loved seeing his people wear his clothes. It sounded stupid, but Bryce felt like he was providing for them—ironic given that they'd earned as much from their business in a few short months as he would from playing football for a whole year.

"Bloody hell," Cole exclaimed, lifting Bryce's arm to get a closer look at his side. "We need to get you checked out. You might have cracked a rib. Are you going in for a recovery session this morning?"

Bryce looked at his phone, checking the time and nodded. "I've got a couple of hours, but yeah, the doc will want to do an X-ray." He pressed his fingers to his side, grateful that the pain wasn't too sharp. "I think it's just bruised. I hope it is."

"Come on, let's go figure out what's so important that we're being woken up at the arse crack of dawn."

As Cole opened the door, Bryce inhaled the unmistakeable scent of excellent coffee. His stomach growled and he grinned at Ava who was already getting bacon and eggs out of the fridge.

She ducked back into their room as Bryce greeted Jake and Phoenix who were standing there in almost matching shorts and hoodies. Phoenix handed him a coffee from the tray he was carrying.

"Thank you." Bryce inhaled deep, waking his body up as the scent of the rich brew filled his lungs. Taking a long drink, he sighed happily before asking, "What's going on?"

Jake's smile was forced but he spun the newspaper sitting on the kitchen bench around and pointed to the page one headline.

Top lawyer charged with extortion. Facing 14 years jail.

The picture was of a cuffed Denyer being led out of his mansion, two uniformed police officers flanking him.

"Woah, she did it," he breathed, shocked and in awe.

Cole wandered in from the bathroom and grumbled, "Why are you awake?"

"You're a tradie. Don't you always wake up early?" Phoenix asked, passing him the remaining coffee. Cole placed a cool hand low on Bryce's hip and took a long sip, his Adam's apple bobbing as he swallowed.

"It's Sunday," Ava explained as she walked back in, dressed in jeans and a lightweight shirt. "His only day to sleep in."

Bryce shifted the paper over so Cole could see, and threaded their fingers together as his man froze.

"Holy shit." Cole pulled the paper closer, his fingers tightening their grip on Bryce's. "Maxwell Denyer, partner at blah, blah, blah, was arrested late yesterday evening after police executed a search warrant on his Bellevue Hill home last week. Officers allege that detailed evidence was found of dealings with both public officials and private organizations spanning decades. These dealings, it is further alleged, are evidence of extortion resulting in the commission of various crimes, including corruption at multiple levels of government, across numerous states and territories. Denyer is expected to apply for bail—"

Cassie called out, "Knock knock," and Jake rushed over to open the door for her, relieving her of the tray of muffins and freshly baked bread.

"He'll be out of the country within hours if they grant bail," Bryce mumbled. "Hey, Cass."

"Morning."

Phoenix smiled, a cold smirk that was pure vengeance. "Read to the bottom. They were monitoring his emails and found evidence that he'd booked a ticket to non-extradition country. There's no way the courts will approve bail without a surrender of his passport."

Cole blew out a breath and rested his forehead against Bryce's shoulder. He reached back, hugging Cole to his body. He grunted in pain as he twisted, pulling at his bruised ribs.

"Bloody hell, Bryce, were you hit by a car?" Jake asked.

He brushed off their concerns. "Felt like it, but it's from the game last night. I took a knee to the ribs. I think it's only bruised but it's sore."

"Are you okay?" Ava asked as she touched his arm before doing the same to Cole. "Seeing this? I mean, does it feel like justice?"

Bryce thought on it for a moment. He was shocked more than anything else. He'd believed Ava and Cole when they'd said Queen was looking into Denyer. He couldn't believe how quickly she'd dug up information on him, and her promise to take it further seemed genuine. But he hadn't really believed it would happen. It seemed like an impossibility. Surely if he'd done all those horrible things, if he truly had friends in all the right places like Cassie, Jake and Phoenix's experiences were with him, he'd be untouchable. Or maybe all those so-called friends were like rats abandoning a sinking ship.

"I'm... kinda shocked that it's actually happening to be honest," he settled on. "You know how you're told something is true, but you don't believe it until you see it? It's kinda that for me."

"Hope the bastard rots in jail," Cole huffed.

"Yep," Jake agreed.

"And you three?" Ava asked. "He's caused you a lot of pain, but he's your—"

"Don't say family," Jake said quietly. "My family are here with me. He's my sperm donor, but he was never my dad. Cassie's and Phoenix's fathers are both more my dads than he ever was. But yeah, for everything he put us through, I'm glad he's going to jail."

"Assuming he doesn't get off somehow," Phoenix added. "I won't get my hopes up until the sentence is handed down and appeals are exhausted."

"We should crack open a bottle of champagne. Have some mimosas," Ava mused as she looked over her shoulder to check on the bacon sizzling away in the frypan. "Do you have any, Bryce?"

"Thanks, we won't have any," Jake said, raising his hands up to stop her from ripping the kitchen apart to find some. Jake gentled his rejection with a small smile tilting his lips and a blush that stole across his face. "We're going dry for a few months."

"Yeah, too easy to drink too much when you're around liquor all the time like I am," Phoenix added smoothly.

"But feel free to have some," Cassie interjected as she finished slicing the bread and putting four slices in the toaster.

Cole shook his head. "Phoenix is right. Let's leave it until the conviction. Anyway, I'll drive Bryce to the recovery session today, and he shouldn't drink in case he needs some painkillers."

"Yes, Dad," Bryce teased, dodging to the side when Cole playfully bit him.

Cole sobered and cupped his face, pressing a soft kiss to his lips. He rested his forehead against Bryce's and whispered, "I just want you to be okay."

Bryce smiled, his cheeks hurting with the grin and the swoopy feeling in his belly from the millions of butterflies doing somersaults. "I know. Now that you're both here, I'm perfect. But I'm also starving."

TWENTY-FIVE

Ava

DECEMBER

Privacy had never been a big concern for Ava. It was always something that just existed in the background. Something she expected. But since their lives were turned upside down, they craved it. They wanted peace and quiet. They wanted to be as far from prying eyes as possible.

She wanted to be able to show Bryce and Cole that she loved them without having to look over her shoulder to see who was watching. It wasn't like they regularly got it on in public, but having a safe space where they could just be had become essential.

The media had hounded Bryce for months after he'd been forced to come out. The questions surrounding their relationship were relentless. She and Cole hadn't had it any easier while they were in Sydney, but at least they'd had each other. Aside from being with family and friends, Bryce had been largely alone for those first few months.

She was so grateful to Bryce's parents. While she had a decent relationship with hers, they were busy, and so was she. They'd never really been that close either. Bryce's family, on the other hand, was always there with open arms for a hug and to lend an ear when they needed it. They all went home to Bryce's parents for a dose of mum and dad love.

But it was their friends' unending support that had made the biggest difference.

Adelaide and Katy had quickly become her besties, while Cassie, Robyn, and Emma were like older sisters to her now. Their guys were great too. Each one brought something different to their friendship—they were all loyal to a fault and would take the shirt off their own back to help. Bryce's friendship with Liam had blossomed, especially since becoming teammates, and they often did crazy adventure stuff together with Levi, Connor, and Mike, the other fitness junkies in the group. The more serious ones — Cole, Ezio, King, Jake, and Phoenix—took the chance to catch up in a more low-key way doing poker nights or, more recently, smoking meat.

King was competing with Cole's smoker fit out, but everyone knew Cole had won that competition, hands down. The giant wood-fired barbecue on their new property was what had sold Liam, Adelaide, and King on moving to a few acres on the mountain. In truth, it was their need for privacy too, but no one liked to dwell on the persistent invasions of space.

Living in the rental hadn't been ideal for them either, and once Cole had seen their friends' rural retreat, there was no question they'd be following suit. Moving out of the city to the hinterland had been a big step for them, especially all having come from apartment-living in Sydney. It was a bit of a drive out and a pain if they ran out of milk or couldn't be bothered cooking—restaurant delivery options were non-existent—but it was quiet, theirs, and their closest neighbours were a mob of kangaroos.

Their property was everything they hadn't known they'd wanted until they laid eyes on it for the first time.

Driving along winding roads, dappled light shining down on them through the towering trees had them wide-eyed. Ava had shifted excitedly in her seat as they'd ascended the mountain—she still did it every time she took the road. They'd fallen in love the moment they'd crossed through the gated entrance to lush landscaping and a view like no other. Spectacular didn't come close to describing it. The crescent-shaped hill undulated before them, covered in tropical native forests. Ferns and palm trees were mixed with giant eucalypts along the drive, and a picturesque white house was perched halfway down the hill. Rich-green lawns gently sloped away from it and at the base of the hill, the land flattened out, culminating in a sparkling lake that the nearby creek fed. Rows of fruit trees and grapevines grew along one side of the property, while sheds and stables lined the other.

The lake was partly theirs and partly their neighbours', none of whom had built on their land. Finding out that it would be partly theirs had sealed the deal. They'd decided to buy the property before they'd even seen a close-up of the house. The cottage was small, but charming, and more than enough for their needs. One day they'd have to add a few more bedrooms for the football team of kids that Bryce wanted around, but for the moment, it was perfect.

They hadn't lived there long, but Cole had already put his stamp on the old Queenslander. He'd restored the original fireplace, crafted new decorative pieces to sit underneath the bullnose wraparound veranda, and extended the veranda out to one side of the house, creating a gorgeous screened-in outdoor area.

It was where they were currently sitting. Boxing Day lunch was the next step in Cole's and King's cooking competition—the giant smoker, pizza oven, and barbecue were getting a workout for a crowd. But unlike the Cole she'd met two years earlier who'd hated peopling, this Cole had spent the last year thriving among friends.

Everyone was there, but unlike those enjoying the warm days, poor Cassie was suffering. Ava turned the fans up from their lazy circling to a quicker spin, and set the mister on Cassie's side of the table to automatic. She was only a week from her due date, and Ava could see her shifting in her seat every few minutes. The discomfort was definitely getting to her.

"Thanks, babe," she said as Ava placed the last remaining salad on the table. "Next baby is coming in winter." She pointed to Jake and Phoenix, narrowing her eyes at them. "Katy, Con, and Levi are doing it right."

Katy's baby bump was still tiny, but she was starting to show more and more every day. Soon there would be no mistaking she was pregnant.

"We'll get pointers from them," Jake teased from his spot at her feet as he rubbed her calves.

"Hey, at least we didn't saddle you with twins during summer," Phoenix argued, pointing to Nick.

Cassie winced and shifted again while Nick held his hands up in surrender. "No argument from me that the timing sucked. Em decided she wanted to try again, and I'd barely kissed her before we were announcing she was preggers with twins and due smack bang in the middle of summer."

"You're doing it wrong if you don't remember it, mate," Con announced, slapping him on the back.

"Not all of us have orgies every night," Nick retorted with a grin.

Ava laughed. That was pretty much their sex life, and she wouldn't change it for the world.

"You're the one who's missing out," Addy teased.

King dropped a plate of snags on the table and high-fived her as he walked past.

"Let me guess, I should try adding a spectator or two," Nick asked, looking at Ezio with an innocence that didn't deceive anyone.

"Hey, don't knock having spectators until you've tried it," King pointed out, waving a set of tongs at him that he placed on top of the sausages.

Ezio choked on his drink, his face going scarlet, and Nick let out a gleeful cackle. "You right, mate?" he asked, biting back another laugh. "You have issues with spectators?"

"Arse," Ezio shot back.

"According to Jax, that was you. Well, actually, it was Mike's arse and your 'huge doodle.'" He uttered the last two words adding air quotes with his fingers and a lewd wink.

"Oh my fucking god," Ezio muttered, hiding behind his hands. "I need a stronger drink."

Ava loved these guys. She loved all of them. They were so much damn fun. No one took themselves too seriously, and they were happy to dish out and receive as much shit as they could pile on one another.

"I need to hear this," Cole teased, leaving the barbecue unattended for the moment. She watched as he sat on the edge of the chair opposite Ezio and rested his chin in the heel of his cupped hands. It was such a Bryce move, right down to the wide eyes and cheeky grin that he was wearing so much more often now. The Gold Coast—their entire lifestyle—looked good on him. He was happier, lighter too. Gone were the days where Cole was a dirty secret. If nothing else had come out of Denyer exposing them, allowing both her and Bryce to acknowledge him as theirs was worth it.

"Apparently, Nick knows all about it," Ezio mumbled, motioning to his partner's oldest friend.

"Well, when people love each other, they like to —" Ezio shot out his hand in a stopping motion and Nick snorted out a laugh.

"Stop. Please, stop." Ezio shook his head, his half-laugh embarrassed. "Jax, the little bugger, has learned how to pick our bedroom door lock. Butt crack of dawn and he's up, breaking into our room to ask if he can play X-box. We were… in a compromising position. Let's just say those kinds of spectators are not recommended."

"What kind of spectators are *you* talking about, King?" Cole asked.

King was staring off into the distance, running his fingers through Addy's hair, a fond smile tilting his lips upward and colour rising in his cheeks. When Cole's question registered, he snapped to attention. "Ah, lunch is nearly ready. You want me to wrangle the masses? Yeah, I think I'll go get them."

"What kind of spectators, King?" Addy seconded in a singsong voice.

"Just you… yeah, you know." King scrubbed a hand over his neat hair, making it stick up every which way as he cleared his throat. He pointed to the soaked group of kids, men-children, and mums watching closely to make sure no one broke a limb or worse, pushed in. "I'd better go get them." King hurried out of there like a fire had been lit under him, and Ava laughed heartily. He was such a shy one and Bryce, and now Cole, loved teasing the hell out of him.

Ava hopped up to help bring the remaining platters of food over to the table. Within minutes, the meal was ready to be served. Robyn and Emma had the kids wrapped in towels, and Levi, Mike, Bryce, and Liam had all thrown on T-shirts and were sitting among them. By the sounds of the kids' colourful retelling of their adventures, everyone had been having a blast.

Cole and Bryce sat down on either side of her, and Ava didn't hold back her elated smile. This was what they'd always wanted—to be together. Never in her wildest dreams had she imagined they would find themselves living and working in paradise and doing good deeds for the local community with their charity work. She had to pinch herself some days just to make sure she wasn't dreaming.

Their group of friends had become so dear to them in such a short time. They were a family by choice. Some of them weren't lucky enough to have ties to their bio relatives. Others had severed their relationships because of the toxicity they'd experienced. But they'd found one another and would never take the others for granted.

No one underestimated the importance of being there for one another.

They loved hard. They loved fierce. They were loyal and true to one another. Everyone in the group were friends who'd become family and family who she wanted to be friends with. And the next generation of kids would grow up knowing how that love and acceptance, how being there for your people through thick and thin would leave an indelible mark on their hearts.

She was lucky to have the friends she had, but she was blessed to have her guys. They were everything to her. Her sunshine and solid strength. The absolute loves of her life. They completed her, and yes, it was in exactly the same cheesy way as the line from Jerry Maguire. Except that it was real. They weren't make-believe; they weren't the product of a script writer's imagination. They were there right in front of her like they always were.

Even when they were apart, there had never been a question they'd be together again.

Fate in the form of a dust storm had brought them to one another. Call it recklessness or faith, but Ava had known her guys were different. Something had told her to trust them. She might not have known Bryce and Cole then, but her soul recognized its counterparts. Her heart recognized the ones it beat for.

Ava stood, raising her bottle. "Before we get started, I'd like to make a toast." A cheer sounded and the others raised their drinks. She opened her mouth to continue when three simultaneous dings went off. Cole picked his mobile up while Ava started, "To fam—"

"Ava," Cole said, a hint of urgent panic in his voice as he tugged on her summery dress. "You need to see this."

"What is it?" She looked around the group and apologized before checking out a notification from their bank. Ava sat down before she fell, slumping into her chair. Surely it was a mistake. It couldn't be right. There was no way. They weren't even properly fundraising yet. There was a sign-up form on their website, but there hadn't even been one hit yet. No one would drop a million bucks on them. But if it wasn't right, then there was something seriously wrong. "Can't be. Can it?"

Bryce was on his phone calling the bank. Was the hotline even open on a public holiday? Cole clicked through to the details of the deposit, but there wasn't much to see. There was no name, no reference numbers. Nothing.

"Who'd give us a million bucks?" Cole asked, mirroring her question. "Well, the charity anyway," he clarified.

"I have no idea." Ava scratched her head and looked to the lawyers in their group. "I think we might have a problem."

Her phone flashed up with a message and Ava picked it up. Cole and Bryce were both there, looking at it over her shoulders. Bryce hung up, the hold music ceasing immediately.

I'm trusting you to help as many people as you can— consider it a gift from Denyer.

The text—with no number displayed—was signed off with a chess piece. Queen. It had to be.

Ava blinked, re-reading the message a few times over, then looking to Cole's phone. There were a lot of zeros on that number.

Holy shit.

Queen had sent their charity a million dollars.

One. Million. Dollars.

They could help so many people. They could do so much good with it.

They'd always been hampered with the extent of repairs they could do because of the limited funds they had to spend. But this... this would be life changing for literally thousands of people.

Tears of joy sprang to her eyes, and she clamped a hand over her mouth to stop the sob breaking free. The others were looking at her like she'd grown two heads, but Bryce's and Cole's arms surrounded her, wrapping her in their brand of love and protection. Now she had everything she ever dreamed of—she got to work with the two loves of her life, creating a home for them and for others. They could genuinely help the people who couldn't afford to buy their high-end products—the battlers, the ones struggling, the ones who were feeling the pinch of higher interest rates and ridiculous rents.

It was the best gift anyone could have given her.

Trust Queen to have delivered.

"What's wrong?" Liam asked, horrified.

"We just got a massive donation," Bryce explained. "We're going to change a lot of lives with it."

"From whom?" Jake asked.

"A... friend." Was it right to call a woman who they didn't know a friend? What they did know was both scary and a mix of intimidating and a bit like taking a walk on the wild side. She'd helped them, asking nothing in return, but she'd cleaned out a shitbag of a person's assets in doing so. Ava should probably be worried about what message that sent, but she focussed on what was important—the people who would benefit from their help. Ava clarified, "They dislike your sperm donor as much as we do."

"Do you need volunteers?" Jake asked, his gaze flicking to his husband who immediately nodded.

"I'll help."

"You might as well count us all in," King chimed in and shrugged. "It's what we do—"

"Ah, guys." Cassie grasped Phoenix's arm and cried out, slapping Jake's leg to get his attention. "I... I think my waters just broke."

Phoenix's squeak was as much comical as panic-inducing. The hospital was nearly an hour's drive from their house. Ava's heart slammed against her chest. Did they need to call an ambulance? When were the hot towels needed? Surely not yet. What the hell did they do?

She sat there frozen, blinking like an owl, and forgetting to breathe.

Jake just grinned, pride shining in his eyes and his smile lighting up his entire being. Never mind Cassie having a pregnancy glow, Jake was incandescent. "Cass, we have plenty of time—"

She groaned, sucking in a breath as she squeezed Phoenix's hand until it turned white.

"How long have you been having contractions for?" Ezio asked, going to her. He rested a hand on her belly before flicking his gaze to his partners, his face a mask of calm but his eyes communicating just how urgent things were. "Rob, I need my bag out of the car. Mike, get ready to bring it down here. We might need to make a dash for the hospital."

"We've got everything in our car," Jake assured him.

"Cassie, I need you to answer me, hon. Have you been having contractions? Or is this a sudden pain?"

"Just cramps," she breathed, gnashing her teeth together as her belly visibly tightened again. "Been getting them since last night. Didn't sleep much."

"I need to examine you, Cass. I need to check how far dilated you are. Going to the hospital isn't a good idea if you're too far along."

"No," she ordered stubbornly. "This baby is being born in a hospital. Calm music and candles burning with doctors and nurses fucking everywhere." Tears welled in her eyes. "I didn't know."

"It's okay. We can do this."

Ava loved how he said that. Yes, Ezio was a doctor, but that was just like their friends. There was never a "you." It was always "us" and "we." Whenever someone was needed, there was never a question whether the others would be there.

"Kids, how about we go and check out the chickens in the coop?" Emma said. "Anyone who's not necessary can come with us." Nick picked up one of the twins and Katy hoisted the other on her hip.

"Come with me, munchkin man," she cooed. Levi and Connor were both around her side of the table before she could even get him settled, Levi lifting the little man to his shoulders. Adelaide and Lexi took Helena's little hand and swung her between them as they walked down the hill, Jax taking off after them wanting to have a go.

Cole picked up one of the meat trays, Liam and King following. Between them, they grabbed most of the platters. "What do you need me to do?" Ava asked Ezio. "I can help."

"Can we use one of the spare rooms?" He turned to Cassie. "I promise, if it's safe to go, I'll come with you. We'll get you to the hospital."

"Absolutely," Ava answered.

Bryce stepped forward. "Can I carry you, Cass? Or would you prefer to walk?" She shook her head so Bryce let Jake help her up. She could see that all Jake wanted to do was pick her up and take away the pain, but Cassie was strong.

She made it four steps, Jake and Phoenix helping her walk before another contraction kicked in. Ava counted in her head. They were getting closer together and more intense. A few more steps and Cassie was crying, her legs buckling under her.

Jake didn't hesitate.

He swept her into his arms and loped to the back door, Phoenix holding it open for them.

Ava led them into the first room with a door. They hadn't yet decorated it, but it had the couch from Cole's apartment in Sydney, a rug and spare pillows and cushions they'd accumulated from their various staging projects. Would a bed be better? She wasn't sure whether it had everything they needed, but when Ezio smiled and nodded at her, she let out her breath.

Ezio instructed Cassie's guys to get her comfortable as Robyn strode in with Ezio's medical bag. Ava pointed out the bathroom so Ezio could wash up, while she and Robyn waited by the door.

"Ava, don't go far," Ezio called out as Robyn shut the door after he'd returned to Cassie.

"Right, I better make sure the kids have eaten or we'll have gremlins on our hands," Robyn said.

"Ava," Ezio called. "We need you in here for a minute." She poked her head in. "This baby is coming now. I need a plastic tablecloth or something to put down on the floor, a bag without any holes in it and a few towels."

"Should I call an ambulance?"

"I'll do that from in here," Ezio explained.

"Can you get the bag out of the back of our car too? It's got a few things in it we need." Phoenix passed Ava his keys.

"Will do." With a nod, she closed the door and dashed into the kitchen, her heart in her throat. Nerves and worry for her friend clawed at her, but at the same time, Ezio's presence comforted her. He knew what he was doing. He would be there for Cassie and her bub. They were in safe hands.

"Cole, can you get the little speaker we have for Cassie. We need calm music. Find something for her to listen to." He nodded and headed for the bedroom they'd set up as a gym. "Can you grab some towels too?"

"Yep," he called out.

"Bryce, where are the scented candles we use for show-ings? We need them as well as a plastic tablecloth or something and a bag."

"I know just the thing. I'll get them."

After dishing out her orders, she dashed to the front of the house, pulling Cassie's bag out of the car and met her guys outside the room. She knocked and passed the items through to Jake as Cassie cried out and breathed hard and fast.

"Thank you," he said, barely looking at her. His gaze was filled with concern, his effervescent joy from moments earlier replaced with fear.

"Hey, Jake," she murmured encouragingly. "You've got this. Go become a dad."

He smiled, stood up straighter and looked over his shoulder again. "Yeah." He nodded and his gaze bounced between his husband and wife. "We're gonna be parents."

Ava closed the door, beaming as she held her hands to her chest. "It's happening."

"It really is. I'm so stoked for them," Bryce whispered, wincing when Cassie cried out in pain.

"That's it, Cass. You're doing so well," they heard Ezio murmur through the walls. "You're nearly dilated enough to start pushing. Only a few more contractions to go before we can get bub out."

Damn, it really was happening quickly if she was already nearly there. Thank goodness for Ezio's expertise—if it wasn't for him, Jake or Phoenix would be speeding down the mountain trying to get them to the hospital. Where were the paramedics?

Cole must have had the same thought, opting to wait at the open front gate for the ambulance while Bryce took off to see if the others needed anything. Ava hovered in the kitchen, wringing her hands and waiting.

She was practically climbing the walls, pacing the length of their little lounge room. Everything in there was a re-minder that they'd made their cottage a home. It was the little things that she noticed—her origami rose and the gor-geous egg-shaped bowl Cole had crafted sat proudly on the mantle, framing Cole's wedgetail eagle. They would always be reminders of their firsts—Christmas and birthdays—and Ava loved that they could create a place at the heart of their home just for them.

But it wasn't only the trinkets that made the house home. It was as much the people around them. Their friends and family. And right now, their friends needed her to be within earshot, but far enough away that she wasn't eavesdropping on them.

Ava waited.

She heard the sirens and smiled as the gaggle of children and adults drifted closer, waiting for news. Mike held open the door for the ambos pushing the stretcher. "Where's our new mum and bub?" the woman asked.

"Right through here," Ava answered, pointing the way as Bryce wrapped his arms around her waist from behind. Cole entered the house a moment later and joined them, leaning in to kiss Bryce's shoulder and squeeze Ava in a cuddle.

They waited. Ava had no idea how much time had passed. Ten minutes? An hour? Three? But she didn't move, standing sentinel in case her friends needed her.

The door to the room finally opened and closed, before water ran and shut off again. Ava couldn't wait anymore, ducking her head into the bathroom. "Is everything okay?" she asked Ezio, interrupting him drying his hands.

He smiled from ear to ear as he tugged his stained polo shirt off. "They have a beautiful baby. I'll let them reveal details." He laughed happily. "I delivered bubs. My first delivery outside of an emergency room."

Bryce waved the others into the house, shushing the kids as they migrated into the lounge room just off the front door. There was an air of anticipation, a quiet excitement that set Ava's pulse fluttering. She couldn't wait to catch a glimpse of the new baby, mum, and the two proud dads. Her pulse skittered in her veins, her heart bursting with joy for the newest addition to their family.

She looked around the room, kids babbling happily and adults whispering quietly as they waited on tenterhooks and smiled. Yeah, they were family.

The door opened and a collective ripple of excitement flowed through the group. Jake came out first, holding hands with Phoenix, tears streaming down his face. Phoenix wrapped an arm around his waist and pulled Jake close. "Cass and bubs are doing great."

"We're parents," Jake babbled with a sob. "We have a baby girl. Little Charlotte Dawn."

Cassie was holding their baby chest to chest, a light muslin wrap covering them both. Although flushed and tired, the love shining in her eyes was like nothing Ava had seen before. Cassie brushed her thumb gently along the tiny bundle's cheek and smiled proudly at her friends. The ambos paused just long enough that she could lift her hand, Charlotte's tiny fingers curled tightly around her pinkie.

Ava's heart was fit to burst. "Congratulations," she whispered, blowing them a kiss.

It might have been an unexpected ending to their get-together, but it was perfect, nevertheless. New life, new beginnings. A new addition to the next generation. Ava couldn't have asked for anything more. Finding the loves of her life, meeting friends who'd become family, finding happiness and a peace within her that she hadn't known she needed. They had a beautiful future together and she couldn't wait to spend it loving her guys.

"To family," she murmured as the door closed behind the happy trio with their beautiful bundle of joy.

And they lived happily ever after.

FIVE YEARS LATER

Gold Coast locals winning on and off field
SPORTS EDITION - GOLD COAST TRIBUNE

Fairy tales do come true for friends and teammates Liam Masters and Bryce Flaharty. Captain and vice-captain of the Gold Coast, the dynamic duo have been a force to be reckoned with since Flaharty signed with the Gold Coast five seasons ago.

Released from his contract with the East Sydney Lightning after a stellar rookie year, Flaharty returned home to the coast. He's joined Masters in cementing their places in NRL history. Both openly pansexual and in polyamorous relationships, they have the player stats to prove their skills. Masters described captaining the Gold Coast to their third premiership win in five years as "bloody brilliant."

Roles were reversed in tonight's State of Origin finale. "I've dreamed of wearing the maroon jersey since I was little. I'll never forget my first call up, but captaining the team to a win on home turf tonight was epic," Flaharty explained.

Maroons Coach, Billy O'Keefe, congratulated his star playing duo, calling them, "undoubtedly men of the series."

The Gold Coast will continue to reap the benefits of the duo's rock-solid partnership having signed both Masters and Flaharty to multi-million dollar contracts for the next five years.

The born-and-bred Gold Coasters have had as much success on the field as off. Masters became a father for the second time this year with his longtime partners, teacher Kingston Vella, and somatic sex educator Adelaide McMahon.

in a Christmas ceremony three years ago, Flaharty pledged his commitment to his longtime partners, project manager Ava Mason and carpenter Cole Saxon. Together, they provide emergency foster housing and farm stays for homeless LGBTQIA youth, undertake charitable renovation work for local families in need, and run boutique renovation company, Triple Threat.

Masters and Flaharty will lead the Gold Coast in a Queensland derby against the North Queensland Cowboys on Monday night. Tickets are nearly sold out.

Thank you for reading Triple Threat. I hope you loved Ava, Bryce and Cole's journey.

Want to find out who Queen is? Keep your eyes peeled for my upcoming Billionaire Boss Girl Series, available for pre-order now:

https://books2read.com/u/bzVQPz

PROFESSORHOLE

I play by my rules. My code.

My police handler thinks differently, but little does he know the extent of my hacking skills. I'm a billionaire because of them.

But the case he assigns me tests me in ways I wasn't expecting. The brief was simple—study a university subject on investigative techniques.

Turns out, it's anything but easy.

My professor is an a-hole. I hate him almost on sight. I want to damage his beautiful face, especially because of the lies he's telling about my late mother. My handler believes him, and my oldest friend Flynn is infatuated with him.

I *will* prove my mother's innocence.

I *will* put his accusations to rest once and for all.

But that means working closely with both him and Flynn to prove him wrong.

My professorhole won't know what hit him.

*****

Billionaire Boss Girl is a contemporary reverse harem / polyamorous series. There is no need for the leading lady (or her men) to choose in order to find their HEA.

Professorhole is book ONE of THREE in this slow build, high heat romantic suspense series.

Pre-order Professorhole now

https://books2read.com/u/bzVQPz

About Ann Grech

By day Ann Grech used to live in the corporate world and could be found sitting behind a desk typing away at reports and papers or lecturing to a room full of students. She graduated with a PhD in 2016 and is now an over-qualified nerd. But the grind got old, and the voices got louder. She still has the librarian look nailed, but she's a little freer to be herself now.

She's never entirely fit in and loves escaping into a book—whether it's reading or writing one. But she's found her tribe and loves her book world family. She dislikes cooking, but loves eating, can't figure out technology, but is addicted to it, and her guilty pleasure is Byron Bay Cookies. Oh and shoes. And lingerie. And maybe handbags too. Well, if we're being honest, we'd probably have to add her library too given the state of her credit card every month (what can she say, she's a bookworm at heart)!

In 2019 she was an Award-Winning Finalist in the Fiction: LGBTQ category of the 2019 Best Book Awards sponsored by American Book Fest for her story In Safe Arms.

She also publishes her raunchier short stories under her pen name, Olive Hiscock.

Ann loves chatting to people online, so if you'd like to keep up with what she's got going on:
Join her newsletter (you'll get two free books!):
https://landing.mailerlite.com/webforms/landing/d8m4r2
Follow her on TikTok or Instagram:
@anngrechauthor
Like her on Facebook:
https://www.facebook.com/pages/Ann-Grech/458420227655212
Join her reader group:
https://www.facebook.com/groups/1871698189780535/
Follow her on Goodreads:
https://www.goodreads.com/author/show/7536397.Ann_Grech
Follow her on BookBub:
https://www.bookbub.com/authors/ann-grech
Follow her on Amazon:
https://www.amazon.com/~/e/B00IJPO3EM
Visit her website for her current booklist:
http://www.anngrech.com/

She'd love to hear from you directly, too. Please feel free to e-mail her at ann@anngrech.com or check out her website for updates.

ANN GRECH'S BOOKS

BILLIONAIRE BOSS GIRL

Professorhole (RH/Polyamorous — FMMMM) coming 2023

RULE OF THREE

Three Hearts (MMF) (Also available in audio)
Yes, Captain (MM)
Triple Beat (MMF)
Threepeat (MMF)
Third Time's A Charm (MMF)
Triple Threat (MMF)

PEARCE STATION DUET

Outback Treasure I (MM)
Outback Treasure II (MM)

SPINOFF FROM PEARCE STATION

Three of Us (MMF)

UNEXPECTED

Whiteout (MM)
White Noise (MM)
Whitewash (MM)

MY TRUTH

All He Needs (MMM)
In Safe Arms (MM)

STANDALONES

Home For Christmas (MM)
The Gift (FMMM - free for newsletter subscribers)
Take Two (MM – free for newsletter subscribers)

M/F TITLES

One night in Daytona
Ink'd

GERMAN TRANSLATIONS

Outback Treasure I
Outback Treasure II